BRIAN LYNCH was born in Dublin in 1945. On the nomination of Samuel Beckett and Michael Hartnett he was elected to Aosdána in 1985. His first book, *Endsville*, was shared with Paul Durcan and published in 1967.

His first novel *The Winner of Sorrow*, based on the life of the poet William Cowper, was published in 2005. His translation with Peter Jankowsky of *Paul Celan: 65 Poems* was published by Raven Books, Dublin, in 1985.

He wrote the script for *Love and Rage*, a feature film directed by Cathal Black in 1998. *Caught in a Free State*, about German spies in Ireland during World War 2, was directed by Peter Ormerod for RTÉ and Channel 4 in 1984.

A long poem on Northern Ireland, *Pity for the Wicked* was published with a preface by Conor Cruise O'Brien, in 2005.

See www.brianlynch.org

First published in this edition 2013 by
The Duras Press, 5 Glandore, Pilot View,
Dalkey, Co Dublin, Ireland.

A CIP record for this book is
available from the British Library

ISBN 978-0-9568379-2-9

Photographs in text: Brian Lynch

Typesetting and Cover Design:
Clare Lynch

Cover Photograph: Ian Pearce

As a member of Aosdána the
author gratefully acknowledges
the assistance of the Arts Council
/ An Chomhairle Éalaion.

For Serena Condon

'When he actually met his duchess,
Proust's image was shattered; he had
to build another, to correspond with
the woman instead of the name... It was
Mme de Guermantes' complexion that
failed Proust. We have found Turkestan
in the full bloom of early summer.'

ROBERT BYRON
The Road to Oxiana (London 1937)

'Carnal pleasures... which are but
welcome pains, draw the spirit inwards
into primal darkness and indistinction...
The chained dogs below keep on barking
in their kennels.'

GEORGE SANTAYANA
The Realm of Spirit (New York, 1940)

THE WOMAN NOT THE NAME

1

WILL FERRIS noticed the man long before he bent the one-legged table in the back bar of the Baggot Inn. The leg was made of iron and bolted to the floor with a steel plate — the man was not as boneless as he looked in his loose blue overalls and brown suit jacket. But his strength would be revealed later. Now he was noticeable because without him Will's audience would have been cut by half. The other half was wearing a raincoat and reading a morning newspaper. Outside it wasn't raining, but a cold breeze was blowing. The bar was warm and gloomy, kippered with cigarette smoke, and yet it did not reek of tobacco and stale beer. To Will the absence of this centuries-old stink was mysterious, but that was because he didn't know that smoking in pubs had been banned since March. It was no wonder then that on this Monday night in November the air would be odourless. The walls and the ceiling though were still brown with smoke.

With a glass in either hand, held out to balance him as if they were weights, the man manoeuvred himself up onto a high wooden stool by the one-legged table and shuffled his hams into its twin shallow depressions. Problem solved, he swallowed most of his pint of stout, then poured his rum and blackcurrant into the remainder and sipped the sour-sweet mixture.

The principle reason for Will noticing the man was his face. It was round, flat, white, dull, moon-like, blank, expressionless. He wouldn't have stood out otherwise. As it is hard to believe the pallor of the moon is caused by the sun, it was even harder to believe that this Moonman's mahogany-coloured hair, which seemed to have tipped slightly to the side, was not a wig; it was his own; there was nothing false about its rigid mahoganic limpness. Was there such a word?

This is how Will Ferris's mind works, or worked, once upon a time. He was also a singer. Singing is what he was really thinking of and waiting to do, but every time he touched his guitar it crackled.

'What's the story?' he said, turning to Ossie Gleeson.

'This thing is history,' Ossie said. 'Try her now.'

The amplifier had stopped crackling, but there was a low hum off it. Will began to play. He hadn't performed in Dublin for more than a year — if busking in Grafton Street for a week could be called performing.

Ossie sat on the amp, propped his chin on his hands and listened. He was twenty-four year old, tall, dark, shaven-headed, doe-eyed, and he would never be poor, because the family business paid for the basics, like rent, and for some recreational work, like the band he had managed until he brought them to London and they signed a deal that hadn't included him. Will wouldn't do that: they were best friends forever. Anyway, the manager hadn't yet been born who could be Will's manager, or get him to do anything he didn't want to do, or that was popular.

The man in the mackintosh folded his newspaper and went out. It was hopeless.

But then Maeve MacNamee and Cory Leary came in and sat on the ragged banquette by the emergency exit. Ossie blushed: he had slept with Maeve on Saturday night, but on Sunday morning when he had asked her to meet him on Monday she had said, 'You must be joking.'

As he hurried towards her she stood up again. Not to kiss him; but to stop him kissing her — she was, obviously, too busy taking off her heavy leather overcoat to be kissed.

Underneath the coat she wore a wrap-around blouse made

of some silky material printed all over with multi-coloured blotty flowers. It may have been opaque in fact, but in Ossie's eyes it might just as well have been transparent. In books, and in religion too, breasts like Maeve's are sometimes said to be generous, a word which, as well as meaning big (because when it comes to bosoms, it appears there can't be generosity in smallness), means promising. Hope for the future. But whose? Ossie Gleeson was confused. Maybe when she had said he must be joking she wasn't being serious. In his confusion her shucking off of the leathery animal-skin to reveal the downy woman-skin beneath seemed an effect she had planned in advance, and her perfume, which smelled as if it had been trapped in a private place for a long time — she must have planned that too.

Will began to sing. Ossie shushed Maeve with an apologetic finger raised to his lips. Looking at him sideways in brief disbelief, she said out loud, 'I have a hangover like a lawnmower. And I'm perished with the cold. Get us a hot whiskey, will you? What do you want, Cory?'

'Ballygowan.'

'Water for the lady and whiskey for me. Make sure it's Jameson. Don't forget the lemon. And the cloves.'

Will, who had stopped singing, now started again. At the bar Ossie had to wait while the Moonman was being served. As the barman put more Guinness and another rum and blackcurrant on the counter, he cocked his head and said, 'That's your lot, sunshine.'

If Maeve's spirit was whiskey, it was raw but not neat. She looked a little unfinished, especially about the mouth; and her wet red lipstick seemed slashed on carelessly, but it was not the stick but the lips that were irregular; at one corner they were turned down sardonically. There was a touch of the gypsy in her high cheekbones, lozenge-shaped violet eyes and tangled mane of glossy hair, which was dyed a colour she called tinker-black. Still, if it wasn't for the sarcastic mouth, she could have been a typical Romany beauty. But it was the crookedness that made her beautiful.

If Cory was a beauty, it was of the unnoticed kind. Like water, she took on the colour of her surroundings. Her eyes and hair were a nondescript brown and her skin was rain-dotted all over with faint freckles. While it was not true to say, though Maeve would eventually say it, that she was 'built like a little heifer', there was something calf-like about her broad-shouldered, narrow-hipped, muscular body — the muscles came from swimming. She was slightly buck-toothed: her top teeth had never been braced and she had a habit of closing her lips over them, though all that did was attract attention to what she wanted to hide.

If it were possible to ask these women about these descriptions it is certain that Cory would make no comment on them, but it is likely she would agree with Maeve who would definitely say, 'Thanks for starting with my brain.' Actually, Maeve probably wouldn't bother her head saying anything. What would be the point? You might as well try to take a case to prove there was a future for the flat-chested. That would be pointless, literally. Anyway, she had studied and understood the dictum, *De minimis non curat lex* — the law does not concern itself with the smallest things.

Ossie whispered to Maeve, 'He's good, isn't he?'

'It'd be a help,' she said, 'if he could sing.'

For someone so tall and with such a deep chest, Will's voice was small and reedy, and he didn't so much sing the song as say it, as if he was telling a story — but the story of this song will not be told for a while yet, except to say there had been no cheese to bait the trap, and Sheevawn means white ghost, which can be of either sex, or none, as indicated by the addition of 'ban', meaning woman, to banshee, who foresees death and cries in foresight.

> *The mouse died with the taste*
> *Of butter in its mouth.*
> *Sheevawn the white ghost raised*
> *Her skirt up and cried out,*
> *What kind of beast are you?*
> *She wasn't alone in the house.*
> *The night outside was blue,*
> *She was in the wrong place*
> *To get what she deserved,*

To be adored.
What a man. What a waste.
And the slain mouse
Lay prone behind the door,
Eyes wide and the taste
Of butter in its mouth,
And otherwise it was
The quiet of the house.

'What was that all about?' Maeve said.

'Search me,' Cory said.

The Baggot was not as empty now as it had been at the beginning of the singing. The front bar was filling up with a cohort of officials from Government Buildings who had been working late on the estimates for the Budget. When a Junior Executive Officer, Cormac Healy, and an Administrative Officer, Ultan McGrath, looked into the back bar to see if there was room they saw Maeve MacNamee. Although she was not in the Department of Finance — she was the most Junior Legal Assistant in the Attorney General's Office — they knew her because all three of them had joined the civil service on the same day in September and had met at a day-long induction course in the Institution of Public Administration.

'After one day,' Maeve said to Cory, 'we were ready to run the country.'

Cormac Healy said, 'Plus we get a pension when we're a hundred and sixty-five.'

'Yeah, right,' Maeve said. She leaned towards Ossie, put her hand under the table and ran it up his thigh. 'Your man,' she said, 'what did you say his name is?'

Will was crouched down at the amplifier, about to turn it off, because of the hum, when he looked up and saw her blouse flowering above him.

'You're Will Ferris,' she said.

'I am,' he said, straightening up.

'Your boyfriend says you're really good.'

'He's not my boyfriend.'

'I can see that.'

'Can you?'

'I can now. Do you play requests? Don't say you don't.'

'Is that an order?'

'Maybe it is. Would you like that?'

'It depends.'

Maeve said, 'Mmmm.'

Will said, 'OK. What do you want to hear?'

'Play us something civil servants can dance to, not some fucking dirge, like the last one.'

'What did you say your name was?'

'I didn't say. But it's Maeve.'

'Well, Maeve, fuck off.'

She said curtly, 'Do what you're told,' and went back to her seat. But before she could reach it, Will turned up the amplifier to ten and struck the strings of the guitar. The thunderous chord had an effect like a magnet on a scatter of iron filings: the attention of everyone in the bar, even on the other side of the partition, turned towards it, and when the babble of voices resumed, they had risen to a different pitch.

Speaking close to the microphone in a prim American accent, he said, 'Just what is it that you want to do?' In another voice, also American but crazed, he whined, 'We wanna be free, we wanna free.' Then he played *I'm Losing More Than I'll Ever Have*, beating his knuckles on the body of the guitar and occasionally howling, 'We wanna be free and we wanna get loaded.'

Civil servants were coming in from the front bar all the time, so the space for Maeve to dance in kept on getting smaller. But all she was doing was standing on the spot with her hands loose-fisted in front of her face, moving her hips as if trying to wriggle out of a narrow passageway. The next thing Will noticed was that the dumpy little girl Maeve had come in with stood up abruptly and went out.

2

AS VANESSA BANIM came into The Clock, next door to the National College of Art and Design on Thomas Street, Harry O'Gara said to her,

'Excuse me. Do you mind if I pay you a compliment?'

'Sorry?' Vanessa said.

'I just wanted to say you look gorgeous.'

'Well, thank you.'

'What kind of fur is that?'

'Rabbit, but it's not real.'

'Well, I think it's divine, and I especially love the bag.'

'Do you? I made it out of a pair of children's slippers. They used to be bunnies, you see, so they go with the coat.'

'That's wild,' Harry said. Then he turned to the man beside him and said, 'Isn't that wild?'

'Bring back myxomatosis,' Emmet Roche said.

By the time Emmet had explained about the disease that had almost wiped out the Irish rabbit population in the 1950s — he knew this because his father was a farmer — it was clear to Vanessa that he did not care for her coat or her bag or her self.

'Don't mind him,' Harry said. 'He's a barbarian.'

Emmet said, 'She likes barbarians.'

'Do you know this man?' Harry said.

Emmet said, 'I never saw her before in my life.'

'I know him,' Vanessa said.

Emmet said, 'You're a student. I don't see students.'

'This is getting very intricate,' Harry said. 'Let's have a drink.'

It wasn't true that Emmet Roche didn't see students: he not only saw but knew some of them, biblically. The intimacy owed nothing to his handsomeness: he had a small head, beady eyes that gleamed behind granny glasses, and a long nose that twitched and sniffed constantly, like a stoat snuffling at a rabbit burrow. But what made the smallness of the head disturbing was the hugeness of his hands and the bigness and the burliness of the rest of him.Every one of his students painted the way he did — thick gouts of primary colour squeezed from the tube and battered into submission on the canvas — but their work did not have his painterly elegance.

'Well,' Harry said, 'at least you two have one thing in common: the Nazi jackboots. But which one of you is the fake?'

Vanessa's boots were the real thing, but they were not jackboots: the silver plates on the heels had Harley Davidson stamped on them. Their biker brutalness, as she well knew, contrasted well with her willowiness and tight-permed blondness and the Meissen delicacy of the polished skin of her perfectly oval face, which was as pink as a rabbit's nose. But her lips were thin and she thought them ugly, which was the opinion she had of herself as a whole, all the more so because one of her baby-blue eyes had a hint of a squint in it.

Emmet's boots were clumpy, too, but there were no logo plates on the heels, the laces were undone, and the tongues, like the tongues of dead dogs, lolled out of them. The boots were speckled with flecks of paint, as was his boilersuit.

Harry said to Vanessa, 'I love that blue, don't you?'

Emmet said, 'What the fuck is all this fucking talk about fucking clothes for? Who gives a fuck?'

'I do,' Harry said. 'And please watch your language; it's vile and completely unnecessary. Actually, the only thing I give a fuck for is frocks.'

When Vanessa learned that Harry was a window-dresser and that the windows he dressed were Brown Thomas's, the most fashionable department store not just in Grafton Street but the whole of Ireland, she said, 'Oh, that's staggering.'

Emmet said, illogically, 'That's because you look like a fucking rabbit.'

Two hours later, as she came through the batting doors of the Baggot Inn, she said out loud, 'I am sooooo cold.'

She was too busy making her entrance to see Cory Leary, head bent low like a swan, passing by with an apology. Vanessa had a lot to do: to not look anyone in the eye; to raise her chin, not too haughty, on the swivel of her long neck; to shiver her shoulder-blades to show they were cold; and all the while to make for the bar with grace and humility. Grace because she aspired to be graceful. Humility because not to be blind to Department of Finance officials falling back and dividing like the Red Sea to allow her pass through them would be like a beautiful woman who knows she is beautiful: just too awful. All in all, making an entrance made Vanessa nervous. She was not as proud as she wanted to be.

As Harry and Emmet followed her to the bar, Harry said, 'Why are you such a terrible man?'

'What?' Emmet said vaguely. He was distracted by recognising Cory and by her not saying hello to him. Not the other way round — why should he speak first? But maybe she hadn't seen him. Of course she had — who could not see him?

'That's Primal Scream,' Vanessa said, hearing the music. So they went into the back bar to see it. When Harry saw Maeve dancing he blew her a kiss and she blew one back.

'Who's the guitar-plucker?' Emmet said.

Vanessa said. 'He's something else.'

Harry said, 'Why is it all the interesting men in the world look like nothing on earth?'

'How would I know?' Emmet said. 'The only man I'm interested in is me.'

Harry said, 'Oh, you devil you.'

'I am a devil,' Emmet said. 'That's why I'm interesting.'

'I don't want to hear this,' Harry said.

'Why not?'

'The devil frightens me, that's why.'

'Well,' Emmet said with satisfaction, 'I think I've hit the shuttlecock back to the lady's side of the net.'

Harry said, 'How is it your most charming trait also manages to be your least charming trait?' He pronounced 'trait' in the French way. 'Now, please, let me listen.'

Will Ferris was singing:

> *If I obeyed you, I can't be me,*
> *So I betrayed you.*
> *I don't want nobody else,*
> *I just want you to myself.*

Harry shivered. This unknown singer was looking straight at him. Not only was he beautiful but he wanted him to himself, and to be free too. Sweet god, Harry thought, I'm so romantic it'll kill me one of these days. But this wasn't true. Still, it felt as if the beast within, that old feeling deep in his heart, which had been dormant for so long it had ceased to be familiar, was stirring to life again.

It was then that the barman burst out from behind the counter and made for the Moonman.

3

SHE WAS GRINNING like a horse chewing thistles. Will turned on the light in the windowless bathroom. The image arrived with the click of the switch. It was given, not found or stolen. The words came to him, he had no power over them — that was the source of his power. This was foolish, like believing water could be turned into wine, but not to believe in miracles was stifling; it stifled what he thought was magical in him. And yet, plainness was truer than any miracle, or any magic, other than itself. So, though he had been for a long time convinced that he was gifted, a genius even, the suspicion that he was also a fraud stayed with him. This awareness had become an essential element of his style; it added an undertaste, dry, bitter and reduced, to the way he wrote and sang.

Now he bent towards the tarnished mirror over the washbasin, rotated his torso and flexed his right arm, like a body-builder, to inspect the ball of his shoulder. The skin had not been punctured, but already a bruise was forming around the toothmarks.

He asked his reflection how many girls he had had sex with. Before the age of seventeen, none. On his seventeenth birthday, one. After that, many. And often. He knew the number, because he had done the count during a long period when he had slept with no one. But this was the first time anyone had bitten him.

Seeing his stubbled chin and the dirty straw brush of his hair sticking up, he thought, You look like you made your entrance through a haystack. This was true, but, even so, girls often thought Will Ferris gorgeous. He had dazzlingly white teeth, a rarely seen but brilliant smile, bright blue eyes; if it wasn't for the twisted drum of his nose and the scar tissue thickening around his eyebrows, his face would have been girlishly pretty. His body wasn't girlish, though. There was something out of proportion, almost deformed, about the bone-ridged barrel of his chest. In his boxing days he had advanced rapidly from welterweight to middleweight, but he had been too lanky for his 154 pounds. He was a southpaw, built for counter-punching, for the art of backpedalling and jabbing, with a whiplash turn of the wrist to add a sting to his long straight right. But he had been too aggressive to exploit his height, speed and reach advantage. He had refused to be taught not to lose his temper: when he was hurt he put his head down and bored in. As a result, his eyebrows had cut badly and his nose had twice been broken. The airways were narrowed, his breathing was poor, he snored in his sleep. But not a few women thought his face looked better because it was battered — they wouldn't have done the damage themselves but they weren't sorry it had been done.

The water that exploded out of the anciently grinding tap was so cold it sent a wooden shock up through the bones of his forearms.

Maeve's flat was in the basement of a tall Georgian house in Waterloo Road. When she brought him back from the Baggot, it was still warm — the gasfire had been left burning. It was the kind of rented place where the process of replacing and mismatching the furniture had been going on for years, maybe a century. She switched on a standard lamp. A weak yellow light strained through a parchment shade that was fringed with tassels and tilted to one side with an air of weary jauntiness.

'Well,' she said, 'what do you think?'

It wasn't the room she was asking about, it was herself, shedding the leather coat and opening her hands like a circus acrobat seeking applause for her first trick, a very simple somersault.

Will said, 'I feel like the Moonman.'

'The who?'

'The guy with the moon face. The sex maniac?'

'What are you talking about?'

Will was amazed. She might not have noticed Moonman playing with himself — though from the expression on his face it was less with than against — but it was obvious enough for the barman to whip away his rum-and-black-and-stout and tell him he was barred. But the Moonman wouldn't budge. He held on to the leg of the table and would not let go of it until two more barmen, hefty culchies with drooping bellies, barrelled out from behind the counter, wrenched him loose and bundled him through the emergency door onto the laneway at the side of the Baggot. This had been done with speed and efficiency — the drinks of other customers had been taken off the table first. The remarkable thing was that at no point had the Moonman uttered a sound.

'OK,' Will said. 'Maybe you didn't notice that, but what about the table?'

'What table?'

'He bent the table to an angle of, it must have been, forty-five degrees. You could hardly not have noticed that.'

'Well, I didn't. Anyway, what's it got to do with me?'

'It was your fault. It was your dancing got him going.'

She made her way across the threadbare carpet, linked her hands around his neck and said, 'Let's dance then.'

They shuffled together in front of the gasfire to her tuneless humming of what might have been the tune of *I'm Losing More Than I'll Ever Have*. Then she pushed him down on the sofa, hiked up her skirt, straddled him and started devouring his neck with kisses.

He groaned.

She stood up, saying, 'You're getting carried away with yourself.'

In the kitchen she stood watching the kettle boil. It was usually her principle that if pleasure was near enough to reach, as it had been just now, it should be reached, but sometimes putting it off made the risk of being dissatisfied worth the wait. This was one of those times. Anyway, she was never not satisfied. She made it her business to come. Or so she had once said to Cory Leary, who had looked at her as if she was a slut and a nympho, or worse, a liar. Well, even if Cory was right, she was wrong. Women were desperate liars, especially when they bunched together, pretending they were sisters, though they actually knew very well what they wanted, and sisterliness didn't come into it, except as a means to an end. Women were single-minded, but they loved to surrender, which was suicide, though they hardly ever committed it, because they were only pretending to love surrendering. Suicide was a man thing. Maeve preferred men.

When she came back from the kitchen with the coffee, Will was writing in a notebook he had taken out of his leather satchel.

'Are you keeping the score?' she said.

But he wasn't marking her out of ten in his little black book. What he had written down had come to him while his neck was being kissed, but since he couldn't tell her she was 'a Dracula of the shiver' he told her a lie. For days he had been trying to finish a song and now an idea had come to him how to do it. The notebook was full of songs by other people, but unless the tune or the words, and preferably both, could be changed enough to be sung in his own style, they couldn't be performed in public.

'That's eejity,' Maeve said. 'And the logic is crap, too.'

'Is it?'

'Of course it is.'

'Why is that?'

'Because everything is logical, except when people like you talk crap.'

'I see.'

'I see, said the blind man. Anyway, sing the song.'

'You like giving orders, don't you?'

'Only to eejits. Sing the song.'

'Do I get paid for it?'

She looked at him speculatively. 'Yes.'

'Can I ask how much?'

'You can.'

'How much?'

'I'll pay your bus fare home. Because that's where you're going, in about five minutes.'

'Oh. I see. So what happens if I don't sing?'

'You can sleep on the couch.'

'I can't lose, can I?'

'Wait,' she said. She went to the kitchen, came back with the stub of a candle in a bottle, lit it, placed it on the coffee table, much scarred with cigarette burns, turned off the standard lamp with the tasselled shade, and sat in a raggedy armchair on the other side of the room.

'Now,' she said.

He couldn't see her face. And she was so far away she heard the whisper of his voice as if at a distance.

> *When they heard that Lewis was dead,*
> *All the womenfolk they dressed in red.*
> *They told each other it sure was hard*
> *To see young Collins in the old graveyard.*
> *Collins shot one but Quinn shot two,*
> *Shot poor Lewis, shot him through and through*
> *Miss Collins weep, Miss Collins moan.*
> *What drove her son Lewis from his home?*
> *Old Quinn it was led him astray,*
> *He paid young Lewis the devil's pay.*
> *And now the women have laid him away,*
> *They've laid him six feet under the clay.*
> *Angels, bear him away. Angels, bear him away.*

'That's weird,' Maeve said. But she wouldn't tell him what was weird was that her mother's maiden name was Collins, and she had a dead brother too, though his name was Laurence. That was none of Will Ferris's business. But it was eerie.

Then they were in her bedroom and she was holding his head in her hands and thrusting her tongue into his mouth like a child trying to lick syrup out of a bowl it can't reach the bottom of. Although she was aware she hardly knew this man, and that his singing a dreary old dirge with her mother's maiden name in it was hardly a good reason for taking the risk of catching some hideous STD off him, she didn't bother about protection. But so what? What was the point of taking a risk if there was no danger to it?

As her orgasm began to arrive, she said, 'Look at me. Look at me now.'

But as soon as she caught his scared gaze, a wave of shuddering washed up her spine and threw her head helplessly back onto the pillow. When the wave receded, she looked at him again. She had been wrong: his eyes weren't frightened. Instead, she saw in them a pity not meant to be shared.

'You're a cruel brute, aren't you?' she said, but he didn't answer. 'Come on then,' she said and got on top of him, driving pubic bone against pubic bone. After what seemed to Will long minutes of this horned combat, she put her hands on his chest, levered herself to the length of her arms and stared down at him.

'Say my name,' she said. 'Say my name.' But he said nothing. The truth was he couldn't remember it. It was at this moment that the image of the horse chewing thistles began to prickle in his brain. The next moment, even before he could realise that the two drops of warm water that struck his chest were tears, she stooped and bit him.

No, it had not been pleasure, and the bathroom was not windowless either. High up over the cast-iron bath, which had greenish-black streaks rivering down from the taps, there was a small square window set deep into the thick wall.

4

MAEVE KISSED WILL on the cheek and on the spot she kissed she placed a cold silver Yale key. 'Leave this under the third stone,' she said. 'And don't think I don't know you're only pretending.'

She wasn't wrong — he was more awake than he had let on. But later when he woke with the key clutched hard in his hand he didn't associate it with his dream of struggling to close a steel door against a storm in a one-roomed house suspended above a calm sea, and then he was opening the door and there, in a grove of elder bushes — it was summer because they were flowering a cream foam — was a black marble sarcophagus, and in it a woman stood, wrapped in black plastic and bound with a white cord. He knew it was a woman because written in gold beneath her feet were the words, 'I Am The Immaculate Conception'.

He stretched out in the warmth of the bed and felt a luxurious sense of achievement. On the bedside table were a cup of milky tea and a slice of toast on a blue plate. Propped on one elbow he ate the toast, gulped down the lukewarm tea, and slept again, dreamlessly, even more luxuriously.

Waking, he was hungry and thirsty. Off the bedroom was a narrow kitchen. While the kettle was boiling, he went to the bathroom. Thinking how generously rounded and yet sharp-edged Maeve was, he opened the wrong door and was surprised by sunlight slanting low through a twelve-paned window. This room, unlike Maeve's, was neat, and no one had slept in the bed. A bunch of withering freesias leaned gawkily out of a honey-jar on the windowsill, but otherwise the room was bare of decoration, cell-like, monkish. A shiver to piss zinged through his loins.

In the bathroom, idly looking up again at the small high window, he shuddered. Then he went back to the kitchen, drank hot tea and ate toast thickly slathered with butter; then sat cross-legged on Maeve's rumpled bed and for an hour practised on his guitar, as usual. Then he dressed and left.

It was the kind of morning he often experienced at this time. Everything passed by in a flash, but slowly. The rawness of the air on Waterloo Road served only to add an outer edge to his inner state. Never wearing a coat and the habit he had of pushing the sleeves of his shirt up over his elbows weren't done for show: his metabolism churned out so much heat he needed to feel the cold. Sometimes, before playing the guitar, he even stouped his hands in icy water to sharpen their touch. But while it was understandable that he might need to shiver, he couldn't understand why other people had to keep warm. It was the same with the weather: nothing was as important in life, or as good, but human beings weren't good and they didn't love it; they stood in the way of goodness without knowing it. Still, he had to feel pity for the passersby in the street: they were going about their business, whatever it was, and they obviously didn't see that this was one of those cloudless winter days that are brilliantly lit and yet somehow the sun itself is nowhere to be seen. It was a miracle, and it was tragic that he was the only person on Waterloo Road who saw it for what it was. This miraculous tragedy was his alone: he had been blessed and had no one to tell it to. No one or everyone. That was his duty.

On Baggot Street he boarded a 46A bus. A pair of old men in dirty raincoats — which smelled of stale smoke and stale beer, that centuries-old stink — occupied his favourite seat, at the front on the top deck.

One of them, wearing a scarlet bandana around his neck, was saying, 'Well, says he, you've even got a little man in the cockpit. I suppose he's steering the boat. It's not a boat, says I, it's a ship; and it's not a cockpit either, it's the bridge.'

'Doesn't know the difference,' the other man said. 'Hopeless, hopeless.'

'Do you know what I'm going to tell you, skipper? Young people these days, they're so intoxicated with themselves, they'd hardly know a bullet if you fired one up their arse.'

'I know, I know, but sure I'm the same. Two pints and I'm the dog of hell itself.'

'You're a martyr,' the bandana said testily.

'And you're getting very red in the face these days. You're a model for a stroke.'

'Model is right.'

After that they fell silent. From his leather satchel Will took out his notebook and wrote down the conversation.

At Merrion Gates he got off the bus and walked through the level crossing to Ossie Gleeson's flat. Ossie had chosen it because the back windows looked out on Sandymount strand. Having slept on the living room couch for three weeks, Will had begun to feel annoyed by the place: the tide was supposed to come in twice a day but the biscuity vastness of the strand was almost always waterless. The level crossing irritated him too: before the gates came down they jerked, but the jerking happened not because there was something faulty with the mechanism but because the engineers had designed it as a warning to motorists that a train was thundering towards them. But how many drivers would be thick enough to stop on a railway track? Maybe one in a hundred million. So, for insurance purposes, the train company had decided to cater for that maniac, and to be absolved in advance of the blame. What use was absolution after the fact of a train making raspberry jam out of a maniac? Not one iota — they'd still have to pay out. No, that wasn't entirely true: absolution mattered if you were truly sorry. In his own case it had mattered greatly, even if it was self-absolution and the sorrow was for himself.

Still, the bloody level crossing and the tideless strand annoyed him. These days he was as often annoyed by the facts of life as he was inspired by them passing him by in a flash.

Ossie had left a note on the kitchen table. It said, 'You're in luck. I've got you that crib. Ring me. Miss MacNamee is some chick. Right?'

Will rang his mother instead. As soon as Polly heard his voice she said, 'What have you done now, you good-for-nothing boy?'

Will's life was disorderly, but schedules, dates, and the awareness of when things should happen wired themselves into his brain. He knew it was coffee-break time in the Cork School of Music and that in five minutes Polly would have to go to her next class. He hadn't planned the shortness of the conversation, but the prevention of things spreading out wastefully was, like his fraudulence, an essential tool in his economy.

Polly had observed this trait in her son long ago. Her first observations of it related to food. As a small boy Will had had a fondness for baked beans with fried bread and a crisp-fried egg, but while all three could mingle in his mouth, they were not allowed to touch each other on the plate. Considering the nature of beans, this was tricky to organise, and if she was sloppy in organising it, he threw a fit. This prohibition had given her a pang: was the child autistic, did he have Tourette's Syndrome, or Asperger's, or was he just mad? Then, when he was older, he had developed a passion for making elaborately gory sandwiches of pickled beetroot, red onions and tomatoes, all smothered with mayonnaise. The problem then wasn't the mingling; it was the tomatoes. The ends of them had to be sliced off and discarded. No matter what she said, he would not, or could not, see the sense in saying tomatoes had no ends.

He was quite happy to eat the whole fruit sliced any which way in a salad, but not on any account in a sandwich, so the discs were left scattered forlornly on the breadboard.

And anyway, he said, the tomato wasn't a fruit; it was a vegetable.

She showed him the definition in the dictionary. It didn't matter what the dictionary said; the dictionary was wrong.

He had proved contrary, too, when it came to music. She had

taught him piano up to Grade Eight, but then he had stopped and switched to electric guitar.

'You'll come to regret it,' his mother had said.

'And you,' he had replied, 'are a stupid bitch.'

Then he had kicked in a panel of the upright piano and gone out to walk around The Lough, a depressing pond near the Ferris family home, another hole, on the Glanmire Road. He had been fourteen then and wholly taken up with indifference, particularly to his hair (teased out with gel and dried soap to the shape of an exploding crow's nest), to his clothes (a long black leather overcoat and chromium-plated boots), to Morrissey of the Smiths (who was by then already an antique), and above all to life as it was lived by his parents. This last indifference was furious.

'You're only consuming oxygen,' he said to his father, 'and if you gave up breathing, you'd have less effect on the world than the beating of a butterfly's wing in the rainforests of Brazil.'

'What are you talking about?'

'I'm talking chaos theory, but you wouldn't know anything about that, would you? And this house, and all these other bloody houses, what are they but coffins? Upright coffins!'

'You try paying the mortgage then.'

'Mortgage! What's a mortgage? I'm sick of this fucking mortgage.'

Paul said, 'Don't swear at me, you brat. I've a good mind to give you a toe in the hole.'

Polly said, 'That'll be the day.'

What was truly infuriating to Will about that period in his life was being aware that it was a period, that it was 'just a phase he's going through', like millions of teenagers.

He wasn't like a teenager; he wasn't like anybody, he hated the word 'like'; and even when he had outgrown the gelled hair, the leather coat, the boots and Morrissey, the conviction remained with him that the worst thing in the world was being like anyone else.

At the age of sixteen he had said to his girlfriend, 'When you say what it is, I know that's what it isn't.'

To this she said, 'I haven't said anything so far.'

'I know that. I'm talking in general, not about you. But, like, take your name, Sheevawn Rogers.'

'That's two names.'

'That's what I mean. You have two names. Did you ever think why? It's really weird when you think about it, isn't it? Everyone has two names.'

'Except Morrissey.'

'Oh him. That's just shite, that's show-business shite. What I mean is, like, Sheevawn and Rogers, they're the names you were given, but they don't say anything about you.'

Sheevawn was a smart girl. She didn't look the least little bit like a white ghost, which is what her name meant in Irish. But, if Will had been able to tell the truth, he would have had to admit that the name actually did say something about her. It suited her and she suited it. Sheevawn Rogers was the springy feel of her rubbery body and the giddy sensation of her tongue leaping around like a new lamb in his mouth — she French-kissed as if she had just invented it. She had been, as she admitted to herself, 'mad for it', but she was wise enough to realise that going all the way with Will Ferris would be bad for Sheevawn Rogers. Which, when it did happen, on his seventeenth birthday, it was. She had learned a universal lesson: sex is the problem but sex isn't the solution. Whatever it was cracked up to be, sex was what it wasn't. Then her boy, her man, her lover, was off and running.

His phone call was now coming to an end. Will said, 'How's Paul?' Paul was his father.

'Why don't you ask him?'

'Is he at home?'

'Where else would he be? Oh god, where am I? Oh yes. Birdie must fly. Bye bye bye bye bye.'

Will said goodbye, but she had already put down the phone.

'Birdie must fly' was a phrase Polly had picked up as a child from a radio serial called 'The Kennedys of Castlerosse'. All her phone calls ended with it, and the number of accompanying bye-byes had increased exponentially over the years. They stopped people chattering when she had decided to stop chattering. Will tried not to find this and her many other mannerisms annoying. But, try as he might, both his parents were beyond redemption. 'Your father,' as Polly called her husband, even when he was in the same room, had once been a draughtsman in the Planning Office of Cork County Council, but he had retired early and his days were now devoted to — to what? It was hard to say. He pottered about and listened to records in his den. At the start a love of music was what he and Polly had most had in common, but it had turned out to be what most separated them. She wanted everything to be just so, but she was incapable of making the arrangements. He had everything arranged; incompetence was incomprehensible to him, especially hers. Being an excellent teacher but a useless administrator, Polly had, of course, been made head of her department. Paul might have become head of the planning department but, without telling her, he had refused to be promoted. Promotion involved too much hassle. Then, even in music they had come to differ. The further back she travelled into the past — by now her tastes were medieval — the more rooted he remained in the present, or rather in the 1960s. He had a particular liking for obscure dead singers, like Minnie Ripperton, and up-and-at-them bands that had never quite made it, like Brinsley Schwarz. And developments in earphone technology now allowed him to sit and listen to his favourites in silence, like God the Father in heaven but without His need to share the joy of the creation with the created, not even with the dizzy young piano teacher Paul had once been pleased to call 'pretty Polly, pretty Polly.'

5

WHEN WILL SAW the girl asleep on the couch, he stopped, bewildered. Maeve had opened the door, folded her arms, leaned against the jamb, like a slut in a soap opera settling herself for a long conversation, and said, 'What kind of omadawn are you?' The fool had forgotten to leave the key under the stone. 'Oh well,' she said, levering her shoulder off the jamb, 'now that you're here, I suppose you'd better come in.'

This was all an act. Early in the morning she had rung Ossie to remind his boyfriend — who refused to own a mobile phone — not to forget about the key, but really to find out more about him. That Ossie might object to being used as a go-between never occurred to her. If it had, she would have dismissed the objection. Ossie Gleeson had got all he was going to get from her, and she couldn't see why he should resent it, or why she should be shy about snaffling his best friend. To her there was no mystery about decisions or preferences — she made them and she had them and that was all there was to it. 'The trouble with you,' her mother had once said, 'is that you take it for granted that everybody is as self-centred as yourself.' Maeve had no problem with that; it was true: people were equally self-centred; it was a law of nature; and if they pretended they weren't, they were pretending; and if they made mistakes because of the pretence, that was their own mistake; it was one she wouldn't be making.

'Wake up,' Maeve said, shaking Cory. 'Wake up and say hello to the stupid man.'

'Hello,' Cory said, but her eyes, refusing to focus, closed again and her head fell to one side.

'She's been awake for thirty-six hours,' Maeve said. 'Would you want your broken leg to be treated by a doctor who's been awake for thirty-six hours?'

'Oh,' Will said, 'she's a doctor is she?'

'No,' Maeve said, 'she's a trapeze artist. Pour yourself a glass of wine and get your brain in gear.' She went into the kitchen and from there said, 'Now that you're here, I suppose you think you'll have to be fed.' After a few moments she looked out with a puzzled look on her face and said, 'Did I say that before? Oh my god, I am so stoned.'

On the coffee table lay a slab of hashish in tinfoil. About fifty quids' worth, Will calculated. But the sleeping girl, who was she? Where had he seen her before? Just then, flexing in the heat, one of the chrome bars of the gasfire pinged loudly, startled him, and he remembered her walking out of the Baggot Inn. He had felt himself withering then, but only briefly because his attention had been distracted by the barman whipping away the Moonman's rum-and-black-and-Guinness cocktail. Maybe she had seen what that brute was doing and it wasn't anything Will had done, or said, or sung, or — worst of all — represented, that she was fleeing from. He hoped so. It was odd to hope when he didn't know anything about this girl with the sticking-out teeth. It was odd, too, that it hadn't occurred to him that the monkish room must be hers.

Why is he glauming at her like that, Maeve thought as she stood for a moment in the doorway with hot plates in her hands.

'Much good it'll do you,' she said.

'What?'

'There's a banana thing on the counter,' she said and made a backward gesture with her head. 'A banana thing with yoghurt. Get it for me, will you? Before I wet myself with the laughing.'

A banana thing with yoghurt sounded funny and Maeve was

funny about food, particularly food she had prepared herself. It was hers and no one else's. Even if she offered you a morsel from her plate, she watched you with a beady expression in case you might think you were going to get away with it. What she wanted from food was like what she wanted from a man: bluntness and sharpness. Only that combination could satisfy her. This particular evening she had made one of her old reliables: chunks of chorizo fried crisp, then an onion melted with plenty of garlic, cumin and chilis, then a tin each of red kidney beans and tomatoes, some potatoes quartered, all simmered with a handful of green cardamoms and a scattering of black peppercorns, which she liked whole for their musty crunch. All dolloped on top of rice boiled bright yellow with turmeric.

'That's what the banana thing's for,' she said when Will waved his hand in front of his face. He drank a mouthful of the red wine. Its taste was blotted out by the spices, but it left a warm earthy feeling at the back of his throat.

This woman, he thought, will still be serving this food in forty years time, but I won't know her then.

Cory had woken up briefly when Maeve brought her a small bowl of the chili. She remembered the guitar-player but not his name — she was too worn out. The hospital had been swamped by old people with chest infections made worse by an outbreak of the winter vomiting bug, and then casualties had come in from a multiple car crash. That was what they were phoning her for in the Baggot. When she explained this to Will, he had an unaccountable feeling of relief, of being absolved of a crime he hadn't committed.

As Cory ate, delicately removing the cardamoms from her mouth and balancing them on the rim of the bowl, Maeve watched her with sidelong glances of disapproval, occasionally turning to Will, pursing her lips as if to say, 'Give me patience.' If Cory was aware of this, she didn't let on, and after a short while the fork fell from her fingers, her chin went down and she was asleep again.

Saving the bowl from sliding off Cory's lap, Maeve said, 'I can't stand nibblers, picking and poking at their food like there was something hidden in it.'

As she got up to remove the dishes she said, 'Now, turn on the box, like a good man.'

The television set stuck out above Will's head. It was fixed to the wall by a double-jointed black metal fixture that looked like the skeleton of a leg. The leg had a hand and on the hand the TV box rested submissively, like a creature that knows it is soon going to be swallowed by some mouth somewhere. If it could have crept, it would have been creepy. Maeve had spoken to him as if he, too, were a fixture, maybe even her husband. What was he doing here? Why was he sitting on a raggedy armchair with his neck twisted to look over his shoulder at a spiderous telly?

'What time is it?' he said when Maeve returned from washing the dishes in the kitchen.

'I don't know,' she said. 'But if the wind changes you'll be stuck like that for the rest of your life. Here, move up there,' she said to Cory, hooshing the leaning girl upright with her shoulder. 'Now, honeybunch, get in here beside me.' Will sat where she patted. She put her head on his shoulder and said, 'You'd think we were married. What a fucking bore. Let's do some blow.'

'No thanks.'

'Why not?' she said, and started softening the hashish with the flame of a lighter. 'Is dope against your principles too?'

'What do you mean "too"?'

'I know what you're like. You're always judging everything, aren't you?'

'No, I'm not.'

'Yes, you are. You're just such a straight.'

'Thanks.'

But he took the joint. He hadn't smoked dope for a long time. The first draw of the smoke went straight to his brain and within seconds he could feel the drugged blood frothing in his feet.

Then he was watching the TV intently, hardly aware that she was watching him.

Well, Maeve said to herself, he's done this before. She was puzzled. The way he had said 'no' she had thought he was straight, but the way he was sucking on the joint you'd think it was the last one on earth.

'Oh, look,' he said. On the screen a ramshackle man wearing a fez and waving a magician's baton was saying. 'My next trick is impossible.'

Maeve said, 'Do you think that's funny?'

'Of course it's funny. That's Tommy Cooper. He's a sack of jam.'

'I don't like comedians.'

Will stared at the screen, then turned to stare at her. 'Do you know, you remind me of a girl I used to go out with.'

'Goodlooking was she?'

'Goodlooking? Sheevawn? I suppose she was.'

'Thanks for the compliment.'

'What? Oh, I see what you mean. Well, Sheevawn was a sack of jam too, but she used to drive me up the wall. She was very critical.'

'Just like me then.'

'Yeah. But do you know what I used to say to her? I used to say. Let me see can I remember it. I used to say, "My moral faults, what you think are my moral faults, are just technical things to me".'

'Technical things?'

'Like watching TV, that's a technical thing. It's work. I'm thinking about work all the time I'm watching. Do you know what I mean?'

'Oh yeah, absolutely. It's as clear as mud. So what happened to your pretty woman? I bet you ditched her.'

A wave of cold guilt-blood surged through Will's veins and he stopped laughing. 'I have to go now,' he said.

'Go? You can't.'

'I can't? Why not?'

'You're being collected, remember. And your driver hasn't arrived yet.'

Will did not understand what she was saying. He looked at his watch. It was eight o'clock. He'd been here for more than an hour.

Whoever it was that was coming to collect him would find

him, and it would be in a room like this one, and with a woman in it as terrible.

'Why did you say "yet"?' he said in a small boy's accusing voice.

'Because,' Maeve said, 'before you go, you have to come.' And then she put her hand into his pocket. 'My word,' she said, 'that's eager. It leapt up like a dog out of a thorn bush. I've never experienced anything like it, so I haven't.'

This wasn't true. There was nothing exceptional about Will's penis for eagerness, size, or oddity — she had seen many an odder one — but it was a compliment she was used to paying, because it paid off, men being naturally inclined to exceptionalism, a term, picked up in her legal studies, relating to the American Constitution, which was only another way of saying Yanks were vain, as if their dicks were the Statue of Liberty. But just because it wasn't true did not mean she shouldn't say, 'It's like a fucking monument.'

Will did not hear what she was saying, partly because there was a ringing in his ears, but mostly because Cory was waking up. Her chin rose slowly off her chest, as if lifting a great weight, until at last the mass of her head was balanced for a moment on the column of her neck before toppling back again. And there definitely was a ringing in his ears.

Maeve stopped. 'Well, sod it,' she said.

'What's going on?'

'Saved by the bell. You answer it, will you?'

'Answer what?'

'The doorbell. What else would be ringing, you dope? And you'd better tell that thing to lie down first, or it'll make him even more jealous than he is already.'

Although the morning had been bright and sharp, in the late afternoon a thick blanket of fog had settled on the city, which was now so thick that Will, opening the door, saw the streetlamps on Waterloo Road as a series of fuzzy needle-balls. A white van was parked on the gravel and a figure was standing in its blazing headlights. It was Ossie Gleeson. Between the fog and the headlights, the freezing air occupied by his shadow was fogless.

The effect hardly registered on Will because a diminutive human being was tugging his sleeve. It was a boy with a harelip and the liquid eyes of a hare. Will took the paper the boy was holding out to him and tried to read the words scrawled on it.

'Who's the kid?' Ossie called out. 'Does he belong to you?'

6

WHAT MADE THE night was the Phillips Dansette. Ossie had loaded into his van the red and cream record player, which was a valued possession, along with some vinyl discs, Will's guitar and rucksack, and driven the short distance from Waterloo Road to Leeson Street. Music was now booming out scratchily from the Dansette and the flatwarming guests were passing around Maeve's big fat joint. How Vanessa Banim in her fake rabbit fur, Harry O'Gara, the window-dresser, Cormac Healy, the Executive Officer, and Emmet Roche, the artist and brute, came to be there was a mystery to Will. While the van was being unloaded in the street, they had come looming out of the fog, but was their arrival merely a happenstance, or had Ossie, or maybe Maeve, invited them? Either way it was annoying — he didn't like people coming into his personal space and lying around in it, smoking dope and burning holes in the furniture.

'It's not your space,' Ossie said. 'This is strictly temporary, right? No lease, no notice to quit, nothing. None of that malarkey. This guy is, like, weird about that stuff.'

This guy, never to be seen, was the landlord. He owned the whole building, a Georgian four-storey-over-basement house in Lower Leeson Street, and now that the sitting tenant had been unseated by death, the landlord, who knew Ossie's father, had agreed to rent his flat to Ossie's father's son's best friend.

'Even if it's only for a few weeks, you're in luck,' Ossie said. 'It's the whole top floor and the street is full of nightclubs.'

'It's just so amazing,' Vanessa said after all six of them, loaded with luggage, had tramped up many flights of dark brown linoleum stairs, passed through a door windowed with frosted glass, climbed another two flights of stairs, and found themselves panting on a landing.

'Somebody here drank,' Maeve said.

'The whole place is freaky,' Emmet said. 'The floor is on the wall.'

In the living room one wall was faced with planks and it did look like a floor. On the real floor of this room, of the landing and of the adjoining kitchen, empty bottles stood in rows, mostly wine but including whiskey, gin, vodka, brandy, sherry, Amaretto, tequila and St Germain, a liqueur made out of elderberries. A dozen of these bottles held a single rose, once red, now brown and withered almost to dust.

Harry said, 'This is nice. Let's have a nice cup of tea.'

'I've a better idea,' Maeve said, producing the slab of hash.

Vanessa said brightly, 'Oh, are we going to do drugs as well?'

To Harry the brightness seemed strained, but then this was only the second time he had met her. On reflection, the first time, in the Baggot Inn, with the rabbits sewn into a bag, had been strained too.

To Ossie 'drugs as well' wasn't enough, and without telling anyone — 'Where's your toyboy disappeared to all of a sudden?' Maeve asked Will, and got no reply — he had skipped down the stairs to the nightclub in the basement next door and soon returned with two bottles of champagne.

'To add to the collection,' Harry said.

'How much did that cost?' Will said.

'I know the manageress in Buck Whaley's,' Ossie said. 'She let me have them cheap. Good as gave them to me. Cost price nearly. And anyway it's only Spanish stuff, about a tenner in the supermarket.'

'You're a liar,' Emmet said.

'Would you believe it,' Harry said, 'we've got Ravel's Bolero.'

Eventually, when the wine had been opened, the flat toasted, and the joint passed round, they listened to the record, as Harry insisted, 'without drug-crazed interruptions.'

After a few minutes, though, it was Harry himself who interrupted. He rushed across the room to Emmet, who was squatting beside the Dansette, removing the records from their sleeves, holding them up close to his pebbly glasses, then flicking them, sleeveless, onto the floor.

'What are you doing, you terrible man,' Harry said, snatching up a disk. 'Sweet mother of the divine, this is Jack Buchanan. You wouldn't do this to a Picasso, would you?'

Emmet said, 'I would.'

'Well, don't do it to Jack Buchanan. He's an artist. Kindly treat him with the respect he deserves. Now, can we listen, please, to the fucking frog?'

So they listened to the Ravel. When the final repetition of the tune began to be played by the whole orchestra, Harry cried out, 'Tutti frutti!' and when the last bang banged, every one cheered and the ground beneath their feet rumbled in triumph.

'Now, ladies and gentlemen,' Harry said, 'let's have something we can dance to before Mr Roche can destroy it.'

On the Dansette Jack Buchanan sang:

> *Good night, Vienna,*
> *City of a thousand melodies,*
> *The world is waiting at the edge of the day*
> *Just waiting to say, I love you.*

Emmet stood up threateningly, advanced on Harry, then took him in his arms. Waltzing together, they swooped and curvetted on the fawn-coloured carpet. To make more space, Emmet kicked shut the door with a tremendous slam. As the song ended, Harry, body hooped back, one arm trailing the ground in imitation of a broken wing, died in Emmet's arms like a swan.

In the middle of the clapping, Vanessa said, 'I think somebody is knocking on the floor.'

Downstairs, of course, it was not the floor but the ceiling that was being stabbed with the handle of a sweeping-brush.

Will opened the door at the bottom of the stairs with difficulty because he was too stoned to find the light switch in the dark, and then he couldn't locate the latch either. Also, the thunderous rapping on the rippled frosted glass was bewildering him. When he did manage to get the door open what he noticed was the rapper's hair. It was dyed a burnished bronze and fitted over her head like a helmet.

'I'm going to call the guards,' she said. 'I'm a respectable woman.'

'But she didn't look like a respectable woman,' Ossie said later. 'She looked like an ancient old whore.'

'Just my type,' Emmet said.

Vanessa said, 'You can't say ancient and old together, can you?' And as she said it, she took Ossie's arm and pressed it to her breast.

But the dancing was done for the night, and though Jack Buchanan sang again, he did so at a lower volume, and when all the Spanish sparkling was drunk, everyone went down the stairs, tiptoeing past the woman's room — everyone that is except Emmet, who clomped his boots on the brown linoleum.

After they were gone, the flat, as well as seeming dingier, was definitely colder. On the bare mattress in the bedroom Will huddled in his sleeping bag. The upper casement of the window was jammed and through the gap an icy breeze was blowing. He thought of the woman downstairs, furious still, and rightly so. Like him she was in bed, or maybe she was squatting on her perch like an old hen, red wattles quivering, clucking indignantly for the want of an egg to be laid, a chick to be reared.

And he thought then of Waterloo Road and how Maeve had brought the boy with the harelip into her flat, read his tattered message and questioned him. What was he doing out in the fog on a night like this? What was his name? Where was he from? His only answer was a brown-eyed stare.

Ossie said, 'Maybe he's a gypsy.'

Maeve said, 'I know what it is. He doesn't speak English.' Then she turned to the boy and said, 'You're from Rumania, aren't you?'

The boy said, 'Fuck Rumania.'

Maeve laughed, gave him a tenner and sent him back into the fog.

7

The boy was a tinker, the season was winter,
And the girl's years were tender.
They smoked a cigaro, they danced the Bolero,
Hi-fol de-lol air-o.
The woman was red-haired, her temper it up-flared,
And no one was dead scared, but, baby, you were,
There was fear in your fur.
So this is what the drugs are for.
The boy is a splinter. The girl is a cinder.
It was writ on her face he was in the right place
For hunting the hare, for hunting the hare.

WILL LEFT THE flat only once, to go to the Tesco supermarket in Baggot Street, and he did that with his head down. If he had met Maeve on the way, he would have passed her by. He had work to do. The song wasn't right. Red-haired and up-flared? What a rhyme. He hated it.

He heated up his dinner. For three days he had been eating the same grey stew of fat lap of lamb. It was on Special Offer in the supermarket, so he had bought it. Bent low over the plate, he growled at the lumpen mess. He was furious at himself, at civilisation, at etiquette, but most of all at Tesco's. Somewhere in Ireland — probably in a Disadvantaged Area, where the poor farmers drove

Mercedes-Benz limousines, grant-aided by the European-Fucking-Union — Tesco had a gigantic boning-hall and in it there were armies of bloody-aproned migrant workers from Brazil, and in charge of these butchers there was a gang of little men from the midlands of Middledom, in white coats and little white trilby hats, and one of them, the big chief of the little chiefs, who wore on his pointy head a slightly whiter hat, was saying to them, 'Draw nigh to me, lads, I have tidings of great joy to impart, for we have here, after we've put the frilly bits of paper on the racks of lamb and sold them to Ossie Gleeson's mother, we have millions of tons of left-over laps of lamb, so get your Brazilians to sharpen their boning-knives and get out those bales of clingfilm and get out those emerald green polystyrene trays, for we are going to make the little people of this country a Special Offer they cannot afford to refuse, and most particularly of all, that pauperised little ferret Will Ferris.'

The flat was piercingly cold. The ferret needed a chill to work properly, but this was too much. So he left on the oven and all the gas rings. Heat snored through the place. At night the noise prevented him from sleeping, so he turned it off. There were no bedclothes, but in a cupboard he found a pair of old curtains made of a heavy serge-like material, decorated with a pattern of blue grapes and maroon roses. Wrapped in their mustiness he would sleep well.

But where to sleep? In the bedroom the window wouldn't close and the wind whistled through it like a train in a tunnel. The couch in the living room was too short. There was another room, which he had thought was empty, but on the second morning he discovered a horsehair mattress leaning against the wall. The sun was shining through the window. And lying side by side on the windowsill were a large hawkwing moth and a swallow.

The bird had more than likely flown in through the open window in the other room and been trapped by a breeze that had slammed the door shut. It had died in captivity. Who knows how long the death had taken? The floor was speckled with bird-shit. And as for the moth, it might have been born in the room, hatched, pupated, grown wings and flown around with the swallow, the two of them swooping and fluttering, then dying and dehydrating together in the sun from Leeson Street. But the moth's body was dry to start with. In all its minute organs there could only have been the smallest droplet of liquid to lubricate them, to stay them from becoming what they had now become, a speckle of amber resin, and the vivid patterns on its wings were dust, a colourless smear on the tip of his finger.

He had bought a roll of plastic sacks for the bottles — there was more than a hundred — and left them out in the street with the bins. Then he had found, in the same cupboard as the curtains, an ancient Hoover, a cylinder on skis, but it worked and he had vacuumed the entire flat. Less the bottles, the bird droppings, the dust and the dander, the rooms had the clean air of an abandoned mortuary. That suited him. But personally he was filthy. So, standing naked on a towel in the bathroom, he washed in the handbasin. Maeve's smell and the smell of sex was still on him, fish crossed with fox.

In the kitchen the dead tenant had tacked cuttings from newspapers and pictures from colour supplements all over the walls. His relatives, if he had any, hadn't thought them worth saving, and the landlord hadn't thought them worth tearing down. There was too much for Will to take in yet. Now he saw just a photograph of Marilyn Monroe glowing vulnerably in a terrycloth robe and, pinned on top of it, a yellowing headline from the *Evening Press* that read 'Monster Walk for the Handicapped'. He was about to turn away when he noticed words, the record of a conversation, faintly pencilled on the wall's damply flaking plaster:

'Are you drinking wine?'

'No, I just poured this little drop for myself.'

'You've had 3 glasses of wine.'

'No, I haven't. I've only had one.'

'You've had 3.'

'No, I just poured this much 3 times.'

It was dated 21st July 1996. This, Will thought, is a story I am never going to be told.

Of course, as he knew she would, Maeve had called. Twice

in the night and once in the morning she had rung the bell and hammered the knocker. And she had left a message that read, 'I know you're in there.' The message was on a postcard that showed Diana the huntress firing an arrow at Actaeon. To Will, who had never seen a Titian before, the painting looked crude, almost cartoonish, but the rose-madder red of the satin robe the goddess wore lodged in his mind and some weeks later he remembered it and went into a bookshop to look up a dictionary of mythology. He'd been wrong: Actaeon didn't have a horse's head but a stag's. Even more arresting was the fact that as well as being the guardian of virgins, Diana was the killer of women in childbirth. And the girls who came to her shrine from all over Greece used to pretend to be men and dress up in the skins of bears. That suited Maeve all right.

He had found the card lying not on the brown linoleum but on the hall table. The old hen in the flat below must have put it there. Ms Geraldine Heneghan R.N. was the name on her mail. What did the letters stand for? The Royal Navy. She was a retired sailor. That suited her.

But there was a mystery about this 'Ms' — she wasn't living alone. She had a man. They came in late at night and went out early in the morning. On the day he finished the Bolero song, Will met them on the stairs. The man was his own age. That is to say Will's in years, but, according to the calendar of reality, he was ageless. He had short colourless scaly hair and a round face, babyish but pimpled. He wore an official-looking blue suit and efficient brown shoes, highly polished.

'I'm sorry about the noise the other night,' Will said.

'It's too late to be sorry,' Ms Heneghan said. 'The time to be sorry was beforehand. We don't deserve to have our night's sleep disturbed by a pack of I don't know what kind of animals galloping over our heads.'

'A pack of buffalos,' the man said. Then added, as if he had gone too far, 'Well, that's what it sounded like to me.'

'Buffalos are animals,' Ms Heneghan said. 'But they wouldn't engage in this kind of behaviour. And as for the guitar-playing night noon and morning, that's more of it, and up with it I will not put. Isn't that right, Sonny?' But Sonny only ducked his head and pawed at the lino with his hoof.

With that she opened her door, pushed him in before her and followed through as small an opening as was practicable to prevent Will from seeing what was no business of his to see: an all-in-one bedsit with a partitioned cubicle in a corner for hygiene.

But Will had seen, and as he walked to Waterloo Road he wondered. It was hardly imaginable that she shared the same bed with her son, if that is what Sonny was — he looked like a premature baby born with pimples, but he was too like her not to be descended from her. It didn't bear thinking of. Anyway, the bed Will had spied, it would be an exaggeration to describe it as queen-sized, even in Lilliput. Perhaps Sonny slept on the floor, or maybe she put him to sleep in the hygiene cubicle, standing up. Will was never to know, and in the eight months he stayed in Leeson Street neither of them ever spoke to him again. Everywhere he went, almost as soon as he opened the door on a new place or switched on the light in an old one, he made enemies. Why was that?

8

CORY LEARY DIDN'T believe in God but she went to Mass every Sunday. On this last Sunday in Advent she was in the Franciscan church of Adam and Eve on the south bank of the river Liffey. In the sense of something good coming, Advent meant to her only the dutiful prospect of going home for Christmas. In the sense of adventurous, the word didn't apply to her either, or so she thought. And yet there were people who believed she was daring and that she represented the possibility of the coming of something good. Amongst these people was Will Ferris. So full of hope was he this Advent Sunday that he was hiding in the north transept, spying on her in the nave.

Also among the hopeful people, though not in the congregation, was Emmet Roche.

Two months earlier, in late October, while painting a ten-foot tall canvas — 'The middle classes won't,' he said, 'be hanging this over their mantelpiece' — Emmet had fallen off the ladder and dislocated his knee.

In the Casualty Department of the Mater Hospital, where she was doing part of her internship, Cory had said, 'We'll bring you into theatre, give you an anaesthetic and sort it out, but you'll have to wait. You can see the madness here, so it might take some hours. Or I could do it now. The pain will be bad, but it won't last long, and then you'll be OK.'

What kind of option was that to offer a Roche?

So, putting one hand on his knee, the other under his heel, she had leaned, jerked and twisted simultaneously. Emmet had screamed. Then he had wept. Not for long, but still he had cried, which he had not done since he was a child, and not much then. All you needed to know about this pain was that it was in the world. Cory had given him a tissue to dry his eyes, said she would have a cup of tea brought to him, told him various things to do and not to do, including dancing, and gone away to the next casualty, all as if she had not seen the tears. But she had. And he had seen the look in her eyes. Cory Leary was noticeable when you noticed her. And her small hands were surprisingly strong. One thumb, though, was raw from being gnawed, and her doctor's white coat was too big for her, and the long-laced trainers she wore made her feet look clumsy, as if she were standing on dilapidated blocks of cement. It pained Emmet to see them, but he dismissed the feeling scornfully. There was no room for sentimentality in his economy. All the same, he had kept the tissue. It bore the faintest trace of her perfume, Chantecaille Frangipane, which was all the more powerful for being faint, like a homeopathic remedy.

Homeopathy, though it was one of his pet hates, was marginally less hateful to Emmet than God, especially the Christian one. The world was, after all, full of evil spirits and it was just possible that if you gave it back a bit of its own medicine, diluted in the proportion of a molecule to an ocean, it could cure you. That is, of course, if you believed in it. Which he didn't. This happened to be true of his own work, or his practise, as he had learned to call it at St Martin's School of Art in High Holborn, where he had studied for three years. As well as a vocabulary, he had acquired there just enough theory to realise that what he had been critiquing all his life was the production of meaning, but what the college called 'the intertextuality of appropriation' was, in his opinion, the shite of a bull — he was a painter, he painted fucking paintings, and if they didn't like it, they could fuck off. But St Martin's, though it had shaken its collective head, had liked the way he appropriated his textualities and awarded him a first class degree in Fine Art. And why wouldn't they? He was absolutely Fine, indubitably. Of course he slathered on the paint inches thick, but the smallest mistake, a dull whorl of colour, a duff curl of impasto, bothered him, sometimes for months, and the botheration was all the more bothersome because in his way of working, mistakes were hard to correct. Correction meant you were wrong from the start. Nothing good could come of going back to the bad. For him everything was advent, or at least adventitious, in the sense of coming from the outside. Harry O'Gara said his work was 'simply divine, sometimes'. That opinion was in Emmet's opinion, 'culture-vulture horse manure'. Harry's pause for the comma was especially galling. What the hell did 'sometimes' mean? Emmet's art was superb, always and forever. It was only on the basis of eternity that people should look at it, and they were too stupid for that. What he needed was praise, yet the only praise that could satisfy him was the equivalent of Cory Leary cracking his knee back into place.

Seeing her again, pushing through the door of the Baggot Inn, had been a shock, and when she passed by, he had let on not to see her. Her seeing him was what he wanted, and planned for — occasionally: he wasn't that obsessed, yet. But had he been told he could be seen by her by going to church he would have been puzzled, genuinely. Was Adam and Eve's a pub he hadn't heard of? And if he had been told that Cory went there to go to Mass he would have said, 'You must be out of your Chinese mind.' Because Emmet was an atheist. Not the sort who starts off doubting that God exists and ends up believing in the doubt; nor the sort for whom God, as the author of the tragedy of history, has become another victim of it, and serve Him right too. No, Emmet just knew there is no god, certainly not with a capital letter. The fact of the matter was that matter was fact. That was it, end of story.

If, though, going to Adam and Eve's had been suggested to him as a stratagem, he would have gone, and gladly. But even if he had appeared as an altar-boy and gone down on his knees on the marble steps, his paint-speckled boots sticking out from under purple skirt and white surplice, with the golden cluster of communion bells trembling with terror in his huge hand, it wouldn't have made any difference to his chances of success — as Cory didn't believe in God she believed even less in miracles. Or in mysteries.

'If everything is mysterious nothing is,' she said to Will after he had sung 'The Boy in Winter Bolero' to her and Maeve in Waterloo Road. His explaining the background of the song hadn't changed her opinion either. In fact it had strengthened it. How could anyone be expected to know the red-haired woman was angry because he had danced on her ceiling, or that the boy had a harelip? The answer was, they couldn't. Such mysteries, she said, were worse than mysterious; they were unfair to the audience. At least religion was upfront about them.

'I'll give him this much,' Maeve said to Emmet, much later, 'Will Ferris has a brass neck.' She was annoyed that Will had come around to Waterloo Road and sung the song.

'I don't get it,' Emmet said. 'Why does that mean he's got a brass neck?'

'He only did it to impress that frigid witch doctor of his. The only reason he was there was to see her. And the worst of it is — anyway, what do you care?'

'I don't,' Emmet said.

Maeve, although she was tempted, didn't say what the worst of it was. That was the way Will had made love to her that last time. That had been the revenge of disappointment, the typical male's brutal fucking of a woman when he's on his way out of her life. But the worst of it had also been the best of it.

'Listen,' Will had said, 'what about, you know, your flatmate? I don't want another couch experience.'

'What?' Maeve had said, thrusting her tongue into his ear.

'Like the last time. She could have woken up.'

'Who?'

'Your flatmate.'

'Oh my God, look at that,' she said after dragging down his zip.

'But what if she comes back?'

'She won't.'

'But she could. You can't guarantee — '

'It's all right. How can you walk around with this thing?'

'But it mightn't be all right.'

'Well, it is. She's gone for good.'

'What?'

'She's moved out. Gone.'

'Gone where?'

'How would I know?'

But Cory had come back. In a matter of minutes — violent ones for Maeve — she was knocking at the door. By the time Maeve let her in, Will had adjusted his clothing and it was more or less without embarrassment that he had followed her in pursuit of a faint chirruping sound.

'There it is,' Cory said opening a drawer in the bedside locker. The chirruping grew louder. It was her phone.

She had stayed long enough to drink a cup of coffee, to hear Will singing his song and to explain why she was leaving Waterloo Road: she was moving into the Rotunda hospital to do her gyney. Gyney? Gynaecology. And midwifery.

'It beats me how she does that stuff,' Maeve said. 'She's so bloody prim and it's so bloody sordid.'

9

THERE WAS, HARRY O'Gara thought, something unearthly about Emmet Roche. For one thing he listened to Kraftwerk. Even more of a give-away, in his studio cum apartment cum derelict warehouse down on the quays, as kraut-rock boomed from the speakers, Harry saw on the floor an open book by William Burroughs called 'Junky'. Maybe Emmet did heroin. No needles were in sight, but the way he was going they were bristling on the horizon.

'You are,' Harry said, 'so evil I don't know what I'm going to do with you at all at all.'

To Emmet to be called evil was a compliment. But he wasn't the kind of person you paid compliments to. Not only would you not take sweeties from such a strange man, you wouldn't give them to him. Perhaps that was the unearthly thing: perhaps he was afraid of being gay.

Harry had considered this possibility when they first met. The meeting had come about because he had had the brilliant idea of asking the College of Art could he borrow some of their classical plaster-casts for a display of swimwear — not wearing the things, or the thongs, just looking on at the mannequins — in Brown Thomas's windows. The College had sent him to talk to Mr Roche in the Fine Art Department. Mr Roche had thought it was funny, as if a De Chirico idea in fashion was original. Nothing had come of it of course: you couldn't rent statues from the State — for a start it wouldn't know what to call the money — but to celebrate the refusal, they'd gone for a drink in The Clock.

Was Emmet, Harry asked himself, one of us? No. Not never no way. But nobody was not gay. Well, that was a prejudice. Which didn't mean it wasn't true. But was Emmet straight then? No. He was bent in some way. Was he, maybe, a chicken hawk? Harry brought up the subject of paedophilia just to see how he'd react. Blank. So, to test him a bit further, Harry had said, 'That's how I started off my own illustrious career, you know. My by now more or less non-career in the priesthood of gaydom.'

Actually, it had been a priest who had introduced Harry to sex. Some years later the priest had become famous by being caught red-handed doing his evil deeds with other, even younger boys.

But were the deeds evil?

'Not as far as I'm concerned,' Harry said to Cory Leary when the subject came up some five months later.

'Why not?'

'Because I'm not the first little boy that was groomed by a pervert and liked it.'

'Liked it? I don't believe you.'

'Well, we all have to start somewhere, and boys, especially boys like me, will start anywhere. Of course, it's different for women, isn't it? I mean it's all water to fish, isn't it? Blood and sex and birth and death. Ladies swim in them things. But men are so — I don't know — narrow-minded. I mean, what we go for is the action, not the consequences. Anyway, I liked being groomed. I don't like it now, but I did when I was fifteen. Sort of. And it was fun. Father Phil — he liked to call himself Father Philomena, but I called him the Druid of Dungarvan — he used to bring down the weirdest boys from Dublin. It really was great gas, camping around in the presbytery dressed up in his vestments and drinking vodkatinis. So not Dungarvan. Except for the vodka.'

'Harry, don't pretend it's funny.'

'I'm not pretending.'

'What did your parents think about this? Did they not mind?'

'Don't make me laugh. My parents were too busy killing each other to notice what their son was up to. So I take a world-weary view of evil men. It's like listening to too much Kraftwerk. I mean, if that's not evil, where does Emmet Roche's unearthliness come from? From being certain, that's where. Did you ever meet anyone so certain in all your life?'

'Will Ferris?'

'But of course. From the start those two were bound to come into conflict. They're like two big distant objects in the universe. You mightn't notice it but they attract each other. Speaking of the Big Bang, do you know where I think the trouble started? The Café En Seine. You know the Insane Café? That cavernous place in Dawson Street. Anyway, there I was this Sunday, just before Christmas, if I remember correctly. I'd gone there to read *The News of the World*, which I do on Sundays, for the book reviews, and then who appears except Emmet. In his boots. I believe he has the paint speckled onto them by a beautician. And then who do you think flurries in, like a hen in a hurry to lay an egg, but Ossie Gleeson. And who has Ossie in tow?'

'Will.'

'How did you know that?'

'He told me.'

'I bet he didn't tell you why Ossie was hen-like.'

'No.'

'Because he'd spent the morning trying to find Will. Looked everywhere, high up and low down. Not to be found anywhere.'

'He was at Mass.'

'Don't make me laugh. Anyway, Ossie had got him this gig in the En Seine for a couple of hours in the afternoon. Strictly the guitar. Background sounds in one of those upstairs galleries. But Will played fantastically well. And then he sang the song about the boy with the harelip. I got so many shivers up my spine I couldn't count them.'

'Harry,' Cory said, 'you're exaggerating as usual. Will doesn't even like the song. He thinks it's crap.'

'He is such a snob.'

'He's got good taste.'

'Same thing. Anyway, Emmet Roche hated the whole performance. When Will came over to our table he just said, "That was very nice — for folk-music." Well, I said, Bach was folk music and so were Bartok and Buddy Holly and, come to that, so is Avril LaVigne. "What's got under your shirt?" says he. And come to that, says I, even your Kraftwerkers are folk, underneath their helmets. "They aren't," Emmet says, "they aren't banjo-players anyhow." Jesus, the guy is pitiable.'

But it wasn't because Emmet was a musical philistine that made Harry think he was pitiable. It was because early on the May morning of the night he was talking to Cory, his doorbell had begun buzzing. At first he had thought it was some other buzzer in the warren of tiny flats he lived in, but then he had realised it really was his. So he had got up, put on a dressing gown — 'a kind of kung-fu kimono, woefully short' — and gone to open the door.

'Emmet,' he said, 'do you know what hour it is?'

But Emmet, who was wearing a tuxedo and a long white scarf, had merely looked upwards, as if to check the number over the door was the one he was looking for, and then he had turned on his heel and walked away. Harry had not said anything to stop him. The look on Emmet's face was too far gone for stopping.

10

IT WAS WHAT Will thought was a harmless remark that caused him to sing with such feeling in the Café En Seine that Sunday afternoon.

Cory often moved house. When she had first arrived in Dublin at the age of seventeen, wearing the wrong clothes and with no money, she had stayed in a student hostel, but in the following six years at medical school she had tenanted many bedsits, flats and shared houses. She was, though, fixed in one respect: she froze at even a hint of condescension. This should not have conflicted with a streak of servility in Will's character — which he loathed — but it did. He was, she said, the only person she had ever met who could bully and cringe at the same time.

The servility manifested itself primarily in his dreams. The night before he made the harmless remark, he had dreamed he was in a Volkswagen Beetle being driven by Hoagy Carmichael at a hundred miles an hour backwards through Bloomington, Indiana. Smoke from the cigarette drooping from his lower lip trickled up past Hoagy's rheumy eye. His head was turned away from the smoke, just as it was when he played the piano, so that Will wondered how he could see where he was going in the rear-view mirror. But Hoagy, who was all old loose bones in his clothes, had everything under control.

Will had intended saying, 'In my opinion, Mr Carmichael,

"When the deep purple falls on the kitchen garden walls" is the best thing you ever wrote.' Not only were there no kitchen gardens in any of Hoagy's songs, but to his horror he had said something entirely different: "In my opinion, Mr Carmichael, the best thing you ever wrote is, "He played his guitar just like ringing a bell".'

Whereupon Hoagy had stood wrathfully on the brakes and drawled, 'Kid, I may be dead, but sure as hell I ain't Chuck Berry.'

Servility of this sort could manifest itself in waking life only as rudeness, and Will, in the presence of the famous, was rude to the point of violence. On the one occasion he had met Bono, for instance, the U2 singer had retreated behind the bulk of his burly manager saying, 'What's his problem?'

Rudeness and servility were not designed to appeal to Cory Leary.

At Mass in Adam and Eve's she neither knelt to pray, nor stood for the Gospel, nor went up to the altar to receive Communion. She sat on the edge of her seat staring intently at the doddery old priest as he faltered through the ritual. The only movements she made were to lean back, uninterested, during the sermon, and occasionally to gnaw at the side of her thumb. On her head she wore what looked like an old-fashioned schoolboy's blue peaked cap; around her neck was wound a thick red scarf; and the rest of her was enveloped in a man's dark brown crombie overcoat, a near-antique by the look of it, which was so voluminous that she seemed to have taken refuge in a crumpled box, with only her nose sticking out of it, like a cartoon character drawn on a wall, a Kilroy Woz Here, not male or bulbous, but female and pointed.

When the Mass was ended, Will followed her again. This time he felt even more guilty and furtive than he had when, hanging around outside the Rotunda in the hope of spotting her, he had seen her but lost his nerve and, instead of saying as planned a surprised 'Hello', he had shadowed her to Adam and Eve's.

Now, going back to the hospital along the new boardwalk by the river, she was stopped by beggars. One was a dirty blonde in a dirty tracksuit, the other a ringletted brunette in a short short skirt. Although they were small and tall and far away, it was clear to

Will that they were mother and daughter. And even at this distance he could sense the electric yet lazy threat that came off them. But before he could decide what to do, Cory had parted with money.

As she made for the exit from the boardwalk, Will speeded up, crossed the road, recrossed it, and deliberately almost bumped into her.

'Hey,' he said. 'Fancy meeting you here.'

'Oh, hi.'

'What are you doing in this neck of the woods?' He hadn't planned saying 'neck of the woods' and when he said it he felt he should be beaten with a short stick.

'I'm going to the GPO.' She took from the big patch-pocket of her coat a padded envelope. 'I don't want to miss the post.'

'You'll be OK. There's plenty of time.'

'It's not for here. It's for America.'

'Oh, that's different. In that case you'd want to send it express.'

'Good idea.'

'Parcel post takes forever. That isn't really a parcel, though, is it? Is it a book? It looks like a book.'

'It is.'

'What's it called?

'*Winnie the Pooh*. It's a present for a cousin of mine.'

'Oh, are you an aunt?'

'An aunt? No.'

'I wouldn't have taken you for one.'

'Why not?'

'Well, you're too young.'

'You could be born an aunt.'

'I hadn't thought of it like that. You could even be an aunt before you were born.'

'Or an uncle.'

'Yes, you're right. Right again. Not me, though. I'm an only child. I'll never be an uncle. I mean I can't have blood relations.' She looked at him, closing her eyes briefly. He knew he was gabbling but he couldn't stop himself.

'Speaking of blood, you're a doctor, aren't you, or a medical student?'

'Yes?'

'Well, I saw this weird thing in the paper yesterday. It was about Yasser Arafat, you know, the Arab, the head of the Palestinians, in Palestine, right? Anyway, it doesn't matter if you know or not. Well, this guy that was with him when he died, he said Arafat had blood coming out of him from everywhere, every opening, ears, mouth, nose, from his eyes for God's sake. Bleeding from the eyes. Have you ever heard of anything like that?'

'No,' she said, 'but I have heard of Yasser Arafat.'

'Oh. I'm sure you have. I didn't mean — '

'Look, there's the lights. See you.'

The traffic lights had changed from red to green. Almost instantly she was swallowed up in the throng of people swarming across Bachelors Walk. As he turned away hopelessly he saw the junky mother and daughter staring at him. More enemies. More hatred. Righteous, though.

11

'ANYWAY, WHY DID you ring me?' Maeve asked Ossie.

'Oh, I just thought you'd want to know.'

This ape slept with me, she thought, and unless I'm very much mistaken he wants to sleep with me again, but he rings me to say that his best friend, a guy he knows I have a thing for, is playing in the Café En Seine and he says he rang because he just thought I'd want to know. That's crap. I don't believe that. So what's the real reason? Her violet stare pierced his doe-eyed gaze. There were three possible explanations. One, he was innocent — but when it came to men, innocence was out of the question. Two, he'd rung because he knew it was too late for her to get to the café in time — but that was more malice than Ossie Gleeson capable of; he hadn't the brains for badness. Or three, he'd rung because he had an obscure desire for her to sleep with Will again in order to be jealous, or maybe even, if he was, like most males, a pervert, to be there while she was being screwed. Yes, there was something of that in it. But though Maeve analysed motives, she didn't give weight to them, and as a result she found no one guilty. People were like weeds: they grew up and bent over with the weight of their own heads — there was no guilt in that, or sorrow either. As a result, she had no time for remorse or grief. Her thoughts were granular, the grains stuck to each other like seeds in a pomegranate, but they were indifferent to the stickiness. Indifference was her best weapon. But although her emotional senses were highly developed, they were also primitive: she was like a lizard sunning itself on a rock whose blood goes cold and slows as soon as the sun is hidden by a cloud.

'Thanks for thinking of me,' she said. 'But I couldn't have made it, even if I'd wanted to.'

She couldn't have made it because she had been out in Blanchardstown collecting her first-ever car, a Volkswagen Beetle, which she had bought off a shady dealer. Her father often put business in the dealer's way, so it was in his interest to give her a good deal, and indeed he had, to the extent of offering himself to her for free. While she was fending him off, Ossie had called and saved her — not that she needed saving. There was no way of getting to the En Seine in time, but she had driven the new car back there anyway. And on her way in the door she had met Will on his way out. He had kissed her coldly on the cheek and then stalked off as if a thundercloud was hanging over his head.

'What a minger,' she said.

'On the basis of what we heard just now,' Harry O'Gara said, 'this minger is hot stuff.'

'Hot my bottom,' Emmet Roche said. He and Harry had already been at each other about Avril LaVigne being a genius and Will Ferris not being even in the same class as her.

'You're just jealous,' Harry said.

'Look at the green in my eye,' Emmet said, lifting up his granny glasses and with his thumb pulling down the pouch of one bloodshot little eye till it almost popped out of its socket.

'In my part of the country a minger is a kind of scumbag,' Cormac Healy said to Maeve.

'A minger is a minger anywhere,' Emmet said. 'Where are you from, boy?'

'I'm from Stab City,' Cormac said. 'So don't boy me, boy. Sure, aren't you from Limerick yourself, except you're only a Rathkeale pisspot.'

Ultan McGrath said, 'Rathkeale is a Traveller town, isn't it?'

'Traveller?' Cormac said. 'Tinkers, tinkers that's the word for them.'

'Who's a tinker?' Emmet said.

'Who's a minger?' Cormac said. This didn't make much sense, but anyway he said it.

Earlier Maeve had asked Harry his opinion of Cormac, and he had said 'Well, he spits when he speaks, and he's wearing a deplorable suit and a manky tie, even though it's Sunday. And he's even straighter than his friend, Mr McGrath, if that's conceivable. But I'm fond of him already.'

Normally, the fact that two men were out stravaging around the city together on a Sunday afternoon meant, in Harry's opinion, that they must be gay, but in this instance the rule didn't apply. No one could ever think of Cormac Healy as not straight. And his friend was, if anything, shorter than the shortest distance between two points, as the crow flies. Ultan McGrath was big, brawny, bearded, as coarse-haired as a badger but fox-coloured. His brain, though, was bigger than a fox's. There were stars all over his first-class degree in economics, and he could have gone on to MIT or Harvard or Chicago, but he had sat the exam for Administrative Officer in the Department of Finance instead. He had done this to please his father, who had entered the civil service by that route and risen to be Secretary of the Department of Defence. Pleasing his father and his mother, who was headmistress in a convent school, had occupied all of Ultan's adolescence, and the only relief from pleasing them had been provided by Orla, his first and only girlfriend, another swot. Unfortunately, or as Harry put it, 'As fuck would have it,' Orla had got pregnant during their first term at UCD, and to mollify both sets of parents — who were old-fashioned enough to be scandalised —they had got married. The child, Dáibhí, pronounced Dawvee, was now a healthy and interesting two-year-old; Orla had found a part-time job as a research assistant and was studying for a Ph.D. in molecular biology; and in the AO exam Ultan had won first place. Within a month of entering the Department of Finance, his superiors had noted the quality of his work and he was on his way, imperturbable as ever, up the ladder. But within another month, in the middle of November, something momentous had happened to him: he discovered he was bored. His work was interesting, the workings of the Department and of power were interesting, but really they were boring. So was everything else. He was lost. He hadn't the faintest idea what to do with himself. All he knew was that he didn't want to go home after work, and when he got there, he didn't want to look at Orla, or — he couldn't bear to ask why — at little Dáibhí.

All the same, although he had little empathy with others and even less imagination, it could not be said of him, as can often be said of the imaginative, that he was an intellectual snob. His new friend Cormac Healy, for instance, was a dunce, and how he had managed to become an Executive Officer in the Department of Finance with only a pass degree in, of all things, Commerce was incomprehensible. That he had a gammy leg and used a walking stick should not have been the explanation, and yet, viewed in the light of the government's new-found commitment to gender equality and disability issues — what one Human Resources officer in Finance called 'cunts and cripples' — perhaps the inexplicable could be explained.

Anyway, Cormac was good company, always around, always on the go, always full of jizz. Besides, he didn't ask awkward questions. For instance, when he said he was thinking of going down to Smithfield to have a dekko at the open-air ice-rink, he hadn't asked why Ultan had instantly volunteered to join him without as much as a by-your-leave from his wife.

Nor, when they wandered into the Café En Seine and met Maeve, had Cormac asked why Ultan's face had turned brick red. Anyway, both of their faces were flushed already — after seeing the skaters at Smithfield, they had gone on a small pub-crawl.

The real reason for the redness was something Ultan had done. He had spent the most of the previous Thursday night searching for a nightclub. That there is a distinction between a nightclub and a club for dancing was a distinction he had forgotten, if he had ever known it. He did know, though, that if you were a habitué of such places there was a strong chance you were the sort of person who had a pass degree in Commerce. But that was the old world, pre-boredom. Now he wanted to go there. But where was there? Wasn't Leeson Street full of nightspots? So he had gone to Leeson Street. But it was closed. It took him some time to realise that it was not yet nine o'clock and that clubs opened their doors only when pubs closed theirs.

Annoyed with himself, he was about to go home to Orla when he was brought up short by the sight of a young woman standing on the edge of the pavement with her hands cupped around her mouth, howling at the top of her voice. Her head was thrown back so far he thought she might be cursing the yellow moon that hung over the city, but then he realised what she was howling at was a lit window, high up.

'Come out,' the woman cried. 'Come out or I'll burn your house down!'

That this woman had an excellent degree in law from Trinity College, that she was a qualified solicitor, that she worked in the Office of the Attorney General, that she was Maeve MacNamee, were only minor amazements compared to the astonishment of her taking him by the arm, dragging him up to O'Brien's on Mespil Road for hot whiskies, and then hurrying him home to her bed in Waterloo Road.

For weeks Ultan's mind had been turning over aimlessly, as if the engine of his intellect had stripped its gears, but eventually he had come to understand that the problem was not mechanical but linguistic. What he was missing was the manual, what he needed were the words, the Directions for Use of the Life Machine. And now, as he sprawled on Maeve's salmon-pink silk eiderdown, naked for her in a way that he had never been naked for Orla, he found them, miraculously, in a memory of Dr Martin Luther King at the Lincoln Memorial in Washington saying, 'Free at last, free at last. Thank God Almighty, I'm free at last.'

It never crossed his mind that freedom for him might be boring for Maeve, just as he didn't pause to wonder, as his old repressed self being was being swept aside by this dam-burst of sexual sensation, why he had kept his socks on. The reason was all too obvious: the floor looked, as his mother would have said, 'a bit germy'.

Actually, Maeve agreed. With Cory going, she would need a flatmate to help with the rent, and, to attract one, a blast of the vacuum cleaner wouldn't go amiss.

But all that was in the future.

~~~

Back in the Café En Seine, Harry stood up abruptly. From the gallery he saw a man he knew, instantly had a bright idea, and ran down the stairs to speak to him.

'Where's your notebook?' he said. 'Doesn't the proprietor of *The Irish Times* supply you with parchment and Mont Blanc pens?'

'I'm perfectly capable of remembering,' said Ernesto de Mahon. 'Just give me the names.'

As his own name suggests, Ernesto's origins were partly Irish but mainly Hispanic. His family had owned land in Cuba, but, before his birth, they had been forced to flee to Miami, thanks to Fidel Castro. By the time he had grown up and gone to New York to study, where he had met Harry, who was still in his teens and working in Bergdorf Goodman's department store, Ernesto had spent most of his inheritance on cocaine.

'The nose,' Harry said, 'was falling off his face.'

As well as telling Ernesto that the land of their common ancestors was full of little people, all called Darby O'Gill and all of them gay, Harry had also done him a favour with an unpleasant drug dealer. 'I merely,' he said, 'interposed my charm between them.' Merely wasn't true: he had paid the dealer five hundred dollars to go away. Belatedly, since by now Ernesto had been living in Ireland for almost four years, payback time had arrived.

The Irish Times was far too serious a newspaper to have a gossip column, and yet, as Ernesto had pointed out to the Features Editor, the avoidance of tittle-tattle about the nouveaux riches and the consequential absence of photographs of blondes dressed in frocks held up by thin shoulder-straps had left an obvious gap in the paper's coverage of social affairs. To fill this gap, the paper had a column called *On the Town*, devoted almost entirely to book-launches and the opening of art exhibitions. Such events attracted some moneybags and some mistresses, but mostly they were attended by bright-eyed women in jumpers and desperate men with wispy facial hair and cheap eyeglasses. Ernesto, whose principal interests in life were 18th-century houses, their 21st-century owners, good clothes, ground-breaking restaurants and scandal, had done his best to add some *bon ton* to the column, but the tone had remained depressingly high. Harry's request, however, was easily met. Nor did it matter that Ernesto had not been present to hear the singing.

B runch in the splendid, almost neo-Baroque bastion of the **Café En Seine** in Dawson Street is proving to be a highlight in the capital's Christmas cultural caravanserai. Sipping a medicinal Alka-Seltzer, actually the Café's curious, if refreshing, Cava spritzer, *On the Town* chatted with noted trend-setter and **Brown Thomas** bright spark **Harry O'Gara** who was positively buzzing with enthusiasm after hearing the Seine début of singer songwriter **Will Ferris**. Originally from Cork, the Leeside warbler has, one might be tempted to say, words at Will and, besides, according to O'Gara, he 'sings like the Angel Gabriel'. Your columnist rather thought that heavenly person was less a vocalist than a tootler on the trumpet, but why quibble when a star is being born? Concurring in this opinion was the fabulously fresh fashionista **Vanessa Banim**, who described herself as 'something of a Ferris fanatic.' You can catch up with the Corkonian caroller on Monday nights in the **Baggot Inn**. [Where's that?]

This last question was intended solely for the sub-editor, but it went through unnoticed in the Christmas rush. The following week, however, in accordance with *Irish Times* policy, the Corrections and

Clarifications panel stated that the Baggot Inn was in Baggot Street.

'A Ferris fanatic? I never said any such thing,' Vanessa said.

'But Ernesto is such a sweetie really, isn't he? And so elegant. I love mature men, don't you?'

'We do,' Harry said.

'But what we really love is mature women,' Maeve said.

Harry's bright idea had not turned out brightly. Ossie Gleeson had rung to say that he thought the piece was grand but Will was throwing up with fury. Harry himself felt slightly sick — 'Brown Thomas bright spark' sounded undesirable, like an electric shock to the colon — and he was more than slightly irritated by the fact that it had not been he but Ernesto who had made the mistake about the angel Gabriel being a singer.

12

GETTING VANESSA TO take Cory's room was also turning out to be not a bright idea. It should have been blindingly obvious that someone who attached herself to Ernesto — 'Gay Chevara' as Harry was now calling him — just to get her name in *The Irish Times* was not a suitable flatmate for Maeve. All she had done since her arrival in Waterloo Road was fill the fridge with health-foods, cover the couch with a 1960s-style polka-dot material, litter the place with samples of cloth, sew on her computerised sewing-machine, and lie in the bath for hours.

'That's a full day,' Harry said. 'She needs the rest.'

'The one that needs the rest,' Maeve said, 'is me.'

'Be patient, pet. She's a bit of a lost soul.'

'I know that.'

And Maeve did know, because Vanessa had told her how her father, a member of the old Northern Ireland parliament, and her mother, a society beauty who had been painted by Lucian Freud in the 1960s, had been killed when their car tumbled down a steep slope in the Alps and landed upside down in a stream. Vanessa had been trapped in her babyseat overnight and had almost died of hypothermia.

'She's supposed to be an heiress,' Maeve said, 'but the dough is in trust until she's twenty-five, and meanwhile she hasn't got a bean. Half the people of Dublin have been touched by her. She's a woeful moocher. And Cormac can't stand the sight of her.'

Harry said nothing, especially about Cormac. That was already a sensitive subject.

What, he had begun to ask himself recently, am I doing hanging around with this gang of senior infants? He was almost thirty years old and had many intersecting circles of friends of his own age and older, and not just in Ireland: anywhere gays congregated, which included, as he put it, 'the whole known universe', he had connections. Of course the only reason for playing around with these often high High Babies was Will Ferris. Will was a rarity. But so, for that matter, was Maeve.

'Men,' Harry told Cory, 'men are like rabbits, they'd get up on a duck. Sometimes I think Miss MacNamee is really a man. She's a man trapped in a woman's body, which is maybe why I'm friends with her. That way Narcissus lies of course. And if not Narcissus then a largish field of daffodils. Maybe I should get her into our collective.'

'Your what?'

'You know this group I'm part of? The Lesbian and Gay Men's Health Collective? How could you not have heard of us? We're grant-aided by the Equality Authority. I ask you, Equality and Authority, they go together like strawberries and spanners. We're supposed to look after sick queers but most of the time all we do is give needles to junkies. Frightful people. It's voluntary work. Once a month. Worse than having a period.'

'Harry, don't be vulgar.'

'Well, vulgar is what I am. I can't help it. As for the volunteers, they're PC like you wouldn't believe. At one of our interminable meetings I proposed we change our name. I mean, I said, putting Lesbian in front of Gay, it's so ladies before gents, it isn't even alphabetical, so I suggest we call ourselves Gay and Lesbian Men.

"Harry," says the chairperson girl, "is that a formal motion? Because if it is, it's frivolous." Of course it's frivolous, I said, isn't that why we're here? Isn't that why we're queer? Because all we want is a bit of frivolity, instead of being straight like the rest of the straights. Not you, Cory, of course.'

'Harry,' Cory said, 'you're tiring me out.'

So he had shut up. Cory was right, but nowadays he only camped it up when he was anxious, which was often, whereas in the old days he did it when he was excited, which was all the time. Hysteria, then, had been his religion, just as sex was for Maeve, but now he was getting too old for the pleasures of homosexual panic.

Which religion did Will belong to? None. He was god-like. So it wasn't surprising that Maeve adored him. She was next best thing to obsessed. 'I feel like a stalker,' she said, because the night after the En Seine experience she had turned up in the Baggot Inn — in Baggot Street — dressed to kill in a Vivienne Westwood frou-frou skirt that Vanessa had lent her, knickerless of course. She hadn't been able to get close enough to tempt him because 'that appalling bully', as Harry described Emmet Roche, had wanted to headbutt the god. But even Harry had to admit Will's song about Emmet's musical tastes was provocative, especially the last verse:

> Hey there, you on your Kraftwerk trip,
> Why is your hearing not so quick?
> Ass-ears on your head, man, that's not hip,
> Even down there in Limerick.

Harry said, 'What did Will expect, a bunch of flowers? A bunch of fives would have been more likely, and Emmet has the most enormous hands — one blow would have creased the Lee-side Warbler.'

It wasn't even, though Harry kept this opinion to himself, a very good song, but Will was so callow and aggressive, everything he did seemed calculated to go against his own best interests.

'Of course,' Harry said, 'I'd be gagging too if Ernesto had alliterated all over me, but it certainly didn't merit being treated as if it was my fault. And Fergus Menton, whom I went to such trouble to get to come to the Baggot because he's a researcher with the *Late Late Show*, the country's major TV gabfest after all, well, Will would hardly speak to him, he was positively sullen. Most sensible performing persons would give their eye teeth to appear on the *Late Late*. But the way Will behaved you'd think poor Fergus, a perfectly inoffensive young queen, was asking him to pose topless for Gaydar Radio.

'Anyway, where was I? Oh yes, Maeve. Well, it had been a fraught night for romance and I can't say I was surprised she wanted to work out her frustrations on someone. But the last person on earth I imagined her slinging her hook into was Cormac Healy. Come to think of it, though, maybe it was the other way round. For a man in a baggy suit, Cormac is not short of self-confidence. It's hard to imagine the word could apply to such a soup-stained person, but believe you me, he's not a man to get on the wrong side of, even if he's only a little wisp of a thing with a limp and a walking stick.

'Still, I thought, Maeve has had more one-night stands than she's had hot dinners, and this one will go no further than that, but lo and behold, a week passes and they can't be prised apart, they're practically living together, except that Cormac has to go back to the boglands for Christmas, and so does Emmet Roche, and Ossie offers to give them a lift to Cork where they can stay in the mews of Ma Gleeson's mansion before going over to Limerick. He has this clapped-out old van his father gave him, surplus to the requirements of the Gleeson haberdashery empire, and when it comes skidding into the gravel in Waterloo Road, who's there in the back of it among the rest of the southern gentlemen — you'll never guess — only your Will, guitar and satchel and all. He and Emmet had made it up. You'd think they were buddies, sort of. And as for Cormac, well, he was triumphant; you'd think he'd ridden the winning horse in the Grand National, which I suppose he had, because Maeve is, if you'll excuse the expression, a ride.

'Anyway, although it was hardly half-past breakfast-time, she gave them this hot punch, a stirrup-cup she called it, made out of mango juice and an absolutely criminal bottle of poiteen, moonshine, real mountain-dew, that she got off the mother of that Traveller child she's taken on as a charity project. She was all over Cormac, like a rash, for the benefit of you-know-who, and when they were leaving she kissed him goodbye as if he was Napoleon going off to the wars and she was the Empress Josephine, hardly able to wait until she could get her hands on his Boney Part once more. Of course, Ossie, being the driver, was sober, but still, imagine heading south to Dixie with that crowd of juiceheads.'

13

'IT'S VERY DARK,' Cormac said, climbing into the front seat.

'Let me concentrate here for a second,' Ossie said, bending low over the steering wheel.

They were running late because, out of a clear blue sky, a shower of hailstones had suddenly descended on the Naas dual carriageway, clogging the windscreen wipers. Ossie had pulled in to the hard shoulder to free them, but then the van wouldn't start again. Luckily, there was a filling station nearby and in twenty minutes Ossie was back with a can of petrol. When he sat into the driver's seat he said, 'Jesus, what's that smell?'

From the dark in the back of the van Emmet replied, 'Mango juice.'

'It's Vanessa's mango juice that Maeve put into the moonshine,' Will said.

'You bastards are smoking dope,' Ossie said.

'You were gone a long time,' Cormac said.

'You dozy get,' Emmet said.

Another shower of hail fell near Kildare and again Ossie had to pull in. This time the wiper on the driver's side was the problem. There was no way he was driving without wipers, so Emmet, who was good with his hands, had to fix it. But since the screw had sheared off, he had to cannibalise the other wiper for a replacement. By the time that was done, the day was darkening.

'Wow,' Will said, 'look at that sunset.'

'Red sky at night,' Emmet said, 'sailors' delight.'

'Red sky in the morning,' Will said, 'shepherds take warning.'

'Where did you get the shepherds from?' Cormac said. 'There's no shepherds in it, there's only sailors.'

'He's right, you know,' Emmet said. 'There is no shepherds in it. Anyway, what the fuck difference would it make to shepherds whether the sky was red in the morning or not?'

'Yes,' Will said. 'I get your point. Maybe it's the other way round.'

'What do you mean the other way round?'

'If it was night-time.'

'What do you mean nighttime? Nighttime, daytime, what's the difference? The shepherds are stuck up the fucking mountains no matter what happens.'

'And anyway,' Cormac said, 'it's sailors. There's no shepherds in it.'

'Are you finished?' Ossie said. 'It's getting dark. I don't like driving in the dark.'

'Hold your horses, you dopey get.'

'Stop calling me a dopey get.'

'I'll call you what I like. It's your fault we ran out of petrol, you dopey get.'

'Anyway,' Cormac said, 'the first few times he said you were dozy, a dozy get, that's what he said, I heard him distinctly.'

'So get it right the next time,' Emmet said threateningly. 'Do you hear me, you dozy fucker? Now,' he said, giving the screw a final turn, 'there we are, right as rain.' He held the screwdriver up to the fading light, looked at it, then fired it high over a hedge into a field.

'What did you do that for?' Ossie asked.

'It offended me,' Emmet said. 'It was ugly. It was an ugly screw-driver.'

This was typical of Emmet: he favoured sensuality over common sense. But while a screwdriver might have been a useful thing to have in normal circumstances, it would have been of no use now, because, just as the van was picking up speed, a clanking noise was heard, followed by an explosion. Under ever-decreasing power, they laboured noisily up to a mammoth new garage glowing blue and yellow a mile off the motorway. The only person there, standing forlornly by the petrol pumps, was a middle-aged lantern-jawed Pole with rings on his fingers, bracelets on his wrists, and thick gold chains around his neck.

Will said. 'Don't put this man in the microwave.'

But the Pole, though he spoke little English, could see the problem and, like a Good Samaritan, was willing to set about welding the van's exhaust back into place. The job took only half an hour, but in that time Ossie, yielding to thirst, drank a mouthful of Maeve's punch. Then, 'to clear my head', he took three quick tokes on the new joint. It was while his head was clearing that he had the idea that led to the change of plan.

From where they were standing, out of sight of the Pole at the back of the garage, they had an unimpeded view of a distant range of mountains against the night sky. It was very Christmassy, an atmosphere made more nostalgic by Will playing on his guitar a reggae version of 'Walking in a Winter Wonderland'. As the last ice-tinkling notes rang through the frosty air, Ossie cried out, 'My God, I've got a brilliant idea.'

By the time he was ready to pay the bill, the brilliance of his idea was as blinding as the lights in the garage shop. The shop glimmered with glassy fridges and brightly lit shelves, from which they amassed a variety of frozen turkey and ham Christmas dinners, four bottles of wine and a bottle of Jameson whiskey 'to light the plum pudding' — a thing the size of a cannonball in a plastic basin wrapped in shiny red paper. In the midst of all this loveliness the poor Pole looked so forlorn that Ossie, even though the bill already amounted to €160, added a tip of ten per cent. The Pole lit up. But it was at this moment that the Visa machine emitted a series of bleeps and thereafter would not, could not, and did not bleep again.

The Pole held up his right hand, rubbing his large thumb and thick forefinger together, saying, 'You pay cash.'

Emmet said, 'Keep your hair on.' Then he turned his head

into his shoulder and in a conversational tone said, 'Right, let's say goodbye to Poland and mad dog it out of here.'

But the Pole seemed to have a better command of English than they thought, for at the mention of mad dogging, he produced from under the counter a baseball bat. So, pockets were turned out and there was plenty of money to pay for everything, after a few adjustments: the wine, the whiskey, the Christmas dinners and the plum pudding were returned to their cabinets and replaced with twenty cans of Dutch beer, which were on Special Offer.

Somehow the higher Ossie got into the mountains, the less sure he was that going to Granny's ancestral home was such a brilliant idea after all. Daddy was very fond of the place and had recently had it refurbished. What if his friends scarred the newly polyurethaned floorboards with their boots and cigarette butts?

It was at this moment that Cormac clambered into the passenger seat and said it was very dark.

'Let me concentrate here for a second,' Ossie said, bending low over the steering wheel.

'I mean,' Cormac said, 'it's very dark on this side. I think your left headlight's burned out.'

'Shit!'

'Sure, it's all right, boy, I can keep an eye out for you. Anyway, I think we've lost them.'

'Lost who?'

'The cops. I don't hear the sirens now.'

'Sirens! What sirens?'

Just then there was a dull thump and a heavy object flew past the windscreen. Ossie stood on the brake; the van hit the verge, spun around in a complete circle and came to a halt.

Emmet roared, 'What are you doing, you dozey get? You nearly killed us, you fucking madman.'

Ossie said, 'What was that?'

'I think,' Cormac said, 'we wasted a pedestrian.'

'Oh Christ,' Will said, 'we've killed somebody.'

Emmet said, '*We* didn't do anything. *He* did it.'

Cormac said, 'I told him not to drink and drive.'

'What are we going to do?' Ossie said.

'You probably only hit the branch of a tree or something, you fucking eejit,' Emmet said. 'Anyway, if you killed someone, there isn't much we can do for him now. So we should drive on like Jaysus.' But there was a quaver in his voice.

'Maybe he's just injured,' Ossie said. 'Oh Christ, let him just be injured.'

'Right,' Emmet said. 'Let's go and see the damage.'

'I can't,' Ossie said. 'I can't face it,' and he put his head onto the steering wheel. After what seemed like an eternity, he looked in the wing-mirror. What he saw there he would never forget. Bathed in moonlight, Will, Cormac and Emmet stood mournfully, heads bowed, gazing at a body in a pool of blood gleaming on the road. Then Will raised his arms and, like Job in the Bible, threw back his head and cursed God in heaven.

Ossie closed his eyes. When he opened them again what he saw was more horrible than anything he had seen before: a bloody hand was smearing blood on the window of the van. Through the smear he saw Emmet's face, bestial, teeth bared. Then Emmet was saying, 'Well, she's dead all right.'

'God forgive me,' Ossie said, 'What am I going to do?'

'Open the door and we'll sling her in the back.'

After Ossie had caught up with Emmet and had finished punching him — Will said he flapped like a girl — the sheep was slung into the back of the van and the last few miles were driven happily enough, all things considered. Even the fact that Emmet had to kick in the front door of Granny's house could not diminish Ossie's relief. Nor was it diminished by the discovery in a sideboard of a bottle of Winter's Tale sherry. By the time this and the Dutch beer were drunk and more dope smoked, his relief was so great he had to crawl up the stairs to bed on his hands and knees.

Downstairs, Will, too, was tired. Slumped in an armchair in front of a roaring fire of logs, the last thing he said before slipping off to sleep was, 'Red sky at night, shepherds delight.'

This mention of shepherds, along with the open fireplace, which had been restored to its original condition and fitted out with hooks, swinging irons, a spit for roasting, and an original bastible for baking bread, led Cormac and Emmet to reminisce about the past. Their grandparents had been brought up in houses like this, at a time before electricity, when people grew their own food, churned their own butter, hung hams from the rafters, and killed their own meat. In fact, Emmet's father was a butcher and Emmet had often seen bullocks being slaughtered.

'Blood doesn't bother me,' he said. 'Not in the slightest. I'm steeped in it. It's what makes me the kind of painter I am.'

'What kind is that?'

'The best kind. I'm the real thing. I've often made black pudding with these hands. That's the way to make paintings. Blood and guts and barley, salt and allspice. Lovely, lovely grub. Loin chops, chump chops, gigot chops. A good leg of lamb with mint sauce. Very juicy.'

'Jesus,' Cormac said, 'I'm starving.'

Will didn't wake up when the body of the sheep thudded softly on the newly sanded floorboards.

'Look at this,' Emmet said after a while, holding up a knife. 'This is Sheffield. Best Sheffield steel. Couldn't be better.' In the kitchen he had found a block of wood impaled with brand-new knives, high quality, very sharp. 'Look at that,' he said, as blood welled from his hand. 'I don't mind that. Don't feel a thing.'

Ossie woke to hear Cormac saying, 'Do you got Elastoplast? Emmet's bleeding like a stuck pig.' And he stayed awake long enough to say, 'Try the bathroom.'

There was no sticking plaster in the bathroom, but there were sheets in the airing cupboard. Cormac tore one into strips, which took time, but Emmet didn't mind, because the work he was doing was interesting. Also, the colours inside the sheep — vermillion, a glary ivory, cadmium blue, Payne's grey, magenta, a fat yellow — were as good as anything you could get from Cornelissen's in London, which was where he bought his paints.

For some reason Cormac didn't like the colours.

'The leg is skinned,' Emmet said, 'but the bone is a problem. What I need is an axe.'

There wasn't much blood on the floor, and most of it was Emmet's. But the sheep was a disturbing sight. Emmet had tried to wrench the flayed leg free of the backbone, but even with his great strength he had failed and, gleaming lividly, it stuck up at a disconcerting angle.

'Emmet,' Cormac said, 'I don't think I'm hungry any more.'

'Slices,' Emmet said. 'I'll cut slices off it. Leg steaks. Get plates. Get big plates. Get platters.'

When Cormac returned to the living room, Emmet had cleaned up. Only a long streak of blood indicated that the sheep had been dragged across the floor and dumped outside on the gravel.

Cormac felt hungry again, unbearably so when Emmet hung the meat on the hooks and the skin turned crispy brown and the hot fat began to fall sizzling into the fire.

'Wait,' Emmet said. 'Wait, you greedy fucker. Make a little spliff first. You do it. I can't. It's the hand, you see.'

Blood was coming through the bandage, but not much, and after some more beer and a smoke, the lamb was ready.

'That was worth waiting for,' Cormac said when they had finished eating.

'There must have been four pounds weight in that little snack,' Emmet said. 'I reckon in Tesco's you'd have paid a good...'

But he never got around to saying how much the meat would have fetched, because almost simultaneously both of their greasy chins sank onto their chests and they were asleep. Soon they were snoring, and, as if commanded to symphony, Will and Ossie began to snore too, and the house was filled with the sound of a quartet of snorers, honking and whistling like a free-form jazz band.

As it happened, freedom had something to do with this indoor concert. After thirty years of communal killing, Ireland was at peace. On the entire island the nearest thing to murder that night was the death of the sheep. But two days earlier the Irish Republican Army had robbed a bank in Belfast. Naturally, Sinn Féin, the IRA's political wing, had denied that the IRA was involved. They had become so used to denying this kind of thing, and the general public so used to hearing the denials, and the British and Irish governments so desperate to avoid returning to war, that it had come to be accepted that though the denials could not be true, they should be treated as if they were not false. But the magnitude of this robbery, a record-breaking £26 million sterling, was stretching credulity, particularly now that a white van, similar to the one used in the bank raid, had been seen driving away at top speed from a remote farmhouse in the Comeragh Mountains which was on fire. This was definitely a case of arson, according to the local Garda superintendent, but he refused to comment on speculation that there had been a falling-out among the terrorists or that there had been an element of ritual sacrifice in the discovery of the carcass of a mutilated sheep in the embers.

Cormac told Ossie there was no way the petrol had anything to do with it, since there was only a drain in the can and they had used that to start the fire, though there might have been a build-up of vapour which then exploded in the heat. Anyway what was he complaining about — hadn't he and Emmet saved his life by dragging him down the burning stairs?

What Cormac couldn't understand or forgive was the way that that snake-in-the-grass Will Ferris had slithered off without a word to anyone.

After running down the mountain, Will stopped for breath, turned and saw that the two windows on the front of the house were glowing, like the eyes of some medieval devil, and out the chimney, as if from the top of the devil's skull, a magnificently long and straight horn of fire was shooting up into the starlit sky.

14

IT WAS THE beginning of March. For days, easterly gales had been blowing showers of sleet and light snow across the city. Then the sky had cleared, the wind had dropped, and there was heat in the sun. At Hawk Cliff the sea was so dead flat calm that when Cory dived into it and swam out towards the horizon, she left a widening chevron in her wake.

Although Will knew where Dalkey was — only eight miles from the centre of Dublin — this was his first time to see it and Killiney Bay. How could anything so beautiful belong to a city so miserable? If Dubliners had eyes, they'd be the happiest people on earth. But they hadn't. And they weren't. But he saw it, first thing. It took a Corkman to do that for them — it was part of his character to feel he experienced his experience in the service of others.

It was his first time, too, to see Cory swimming. Back in the city, unknown to him, she often swam in the Markievicz pool in Townsend Street. Weeks had passed before he found this out. She was secretive; she operated on a need-to-know basis and, as is usual with such people, she believed that no one needed to know much of anything about anything much, certainly not anything to do with her.

Will could have known Dalkey for years but without Cory as a guide he still might not have found Hawk Cliff. Hidden under the rocks, it had once been a men-only bathing place. Nowadays women used it too, though only if the sight of cold-shrivelled penises, mostly ancient, did not drive them off. In Hawk Cliff's heyday there had been a diving board, but now all that remained of it was its concrete base, which Cory had dived from. Far out, she turned, waved at Will, then started back to the shore.

Will, waiting on the steps, saw what was happening and shouted a warning. But it was too late. Just as she grasped the rusty iron rail set into the rock, the sea rose suddenly and silently, broke her grip, carried her up the steps and set her down, miraculously, on her feet, before collapsing with a sucking roar back onto itself.

What could just as easily have smashed her against the rocks and killed her was the bow-wave from the SeaCat car-ferry, dwindling now on the horizon on its way to Wales. But when Will said, 'You had a lucky escape,' Cory said, 'If it didn't happen, it doesn't matter.' He had a feeling not unlike the one he had felt when he had told her who Yasser Arafat was. But there was something added to it. Not only would she not put up with being condescended to, she allowed the past no place in her imagination, and she was secretive, reticent as a reticule, rather in the way she constantly pursed her lips over her sticky-out teeth.

The sun was hot for March, but the sea, after cooling down all winter, was at its coldest. As she stripped in the shelter, Will could see she was shivering. Aware of being watched, she frowned, crossed her breast with one hand, held out the other in front of her, palm down, and motioned twice with her fingers to instruct him to turn away.

As he did what he was told, Will felt unaccountably guilty. Not the guilt of a Peeping Tom but of a SeaCat sinner. He had already tried to tell her about this sin, on the first night she came to Leeson Street, but she had not wanted to be told. Now, instead, after she had dressed and they were climbing the steep path towards the road, he told her the story of another sin: how Cormac Healy and Emmet Roche had set fire to the house in the mountains. It was an economical version of the truth: he left out the mango punch, the fact that Emmet had dropped three ecstasy tablets into it, the hashish and the reason why he, Will, had run away. Even so, Cory was not amused: there was nothing funny in killing an innocent lamb, and as for abusing a harmless Polish worker, that was disgusting.

Will said, 'Well, I agree with you of course, but, you know, I don't think that was why Ossie's father was disgusted. He didn't care about the lamb. What he cared about was his house. There was ill-feeling in the Gleeson family.'

'I'm not surprised,' Cory said.

She might, though, have been surprised at how the ill-feeling resolved itself. After some days biting her tongue, Mrs Gleeson had reacted furiously to Mr Gleeson's fury.

'If there's one thing wrong with Ossie,' she said, 'it's that he's too trusting of people. Wasn't he very charitable to be giving lifts to hitchhikers in that dreadful van you forced on him? Humiliating your son like he was a messenger boy. If he had a proper car, it wouldn't have happened.'

The logic of this argument Mr Gleeson was unable to follow, just as he had never followed or believed the story his son had told the police. Subsequently he regretted saying so, since the upshot of it was that he had to buy Ossie a new car, though he had to give way on that too when Mrs Gleeson made it plain that Osmondo, as she sometimes called him, had intimated he was willing to put up with a second-hand vehicle, a cheap thing with only two seats.

'He's so considerate,' his mother said. 'He hasn't a mean bone in his body. Unlike some people I know.'

Ossie's consideration had reduced his needs to a 1964 Mercedes 230 SL California Coupé with four-speed manual transmission.

'I prefer yours to his,' Will said as they puttered along the Rock Road in Cory's 1974 Fiat 500. 'It's like a Dinky toy. If I ever write a fairytale, this car will be in it. And I'll put you in it, too. Would you like that?'

'No thanks.'

'Why not? Don't you want to be famous?'

'No.'

'Well, you might have no choice. Hey, let's turn here. I'll show you where Ossie lived.'

The past tense was no mistake. Mrs Gleeson's fury at her son being humiliated had not been assuaged by the purchase of a forty year-old jalopy. Mr Gleeson, who was an honorary life member of the Cork Yacht Club, had his heart set on sailing across the Atlantic in an aluminium-hulled sloop, to be built to his own design and called 'Blue Bolt' — winning the contract for police uniforms was the basis of the Gleeson fortune — but he was now obliged to put these plans on hold while his wife bought, with his money, a one-bedroomed apartment for their son in 'The Gallops,' Ballsbridge, Dublin 4, a very decent address.

Two bedrooms, in Mrs Gleeson's opinion, would have been more economical in the long run, but Osmondo had plumped for the smaller place, partly because he was so considerate of his father's purse, but also because, being his father's son, he was developing a hankering, if not for sailing across the Atlantic, for not having his mother to stay with him. He had not yet begun to think of living further from Cork than Dublin is — Goa, say. That move, when it was made, would have less to do with her embarrassing him in private than with the police doing it in public.

As Cory's car approached the Merrion Gates the barriers were trembling to descend and the red lights were blinking.

Will said. 'Go on, you'll make it.' Cory put her foot on the accelerator. 'Isn't that weird?' he said idly. 'There's a wheel — ' he was about to say 'rolling across the line', but before he could utter the words, the Fiat stalled and stopped on the railway track. Meanwhile the front wheel on the passenger side sailed on through the level crossing, traversed Strand Road and struck the gate of the house where Ossie used to live.

'There's a train coming,' Will said.

'You can't always be telling stories with false endings,' Cory said after he had told this story too often. 'If you keep people hanging on to find out what happened, and giving them hints that there's some huge structure to everything, eventually they'll get browned off. And that goes for your songs too.'

'Maybe the hints are the structure,' Will said, blushing.

'Oh, come on.'

Will blushed because she had put her finger on a sore spot: half the time his audience had no idea what his songs were about, and the other half neither did he. This was a poor excuse for acting as if the cloak of mystery had anything underneath it. But poor as it was, it was all he had.

Similarly complex confusions had marked the beginning of his relationship with Cory, as they would mark its end. If, for one thing, he had not refused to have a mobile phone, he would have got a call that would have saved him a lot of trouble. And if he hadn't been in a fury of despair, he wouldn't have gone to Cork in Ossie's van four days before Christmas — the last bus on Christmas Eve would have been early enough.

To any sort of 'if' Cory had an answer: 'If your aunt had balls she'd be your uncle.' It was one of her general principles, often applied.

Nonetheless, everything, including the sex, might have turned out otherwise if Will hadn't told her who Yasser Arafat was. Cursing himself for his condescension, he had wandered through the teeming Christmas shoppers, met Ossie, sung in the En Seine, insulted Maeve, and gone off into the crowd again, still cursing. How could he make it up with Cory? Eventually it came to him that the solution should have something to do with the book she had taken from her pocket. Obviously she wouldn't be sending *Winnie the Pooh* to America unless it was a favourite of hers. So he had bought a cheap edition in Eason's, sat in the Oval Bar in Abbey Street, drank three pints of ice-cold Guinness, and read it intently.

Late that night when Cory returned to her room in the doctors' residence she found on her bed a peculiarly shaped package, clumsily wrapped in sheets of newspaper and bound with crinkled Sellotape. Inside the package were a bundle of twigs, a pot of honey and a Christmas card with robins on it. Inside the card there was a message, wobblily handwritten:

Dear Doctor,
I broke these twigs off (of) one of the new trees in
O'Connell Street. I could have been arrested for a
vandal — maybe I should have been — instead of
for the Haughty Idiot which I am. The honey I got
from the Boyne Valley company. You will notice the
jar is full. The bear licked his clean. I hope you will
find it nice and sweet. I am hoping too that when
you throw the sticks off the bridge, they will come
out the other side. Do you mind if I try to ring you
tonight? I would like to talk to you. I think we could
talk. Sorry for being such a H.I., and an Arafat
Head, and Happy Christmas!
Yours sincerely, Will (Ferris)

He had rung. The operator on the Rotunda switchboard was a nice woman and on the third occasion she said she would make sure the phone number of his flat was passed on to Dr Leary.

'Well, I did call you back,' Cory said later. 'I rang that same night.'

'Did you? I suppose I didn't hear. The phone is down three flights of stairs.'

'I've noticed. You should have a mobile.'

'No thanks. I hate mobiles. They make me shy. That's why I said that stupid bloody thing about stupid bloody Yasser Arafat: shyness. I break out into a cold sweat when I think of it.'

'And so you should.'

'But, anyway, the present worked.'

'It didn't.'

'But it did. You rang me, so it must have.'

'It didn't. I've never read *Winnie the Pooh*. I had no idea what the sticks and the honey meant.'

'My god. Why did you ring me then?'

'Do you really want to know?'

'Why?'

'I was worried about your mental health. The whole thing

freaked me out, especially the Christmas card. But what was really freaky was how you managed to get into my room. If I'd known that when I rang you, you'd have got a flea in your ear, and that would have been the end of that, probably.'

'If my uncle had no balls he'd be your aunt.'

'Exactly.'

'Well, that explains one false ending then. A car can keep going on three wheels.'

'Will,' she said, 'that's a red herring.'

When Vanessa, who had been told the story by Ossie, retold it to Maeve and Cormac, she said, 'Isn't that romantic?'

Maeve said, 'It's so romantic it makes me want to throw up all over my suede shoes.'

Vanessa said, 'I just adore suede shoes, don't you? They're so kitsch they're cute.'

'Kitsch, my arse,' Cormac said, without knowing he had made a pun.

But what they heard wasn't the whole story. Will didn't tell that to anyone, certainly not to Cory.

When he arrived at the hospital and said he was delivering medical equipment for Dr Leary, the porter had just lifted his nose to indicate the way and said, 'Third floor, number nine.'

Neon lights and the headlights of passing cars shone flickeringly into Cory's room. Big drops of rain were beginning to splatter against the window. Below, matching the curve of the Rotunda Hospital, was a crescent-shaped parking lot that had once been a garden. Will remembered a school trip to historic sites in the capital city during which his history teacher had told the class that at the end of the 1916 Rising the rebels in the General Post Office had been herded into this garden and held there overnight under armed guard. Amongst them was Michael Collins, 'the greatest rebel of them all,' the teacher had said, 'and he was a Cork man like you, Ferris, and he didn't put gel in his hair.'

In 1922, a mere six years later, Collins, having driven the British out of the south of Ireland and having become the head of the new government, was shot dead by a fellow Irishman at a place called Béal na Bláth.

Béal na Bláth means the Mouth of the Flowers. The music of the sound, Bale na Blaw, and the poetry of the meaning, which was so suitable for the death of the tragic Collins, had made a rebel of Will. Of course, his father's denunciations of the Provisional IRA had helped too. But it was his mother's distaste for the Provos — 'a gang of corner-boys' — that drove him across the city to Ballyphehane, a working-class housing estate, to join Na Fianna, the youth wing of the IRA. The self-satisfied sanctimonious bourgeois fatness of the Glasheen Road set against the anarchic wildness of Ballyphehane and the ugly poverty of the place, which was the result of free-market capitalism and globalisation and McDonald's 'hamburgerology,' plus a TV programme Will had seen about liberation theology in Latin America and 'the option for the poor,' which had been suppressed by the Pope, 'that cunt', meant that the only thing to be in Cork in 1997 was a revolutionary.

There was a problem, though. The revolution was on hold. The Provos were on ceasefire. At the one meeting of Na Fianna that Will attended, the man in charge had kept ranting on about the 'peace process', which had nothing to do with the overthrow of the established order and the destruction of the Glasheen Road. Anyway, Ballyphehane was a nuisance to get to; the bus service was crap. So Will hadn't gone again.

Now the rain was beating down on the Rotunda. In the heroes' garden, which had been turned into a car park, puddles were puddling. Will turned away from the window, found the light and switched it on. The sudden glare of the bare bulb lit up the 18th-century oldness of the room and the newness of what was in it. The grey metal bed dated from the 1950s, the green candlewick coverlet from the 1980s, and the melamine bedside locker was already older than the century, and looking it. The mismatch, as in any institution, was sad. On the bed lay a pair of thick black tights that still had in them a pair of thin white cotton pants decorated at the waistband with a tiny pink ribbon tied in a bow. He buried his face in the pants. There was an intimate, faintly harsh, blackcurrant odour off them. This was the real revolution. This was the secret of life. This was Woman.

15

IN THE TSUNAMI of apprehensions that swept over him as he watched Mrs Molloy being cruelly stretched to expel the baby from her body, Will noticed, without being aware of noticing, one absence: there was no smell, neither stink nor perfume. The faintest trace of female scent had made him forget shame, and yet childbirth, which opened up the source of it, was odourless.

It was New Year's Eve, hardly a week since the tsunami had swollen the Indian Ocean. Will took pleasure in disasters, a pleasure that was intense, because catastrophe was creative, but shameful too, because it was wrong. The tsunami, though, was different. While he was still trying to get used to the word, he had the feeling he would never be able to use it.

What had been so shaming about his fling with Na Fianna was that, though he had almost immediately turned against the IRA, he was still what his father, accentuating his Cork accent, called 'a shnakin' regarder'. Paul meant that Will still had a sneaking regard for the IRA. Their snake's eye view of the world, the glamour of being unmoved by the terror they inflicted on others, had hypnotised him. Like most revolutionaries they were exhilarated by indifference — they were thrilled by something they were indifferent to. For Will, if not for them, such serpentine pleasures were aesthetic. That was why they were hypnotic.

When his father called him down from his room on 11

September 2001, he was just in time to see the World Trade Center being struck by the second plane. What first appeared as a noiseless, distant dart had turned in an instant into a lumbering thunderbolt, and the next instant into a bow-wave of flames tumbling over itself in the golden autumn air. Will felt a charge of icewater dash through his veins. And later when the people began throwing themselves off the buildings they seemed to him to be falling merely a matter of inches, the distance to the bottom of the TV screen which, on Sky News, meant into the station's brand-mark banner, a red bandage with white lettering, which no catastrophe, not even the end of the world, could tear off.

Then, when the West Tower came down, he had the sensation momentarily that everything, except for the plummeting antenna on the top — which, somehow, had been invisible before it fell — was going up, rising slowly relative to the boiling dust and smoke, like the illusion at the beginning of a journey that it is the station and not the train that is moving. For Will the whole of 9/11 was like that: the reverse of itself. This was a destruction that could be built on. Without reversal, there could be no hope in creation. And to him the great mystery, the revelation of New York, like the infinitely small space the Big Bang had burst out of, was that there was so much dust in it.

But the tragedy of the tsunami had had a different aesthetic effect on him.

When he had arrived home after five hours of hitchhiking, and while Granny Gleeson's house was still smouldering, his mother was astonished by his fury. Polly hadn't seen anything like it since his teenage tantrums, when he had kicked the piano.

'Look at the cut of you,' she said. 'Were you out in the streets in this state?'

He had gone straight up to bed, slept for almost twenty four hours and woken up still furious, but listless. Christmas Day had passed painlessly enough, though Polly had miscalculated the cooking of the turkey: it emerged from the oven golden brown, but when the skin was pierced bloody juices spurted, and the brussels sprouts and roast potatoes were as hard as bullets.

Then, on the night of Stephen's Day, the first reports of the tsunami came in. As the death toll rose over the following days, Will became increasingly miserable. What depressed him was that he had initially imagined the wave as a Hollywood wall of water, a glassy disintegrating skyscraper, crashing across the ocean. Instead, it turned out to be an almost imperceptible undulation, a slop that kept low until it made landfall and then killed without drama, fuss or glamour. It wasn't a bomb; there was no explosion. Its indifference, unlike that of the fanatics of the IRA, was genuine, not thrilled with itself. To Will, who had until then thought that drama was essential to creativity, the tsunami, despite the hundreds of thousands of casualties it caused, was of no consequence. The lack of drama dislodged something essential in his soul. He would never be able to get over it.

Or so he thought when he went back to the cold flat in Leeson Street. For three days he did nothing. He didn't even practise the guitar. He couldn't.

And when he looked at his diary he felt even sicker. Each page was 26 lines long, and at the beginning of 2004 he had resolved to write a poem of that length every day. Multiplied by 365, this would produce 9,490 lines, an epic achievement which would make his reputation forever. But on the first of January all he had written was:

> *Empty is the road on which I start.*
> *The second day must be the first.*

Thereafter whole months were entryless. He closed the book with a bang. But as he did, he saw a flash of colour. On the inside of the cover was a map of Ireland. He counted all the counties he had never been in. Only once had he been west of the Shannon: when he was twelve, his mother had brought him to Galway and in Eyre Square he had seen the statue of Padraic Ó Conaire, a giant concrete leprechaun sitting on a cement stone. He had fallen in love with the idea of the writer rambling around Ireland with his little black donkey, sleeping at night under his cart with a canvas sail for shelter against the wind and rain. That was the life Will wanted, and now he would never be able to have it, because he would never again play the guitar and never again write a song, and all because of the tsunami being so boring.

Two finds affected these nevers. On the Friday afternoon, he found, stuck down between the cushions of the couch where Maeve had lain with her head in his lap, the remains of her hashish, wrapped in crinkled tinfoil.

He wolfed the smoke down into his lungs. Immediately a wave of blackness came over him. The yellow slab of foam in the corner by the window was covered with an old green quilt. He lay down on it, curled up in a fetal ball. The room was revolving. He closed his eyes. In his head an old black sun was spinning. Everything was old, cold and ragged. That was how everything was made, raggedly and in a rage, milling around wildly, milled at the edges, spinning like an ancient coin. The only legal tender was terror. The creation was fright in action.

Here it comes, here it comes.

When the wave of fear had passed over him, all his energy had drained away with it. But it was such a relief to be staring at the silkiness of the quilt where his open mouth had drooled on its greenness a darker green irregular stain. He closed his eyes and slept. When he woke up, chastened, the sun had passed by the window, and in passing had turned the room to stone. He had to get out.

That was when he made his second find.

At each turn of the stairs there was an old-fashioned Bakelite cylinder fixed to the wall that turned on the light. After as many seconds as it took to go from one landing to the next, the cylinder, easing out from its pressed-in position, turned the light off again, making a gasping click. As Will pressed the button outside his door something white moved on the brown linoleum and caught his eye. It was a piece of paper. The draft made by the door closing had caused it to come out of hiding and to lean nonchalantly against the skirting board. He picked it up. It was the triangular flap of an envelope, torn off. On it was written:

'Dr Leary the Rotunda Hospital rang.'

As Will read this message — understanding it took long enough for him to realise that, because the adhesive was unlicked, the envelope must have held one of the cards, possibly the only one, Ms Heneghan had got for Christmas — the time-switch gasped and he was left standing in the dark.

The way that he went, which he was soon to know well, brought him as fast as he could go from Leeson Street to Stephen's Green, down Grafton Street, across College Green, through Westmoreland Street, over the Liffey and up O'Connell Street into Parnell Square. The Rotunda Hospital, though he had expected it not to be, was still there.

'Why not?' Cory said.

'I was so anxious I thought it might have disappeared.'

'You're a romantic,' she said flatly, as if stating a matter of fact, which flattened him even more than any intonation of disapproval would have done. If he had been able to reply, he would have said, 'You could have said I'm a road sweeper, or a robber, a rapist or a rich man, but a romantic? I ask you, what's a romantic? He's someone who thinks there's somewhere better than this is. A world where men are just and women are free. But I don't think that, or if I do, I think it only because it's impossible. No, not impossible, because there's nothing more romantic than an impossibilist. Really, I don't believe in anything. I do believe in you though; you're the one that makes my dream come true. That's a song. Do you know it? I'll sing it if you like.' But she hadn't asked him to sing it. How could she? He hadn't said anything.

He had waited impatiently in the hall. The hospital was there all right but Cory had ceased to exist. The porter said there was no such person on his list. Will insisted that there was. Just then she appeared at the top of the stairs, saw Will, didn't stop descending, and as he went towards her, said evenly and without surprise, 'There you are.'

They crossed the road to the Parnell Mooney, a pub that had gone downhill since a man she referred to as Walter had taken her there many years ago. What was now crammed with soft furnishings and lit by concealed lighting had then been a pillared terrazzo-floored cavern smelling of Jeyes Fluid, dominated by a sinuous mahogany counter topped with black-flecked brown marble. It might have been the very counter, Walter said, down which Samuel Beckett's Murphy moved over the course of a day from one stool to another, sitting in front of a succession of half-pints of stout, untouched.

'Who's Walter?' Will said at last.

'My father.'

'Oh. Well. That's funny, you know, because I call my old man by his first name too. His name is Paul. And my mother's name is Polly. When I was a kid, I thought that that was what all grown-ups were called. I used to call complete strangers Paul or Polly. I was a talkative child. But I wasn't as nervous then as I am now.'

'What have you got to be nervous about?'

'You. You make me nervous.'

'You're wasting your time.'

He couldn't see the expression on her face as she leaned forward to sip from her cup of coffee, but the leaning was expression enough. Everything she had ever said to him since they had first met had been in some way off-putting and critical. Saying he was wasting his time was a complete rejection. And yet it was also somehow neutral, not intended to get in his way. This encouragement, if that is what it was, led him, after a pause, to say, 'What does Walter do?'

'He's retired.'

'From what?'

'The theatre.'

'Hey. Walter Leary? I think I've heard that name. He's an actor, isn't he?'

'No, a producer. He used to run a theatre.'

'Really? That's great. Which one? Not the Abbey?'

'No. In Galway.

'The Druid?'

'No. The Belacqua.'

'That's very good, isn't it? Sort of experimental.'

'You could say that.'

'Why is he retired? He can't be that old.'

'He can.'

All of her answers were flat calm, but the way she said 'He can' was also dead. When he got to know her better, Will realised how far she had gone in giving out information — not only did she not answer questions about her private business, she prevented them arising in the first place. This required effort, but she had practised evasion for so long, it was second nature to her now, like breathing out and breathing in, which was a song if you could sing it.

Before he could quiz her further, her bleeper bleeped.

'Is it an emergency?'

'No. But I'm on call. I have to go.' She was, yet again, exhausted. She had been up most of the previous night, and during the day had done a round of the wards with a consultant and attended her first emergency caesarean, which had been as chaotic as a brawl in a pub: panic and shouting and blood on the floor. Although she had been studying medicine for six years, observing physical suffering on the ground, in the rough, had affected her deeply. What she found hard to take was the helplessness of personality near death, the scrawniness of it, especially when it happened in the fatness of life. There were grossly obese people everywhere, waddling through Casualty, wallowing breathlessly on trolleys in cubicles, their heart muscles thickened, their weakened nerve impulses flaring desperately, their blood-vessels congested — when such people had a heart-attack it was, the consultant had said, 'like a lightning storm in clouds of gravy'. Worst of all were the smells. Really sick people, like really poor people, stank.

It was eleven o'clock on New Year's Eve, but Parnell Street was empty, as if the drunks knew 2005 was going to be the same as 2004 and had lost interest in pretending there could be a difference between one year and the next.

At the side-door of the hospital Will said, 'Every time I see you, you're either asleep or rushing off somewhere. I wish you didn't have to go.'

'You're very romantic.'

'You say that as if there was something wrong with it.'

'Maybe there is.'

'But maybe there isn't. Maybe something impossible is going to happen to us. Maybe we're going to be struck this minute by a meteorite and vaporised, turned into tiny glass beads.'

'Why do you exaggerate all the time?'

'All the time? That's an exaggeration.'

She frowned. 'I have to go. I've got a baby to deliver.'

'That's an excuse I haven't heard before.'

'Oh, sod off.'

'Why do I keep on feeling you're criticising me?'

'Why are you so sensitive?'

'Listen, what time are you finished? We could go up and hear the bells at Christ Church.'

'Will, I can't. I'm on duty.' It was the first time she had said his name.

'Well then, I'll have to spend the night in the street, looking up at your window.'

'You're pathetic.'

'I know. But I want to be with you. I want to stay with you forever.'

'Oh come on then,' she said.

Afterwards she thought it was simply annoyance that made her do it. Not only was he playing the romantic but he was keeping her from her work, which was real, and a bit of realism would do him good. Maybe that was cruel. And yet there was more than cruelty in it, more even than the desire to observe him when he came up against the actuality of a labour ward.

She had, though, no time for observation — she was too busy seeing to Mrs Molloy. It was her first pregnancy; she was what the textbooks called an elderly prima gravida, thirty-one years old, a chronic smoker, who had been treated successfully for pre-eclampsia, but she was two weeks premature and the lab had screwed up the test for protein in her urine. She needed watching.

There was no difficulty getting Will into the delivery room. Cory told him that all he had to say, if anyone asked, was that he was a student; he'd be starting his stint soon, he just wanted to have a look at the set-up. Finding a white coat that fitted his gawkiness was harder. The one she got him was too small and would not button across his pigeon-chest. With his stiff brush of blond hair, almost a Mohawk, he looked startled, a bird about to fly out of the nest.

The delivery room was windowless, little more than a cubicle, its fourth wall a curtain.

Clustered in a corner were a midwife and two nurses. The midwife was middle-aged, had thin hair, a pale oaken colour, and an impatient expression. Having made a decision for the nurses she went out, sweeping past Will without a second glance. But the nurses smiled at him. They were Filipinas, and when they spoke they chirruped like birds in the hospital's tropically hot smothering air.

Beside the bed stood an ancient heart-monitor: its oscillations glowed the worn-out green of the early age of computers. Another scuffed machine delivered gas from a cylinder to a black facemask, which looked like a hari-kari pilot's helmet. From a steel stand a drip was suspended, a gleaming bag of thick transparent plastic with an opaque tube worming out of it into Mrs Molloy's arm.

Afterwards Will was surprised how vague her body had become in his memory. Part of the reason was the greyness that had taken her over. She had dyed blonde hair, but after twenty hours of labour it was grey with sweat, and her face had broadened out and turned the colour of dough. Her housecoat was made of quilted polyester with a pattern of pink flowers on it, but the colour had been washed out of them too. Her swollen fingers were heavy with rings, including one on each thumb, and this could only mean that she was poor. Her accent was inner city Dublin, and when Cory, who was giving her an injection, a muscle relaxant, asked what her first name was she said 'Betty', pronouncing it without a 't' but with an 'h'. Behhe.

Seeing Will, she had covered herself with the housecoat, but then with the arrival of new contractions, her hands had opened and the thin material had fallen away to reveal spreading flaccid breasts, drained, damp and grey — even the pink of the nipples had greyed.

Then the midwife came in, whipped away the green sheet tented over Betty's flexed knees and bent to inspect her.

'That's a good girl,' she said and went off again.

'It won't be long now,' Cory whispered. 'You'll see the head soon.'

Will did see it. Everything else about Mrs Molloy was grey, but this opening was red and raw. This was what sex was for. This was why he loved loveliness, perfume, skin-glow, breast-slump and pointedness. They were his magic, but, he now realised, to women there was no magic. There could be no revelation when you knew in advance what was going to be revealed. He felt a shiver in his bones, as if the marrow in them had been turned around. All that the elusive sensitivity of women covered up was cunt — the worst curse of all curses. 'You only want your hole, you cunt.' That was what they used to say to him, his friends from the Glasheen Road, gathered around the Lough. And he had said it back to them. Cunt, hole, twat, slit, crack, gash. He remembered the first time he had seen one; it was Sheevawn's, which she called, not embarrassingly then, her honey-pot. But what desire desired was not a honey-pot; it was a hole dilated, distended, stretched, peeled back, turned inside-out, and all to make way for the descent of a hairy black bone matted with off-white cheese. He looked away. The Filipina nurses saw his face and smiled at each other, faintly.

How long this went on Will could not say. Mrs Molloy was told to push hard but nothing happened. She grabbed at the mask, breathed in the gas frantically as if she was drowning, then threw it down, moving her head from side to side on the pillow. The mid-wife returned.

'This won't do,' she said.

Mrs Molloy cried out, 'The Jaysus thing is killin' me.'

'Taking the Holy Name won't do you any good here.'

'Fuck off.'

The midwife slapped her sharply on the leg. 'Stop your nonsense,' she said. Mrs Molloy uttered a noise halfway between a groan of fury and a laugh of disbelief. Turning her back so that the woman could not see her, the midwife took up a pair of shining tongs and said to Cory, 'Have you used one of these before?'

'No.'

'Well, you have to make a start somewhere.'

With that she brushed the young nurses aside, inserted the forceps into Mrs Molloy and clamped them around the head of the baby.

'Now,' she said to Cory, 'put your hands on mine, OK?'

'OK.'

'Don't jerk. Just draw it towards you.'

'Christ almighty,' Mrs Molloy said,

'You're nearly there, ma'am,' the midwife said. 'Take a deep breath. Push. That's good. And again. Deep breath. Push! Push hard!'

Mrs Molloy pushed. Cory and the midwife pulled. There was a small rush of watery brown fluid and the baby's head popped out like a hard seed squeezed from a fleshy pod. On its stone-blue face was an expression of sullen indignation.

Outside, the streets were full of drunken people capering. Church bells and sirens were going off to welcome in the New Year and fireworks were lighting up the sky.

In the delivery room, no one could say whether the child was a boy or a girl because there was a lot of swelling in its genital area. But that was not why Cory and the Filipina nurses were panicking. The child was not breathing. The midwife, who had thrown the bloody forceps with a clatter into an enamel bucket, seized it, thrust the gurgling vacuum tube further down its throat, then held it upside down in the old-fashioned way by one heel and smacked it hard. The sullen look turned to one of rage, the child filled its lungs with air and bellowed furiously.

As he walked home through the now empty streets, Will remembered that as the baby emerged into the world, one word, for no apparent reason in the plural, had come into his mind. The word was 'bastards', and he might have uttered it, but, before he could, he had caught Cory's eye and the word had been replaced by a fleeting sensation: that they forgave each other.

16

'THIS DEATH THING is very unsatisfactory,' Harry said. He was standing at the window looking out at the back garden in Waterloo Road. It was a wilderness of straggly shrubs, mostly buddleia, which the spring had not yet revived. 'This death thing is very unsatisfactory,' he said again after a while.

A creak and a gasp of yielded mattress air told him Maeve had sat down on the stripped bed. A jumbo-sized black plastic sack, stuffed with clothes, sagged in the middle of the floor.

Harry was given to surges of enthusiasm and to splurging on them. Often, the enthusiasm was sparked off by some fleeting notion, which he paid no attention to until it suddenly demanded satisfaction. Now. Immediately. Completely. His most recent passion had been satisfied at Christmas when he had spent a small fortune buying Handel oratorios. His listening was avid, but the avidity was as inattentive as it was attentive — he played the music over and over, waiting for the stuff he needed to turn up of its own accord. In a six-CD boxed set recorded by the Monteverdi Choir and Orchestra, conducted by John Eliot Gardiner, he had found what he had not been looking for: it was a line from 'The Funeral Anthem for Queen Caroline', which he was now humming.

At the same time he was remembering something he had seen almost half his lifetime before. Then, inspired by what he felt was a genetic memory of ancient Greece, where it had been noble to be homosexual, he had gone off, alone, to celebrate his seventeenth birthday, on a walking tour of Crete. The aloneness was important and romantic, but it also related to an image of how Byronic he might look in a loose white shirt, short shorts, good leather boots and white socks, white only for the contrast they would make with his legs goldened all over by the sun. And so it had turned out, though of course there had been no lengthening of his stumpy stumps — as he said, 'My royal Irish arse is built too close to the ground for that.'

Now in his mind's eye he was walking across a great inland plain, an unpeopled desert, houseless, appallingly flat, an ocean of grey earth. The greyness was punctuated by myriads of bushes, a different grey, leafless, crackling, dry as dead bones and smelling of creosote. In two hours only a single solitary car had passed. He had seen it coming, trailing a cloud of dust that seemed still at a distance but that billowed and boiled tormentedly as it got nearer. As the car slowed, Harry saw that there were two couples in it, northern European by the pale red look of them. The couples laughed at him. Then the car accelerated, skidding a little on the loose stones. The roar of the engine faded as suddenly as it had arrived. The certainty that struck him then, and that struck him again now as he looked out at the garden, was that this state of affairs was temporary. It simply could not go on. But it did.

As for Queen Caroline, she had been, according to Handel, 'princess of the provinces'. That could not be said of Vanessa Banim. And yet in Harry's mind they had had something in common. What could it be? Maybe it had to do with Handel's cloth ear for the English language.

> *How are the mighty fall'n.*
> *She that was great among the nations*
> *And princess of the provinces!*

The music obliged the choir to emphasise the last two syllables of 'provinces' so that they came out as 'Vince says'. All Handel's might and majesty amounted to was a joke. For all the world and for all time, the truth was that what Vince says goes. Harry felt sick.

Vanessa Banim had not been princess of the provinces, or even of the presses that printed the daily newspapers. True, Ernesto de Mahon had mentioned her in *The Irish Times* four Saturdays in a row, once as 'seemstress to the stars' — which the now alert sub-editor had altered to 'seamstress' — on the basis that the ex-wife of the drummer in a once-famous heavy-metal band had appeared at a party wearing a pair of jeans the crotch of which Vanessa had cut out and replaced with a panel of antique Carrickmacross lace. But that had provoked the gossip columnist of *The Irish Independent* to describe her as 'ditzy' and Ernesto, unnamed, as her 'epicene escort'.

All this was bad enough, but it coincided with an unpleasantness that arose following a weekend Ernesto and Vanessa had spent in the Georgian home of an ancient Anglo-Irish baronet. Although he had a cocaine habit and was half-blind from diabetes, the baronet was fanatically watchful and possessive of his possessions, which led him in jig-time to notice the disappearance from his drawing-room of a tiny Meissen figurine, a pink-cheeked shepherdess. Vanessa had denied the charge point-blank, but Ernesto, who had learned how to curse in the Dublin manner, called her 'a black-enamelled cunt' and dropped her like a stitch.

'Maybe,' Harry said, 'the future is like what we want now.'

He had spoken without thinking while watching a pair of magpies hopping on the grass and chackering at each other before rising jerkily into a tree as if drawn up into it by the tugging of an unseen string.

'What did you say?' Maeve said.

He turned to her and said brightly, 'Me speak Nescafé.'

She said, 'If I didn't know you, I'd kill you for talking like that.'

So they had more coffee before continuing with the bagging of Vanessa's effects.

It was her effects that, initially at least, had queered the pitch with Ossie's mother. On the occasion of her first field trip into the Dublin property market, searching for a flat for her son, Mrs Gleeson had arrived at his Sandymount hermitage unannounced, at ten o'clock in the morning, in a chauffeur-driven limousine.

'Have you seen those Dublin taxis, boy?' she said. 'They're worse than a fright. People get sick in them. And the drivers? You know very well I've nothing against asylum seekers. Isn't Dublin full of Cork people? And your father has a rake of Latvians in the cutting room. Very good workers they are too. Wouldn't they want to be, with the wages they're getting? But, really, I ask you, Nigerians driving taxis. That's beyond the beyond.'

Since there was no need to knock — the door was open — she had walked into Ossie's flat and there, sitting on the couch wearing only a skirt, with one foot on the coffee table, the knee propped on her chin to facilitate the re-touching of her toenails with varnish, was a strange woman.

'And who might you be?' Mrs Gleeson said.

What brought Ossie hurrying out of the bathroom was the sound of Vanessa wailing. She was standing with her hands extended downwards, close together, palms out, thumbs cocked, like a mother in a Victorian painting indicating her infant expiring in its bassinet.

'What am I going to do?' she asked him, hopelessly.

What had happened had happened as a consequence of surprise and modesty. When Mrs Gleeson, who was light on her feet for the bulky woman she was, came in so unexpectedly, Vanessa had leaped to her feet and modestly crossed her hands over her bosom. In doing so the brush she was using to varnish her nails had struck the squareish tip of one pink nipple and in consonance with Newton's third law of motion — every action gives rise to a reaction of equal strength but opposite direction — had cartwheeled upwards, stopped briefly, then, in accordance with the general tendency of everything to return to a state of inertia, it had fallen, splot, on the lapel of the jacket of Vanessa's suit.

'Coco Chanel!' Mrs Gleeson cried.

'It's ruined, so it is,' Vanessa said in an accent that came out as a cross between John Millington Synge's Mayo and nobody's Belfast, and that Ossie only later remembered noticing.

But the disaster resolved itself. Mrs Gleeson was a woman of the world, albeit her world was confined to the Cork bourgeoisie — 'That word,' she said to Will Ferris, who had used it in her presence, 'that word is a Communist word' — and when she weighed the presence in her son's apartment of a naked woman against an original Coco Chanel suit, the scales were tipped in favour of the suit. Osmond was sent to his bedroom to get something to cover his guest and when he returned with a silk dressing-gown — 'I got you that in Hong Kong' — she sent him away again immediately, since, even if he had recently broken the Sixth Commandment with a lassie, it wouldn't be proper that he should see her dressing herself. Then, ever so carefully, she blotted the blob of varnish with a tissue, rang directory inquiries, discovered the name of the very best specialist dry cleaners in the city, and ordered the limousine driver to transport the suit there. This instant.

What a wonderful garment it was. Where Vanessa had come by it? At an auction in Sothebys. Oh, go on with you!

Mrs Gleeson had then advanced to discover, by speedy degrees, what Vanessa's origins were, seed, breed and generation.

'In all my born days,' she told Mr Gleeson on her return to Cork, 'I never heard a sadder story. Imagine, in the Alps, upside down in her carrycot, the craythur.'

17

VANESSA HAD BOUGHT a book that cost one euro. The cheapness was unusual for her. Most of the few books she owned were expensive: lavishly illustrated histories of clothes, hats, shoes, fabrics, cosmetics, jewelry, perfume — anything worn by humankind. She had also amassed a collection of material to do with Leigh Bowery, the polysexual body artist. Ever since she had seen his photograph in *Vogue,* a huge teardrop of nude fat modelling for Lucian Freud, she had adored him. Lucian, of course, had also painted her mother, so the adoration was, as Vanessa said, 'kind of personal'.

Anyone Vanessa adored, the obscurer the better, she referred to by their first name; thus Clarice (the industrial potter Cliff); Gloria (the film star Grahame); Madelaine (the couturier Vionnet), and so on. So she would say, 'Leigh was divine; he was just so divinely damned.'

That was as far as Vanessa went with theory. A mild dyslexia, less noticeable than her squint, meant that she preferred looking at pictures to reading words. Anyway, Bowery's nihilism and his sado-masochistic performances — one of which involved giving birth to Nicola (Bateman, his wife) — bewildered her. Bewilderment, however, wasn't the reason why she had sold her collection of his work. There was a problem with her inheritance, the trust fund she would come into when she had reached the age of twenty-five, and she needed the money.

The one-euro book was *The Wordsworth Book of Humorous Quotations*. She had bought it for the Victorian painting on the cover, 'The General Post Office', by Frederick Goodall, which showed a group of people and a bulldog in a gloomy hall listening to a man reading a newspaper. One of the listeners was wearing an ankle-length leather apron. As soon as she saw it, Vanessa saw soft puffs of white organza or maybe chiffon bursting out of it. But where was she to find a leather apron?

The morning after their first night together, she asked Ossie this question. He had no idea. Instead, he had begun to read to her quotations from the book. With one interruption for tea and toasted sultana loaf and another for lovemaking, that was how they had spent the morning.

Over the window Vanessa had tacked a length of super-fine muslin and through it the strong light of a low winter sun was glowingly diffused. Ossie felt similarly sunny and powerful, his masculine heftiness softened by Vanessa's feminine frailty. Propped up against the pillows, reading aloud while her frothy blonde head rested on his bare chest, light as a piece of pumice stone, he had an impression of himself as victorious. She was laughing, he was the winner. That was the way victory worked.

The night before, though, it had been different. Then he had been the loser.

Vanessa had gone to bed with him without having to be asked, quite naturally. But she was not into kissing or even being kissed. Instead she lay on the flat of her back with her arms by her sides, like a lukewarm corpse. After he had worked on her for a while she had begun to tremble with what he thought was excitement, but then he realised she was afraid of what he was doing. He stared at her, aghast. All of a sudden he was aware that the room, though lit by the bedside lamp, was dark in the corners, and that she was quivering like a rabbit hypnotised by headlights. If he hadn't been dismayed he might have recognised what he was feeling as pity, but because pity is usually weaker than embarrassment, he didn't recognise it. Anyway, it was too late for making such fine distinctions. He had already driven too far and too fast through the sexual sequence to stop now, he was so enflamed with lust nothing could stand in his way, nothing could prevent him from overwhelming this woman and consuming her with the power of his passion — or so he pretended to himself. Actually, if she had indicated in any way that she preferred to him to stop, he would have given up immediately. Giving up was something he was used to. In school Will Ferris had made up a rhyme:

> *In the tussle for possession*
> *Ossie Gleeson lacks aggression.*

This was true. But it would have been far more embarrassing to question Vanessa about her fear than nearly to rape her. And it really was exciting when she whispered, 'Turn off the light', and her breathing grew laboured and she raised one arm from her side and tentatively placed the tips of her fingers on his back, as if she were, absent-mindedly, steering the bull into her china-shop.

In the morning when he made love to her again, she was still passive, and silent too. But now she wasn't afraid. And afterwards she laughed at the humorous quotations from the book. Ossie was delighted with her intelligence and ironic knowingness. About his own intelligence he was humble, but, like not a few of those who are humble, he was over-generous in estimating the intelligence of others. On this occasion his generosity led him, as her chortling head vibrated ironically against his chest, to say to himself in all humility, 'Hey, this one is as bright as me.'

Which, in some respects, was true.

18

AN OBJECT STRUCK the door of the boxroom with a tinny thump and made a smaller muffled thump as it landed on the landing. Although Ultan McGrath had no idea what had happened, he instantly foreboded, and this foreboding caused his heart to leap electrically in his chest and then to bump-bump-bump down to a near-halt. He stood up, knocking over his chair, and backed towards the door. The backing was necessary because the space between the bed and the wall was so narrow.

The whole house was narrow. It was one sliver of many slivers of beige brick stuck together out in Firhouse, an area his parents would once have found it laughable to imagine their son living in, since they associated it with encampments for tinkers, itinerants, travellers — the politeness of what these people were called was exactly contradicted by the accelerating increase of their degradation. It was very regrettable. Something should be done about it. Anyway, because house-prices were soaring by ten, fifteen, twenty per cent a year, the parents had approved the purchase of the sliver and even put down the deposit on it. Actually, the boxroom was a decided plus: it meant Firhouse could be sold, soon hopefully, as a 'spacious three-bed family residence', and then Ultan, Orla and Dáibhí could buy a proper house in a proper place, like Dundrum or, even, at a pinch, Drumcondra.

Ultan used the boxroom as his office. Tonight he was engaged in some quite tricky econometric work on health expenditure. That was one of the problems with being a bright star but low down in the sky of the Department of Finance: not only were you put to counting the beans but you were expected to model the maths for the way you counted them.

He opened the door. At his feet, on the hairy but durable grey-blue carpet, lay a cylindrical metallic object, about nine inches long.

What most attracted Ultan to Maeve, apart from the availability of her body, was her mind. Mentally, she was a uniquely free spirit. Her devil-may-care attitude took his breath away. Cormac Healy was drawn to her for the same reason. In their case, though, the attraction was mutual — she saw that Cormac, although he didn't leave her breathless, didn't give a damn about anything and she loved him for it, in her own way. But she also saw that while he was down-to-earth, he lacked calculation, a quality she was not short of — her devil didn't care where she planted her hoof, as long as she had made sure in advance that the ground could bear the plantation. She was, though, inclined to be indifferent to the kind of mark made or the damage done, especially after the event.

Cormac had another fault she didn't have: he was improvident. This failing he shared with Emmet Roche. Both of them were reckless about money — about rather than with, because they never had much of it. Emmet's scorn was ideological: in his opinion only fat fools and thin ones, which meant everyone, were interested in the stuff. Cormac's contempt was untheoretical, which was just as well because at some time in the future he was going to come into quite a lot of it.

The accident that left him with a limp had happened at the start of his second year in college. On a wet September night on the road between Limerick and Dublin, at the turn-off to Killaloe, a notoriously dangerous junction, two cars, one of them driven by Cormac, had collided at speed. The cars were packed full of young men, twelve in all. The only sober one amongst them, a barman, was getting a lift from Cormac to his nearby home. Eventually, after a great deal of panicky shouting and the offer of a large sum of money, the barman had been persuaded to tell the guards, if they ever arrived, that he had been driving the car he hadn't been driving.

'The deal had nothing to do with me,' Cormac said later. 'I didn't bother my brown bollix about it.'

The reason it had nothing to do with him was that the engine of the car he had been driving had broken free of its moorings and trapped his legs. Cutting him free from the wreckage had taken a long time. But the insurance companies involved had got wind of the deception in the other car; prosecutions had been threatened and liabilities contested. Cormac, though, was innocent of changing places, so his compensation was coming for sure. But it would be a slow process, there were years in it yet. Somehow the prospect of the bonanza had failed to register with him. At first Maeve thought that his lack of interest might be due to his brainbox having shifted in his head, like the engine under the bonnet, but she soon realised the explanation was not injury but character. It was in Cormac's character not to be excited by anticipation. Nor had the crash made him anxious. All that disability had done was to exacerbate the irritability that anyway went with his natural recklessness. By and large his anxieties were as limited as his imagination — with one exception: almost as soon as he had got hold of Maeve, he had begun to dread losing her. Normally, the jealousy that followed from this fear would have alienated her immediately, and yet it hadn't. In fact, because he continued not giving a damn about anything else, it increased their closeness: the tie that bound them was the tension between them.

Cormac lived in a bed-sit on Nelson Street, near the Mater Hospital, on the other side of the river from Maeve. It was what the letting agency called a luxury hall-door flat, which meant two rooms off a hallway and a shared bathroom. But the flat did have its own private toilet: it was beside the kitchen-sink and ingeniously disguised as a bench by hinged and liftable planking. Harry said it was very convenient: you could cook and crap at the same time. Still, the place was cheap and close to the stop for the bus that took Cormac to work, which meant he didn't have far to walk. Its proximity to the Mater also turned out to be convenient: not for the first time, his more badly damaged leg, the left one, needed repair work done on the titanium scaffolding that connected the knee-bone to the ankle-bone. After some toing-and-froing with Barrington's Hospital in Limerick, a surgeon in the Mater had agreed to do the operation. All it involved was a two-night stay, possibly three, and then Cormac could limp on as before, one leg shorter than the other.

And so he would have done had it not been for Will Ferris.

The unspoken was something Maeve did not go in for. The second night she slept with Cormac she told him if the Ferris Wheel came round again, she would, if she wanted to, jump on it. 'And,' she added, 'don't you forget it.' At that stage the challenge hadn't mattered to Cormac: he was the cat who got the cream, and he cared less than ever about the devil taking the hindmost. Anyway, Will Ferris was a freak with a yellow streak. Hadn't he done a runner from the burning house and never explained why? And hadn't he taken up with Cory Leary — that watery thing, that chilblain?

Cormac had nothing against Cory. It was Maeve who called her a chilblain. Long before then she had grown scornful of Will too. But she kept the scorn hidden, even from herself, because although she could have shot the bastard through and through, she also felt pity for him. Was there cause and effect involved here? No. What had the pity she felt for Will Ferris got to do with him running away from her? Nothing. Nothing determined nothing. Anyway, it was an unusual kind of pity, the sort which, when it is directed towards the wicked, is a crime against the righteous. Ferocious, for that reason.

This was hard to understand, but for what Maeve understood she didn't need words. So she convinced herself that if she ever slept with Will again, it wouldn't be because she was in any way submissive, but for the pure sex of it, which by the nature of its purity was female and had to remain unspoken — that was the excitement of it. She had bitten him once and, given the chance, she would do it twice, with a vengeance.

Maeve had not given this recital to Cormac. But he had soon begun to brood about the subject of it.

What she did say was, 'For Christ's sake, give over. You look like the Incredible Hulk.'

They had met, unexpectedly, at a meeting in Dublin Castle. The purpose of the meeting, which was chaired by a fish-faced official from the Protocol Section of the Department of Foreign Affairs, was to brief a large cohort of civil servants from every department of state about the duties they had been drafted in to carry out in connection with the accession to the European Union of ten countries, mostly from the old Soviet bloc. The accession was not happening until May Day, and this was still March, but heads of state and heads of government of twenty-five countries, accompanied by Foreign Ministers, as well as by wives, some husbands and a few same-sex partners, plus delegations of civil servants and advisers, were coming to Dublin for the ceremonies, along with a vast rabble of press persons. Faced with this priceless opportunity to promote Ireland, the government was determined to show that when it came to a Céad Míle Fáilte, a Hundred Thousand Welcomes was what the visitors were going to get, and then some. The boat was going to be pushed out big time. All this carry-on was, in the opinion of Departmental Human Resources sections, a bloody nuisance, but if it had to be done, and it did, then only the most useless civil servants and the newest recruits were going to do it. Cormac Healy, it had already been decided, satisfied both criteria. About Maeve MacNamee nothing had been decided yet — in the Attorney General's Office judgements were slow in forming — but her newness was not in question.

After the meeting, much of which had been taken up with the intricacies of the distribution of sides of smoked salmon to journalists, she and Cormac had gone for a drink in a dingy pub off Werburgh Street. It was the middle of the afternoon and the bar was empty. As Cormac was swallowing his second pint of Guinness and Maeve was sipping a coffee, he told her that for one of the functions he was involved in, a major do at Farmleigh, the government's new guest-house in the Phoenix Park, the list of entertainers included the name William Ferris.

Maeve knew this already. How did she know it? Harry O'Gara had told her. He had set up the gig through yet another of his gay friends, an old flame in Foreign Affairs. Why hadn't she told Cormac? No reason. There were lots of things she didn't tell him. Anyway, Will wasn't singing, just playing the guitar.

'Pulling his wire more like,' Cormac said. 'It wouldn't surprise me if he didn't do a bit of shirt-lifting to advance his career. And as for Harry, he seriously wants to get into the same William's knickers.'

Maeve said she wouldn't blame him. It was this opinion that led to the remark about the Incredible Hulk. The Hulk always managed, as Maeve was about to add, to burst out of his clothes without ever bursting out of his dark blue shorts, but she didn't get the chance.

As they were talking, five men had come into the bar, sat down at the next table, ordered pints, and begun organising themselves to play poker. But their leader, a bullet-headed brute whose gross body, as if under pressure from above, had spread itself out elliptically, hadn't approved of the seating arrangements.

'No, no,' Bullethead had said, 'yer man can't sit in the middle, slobberin' and spittin' into the drink. Move him out there to the edge.' Yer Man, who had a ruined mouth, was mentally disabled. As he was being moved along to the next table he said something. 'What'd he say?' Bullethead said. 'Somebody give us a bloody translation.' Yer Man said something else. Bullethead said, 'Foul language is the sign of an unformed mind.' The other men nodded sagely.

The barman put two pints of stout on the counter and said, 'Three more coming up.' There was a warning in his tone.

Bullethead turned around on his stool slowly. His eyes widened and his mouth dropped open in mock-astonishment. One of his men, who had stood up to collect the pints, was halted with a wave of a hand. 'Well,' Bullethead said, 'what kind of place is this? Do we have to carry our stout as well as pay for it?'

'Ah for Jaysus sake,' the standing one said, 'let's have our bleedin' drinks.'

'No way,' Bullethead said. 'That's why we have barmen. I don't want to put anyone out of a job. I'm a union man, not a dummy, like Yer Man.'

This declaration was greeted with a crash of breaking glass. Quicker now but still slow, Bullethead turned towards the source of the sound. What he saw was a gorgeous bird slapping stout off her skirt and a little how-ya of a young fella whose face was as pale as paper. On the table a pint-glass lay in smithereens. Bullethead had not seen Cormac raising his walking stick and slashing it down on the table.

'It's his leg,' Maeve said.

'What?' Bullethead said. He really was genuinely asking.

'Sorry about that,' Maeve said, adding in explanation for her sorrow, 'I can't bring him anywhere.'

'What's going' on?' Bullethead asked his gang. The man with the ruined mouth said something unintelligible. 'Who's askin' you?' Bullethead said. 'Did I ask you anything?'

'Don't mind him,' Maeve said, referring to Cormac, taking his arm and moving him towards the door. 'He's in terrible pain. He's disabled, you know. Bloody eejit. He has to have an operation. Sorry about that.'

And she bundled him out the door, successfully too, because all that Bullethead did, or could do, was look into the faces of each of his men individually and in turn, and then turn again, slowly, to look again at the barman, his mouth this time hanging open in true bewilderment.

But his bewilderment lasted longer than Ultan McGrath's. It took him only a few seconds to back away from his computer, knock over his chair, and open the door of the boxroom. And there was no doubt in his mind who had thrown the object that lay gleaming dully on the blue-grey landing — his wife. Nor was there any doubt what the object was — a vibrator. Bullet-shaped. Just like pleasure. And the price of it!

19

The drunkenness that makes you bite
What you should kiss
And shoot at your enemies — and miss.

Saints of god, come to my aid, he prayed.
Three middle-aged men came in instead.
They were worn by long black coats,
Which they never took off,
And in their throats
Was a well-used professional cough,
Which they made good use of.

Will Ferris was in a fury. How had these two verses come to be yoked together in his notebook? And how was he supposed to make a song out of them? He was also furious with Frank Sinatra. In a book by Anthony Summers he had read the singer saying that the words always came first and the music was only a curtain. A curtain! Any fool could rhyme 'kiss' and 'miss,' or for that matter 'prayed' with 'instead', if you came from Alabama with a banjo on your knee, but the days he had lost trying to draw a curtain of music across the window! But then Frank had never written a decent song in his entire life.

At the top of the page Will wrote, 'Sinatra: his brains were in his bawls.'

He knew where the first verse had come from. It was to be found in the previous year's diary, the one with the map, which was now at the bottom of the leather satchel Sheevawn had given him long ago. He turned back the pages of his current notebook until he came to the place where Maeve had bitten him for the second time. Although there were no actual toothmarks this time, it had still been a disaster.

> JAN 28 FRIDAY. Doorbell rang. I answered. What kind of fool am I? It was Maeve Mac. Why can't she leave me alone? Her car had got stuck up against a lamp standard in Fitzwilliam Sq. With the aid of a passing hippy, I lifted it out. Then of course I had to go with her to the Baggot. Harry was in the snug. Eating Polo mints and drinking coffee. He said, 'I'm a one-man detergent.' When he heard about stuck car he sd to Maeve, 'You should be polishing Wellington boots for a living.' Funny man. A born fan. Mine anyway.

When, months later, Harry read this description of himself, he was brought up short.

> Just then Cormac rang. After the call she launched into a long tale. Absolutely scabrous. At one stage Harry sd, 'I don't believe you're a woman at all. I think you're a man's fantasy of a sexpot.' She sd, 'That's what Ultan thinks.' Why? Because she went to bed with him! And he was hopeless in the hay. She gave me a significant look. Harry offered her a Polo. I laughed. She didn't cop on. Polo the mint with a hole in it. Harry sd, 'This is an irony free zone.' That nettled her — doesn't like being made fun of. She sd, 'Irony, how are you. That's the only way you're going to get your hole.' Then she told us how Ultan sobbed after sex. Why? Because he wasn't bored any more! So she advised him to gee up his sex life with his wife and this preposterous puritan took her advice and went out and bought her an enormous vibrator! Not only that, he then went to Cormac H in his office in Dept

Finance and asked him why it wdnt work — he hdnt realised
the thing needed batteries. Most grateful for the info. Went
out and bought one, plus some spares. Just in case. Harry
said, 'Ultan takes the belt and braces approach.' Off home
with him then where he presented the whole kit n caboodle
to Mrs McGrath. And she promptly threw them in his face.
So he told Maeve. So what did she do? She told Cormac. 'Jesus,'
Harry sd, 'are you mad?' I didn't get it for a minute. Forgot
she and Cormac are a couple. Dimbo! It's only because I'm
stupid that I understand.

> *It's only cos*
> *you're thick to beat the band*
> *You bite instead of kiss*
> *the undertaker's hand*

Anyway, Cormac asked Maeve how she knew about the dildo.
And she told him. Harry sd you didn't! But she did. Just then
into the Baggot comes Cormac. Three days out of hospital
and still on a crutch. Harry sd, 'You look like Tiny Tim.'
And he did. Very wan.Not too sober either. Almost
immediately he left again. I thought to order drink. Did
this 3 times in 10 minutes. Very mysterious. On the last
occasion Harry went after him. Didn't come back. Left
alone with Maeve I was sage, old and pompous. I sd how
wd you feel about being rejected. She said, 'I'd say, Pity about
you, whoever you are.' Whoever? Then I got it. Cormac's
exits were because he's jealous of me. Just because I was
there with his squeeze! Jesus, I'm so slow.

> *Jesus I'm so slow*
> *I'll come and I'll go*
> *Last in the queue*
> *At my own funeralio.*

Maeve then put her hand on my leg. Seriously high up. So
I made myself scarce. Met Harry coming back across the

road from Doheny's. Cormac ws there skulling whiskey.
Harry sd: I've heard of kicking a man when he's down but
she kicked his crutch from under him. I sd Maeve was hard.
Harry sd, 'She's not hard, she's a sceptic.' Is scepticism a
woman's thing — not to believe? Intelligent women like
her don't believe, because they're still at the tail end of
dependence. But when they're totally independent won't
self-pity make them do exactly the same things as they
have always done? Yes. Just like men. Not Harry though.
He's too bright to be a man. Or a woman.

This was terrible. And nothing could come of it either, at least by
way of a song. Will crossed out the entry so violently that where
the X of his pen met, the paper was pierced through.

20

CORMAC HAD GONE back to the Baggot to tell Will Ferris a thing or two and, if he didn't admit to whatever it was he was guilty of, to give him a dig in the snot. But the bastard, like the coward he was, had done a runner. So Cormac had insulted Harry instead. He wasn't going to be told to take it easy by a fucking bum-boy. He'd shoot him first. To illustrate the point, he had lifted his crutch to aim it like a rifle and in doing so had shattered Harry's coffee cup. Then he had fallen asleep in the corner of the snug. Maeve had said he was a pain in the neck and gone off to the cinema. When Harry said she was a hard-hearted witch, she said, 'I'm not his mother.'

After a nightmarish journey from the Baggot Inn to Harry's flat in Aungier Street — Cormac insisted on pointing his crutch at the policeman on duty outside the Department of Justice as if it was a gun — Harry had put him to bed and gone out. Every fourth weekend he manned, or personed, the phone in the office of the Lesbian Men's Health Collective. After that he had returned home and slept on the short couch in his tiny living room.

The next morning Cormac cured his hangover by eating two fried eggs, three slightly mouldy rashers of bacon, four sausages, some black pudding, a lot of fried bread and an amount of extra spicy pepperoni, washed down with about a third of a bottle of Bols Advokaat, the only alcohol Harry had in the flat.

In the veils of blue smoke — to hurry things up Cormac had

done the cooking at the highest possible heat — they had had a conversation about Maeve, love and sex. Although Harry had tried to warn him against getting them mixed up, Cormac could not be persuaded that they were not indivisible, a sort of Blessed Trinity. To him Maeve was God the Mother, her love was his Saviour, and sex was the chewing gum that held the Mystery together.

Harry said, 'Cormac, you are confused.'

Then, as if in answer to his prayers, Maeve had rung to remind Cormac that she was to bring him to the Mater Hospital and from there out to the Bull Wall. She had owned her car for almost three months, but it was only now that she was doing her test, and she needed to brush up on her driving, especially her three-point turns. Dollymount Strand was good for that kind of thing.

As sometimes happens, everything went miraculously well. At the Mater, Cormac's dressing was changed without delay and, because the wound showed signs of healing, reduced in size. Even more miraculous was the fact that the mixture of fried fat and Bols Advokaat had cured his hangover. Although he felt as heavy as a lead balloon in his body, he was as light as a cloud in his head and too floaty with love for Maeve to remember that he hated her for sleeping with Will Ferris. As in religion, everything negative was reversed: it was because of death that life was eternal and not the other way around. He felt too spiritual for anything but repentance, too overcome by relief that he could hunker down in the passenger seat of an old Volkswagen and be scooted up and down a bumpy beach by a voluptuous hard-swearing devil-may-care goddess, and then get out of the car and limp with her into the dunes and lie down and breathe in the sun-warmed salt air. And kiss her. The salt cleansed the wound. The kiss cured it. He did believe. The grace was amazing.

Amazing, too, was his hunger for more grease. So they went to Kinara, sat at a first-floor window looking out on the sea and ate the nicest fattest tandooried lamb chops, the hottest, sloppiest chicken vindaloo, mopped up with pillowy naans stuffed with almonds and slick with ghee, and drank ice-cold bottles of Mexican beer by the neck. On the way out Cormac told the doorman, statuesque in a dazzling white turban, that he looked like a Nubian prince and that Kinara was the best Indian restaurant in Ireland, maybe even in the whole of Africa.

He was amazingly sex-hungry too. And dirty. Dirty in body, but pure in mind. A filth that anyway yearned ravenously for purity. It didn't matter — or did it? — that he knew his desire had a simple origin: he had poisoned himself with drink, and the residues of the poisons had simply irritated his extremities, or rather his extremity, the one and only priest of his religion. The sole solution to such suffering was an explosion. And back in Waterloo Road he did explode. Maeve stripped him of his drink-stinking suit, helped him into a hot bath, propped his newly dressed leg on the soap-stand, and washed him, thoroughly, with a big sponge, which she had bought on holidays in Crete the previous year. Aghios Nikolios was the name of the place. Somehow it had a flying sound to it, but it did not fly as far or as high as Cormac's seed did: it flew across the room, almost as high as the ceiling. Maeve, who had dressed for the occasion in a bright red glossy satin one-piece jump-suit — the bottom half was skin-tight and the top half so deeply vee-slashed, almost to the navel, that her generous breasts were barely contained by it — jumped up from being hunkered down by the bath and cried out, 'Look at that! You should be in the Olympics.'

With every explosion Cormac's loss was lessened, and by the time he fell asleep for the last time that night, he had forgotten the defeat that had brought him so many victories (five in all). But in the morning, when he woke up and discovered he was wearing Maeve's jump-suit, his brain was invaded by horrible memories, too real to be fantasy, though he had not witnessed them, of her being raped and pillaged by Ultan McGrath, that lumbering Nazi badger, and by Will Ferris, that filthy Whistling Gypsy. About Ultan he said nothing, but about Will he could not restrain himself.

'Why,' he said. 'Just tell me why. That's all I want to know. Why did you sleep with that chancer?'

Maeve, irritated at last, said, 'Because he's sexy.'

The sex that followed the row that followed this remark should have led to a truce, or at least to the lull of more sleep, but it had not done so. Instead, Cormac had cried out in the arid waste of his dry orgasm, 'You're killing me!' And when she asked him what he was talking about, he said he loved her to death, that he would die if he lost her, that he was dying all the time, dying and losing.

To this Maeve made the worst possible reply: she laughed. But, to lessen the scorn, she said, 'And if I ever hear you talking such shite again, I'll break your other fucking leg.'

Until now the general level of Cormac's misery had been jagged, like early mountains, but when Maeve uttered this ironical threat, an Iron-Age-old understanding passed over him like a glacier, gouging the valleys of his despair down to the bedrock. As well as being destroyed he was irritated.

Ossie Gleeson was also irritated. His mother, after spending Monday to Thursday completing the purchase of his new apartment with her solicitors and all Friday and Saturday buying soft furnishings from Habitat and pottery from the Crafts Council, had returned to Cork on the last train.

'Pottery?' Mr Gleeson said as he drove her home to Montenotte, 'What does the boy want pottery for?'

'Osmond needs bowls,' Mrs Gleeson said. 'And they're not all ceramic. No, no. Some of them are wooden. There's a very good man called Liam O'Neill who makes them. Vanessa picked out some lovely ones by him. She has a great eye. We'll put dried flowers in them.'

Sometimes, usually in the afternoons, Vanessa was elated. This was one of those times. There was a reason for the elation: at the station Mrs Gleeson had given her a boxed bottle of vintage champagne, Cristal, and a thank-you card with a Brown Thomas voucher in it.

'Two hundred and fifty quid,' Maeve said to Ossie. 'Your mother certainly knows the way to a girl's heart.'

'You look like death,' Ossie said to Cormac, changing the subject — he was infuriated by the way his mother constantly reduced everything to money. Anyway, Cormac did look like an unshaven corpse tormented by the memory of wearing a scarlet satin jump-suit.

'Let's celebrate,' Vanessa said.

By the time Harry O'Gara arrived, the Cristal was finished. So was the celebration. But Vanessa had not noticed. There was hardly any food in the flat and she had volunteered to make up for the lack from her supply of rice-cakes and packets of dried miso soup, each bowl of which she decorated with spring onions cut and splayed to look like Japanese flowers.

'They're not spring onions,' Cormac said. 'They're scallions.' And he doused them with tabasco sauce and gouts of thick Yorkshire Relish.

It was the tabasco that led to the humorous quotations. Maeve had drawn the curtains and opened the window to let some air in on the frowstiness of the flat, but with the air came a grey wintry light that made the tasselled standard lamp shining in its corner look even more forlornly cocksure than usual. Harry thought that the way the five of them were sitting — Ossie, Vanessa and Cormac on the couch; Maeve, wearing her pink robe, in the ratty armchair; himself on the edge of a kitchen chair — was ill-arranged, uneasy. Everyone looked faded and drained in the glow of the lamplight. The gas fire hissed and occasionally pinged its guard wires. There was something Asiatic about the yellowness of the scene, as cold as the beige miso in the bowls. Not for the first time in recent months, Harry felt continentally older than these young people.

Holding up the tabasco, Vanessa said, 'Isn't it an adorable bottle? Iconic, actually. Henry always had the best taste.'

'Who?' Cormac said.

'You know, the man who invented tabasco sauce: Henry McIlhenny.'

Maeve said, 'You sound like you know him personally.'

'Oh,' Vanessa laughed, 'I don't think so.'

'What's so funny?'

'Well, he's dead, you see, that's why. My folks were chums with him though.'

Harry said, 'Dear old Henry.'

'He was a dear. We used to go up and spend a week with him every summer in Glenveagh. This absolutely fabulous house he had? In Donegal?'

Ossie said, 'Greta Garbo used to visit him there.'

Maeve said, 'Now I am impressed. Did Miss Garbo dandle you on her knee?'

'No, silly. That was before I was born.'

Cormac said, 'Who's Miss Garbo?'

'Oh Cormac, you're a scream,' Vanessa said.

Harry said in a Swedish accent, 'I vant to be alone.'

'Look her up in your book,' Ossie said.

Greta Garbo wasn't in *The Wordsworth Book of Humorous Quotations*, surprisingly. But Archbishop C. Garbett was. The Archbishop had once said, 'Any fool can criticise, and many of them do.' Below Garbett was Jerry Garcia, who said, 'Truth is something you stumble into when you think you're going some place else.' And below Garcia was Ed Gardner, who said, 'Opera is when a guy gets stabbed in the back and, instead of bleeding, he sings.'

'Hey,' Ossie said, 'that is witty.'

Maeve said, 'Hilarious.'

Cormac said, 'Opera is for pansies.'

Harry said, 'It ain't over till the fat lady sings.'

'Thanks,' Maeve said.

'Oh Harry,' Vanessa said. She had been on the point of saying to Maeve, 'Men are awful, aren't they?' but instantly she knew better: her fatness was the one thing that was guaranteed to drive Maeve demented, she obsessed over it, though the problem wasn't so much her weight as her insistence on wearing stuff that accentuated her generous curves, tight stuff and bright stuff and stuff with stripes, which, if they didn't hang straight down, swelled out and made you look like a balloon. That was elementary. Everyone knew that. Except Maeve. She wore stripes and checks and floral patterns and plaids and polka dots all together. Frankly, she looked like the foyer of an Irish hotel.

To have something to say, Ossie said, 'Are you guys going to Will's Farmleigh gig?'

Cormac said, 'No.'

'Of course you are,' Maeve said.

'I'm not going to a gig. I'm working. It's my job.'

Maeve said snappishly, 'It's mine too.'

Ossie said, 'Will says I can be his sound-man and Vanessa can carry his guitar, so we'll get in that way.'

Vanessa said, 'It's really cool the way this book works.'

'How so?' Maeve asked, and for the first time Ossie had an inkling that Vanessa was not as clever as he thought she was.

She said, 'It's not just people. You can look up, like, the names of things too.'

Maeve said, 'What things?'

'Things like opera,' Vanessa said. 'You see its number and then you go to it.'

'I don't get it.'

'I didn't either at the start. But you look up, say, opera in the back and go to number ten sixteen and you see it was — hold on — some guy called Dan Cook was the guy who said, "It ain't over till the fat lady sings".'

Harry laughed, against his will.

'Amazing,' Maeve said.

'"Life's too short to stuff a mushroom,"' Vanessa said. 'That's ten fifteen. Shirley Conran. It says here she was Superwoman.'

Harry said, 'I don't think she was in the film.'

Now in something of a panic, Ossie said, 'She wasn't Christopher Reeve anyway. Wrong sex.'

'What are you talking about?' Cormac said.

'Come on, Cormy baby,' Vanessa said. 'You know what sex is.' And went to the index.

Harry said, 'This is too rich for my blood.'

'Number nine nine three,' Vanessa read. 'Somebody called Alex Comfort — now that's a great name. He says, "Sex ought to be a wholly satisfying link between two affectionate people —'

Maeve interrupted, 'I hope you're listening to this, Cormy baby.'

Vanessa said, 'Yeah, but that isn't the whole of it. "Sex ought to be a wholly satisfying link between two affectionate people from which they emerge unanxious, rewarded and ready for more".'

'Oh come on,' Ossie said, but Vanessa didn't pay him any attention.

'I think we've had enough laughs for one day,' Harry said.

But Vanessa didn't think so.

And when she saw Cormac rising to his feet she assumed he was taking his bowl to the kitchen for more delicious miso.

So she went on. 'Compton-Burnett, Dame Ivy, number nine nine seven, "There is more difference within the sexes than between them".'

Ossie said, 'That's enough.'

'I can't stop now, I'm on a roll,' Vanessa said and she laughed what she thought was her most cynically tinkling laugh. 'I hope everyone is listening to this. Colton Charles Caleb, number nine eight seven. "If you cannot inspire a woman with love of you, fill her above the brim with love of herself — '

She was so intent on working out the meaning of this humorous quotation that for a split second she went on reading from the space between her hands without noticing that the book was no longer cradled in them.

Cormac had snatched it from her and, with an awkward turn on the heel of his injured leg, which caused him a furious twinge of bone-pain, had flung it across the room.

The poor quality paper of the pages flapped and made a sound like that from the wings of a flock of starlings, and, miraculously, because such a feat could not have been repeated in a month of Sundays, the book flew out through the window which Maeve had opened from the top about six inches to let in the air.

If Vanessa had been given the time to finish, she would have read on to the effect that after the woman uninspired with the love of you was filled up to the brim with the love of herself, the brimming would have a result: just then, at the very moment of overflow, 'all that runs over will be yours.' But she had not been given, nor did she have, that much time.

21

THROUGH THE SKYLIGHT window Emmet saw yet another High-Sided Vehicle manouevering around the corner of the street where he lived. Beyond the high wall topped with barbed wire he could see a mercury-coloured sliver of the river Liffey. He lived on a rat-run. Trucks that came over the East Link toll-bridge, in order to avoid the permanent traffic jam on the East Wall Road, often trundled down the quays past the Point Depot, turned on to New Watling Street and — huge filthy small-brained rodents that they were — got caught in the narrow streets with their little houses and their little cars parked on both sides so that only other little cars could get through. Then everything stopped and nothing happened. Nothing was happening now.

It was nine o'clock in the morning of the first day of February. Springtime. Emmet had been looking out the skylight since daybreak. On his feet were his unlaced boots, their dead-dog tongues lolling and panting. He was wearing a smock so thick with paint it looked like a work in progress. These were his work clothes — Tuesdays he had no teaching until three. Downstairs was his studio. The stairs was an aluminium ladder. In the studio a long slitty window looked onto the jumbled yard. At the end of the yard was a hutch of corrugated iron, its door always ajar, home to a seatless lavatory. The studio was an ugly space but spacious. Emmet kept it warm with an industrial blow-heater, a menacing thing as big as a fridge and the shape of a jet engine. There was a kitchen sink, which, because there was no bathroom, also served for shaving and washing. A camping cooker with one ring over a blue metal bottle of gas did his cooking. A mattress covered with a tartan rug served as a couch.

A two-tiered metal table, hospital surplus, was crowded with tubes of oil and acrylic paints, bottles of linseed oil and turpentine, pencils, gouache crayons, sticks of charcoal, stubs of pastel, jamjars containing brushes soaking in white spirits, pots of glue, encaustic, beeswax, masking tape, a staple gun, thumb-tacks, Blutak, a hammer and nails, assorted Stanley knives and scalpels. On the floor were cans of paint, household and industrial — oil, emulsion, vinyl, polyurethane, powdered — many with cheap brushes stuck fast in them. In a corner there was an ancient easel, liberated from the National College of Art and Design, which he rarely used, on principle. By the window was an equally ancient draughtsman's table. Under the table were collapsed stacks and jumbled heaps of sketchbooks, notebooks and drawing pads. The studio was illuminated by the kind of lamp known to film technicians as a brute, the stark white glare of which Emmet sometimes interrupted with homemade filters. The filters helped him to avoid the day coming in from the window — if he was using blue, say, a red filter could produce a Permanent Rose, which killed the actual pigment stone dead. Stone dead was good. He often told his students, 'We're making stuff here. Art is stuff. Stuff is made. There's no such thing as natural light. Your eye is a social construct. You have to paint as if you were blind.' The social construct came from St Martin's, the blindness from his own brain.

His bedroom was in the attic. Standing up there was only possible beneath the apex of the triangle of steeply pitched roofs, or with his head protruding through the skylight, as it was now. Apart from the bed, a 1920s tallboy, lying on its side, in which he kept his clothes, took up most of the space. The floorboards were painted a glossy earthen red. The walls and the ceilings were also painted red, but matt and of a lighter shade, getting on towards vermilion.

'It's like being inside a heart,' one visitor had said.

'Not a heart, babe,' Emmet had replied. 'Lower your sights a bit.'

Many babes had been made uneasy by the ladder up to the attic but a surprising number had accepted the invitation to climb it. The uneasiness was not unjustified. Emmet acted there like a drunken army marauding through a town and leaving behind it gaggles of dazed former virgins. It was peculiar how many of these women, not all of whom were young and immature, enjoyed the experience. Fewer of them, though, relished discovering that Emmet was given to describing in precise detail to third parties what had happened to their bodies up in the red room. Even so, some of the ones who loved danger more than safety came back for more, a test of character that often involved having their post-sex portrait painted.

'That's rather at the barbaric end of things for my taste,' Leonard Rivers said, hearing one of these precise details, languidly adjusting with a long limp white hand the cascade of silky, corn-coloured hair that fell, utterly straight, to his fine, square, sharp shoulders.

'That's because I am a barbarian,' Emmet said.

'Well, I wish you a happy New Year,' Leonard said.

'I'd pay your bus-fare home,' Emmet called after him, but Leonard was already out the door of the Apollo Gallery and heading for a 500cc motorcycle parked in the gutter of Dawson Street.

Leonard taught graphic design at the NCAD but he was also an influential theorist and had an international reputation as a photographer of everyday objects and microscopic insects, juxtaposed and blown up to heroic proportions. One of these photographs had recently sold and he had come to collect the cheque from the Apollo's veteran owner, Hugh Charleton.

The reasons for Emmet being in the Apollo involved a number of firsts. Although he had shown at group exhibitions since he was eighteen, this was his first time showing in such a decidedly commercial space. And it was the first time he had tried his hand at making a carborundum print — James O'Nolan had recently taught him the technique in the Graphic Studios. It was also the first time he had allowed thoughts of profit to undermine his hatred of money. Selling the print at €200 a knock meant that an edition of one hundred would gross twenty thousand quid. Even after the gallery had creamed off its fifty per cent, that was a lot of cabbage. It was also his first time assaying a classical subject — what he had done was to take 'The Rape of the Sabine Women' by David, reduce the colour range to black, red and blue, and eliminate all the figures except for a woman, whom he depicted with her arms and legs making an x-shape, and a man, whose sword and enormous phallus made him appear to have six limbs.

'It's very energetic,' Hugh Charleton had said. 'But I don't think we'll put it in the window.'

That should have led to a denunciation, and yet it hadn't. Emmet was feeling too buoyant. And when he met Will Ferris on the street, he was buoyed up even further. They hadn't met since the fire. It was good to meet a coward. Will had left Leeson Street to buy a guitar string. A new string didn't mean he was playing again; it was a way of avoiding playing. Emmet told him he was probably the only man in Ireland who looked more woeful than Ossie Gleeson — Ossie had made so many statements to the police he didn't know whether he was coming or going. But he had fingered no one. Yet.

'Why are you buying me drink?' Will wanted to know as they waited for their pints of stout in Kehoe's on Duke Street.

Emmet tapped his nose with an enormous index finger.

'That's for me to know and you to find out,' he said. 'What did you make of Miss Rivers, the lady on the bike?'

'There's nothing wrong with being gay,' Will said.

'Gay? Leonard isn't gay. He's married with six kids.'

'That wouldn't stop him being gay.'

'It wouldn't stop you either.'

'What do you mean?'

'It wouldn't stop anyone. It wouldn't stop me. But Rivers isn't queer. Anyway that isn't what I've got against him.'

'Why have anything against him?'

'I'll tell you why: he's a Brit. I don't know from where, Islington or the Isle of Dogs or somewhere, and he comes over here and he flutters his hands and he squeaks to himself, "Oh my god, these Irish, they're so backward, they paint pictures." And he's quite authoritarian about it, he thinks doing anything figurative is old-fashioned, out of date, hackneyed, just so provincial, and then here he is and he meets me and he sees what I do and he's amazed by this figure of the naked body and all the sex and the hostility and aggressiveness of it. He can't believe that that's what real painters think of when they paint a naked woman.'

'Sex and hostility? Is that why you paint women?'

'Of course it is.'

'Isn't it a bad idea to paint a thing because of its sex?'

'Not at all. Why would it be?'

'Well, sex is not just an it.'

'What?'

'Sex isn't just sex.'

'Of course it is. What else is it? Why else would I do it?'

'Well, it doesn't sound like art to me.'

'Does Christianity sound like religion to you?'

'Yes. More or less.'

'Well then, there you are.'

'But,' Will said, 'we're not anywhere.'

Emmet laughed. It didn't matter that he didn't know what he meant by comparing Christianity to religion — it had just come to him. Will was his rival, they were enemies armed with similar desires. Victory went to the man with the quickest reply. And he had won the exchange.

'What's the joke?' Will said.

Emmet didn't usually laugh, but now he laughed again. The sound was like the snort of disbelief he would have snorted had Cory Leary said she couldn't come to his studio to have her portrait painted because she had to go to Mass. She hadn't made that excuse. Actually, she hadn't made any excuse at all. Actually, she was coming to the studio, at twelve noon, on the first day of the New Year. The end of the old year was the beginning of spring! Fuck you, Will Ferris! That was why he was laughing. What a difference a day makes! But twenty-four hours earlier he had been dying.

22

AFTER BURNING OSSIE Gleeson's house down, Emmet had spent Christmas with his parents and five brothers on their farm outside Rathkeale, Co Limerick. Sickness, like God, was another thing he did not believe in, and yet he had been undoubtedly unwell. It was not the alcohol or the drugs that had caused the illness — he was used to the desert-dry gawks and the black-brained Tuesdays, and all such hangovers did, if he had the strength to stand up, was make him stronger and paint better, like an animal.

Emmet had an animistic view of animals. The fact that the cut on his hand had become infected was the sheep's revenge for being murdered. He hadn't formulated this idea rationally; he just believed it, wordlessly. His belief was homeopathic, sort of, in reverse. Anyway the infection wasn't a matter of faith, it was a matter of fact, or rather a fact of matter. When he finally unwrapped the bandage of torn sheet in Rathkeale the wound was livid, blue-white, oozing pus. He had drenched it in Dettol, but it was too late; the sheep had got its own back.

Still, to spite the poison, he ate his Christmas dinner. He was a Roche and that was what the Roches did. But what he swallowed soon came back up again, proving the truth of another of his core beliefs: man is only a bloody tube, valved at both ends.

In the Roche household 'man' was the word. Maleness scowled and loured over the festive table, which creaked under the leaden weight of muscle-bound arms. In the case of Mickeleen, Little Michael, the eldest of the brothers, the arms were, maybe, loaded with real lead. Mickeleen was, maybe, in the IRA. He had certainly been running around for years with a variety of raparees and republican go-boys.

In the middle of all this maleness was their mother. Lily Roche was small, lazy, slovenly, a constant smoker of cigarillos, a slow reader of thick books by quick writers. She was also a believer in 'another martyr for old Ireland'. This belief, although she didn't want him dead, had found expression in Emmet, her last-born son, whom she had named after Robert Emmet, 'the darlin' of Erin', executed by the Saxon in 1803.

On the outskirts not just of all this but of everything else was Mickey Roche. Mickey was big, fat, industrious, diffident, depressive, a believer in schemes for making money, a martyr to piles. He was in awe of his wife's cleverness, though he had no clear idea what Lily was clever at, except being awe-inspiring .

Emmet's illness spared him from battling with his mother, being contemptuous of his father and drinking hundreds of bottles of stout with his brothers. But when he went back to Dublin the day after Stephen's Day, the short walk from the bus station along the river to his studio seemed endless, a lethargic trudge through porridge, each fudged footstep slowed to infinity. The desire that kept him going had a visionary certainty about it: he knew that lying on its side in his miniature fridge there was a two-litre bottle of Coca-Cola, which he would swallow in one go. The Coke, when he did eventually drink it, was even more brownly sharp than he had thought it would be. But as soon as he downed it, up it came again, in a blinding fit of vomiting that was followed by a blinding headache.

He sank onto the mattress on the floor, dragged the tartan rug around him, and fell asleep in his boots.

Eighteen hours later he woke up, a new man but weaker, drained of the aggression that fuelled his creative energy.

In this state of mind he walked through the cold blue afternoon to the Graphic Studios to oversee the pulling of his print. When that was done he did not know what to do. Aimlessly he drifted onto Anglesea Street. There, outside the Mongolian Barbecue Restaurant, he leaned the flat of his hand against the plate-glass window. That was how Cory Leary saw him.

'Are you all right?' she said.

'Me?'

'Yes,' she said. 'You look pale.' As she said this, she put her hand under his elbow and there came to him a waft of Chantecaille Frangipane, the perfume on her tissue.

'I feel weak,' he said and sat down on the pavement,

She hunkered down beside him. 'What's the problem?'

He held out his bandaged hand. 'I cut myself. I have some kind of a virus.'

'A virus? I don't think so, Mr Roche.'

Instead of asking how it was she remembered his name, he said, 'That's a nice shade of red.' The tights she was wearing were a deep alizarin crimson colour.

'Try standing up,' she said.

He stood up. 'I'm grand,' he said. 'What are you looking at?' He was addressing people who were passing. They veered off the pavement, scared.

'They think you're a junky,' Cory said.

'I'm not, but I don't know why I'm not,' he said piteously.

'Do you want to go to hospital?'

'No, no, I'm all right.'

'Have you eaten anything? When did you eat last?'

'I don't know. I had some Rubex for breakfast. And yesterday I had some boiled apples.'

'Rubex and boiled apples? Well, you'll live forever on that diet.'

'I'll live forever anyhow.'

'That's a very peculiar thing to say.'

'I'm a very peculiar man.'

'Well, I think you're hallucinating. Your blood sugar must be low. Here,' she said, fishing in her handbag. 'Eat this,' and she handed him what was left of her lunch: half a bar of Bournville dark chocolate. As she watched him breaking off the squares and flinging them disdainfully into his mouth she thought that if she had hands like these, big as shovels, they would change the way she lived her life.

At the same time Emmet was thinking that the freckle-dotted paleness of her skin, the whites of her eyes, the rose-madder red of her lips, the mouse-brown of her hair as well as the crimson of her tights made up the most beautiful combination of colours he had ever seen. And that his energy was returning. But also that she was leaving him forever. Whatever about the forever, she had certainly said something he hadn't heard and was now walking off up the street.

'What did you say?' he called after her.

'I'll be late.'

'Late? For what?'

'For the pictures.'

'Oh,' he said. 'Oh. So am I.'

'Really? The IFC?' He stared at her. 'The Irish Film Theatre?'

'The IFC. Of course. Absolutely.'

'Are you a Bergman fan too?'

'Oh yes,' Emmet said, walking along beside her, elbows out, clearing the way, as of old. 'Oh yes, big-time. I'm crazy about it, you know.'

This 'it' was slurred by a cough because it had occurred to him he didn't know what the hell the sex of this Bergman person was. Was it Ingmar or Ingrid? The film they were going to see, Cory told him, was called 'Cries and Whispers'. Wasn't Ingrid in that? Perhaps it was safer not to ask. So he didn't.

The cinema was half-empty. The audience behaved in an unusually unironic way for an IFC audience: when the corpse in the film woke up, they shrieked, and when a tear came out of its eye, they giggled. Cory slumped down in her seat, gnawing her thumb. Emmet wanted to take the thumb out of her mouth and kiss it, but when, after some minutes looking blindly at the screen, he decided he would, and turned to her, he saw that she was asleep.

He wasn't to know that this time it wasn't overwork that had tired her out.

When the film was over Cory woke in a panic — she was due back in the Rotunda — dashed up to Dame Street and joined a queue boarding a bus for Parnell Square. Before the bus moved off, the muscled club of Emmet's index finger pounded the number of her mobile into his, and he got her to agree to come and sit for her portrait. Tomorrow. Twelve noon. He would text her the directions.

The text, entirely factual and, he thought, a little offhand, was the longest he had ever sent in his life. How sweet it was then to meet Will Ferris.

Emmet didn't clean up the studio — he didn't believe in cleaning — but he spent so long moving things around, he might as well have done so. Then a thought occurred to him: food, she would need to be fed. So he bought a Cuisine de France baguette, a packet of ham, one of salami, one of corned beef, a tin of smoked mussels, a jar of piccalilli, a tray of tomatoes on the vine, and a head of butternut lettuce, a bit wilted because of the holiday season. But, of course, she would expect, being a woman, cheese and biscuits, so he got her a polythened triangle of Roquefort and a packet of Jacob's cream crackers. And fruit: four Granny Smith apples, two bananas, a kilo net of clementines, a pineapple, and a grapefruit, which he cut in half for a starter. No bloody cherry, though. For dessert Häagen-Daz strawberry ice cream. And a McCambridge's porter cake. That would do. No, he had a marvellous idea. A super-sized bar of Bournville dark chocolate. Brilliant!

Because he had no serving dishes, he cleared the stuff off the hospital surplus table, tented the whole thing with bubble-wrap, covered a small painting that he didn't like with tinfoil and then spent half an hour arranging the food on the crinkly reflective surface. There was a subject here: he would do a still life in which the paint was exactly as thick as the objects depicted. Had somebody not done something like that somewhere before? He had a suspicion that somebody had — but he put it out of his mind. Actually he was out of it already. Cory was late. By almost an hour. Even before that, his nerve had begun cracking. He had been, in a different sense, cracked for a long time, but he took being crazy for granted; it was part of the condition of being a great painter. So, if he had preserved the tissue that Cory had given him in the hospital, well, that might be a little mad but it was also practical. And to prevent the scent fading it was practical, too, to wrap the tissue in gauze and keep it in the clear plastic of an old Faber-Castell pastels box. It was, admittedly, a bit Jacob's cream crackers to plan on giving her the box and asking her to open it, as if she were a contestant in some kind of religious game-show, a goddess opening a prize which turns out to be a relic of herself. But with the thought of this gift, his strength had returned in full force. He was completely restored to health. And exultant. He was going to do with Cory Leary what he always did with women: screw the socks off her. The tissue would be a little spicy gift to get her worked up. But as he waited, the practicalities of the plan nibbled away at his nerve. Should he bring the box up the ladder and leave it on the bed? Or present it with the food? Or place it on the mattress in the studio where he was going to pose her for the painting? He tried all these places but none of them worked.

By the time Cory arrived, he had forgotten her. And when he opened the door, he did not recognise the small white face peering out of the boxy overcoat. He stared at her. She was a perfect stranger. A messenger from the gods. To the message she delivered — 'Sorry I'm late' — he made no answer. Instead, with head lowered, eyes raised, and on his face an expression of unworthy supplication, he held out to her, dumbly, with both hands, the Faber-Castell box.

This lasted the merest moment. As soon as he offered the sacrifice, he withdrew it. Startled, she tried to make a joke out of the withdrawal. He said nothing. What could he say? That he was madder than he thought? Somehow he had got hold of an absurd notion, absurd as thinking that the pigment could be squeezed back into the tube, or that a mistake could be corrected, or that a gift could be returned in the same form as it was given. That was stupid. He could give her nothing, or take nothing from her. His eyes swam, his ridged eyebrows, thick inches of bone, blocked his view with their bristles. He couldn't speak, his jaws were clenched shut. Cory walked around the studio, passing incomprehensible remarks about it. Did she say something about the still life on the tinfoil? If she did, she hadn't eaten any of it. Did he ask her did she want a glass of wine? He must have because he had opened the bottle and drunk half of it. But the only thing she drank was a cup of water from the tap. A cup, not even a glass.

Usually when Emmet did a portrait, he worked directly onto the canvas, but now, as Cory sat on the mattress, knees up to her chin, skirt drawn down to her ankles, all he could do was make an ink and conté crayon sketch in a notebook. It was realistic, academic, the sort of thing he hadn't done since he had assembled his portfolio for art school. It had charm. He hated it. She wanted to see it. He wouldn't show it.

Usually, too, when he did a portrait, he had Kraftwerk on loud, to avoid having to talk to his eejity sitter. But this time he forgot the music, and she asked questions, and he answered them. He heard himself telling her about each of his brothers in turn, and then, as if from under a mile-deep sea, about his mother and father. Saying such things angered him, and his anger, he knew, sounded self-pitying, which made him angrier, and so on.

After an hour she said she had to get back to work, that it had been an interesting experience and very nice. Then, at the door, she said thank you and kissed him on the cheek. Her perfume was the one he had trapped in the box. No light could reach it there. He felt like a robber caught red-handed in the dark. His guilt was not secret. But because being guilty was a feeling he had never felt before, like Ultan McGrath being bored, Emmet did not recognise what he felt for what it was. Nor, because it was not in his nature, did he reflect on it. Nor, not reflecting, did he continue to feel it.

What had happened after that was that he had slept with Vanessa Banim, twice. On the second occasion he had not bothered to paint her portrait. She wasn't worth it.

Today, though, with his sandy head stuck out the skylight, he reflected in a general and abstract way about the beginning of spring, the end of winter, the feeling of the closeness of deep feeling to nothingness. But in these reflections, which included thoughts about the Cory Leary disaster, which he did not like thinking about, a minor thought troubled him. Something was wrong. Something was missing.

23

I'm getting tired of sipping wine
And seeing it bubble.
Why did our dreams get of line
And end up in trouble?

MAYDAY 2004. Why did I sing this at the Farmleigh Fiasco?
I don't know. Let's see can I work it out. In any case I shouldn't
forget any of it. Now it's the middle of the day and the sun
is streaming in the window so hard I can hardly see the
TV. They're showing President MacAleese live from Áras
an Uachtaráin as the flags are being raised for the ten new
countries of the European Union. Behind her are Blair and
Berlusconi and Bertie Ahern and all the rest of the Bastards.

What kind of republic is this?
What are your flags to us but filth?
Why can't we stand on our own two feet
Wrapped up in our own green guilt?

Where to start? I knew there was going to be trouble even
before we got to the Phoenix Park. It was sealed off like a
concentration camp with gangs of guards and battalions of
soldiers and a fence that cost 5,000,000 quid to put up. Even
the Zoo was closed down.

I imagined the lions roaring, 'Let us out of here, for Christ's sake!' The whole place was ringed with steel and all to deal with about a hundred Grassroots people, Socialist Workers, anarchists and the odd Womble or two. One guy had a placard, 'Embrace Your Desires — Burn Banks Build Playgrounds.' He looked at us with hatred. Why? Because Ossie was driving a red Mercedes with the roof down, and Cory was driving a Fiat 500 with four wheels, that's why. Plus the two of us were in tuxedos, that's another why. Another guy, a big boney Blade One head, kept shouting at me, 'Parasite, parasite.' So I shouted back, 'Get a job.' I could hardly tell him I'm your side, could I? Why not? Anyway the cops told us to drive on.

When we reached Farmleigh, the real trouble started. At the gate they said no way were we getting in. We had to pull over to the side while they called this guy from the Department of Foreign Affairs. A thousand-year old relic with a face the colour of a sardine's belly. My name and Ossie's were on his list. But there was no provision for equipment. I said, 'I could play air-guitar if you like.' He just looked at me; he had no idea what an air-guitar was. Anyway, the guitar was permitted. But there was no question of allowing in 'this thing' — he waved at the amplifier as if it was the coffin of a black midget. 'And as for the young lady — '

'She's not a young lady,' I said. 'She's a medical doctor, you pompous sprat.'

Luckily enough, I think fish-face didn't hear the sprat bit because Cory said, 'That's enough.' And off she stalked back to the Fiat bright as a beetroot. I didn't know what to do. Ossie was faffing around and Fishface was looking at me as if I'd invaded Poland, but give him credit because he said, 'If I were you, I'd stop digging.'

So I went to the car and said, Cory, for god's sake, give me a break here. And she said, more or less, that it was one thing to be condescended to by a 'pompous sprat' but it was another thing entirely for me to lower myself by saying she was a doctor, a medical doctor at that, when she was hardly even qualified, and if she were a waitress or a charwoman, would I have said that, and if not, why not? And she wasn't impressed either by me insulting a man who was only doing his job. Did I understand that? I did. It was Yasser Arafat all over again. Now, she said, I'm going home and you're staying here, because you have work to do for which you are getting paid, work which is important for your career. I said, fuck my career. Was that a clever thing to say? It wasn't. So that was that, and off she drove, mad as a bat in a bucket of rust.

Anyway she was embarrassed at not being properly dressed. She'd come straight from work and it was only when we met up in Bongo Ryan's and she saw me and Ossie wearing tuxedos that she realised this was a state occasion and not what I'd told her it was, 'some fucking cocktail party'. I hadn't even told her it was in Farmleigh. To tell the truth, I hadn't thought about it. The dress code, I hadn't thought about that either. When Ossie came to pick me up I told him there was no way I was getting into a monkey-suit, but he said I had to. In the heel of the hunt out he went and rented one. The buttons wouldn't close across the chest and the sleeves were too short and they got caught up under the armpits. It was like being sawed in half by two circular saws. I said it was grand, perfect, fitted me like a glove. Then I went to the bathroom and cut the stitches with a razor blade. Of course Cory instantly spotted the slashes. Ossie nearly freaked because he'll have to pay for it. And why not, he's loaded? But the silly bugger hadn't rented me a shirt and the nearest thing I had to a white one was sort of grey and had a green stripe to it. It didn't go with the burgundy bow tie. And Cory said, 'You haven't shaved either. Look at the cut of you.' Just like Polly.

When we got into Farmleigh and started to set up, Fishface kept fishing to find out why I was there. I said because I'm cheap. The room I was playing in is a kind of shrine to our Nobel writers. Who's the pixie with the beard I asked. Fishface looked at me pityingly. 'George Bernard Shaw,' he said. Never heard of him I said. Can a sardine turn puce? Anyway, to show him I wasn't a complete muck-savage, I said, you've got James Joyce in here and he never won the Nobel Prize. 'I know that,' says he, 'but he wrote *Ulysses*.' Well, I said, he didn't win it but he should have done, is that what you're saying? 'It's immaterial,' says he. That's a bit Irish, I said, but it reminds me of what Louis Armstrong said when President de Gaulle presented him with a Sèvres vase: 'The King of France gave me a jug.' Fishface said, 'Very amusing.' But I don't think he meant it.

Anyway I suppose it was a privilege to play in the Nobel Room. But my hands were so sweaty I couldn't get the guitar tuned. Then there were all these women going in and out of this massive ballroom next door to the Nobel Nook. Not one of them paid the slightest heed to me. So I started to play, a bit of Bach. No amp of course. They couldn't hear a note; I might as well have been miming.

Every two minutes Fishface came in to check. Kept on giving me this sardine smile and nodding as if he was just so glad I was not blowing my snot on his gorgeous curtains, or what do you call them? Tapestries. Fantastic things they are too. After about the fifth time he came in to inspect me, I abandoned Bach and gave him some Django Reinhardt instead, as fast and jazzy as I could make it. Bugger just clicked his fingers. Cool as a dead cat. And off he shimmied, twitching his ass like he was doing the foxtrot or going to get his hip replaced. I don't think he saw the glass of champagne under the chair. By this time I'd had three or four of them. I was flying. Ossie got them for me. And canapés. Thai things on sticks with a little pot of chili sweet and sour. Very nice. Stuck to my fingers though, so I had to lay off.

'Where's your sweetie?' I said to him. 'She's not my sweetie,' he said, 'but she doesn't know it yet.' And right on cue, there was Vanessa coming in the door, and there was Ossie doing a runner out into the ballroom. He scarpered so fast he nearly knocked over the statue of Seamus Heaney.

I said, Vanessa, my god, you look amazing. And she did. She was wearing a butcher's apron. It should have been leather, but she couldn't find the real thing, so this was some kind of dirty white rubbery stuff, and she had a whole load of white material — chiffon she said it was — foaming out all around it. But when she turned around — and she did — she had nothing on except this full-length body stocking, so lacey you could see her cute little ass through it — and I did. And these skyscraper shoes, genuine 1970s platforms she said. And her hair was done up in a bundle on top of her head with white flowers in it. They looked real but they were probably plastic too.

I said it again, Vanessa, my god, you look amazing. And she said — I swear — without stopping for breath, 'I just love your shirt it's so real my heart is broken why is Ossie trying to avoid me?'

Just then Maeve and Cormac came in. When he saw Vanessa, he stopped, leaned on his walking stick, shook his head and went out. Maeve came over, pretended she didn't see Vanessa, kissed me, then turned around and said as if she'd just seen her, 'Oh, there you are, we've been looking for you all night.' Which was a lie. Then she said, 'Your dress is lovely.' Vanessa had a look on her face like a chicken looking at a snake.

Just then there was this big kerfuffle and all these people were rushing along the corridor outside, like a blockage clearing out of a drain. Mostly men, bodyguards I suppose, led by Fishface looking like he was about to give birth to a shoal of sardines. And after them, slower, came President MacAleese and Cherie Blair, chatting to each other and laughing like there was no tomorrow. Then, when they got into the ballroom, there was this burst of applause. Irish women are desperate slaves. You'd think Cherie was Christopher Columbus coming back from America with the news that she'd discovered George Bush. So off she goes around the ballroom with Mary Mac shaking hands and grinning like a Cheshire cat. Vanessa said she wanted to meet Mrs Blair, so I bullocked my way into the front row and put her in front of me. The next bit I can't be certain about but I'd swear that Mary Mac saw us and said to herself, 'I'm not introducing the wife of the British Prime Minister to this scruff-bag or that weirdo,' because for a split second her eye looked like the Arctic Circle and she turned Cherie to meet people on the other side of the room. But Cherie looked back over her shoulder, really sweet, all winsome, as if to say, I'd-love-to-meet-you-but-I'm-being-dragged-away-by-this-wagon. And Vanessa — give her credit, I suppose it's from being brought up in an aristocratic family — she made just such an exquisite proud little inclination of her head. Very dignified and sad.

Then this man going by said, 'What a wonderful outfit.' Vanessa was pleased as Punch. Maeve — she'd come up behind us — said, 'Do you know who that is? That's the British Ambassador, Sir Something Something.' Vanessa gave her this big blind dazzling smile like a kid who's done something daring, like showing off her bum at a garden fete and hoping she's going to win a prize for it. Then Maeve said something really weird, 'I bet he'd pay you to take his picture.' What could that mean? She was looking at Vanessa as if she was — what? I don't know. A prostitute? A clown in a circus? No, the person a clown picks out from the audience to beat up with a balloon.

Anyway, before I could work it out, Fishface was making desperate signs to get back to the Nobel Room. Later he said the crowd was getting out of hand and he wanted, as he said, 'music to soothe their savage breasts'. So I did 'An English Country Garden' the way Terry Wogan sings it, but even more sarcastic. It was the only thing I played all night that was greeted by applause. Some send-up. Some country.

No sign of Ossie. I suppose because Vanessa insisted on sticking to me like a postage stamp all evening. The place was incredibly hot, and my fingers were slipping on the frets, which I hate, so I asked her to get me some ice. While she was gone, this skinny berk comes up to me and says, 'You must be the cabaret.' Then he takes out this little black notebook and a big fat fountain pen and he says, 'Harry told me your name. I have it here somewhere. Oh yes,' he says, 'it's Will Ferris, isn't that right?' No, I say, my first name is Gabriel, like the angel. 'Really,' he says. So I say, Do you know how to spell Ferris? 'I believe so,' he says, all haughty. Well, I said, let me help you, and I was just about to say, It's f-u-c-k-o-double-f, but just then Vanessa comes back with ice in a pint glass, sees him, stops dead in her tracks, and says, 'Oh, hi, Ernesto.' He just looks at her, says, 'No thanks, cuntooks,' swishes around on his heel, camp as a giraffe, and stalks out of the room. Whereupon Vanessa drops the glass and it smashes on the parquet floor and a cube of ice slides across it and hits me on the foot. Whereupon she bends down to pick up the pieces and the next thing is she's standing up, white as her chiffon, and there's blood spilling out of her hand down the front of the butcher's apron. I have to say Fishface was very nice to her. He wrapped his big old hanky around it, and then some napkins and then he took her away to the St John's Ambulance people outside. The last thing she said was that she wanted to thank me because I'd stopped her being a wallflower all night. But I didn't do anything.

Anyway, by then it was nearly over, at least on the official side, because unofficially it seems what happens is that the civil servants have what they calls 'the afters,' which means finishing off all the bottles that have anything left in them. Which we did in a place called the Boathouse which they're doing up to be a café for the plain people of Ireland. Old Fishface turned out to be quite a decent skin. De Burca or something is his name. Told me an interesting thing: Farmleigh had this 500-year-old oak tree on the lawn and it was getting in the way of the TV signals and so what did they do but cut the whoring thing down. Typical. I said instead of cutting it down they should have taken the guy who suggested it and hanged him from one of the branches. He gave me this Oh-grow-up look — I think it was him that deserved the hanging.

The other thing that happened was that I went out to look at the tree, got lost in the moonlight and who did I meet except Maeve and Cormac and Ultan McGrath. They were smoking a joint, which might have been nice on top of the about ten glasses of bubbly I'd had, but there seemed to be some kind of row going on between them. Strained atmosphere. We were in this sunken garden beside a statue, and there was a streetlamp near it so I could see their faces. Anyway I told them about Vanessa's cut hand and Cormac said, 'If she didn't do it herself, we'd have done it for her.'

Ultan laughed but from the look on his face, I don't think he knew what he was laughing at. I said I don't know what you've got against Vanessa; she's only a kid. Cormac said, 'She's a bloody nuisance.' 'Ask Emmet,' Maeve said. I was going to ask what Emmet had to do with it, but before I could say anything, she said to Ultan, 'Tell him what Vanessa told you.' Ultan said, 'She said you were the best dressed man in the place.' Cormac said, 'Yeah, you look lovely.' And Maeve said, 'Yes, very lovely. Very effeminate. But that's our Will, isn't it?' I thought she must be joking, so I said, Can I pull your leg too and put my hand down and lifted up the hem of her skirt. Very slow. But she just looked at me without moving and said, 'That's too late.'

I felt as if cold blood was running down the backs of my legs, so I just turned around and walked away.

Back in the Boathouse Fishface said, 'What's wrong with you? You look like you've seen a ghost,' and I said I think I have. So I had more champagne and that's when I sang the Johnny Mercer bubble trouble song to the civil servants.

What's happening? What is it I don't know?

24

'THE GAY PLAGUE made me a rich man,' a man called Brad said to Harry late one night in New York. Brad was a native of San Francisco and old enough to remember when the virus was called a plague, even by gays. 'What age were you in 1991?'

'I was sixteen,' Harry said.

'Lucky you,' Brad said. 'In 1991 I went to Malaysia and bought a latex facility. I knew it was good business but I didn't know how good. That year Malaysia sold the US four billion gloves. In '92 it was eight billion. I'm not Malaysia, Harry, but this wasn't a plague for me, this was a gold mine. Now paramedics all over the world wear them, whether or not there is a blood injury. Even in Africa they're starving to death they wear gloves. And do you know what, it wasn't us the paramedics were scared of back in San Francisco when the plague started. It was everybody. If you secreted bodily fluids — spit for god's sake — they wore latex gloves. The world changed. The whole world was infected. Still is.'

Harry was reminded of Brad when he noticed the hands of the ambulance crew in Waterloo Road sheathed in a second skin, flimsy but impermeable, a skin with a nacreous sheen off it, the dull shine of exposed bone. One of these hands grasped Vanessa's jaw and waggled it to test its stiffness. Then the hand slapped her cheek, almost playfully, the way a runner might slap the bottom of a fellow competitor lining up for the start of a marathon. Good luck! Then it briefly palped the side of her neck for a pulse.

Now, resting crosswise on its fellow, the better to distribute the force, the gloved hand was pressing at regular intervals on her breastbone. Springy and all as the ribcage was, the bones cracked loudly and went on cracking until the other ambulance man returned with the defibrillator.

Everything about the scene reminded Harry of Brad, who had lost his lover, a senior executive at Bergdorf Goodman's, to Aids in 2000. The first time Harry had rung their Upper East Side apartment after the cremation, he had got the answering machine. The message had been changed. It was unemotional, business-like, but after Brad had finished recording, he had unthinkingly let the tape run on, an interval of silence broken with the who-who wail of a siren far down in the city's canyons of steel and, just before the automatic cut-off point, a close-up groan of animal misery.

Harry had also witnessed drug overdoses in New York. To his eye what ODs and virus deaths had in common was poverty. Whether the event occurred in a rich man's apartment, a junkies' shooting gallery in Harlem, a busy Emergency Room, an exclusive clinic, or this basement in Waterloo Road, everyone and every object looked dirt-poor, scratched, blotched, worn out, used up. That all this ugliness was caused by an immobile person stretched on a bed, slumped in a chair or crumpled on a floor was remarkable. You have to give the body credit, Harry thought.

In this instance the body was clothed in a peach-coloured 1940s crêpe-de-chine nightdress, trimmed at the neck with lace. Its slipperiness looked squalid against the pearliness of the ambulance man's gloved hands as they clamped the pads of the defibrillator to the region of the heart. The brief leaps of the body were squalid too, and the spine arched gracelessly.

Had Vanessa foreseen this, she would not have attempted suicide, but somehow she had envisaged her body, that is her self, as continuing after death to be graceful, perhaps even more so than before, ideally. There was much else she would not have liked. The way, for instance, Ossie, summoned from his flat, came into the room, stared at her twitching feet, horned with bunions, and after less than a minute went out. The way the bedside lamp, knocked over by Cormac trying to wake her up, had been righted but stood on the floor, still lit, shining still, just as it had shone all night. The way Harry and the ambulance men, simultaneously and inexplicably, because his entry had been noiseless, turned and saw Thomas the Tinkerboy standing in the doorway, an arrowroot biscuit in one hand halted half-way to his mouth and in the other hand, held at the ready for choosing from, the packet of Marietta.

Maeve said he must have just walked in the front door, which, after all, was open, and gone straight into the kitchen. Maybe she had given him the biscuits, but she couldn't recall, just as she couldn't explain why she had gone to fill the kettle, unless it was something to do with seeing old cowboy films in which a doctor, arriving in a hurry, rolls up his sleeves and demands boiling water because some frontier beauty in a gingham dress, not Greta Garbo, has suddenly gone into labour. Why water had to be boiled for giving birth was a mystery Maeve could not fathom. Anyway, whatever else Vanessa was doing she wasn't having a baby. Or maybe she was. Could that be it? In any case, a watched kettle never boils. Maeve had found out the truth of that proverb.

When she had sent Thomas on his way, Maeve returned to the bedroom to find Harry on his knees. What he was looking for, at the request of the ambulance men, was some evidence of the tablets she had taken. Pharmaceuticals were most likely because there were no wounds, except the stitched and bandaged hand. Nor were there needle-tracks on her arms, so she wasn't an IV drug abuser, nor any signs of searing around the mouth from the swallowing of raw bleach or caustic soda, which, funnily enough, quite a lot of suicides went in for. Could she have taken paracetamol? There were all sorts of vitamin pills, food supplements, homeopathic and herbal remedies, but no paracetamol. Was she on any medication? No, Harry said, not as far as he knew. At this moment, just as Maeve came in to say the kettle was boiling, Harry found, between the locker and the wall, an envelope bearing his own name, which he put in his pocket without thinking, and a box that bore the trade-name Diamicron. In the box were two blister packs of pills, both empty. This was the drug Vanessa had overdosed on. She was a diabetic.

For some minutes after the ambulance had driven up Waterloo Road heading towards St James's Hospital, Harry, who had stayed on the pavement when Maeve and Cormac had gone back indoors, could still hear the siren's who-who fading away on the warm summer air. He sighed an unremembered sigh of animal misery. Unheard though.

25

THE BED IN which Vanessa was lying began to rise. Noiselessly.

Harry said, 'I got such a fright, my soul nearly jumped out through my ears.'

Will said the feeling he had was how he imagined primitive human beings felt when they experienced an earthquake for the first time in the history of the world — there had to be a first time for everything, after all.

Harry said, 'Maybe. But we're quicker now than we're primitive.'

This was true: long before their terror could become either religious or historical, they understood that the bed was engineered. Somewhere in it or underneath it there was an engine that was causing it to rise, to pause, to fall back, to pause and rise again — but this time it was the foot of the bed that rose, and when that sequence was completed, the whole bed began to sway from side to side.

The engineers must also have calculated that the swaying would not cause a human body to turn over and tumble out of the bed onto this or any other dull green marmoleum floor, certainly not if the body was a dead weight, as Vanessa's was. What the swaying did was wash her blood around, to stop it pooling, sedimenting and clotting. A clot could kill her. As to whether or not she was already dead, it was too early to say — death was not easily definable in these circumstances. Her brain felt no pain, there was no response to stimuli, she was unconscious. But she was breathing for herself. In Waterloo Road her heart had stopped, but not for long, and the ambulance man, though he had broken her breastbone, had started it again. Strictly speaking, a month had to pass before it could be said that she was in a proper coma, and there were nearly two weeks left in May. But already it looked as if she was in a Permanent Vegetative State.

Meanwhile the Rotabed continued to rotate.

~~~

On the afternoon of the last day in April, as Vanessa was shaving her legs in the bath, the doorbell buzzed. After the third buzz, which was prolonged, Cormac, coming sleepily to answer it, paused to hammer on the door of the bathroom with his fist and to say, 'Move your arse, you stupid bitch. There's other people in the world, you know.'

It had already been a heavy day for him. Before lunch there had been a reception for the international press in Dublin Castle, which he had gone to, though he, unlike Maeve, had no official business there. In the high and gilded hall they had drunk a lot of champagne and Maeve had introduced herself to an unusually gorgeous man. Nikolai had big liquid brown eyes in a high cheekboned face, and he had recently acquired, at the age of thirty, a string of newspapers all over Eastern Europe. Shortly afterwards, in a hurried consultation with Cormac, which gave him an erection so powerful it was painful, Maeve said the magnate wanted to get into her pants and in return for the promise of paradise, she was going to con him into buying them lunch. Cormac had gone along with the joke without stopping to wonder why the last thing he wanted on earth could be so exciting.

The plan had succeeded, but it had not been a success. Lunch, at a posh restaurant called Thornton's, had turned out to be peculiarly decorous. The grub, Cormac thought, tasted all right but there was an awful lot of very little of it. The other thing was that Nikolai was a bore. His English, which seemed perfectly idiomatic, was in practice incomprehensible. You couldn't knock any fun out of a sham whose answer to everything was the equivalent of an Estonian bus timetable or a pocket history of Latvia, or wherever it was he came from, and who was actually only interested in riding your girlfriend. Actually, Nikolai was not interested in that at all. Instead, he appeared to have got it into his head that Maeve was an aide to the Attorney General and could influence the attitude of the Irish government to the application of EU laws on the monopoly ownership of media outlets. Zzzzzzz.

Cormac was bored stiff, or rather he was bored limp. Plus he was annoyed. He was annoyed because in the middle of the main course — a duck thing with some kind of jam on it — the Assistant Principal he worked to had rung to ask why, at three o'clock in the afternoon, he wasn't at his desk. To Cormac's excuse that his leg had flared up, the AP said that for a hospital casualty department the background noises sounded remarkably like a pub, which Cormac had truthfully denied it was. The AP had ended the call by reminding him that the regulations laid down that absence due to illness had to be supported by a medical certificate.

When Harry told this story to Will on their way out to visit Vanessa in the National Rehabilitation Centre in Dun Laoghaire, Will said, 'The three of them should be ashamed of themselves.'

Harry said, 'That's a bit harsh on poor old Nikolai. His only crime was being loaded.'

'I don't mean him. I mean Emmet. He's a thug. The whole business is disgusting.'

'You're becoming very earnest,' Harry said.

It was Emmet who had buzzed the doorbell. And when Vanessa emerged from the bath some minutes later, smooth-legged and damply rosy, ready to begin applying her make-up — she was thinking of going the whole Leigh Bowery hog with a matt white mask and a shower of mascara tears on her cheeks to match the new black of her hair — it was Emmet she found in her room.

It was true that he was obsessed with Cory, but it was equally true that he didn't think about her much. Being unthought of she had become liquid, a kind of breathable water, the atmosphere of a planet that was not solid, around which he revolved in an elliptical orbit, sometimes near but mostly far.

January, February, and March had rolled by in this fashion. Then on this last day of April, Emmet, his head sticking out through the skylight in his red bedroom, had found himself thinking about the drawings he had made of Cory the day she came for lunch. The one he made after she had left he found with no trouble — he often looked at it. After searching for the academic one without success, he spent an hour looking out the skylight. Then he had taken a taxi to Waterloo Road, rung the bell, brushed past Cormac, burst into Vanessa's bedroom and begun emptying onto the floor the contents of the suitcases, holdalls and plastic sacks that contained all her earthly possessions. The commotion had brought in Maeve from her bed, eye-caked with bleary sleep, clutching her pink silk robe about her nakedness.

By the time Vanessa arrived, moments later, Emmet had found what he was looking for. Advancing on her, kicking his way through the debris, he growled, 'You're a fucking robber, you cunt.'

Maeve had eventually added her own accusation. 'Look at her stupid hair,' she said. 'Where do you think she got that from? I'll tell you: she stole it. That's my dye, you slag.'

Cormac had joined in too, but his accusation was delivered as an aside. 'She spends so long in that bath,' he said, 'I can't even have a piss in peace.'

To this Vanessa said, 'Oh Cormac.' It was a rebuke, quite proud.

Otherwise she had no answer to the charges against her. All she had to offer was a look of brazen innocence — she was used to being caught red-handed. The only thing she was afraid of, really, was that she might wet herself. That would be a worse indignity than being hit, which, come to think of it, would have been a relief. Being hit turned the tables and earned you sympathy, or gave you the chance of it anyway. If only, if only. But wetting yourself, the tables would never be turned after doing that.

Afterwards, when Emmet had stormed out of the flat and

Vanessa had been left alone in her bedroom, Cormac told Maeve he had caught a glimpse of the picture. A portrait of Cory Leary? Was he sure? Maeve was amazed. It had never occurred to her that Cory was Emmet's kind of woman. Which led her to the realisation that, strangely enough, Emmet wasn't her kind of man. Why was that? It was a mystery. But soon to be resolved.

Will and Harry sat in silence by Vanessa's bed. Her face, usually so polished and poreless, was coarsely pitted and puffy and her newly tinker-black hair was beginning to show its blonde roots. She was wired to a machine monitoring the electrical output of her brain. Another machine showed her heart beating steadily. A bag dripped clear fluid into her. Another bag collected cloudy yellow fluid out of her.

But as they turned to go, Harry once more felt as if his soul was trying to leap out through his ears. And Will again felt as if he was an early human being, but on this occasion the first one in history to see night falling in the middle of the day, a total eclipse of the sun.

What happened was that as they turned away from Vanessa they saw Vanessa.

Will said, 'Christ almighty!'

A few primitive seconds later he and Harry realised that, just as the moon moves and the eclipse fades and the old day returns, it was not Vanessa but a shadow of her that they were seeing. This woman's face, too, was puffy, but the puffiness had come with age.

'Call her by her proper name, for God's sake,' the woman said. 'Call her Betty.' In her Belfast accent Betty came out as 'Beddy.' Will thought of Mrs Molloy in the Rotunda and shivered, yet again.

The woman's own name was Doris Dalkeith. She was now walking around the hospital's inner courtyard garden with Harry and Will. The reason why they were not in the hospital cafeteria was curious: Doris had such an aversion to coffee that even its smell gave her the most terrible migraine. The garden was also curious. There was hardly a shoot of green to be seen in it. Everything was brown. The paths were paved with brownish grainy slabs and the only plant, or so it seemed, was cotoneaster, which was brownish too, except for some inconspicuous red berries.

'Dressing up and making up stories, it was all the same to Betty,' Doris said. 'That's what Mr O'Hara used to say.'

Mr O'Hara was Betty's father. Doris's sister Elizabeth was her mother. Mr O'Hara was a Mayo man — that was where Vanessa's accent came from on the day the nail-varnish splotted onto her Coco Chanel suit. Although he was always very formal, Doris said, Mr O'Hara was no snob, but he was entitled to be one, since he had been head butler and chauffeur to a lovely old family in Donegal, the Banims. But Elizabeth was delicate and Mr O'Hara had taken her home to Belfast where she had died when Betty was seven. As for the Banims drowning in the Alps and Vanessa hanging upside down in her baby-seat, that was a fairy tale. But if Betty made things up who could blame her? After all, when she was fourteen her father had been badly burnt driving an Ulsterbus which had been hijacked and set on fire by the IRA. He had died within the year, but not from the burns, so officially he wasn't in 'Lost Lives,' the big book with all the names and histories of the murdered during the Troubles. Even so.

Anyway, Betty was the loveliest wee thing, sharp as a pin so she was, and it was very good of her friends to come and see her. Doris would remember them. Sure, how could she forget? Wasn't Harry and Will the names of the sons of Lady Diana, the Princess of Wales?

On the nubbled brown flagstones amid the monstrous cotoneasters, Doris Dalkeith stood and wept.

The envelope that Harry had put in his pocket he had forgotten about for three days. Then he had been nearly afraid to open it, but curiosity or duty had won out. The note was written on one side of a piece of handmade notepaper, nubbled with real flower petals. The writing was clear at the beginning, but as the drug had taken effect, it wandered...

Dear Everyone,

It's my fault I didn't get the joke. Remember when I'm dead I'll be glad to be dead. I mean this really seriously. I don't blame anybody not even Doris only me. I didn't like reality so I thought I'd change it. But everything looks like it's walking on tiny white legs. Tell Maeve I'm sorry about the dye. I know this is stupid but it's better this way. Sorry.

Love xxx
Vanessa

When Mrs Gleeson heard the news, she said, 'Oh Osmond, the poor girl. She was so lovely. What possessed her? And to think of her now, in a coma. But there was always something about Vanessa. She was needy. Needy, that's what it was. But she was so generous. That little figurine she gave me, the shepherdess, do you know I had it examined, and it's real Meissen. Wasn't it very thoughtful of her? And her poor family, they must be heart-broken, the creatures. Mixed of course. You can tell from the names. O'Hara and Dalkeith. Wasn't it very nice of them to send you such a lovely memorial card? The hymn there at the start, it's very Protestant too, isn't it? You can tell from the sound of it.'

> *Sleeping safe, secure from all alarm,*
> *What a fellowship, what a joy divine,*
> *Leaning on the everlasting arm.*

26

'HER DESPICABILITY didn't stop you borrowing her car,' Harry said on the way back to town from the hospital. By now he was well aware that there were many sides to Will's sensitivity. He was skinless when it came to being laughed at, but when you criticised him outright for being what he was — in this case, hypocritical — he didn't mind. He was like the man in the nursery rhyme who wore breeches made out of goatskin.

> *With the fleshy side out and the hairy side in,*
> *They'll do for the winter, said Brian O'Lynn.*

For Will empathy rhymed with expediency. He might have decided that Maeve was — to use a Billy Bunter word that Harry had recently become fond of — a rotter, but that didn't mean her rottenness should spoil her good qualities, such as owning a car. Admittedly, she hardly ever used the Beetle. In fact it had been sitting in the gravel garden of Waterloo Road for weeks, coating itself with a film of dust, merely because one of its tyres was flat. Maeve thought she'd picked up a nail on the beach at Dollymount. Of course Will could borrow the car on one condition, then two, then three. First, he had to change the tyre; second, go to her father's garage and get a replacement; third, when he brought the car back, wash the dust off it. And — a fourth condition for luck — wax and shine it till it shone.

The reason Will had to borrow the car in such a hurry was that Cory's rust-bucket had failed its roadworthiness test. She had been disheartened, not because the tester, a Nigerian, had laughed at the state of it, but because another motorist at the National Car Testing Centre had whispered, 'These people, they're everywhere. What's happening to our country?' Cory was ashamed that that 'our' should include hers. Failing the test was inconvenient because she had to go to Galway to visit her father, who needed an immediate heart bypass operation, and she was bringing Will with her. Even though they had been living together, or sharing a flat, since New Year's Day, this was a first. Will was looking forward to it. From what Cory had said to date, which was almost nothing, Walter Leary was an interesting person, maybe even the man-key to her woman-lock.

Jimmy MacNamee, Maeve's father, turned out to be interesting too, in his own way. The garage he owned off the South Lotts Road was down a laneway at the back of the house he had grown up in. After many years he had managed, with the legal expertise of his daughter, to secure outright ownership of the plot of land — something to do with the law of adverse possession, whatever that was — and also to sort out a public access issue.

The garage, a kind of hangar with a barrel roof, stood in a yard stacked high with cannibalised spare parts and remould tyres. Towering over it was what had once been three Victorian gasholders enclosed in decorative ironwork. The ironwork had been kept but glass-walled apartments had replaced the rusty gasholders. If Jimmy MacNamee could get planning permission to build on the yard, he was going to be a very rich man.

Inside the hangar the chipboard counter, the grey filing cabinets, the ancient computer, the untidy stacks of ring-binders, stock catalogues and invoice books, even the calendar showing a naked woman leather-browned by the sun, seemed smeared by oily hands. But Jimmy's hands, one of which was holding a phone while the other was waving Will to come in, were as immaculately clean and pink as the cuffs of his shirt.

He was saying into the phone, 'Tubeless? No, haven't got tubeless in stock. I'll get them for you. You want me to go out to the Longmile Road? I will in my bag of coal. All right. This afternoon. I'll call you back.' He put down the phone. 'You're the guitar player,' he said. The phone rang again. He said to it, 'Hold on,' opened the window, leaned out, shouted, 'Moose,' then spoke to the phone as before.

Everything about Jimmy was Maeve made male, but jowlier, like a bag punched out from the inside. His hair was dyed too, not Maeve's tinker-black, but the caramel brown of Grecian 2000, and he had trained it into wings, which he allowed to be silvery, over his ears.

The door opened and a mechanic came in. Jimmy put one hand over the mouthpiece of the phone, held up the other hand with the fingers splayed and said, 'Fit four new tyres on that thing out there. Right? Four? New? Plus a spare. OK?'

The mechanic gave no indication that it was OK, took the keys from Will, went out, got into the car, drove it at a furious pace the short distance into the dark at the end of the hangar, stood on the brakes, which squealed, got out, prised off the hubcaps, which fell with a wobblingly metallic clatter, loosened the nuts on the wheels with a pneumatic gun, then levered up one side of the car with a long-handled manual jack.

Jimmy, finishing his call, got up and looked out the window. He shook his head and said, 'God knows how many years that ape is in Ireland and he still doesn't understand a word of English.'

'What did you say his name was?' Will asked.

'It sounds like porridge. I call him Moose. Because he's horny. And thick.'

The phone rang again.

Will went out into the garage. Moose was a good name for the mechanic. His hair resembled the tuft a moose sports between its horns, and his face bore the same look of evolutionary foolishness, but darkened by human knowledge.

Will asked, 'How's it going?'

The mechanic gave no indication of having heard. Instead he

threw one of the wheels onto a steel machine, which issued a giant hiss that blasted the tyre off the rim.

Will went back to the office. Jimmy put down the phone and said, 'Another gobshite.'

Will said, 'I've seen your Moose before.'

Jimmy said, 'I'm not surprised. He's the kind of fucker that's invisible, then you see him and then you can't stop seeing him. But I'll say this for Moose, he works his arse off. Or he used to. Last week I found him looking at the clock. It's twenty past five and he wants to go home already. I said, "I'm going to get rid of that fucking clock — and you." He just looks at me.'

'He doesn't say much, does he?'

'No, and do you want to know why? Because he's a cute whore. I got him off the streets. Thought he was a charity case. I even gave him a room in the old house. No rent. Then it turns out he's been in Ireland longer than me. And he has a wife. Doesn't live with her. No surprise there. One of his kids has the brain of a six-year and the body of a sixteen-year-old. Trouble, big trouble.'

Will said. 'I see what you mean by work.' The car had just shot past the window into the yard.

'Five new tyres,' Jimmy said. 'I suppose you want me to give you a discount. Right, let me see. That'll be four hundred quid.'

'Four hundred quid!'

'That's a bloody good price.'

'But I haven't got four hundred quid.'

'You what?'

'I haven't got that kind of money. I thought —'

'How much have you got?'

Will put his hand in his pocket and came up with a crumpled ten-euro note and some coins.

Jimmy's face darkened with rage and he roared through the window, 'Moose, get those fucking tyres off that fucking car!'

~~~

Denis Mulqueen, a Customs and Excise official from County Monaghan, was a man of extreme inoffensiveness. He was so unaggressive, so delicate in his manner, so timid in his little person, that his colleagues called him Denis the Menace. Today Denis had come up to Dublin to visit his eldest daughter, who was living in Sandymount. The car Denis owned was a Lada, which was slow, heavy and almost half as old as Denis, who was getting on for sixty.

'This car of mine,' he would often say, 'is in perfect working order and it's in perfect working order because I never exceed thirty miles per hour.'

Denis had, though, one foible as a driver. He would be trundling along at thirty miles per hour, telling whomsoever it was that was with him how the company that manufactured the Lada car under the communist government of a now non-existent country called Czechoslovakia had been taken over by Fiat, the company owned by Gianni Agnelli — 'a kind of Italian Tony O'Reilly' — and then, while trundling and talking, he would see ahead of him a junction and a set of traffic lights. If the lights were red, he would stop. If the lights were green, he would go on. But if the lights were amber, Denis would tighten his grip on the steering wheel, lower his head, and trample the accelerator to the floor. Whereupon the Lada, as if suddenly freed from capitalist captivity by a memory of the socialist fervour that had brought it into being in the first place, would make an almost Chinese Great Leap Forward and, with a roar of its under-used engine, burst through the lights, before the amber could turn to red. Hopefully. Which modifier, though it dangles and is disdained, will continue, whether grammarians, who know their whole enterprise is hopeless, like it or not, to be used, regrettably.

As Will drove away from the garage he was in a fury. To have been taken in by Jimmy MacNamee, admittedly a brilliant actor, about the price of the tyres, which were free, was mortifying. Maeve had inherited more than her father's brains — she had always been able to make Will feel stupid. And to be obliged to join in with Jimmy's laughing had been made the more demeaning because Moose — who was the Moonman — had come in to discover why he had been shouted at and had stood up close, too close, to Will in the narrow office, not laughing, expressionless. Will felt mortified, demeaned, unnerved.

All these diminishments came together at the junction of South Lotts Road, Grand Canal Street, Beggars Bush, Shelbourne Road and Bath Avenue. When the lights turned green, Will drove out of South Lotts Road. But just as the lights turned red on Grand Canal Street, Denis Mulqueen came roaring through them. Will wrenched his steering-wheel left. Denis wrenched his right. The Lada's left front mudguard — wing would be too bird-like a word for it — struck the driver's side of the Volkswagen. Heavily imperturbable, the Lada mounted the footpath and cannoned into the chained cannons, stuck barrel-down into the ground, which keep pedestrians off the patch of lawn that fronts the high grey stone walls of Beggars Bush behind which are housed some of the offices of the Revenue Commissioners, as well as the Labour Court, the Irish Labour History Society, the National Print Museum, the Irish Geological Survey and a terrace of privately owned apartments, Georgian or perhaps early Victorian, that had once been home to the Government Publications Office, a subsidiary of the Office of Public Works. For centuries Beggars Bush had been a military barracks, but after the War of Independence the new Irish army had taken it over, and it was there on 24 November 1922, at the height of the Civil War, that the irredentist republican Erskine Childers, the English-born author of the thriller *The Riddle of the Sands*, was executed by firing squad.

Denis Mulqueen, who had once upon a time actually seen the 1979 film of the thriller, starring Michael York and Jenny Agutter, and who had as a result harboured romantic feelings for Jenny, and who was at this moment in time not interested in history or romance, who was in fact beyond knowing whether he was already dead or just waiting for the sentence to be carried out, sat clutching the steering wheel of the Lada with nerveless little lady's hands, ashen-faced, horrified, unhurt.

Meanwhile Maeve's Beetle had struck the pedestrian island in the middle of Shelbourne Road and spun around so that when it came at last to rest on the pavement at the corner of Bath Avenue, its nose was pointed back the way it had come.

Will Ferris did not sit clutching his, or rather Maeve's, steering wheel. The door of the Volkswagen, which was jammed, he burst open with his shoulder. Then he raced across the road to the Lada. Smoke was pouring from underneath its bonnet.

A Mrs Kirke, who was going in to do a shift as a cleaner in the Beggar's Bush bar, said afterwards, 'I thought the whole thing was going to go up in flames and roast the poor unfortunate that was trapped inside of it. But didn't the young fella race across the road and grab hold of the door and start pulling at it. There was smoke everywhere, and Oh Jesus, I couldn't bear to look. If there's one thing I can't stand the sight of, it's a man on fire.'

By the time Will got back to Leeson Street, Cory was home from the hospital. He had to tell her the story of the crash because she met him on the stairs and wanted to know what he was doing with a hammer in his hand — he intended using it to beat the Beetle back into shape. What he did not tell her was what happened when he had torn open the door of the smoking Lada.

'Help,' Denis had said.

'Get out,' Will said. 'Get out of the car!'

But Denis could not get out because he was held in by his seatbelt and he didn't have the strength to unbuckle it. But Will did. He leaned across Denis, unsnapped the catch, hooked his arm around Denis's neck, dragged him out of the smoke, propped him up against the side of the car with one hand and aimed a right fist straight at his head.

But then he noticed that Denis was to all intents and purposes a dwarf.

And then the thought occurred to him, 'If I hit this midget I'll kill him stone dead and then I'll go to jail again, but this time for the rest of my natural life.'

Again?

27

THERE ARE PEOPLE, usually men, whose personalities are revealed by the houses they live in. This was true of Walter Leary. Such houses have usually been lived in by such people from an early age. This was not true of Walter Leary — he was thirty-seven years old when he first saw Bunnahowan.

Frances Dirrane, who was to be Walter's wife, was a last child, separated from her twin brothers by a gap of ten years. She had trained in nursing, which tied her down when she had to look after her parents while they were dying from respiratory illnesses. Long before then the twins had emigrated to America. They had prospered in the States, so they had no problem with Frances inheriting the house and the twenty acres of rushy bog and yellow gorse that surrounded it. This was at the end of the 1970s and such land — three miles out of Kinvara on the road to Gort — had not yet become attractive to Galway city commuters as building sites.

When Walter saw Bunnahowan, he thought immediately, 'This suits me.' If something suited Walter he often got it. But he was lazy, and the laziness sometimes led to jumbled last-minute manoeuvrings and to disappointments, which were bitter because what he didn't get he deserved.

After six years at University College Galway Walter had only managed a pass degree in English. This had been followed by a job in the New Ireland Assurance Company, which was boring for him and irritating for his employers — he condescended to them like a butler in a West End farce who has got drunk on his lordship's brandy. Actually, gin and tonic was Walter's drink. But he was not often drunk in the office, at least not until the months before he finally departed to work full-time in the theatre, where he had been directing since his college days. Unlike Gary Hynes, who was then making her name with the Druid Theatre, Walter ignored Irish playwrights, except Samuel Beckett, in favour of the likes of Ionesco, Jean Genet, Edward Albee and Harold Pinter. In successive years he had taken Genet's 'The Maids' and Pinter's 'The Caretaker' to the Edinburgh Festival. Both productions had won awards, but though the honours were for acting and went to a menacing-looking carpenter called Myles Fury, Walter had got credit for them too. *The Irish Times* had hailed him as 'a Shannon-side Stanislavsky' and as a consequence the Arts Council had given his company, the Belacqua Players, a sizeable two-year grant. Now, in 1978, if capital funding were forthcoming and a suitable premises found, the Players would become a Theatre, with Walter as Artistic Director, salaried. A lot depended on his next Edinburgh production, another Pinter play, 'The Dumb Waiter'. A lot depended, too, on Myles Fury. But Myles found himself teetering on the brink of fame elsewhere: he had appeared in a TV commercial as a saturn-ine airline pilot under the slogan, 'There's a world out there that the Irish people want to share in.' In the advert the pilot had a wife desperately waiting all day in her apron for him to come home to her. What the couple looked forward to sharing were 'Two ham steaks, individually wrapped in polythene — for people who can't afford to hang around.' Polythene was the future then. Although Myles had only one line — 'Thanks, Ireland' — he had delivered it to the bedazzled wife with such brooding intensity that he had been asked to audition for the part of a psychopath in a TV soap opera in London. But in the real world Myles was neither saturnine nor psychopathic. If anything, he was over-socialised, kindly, naïve, gentle — he had a habit of saying 'I'm sorry' in Irish, 'Tá brón orm,' pronounced 'Thaw brone urrum,' literally 'Sorrow is on me,' in a way that was so heavily true it made one want to console him. His dominant trait, though, was indecision: giving up a steady job as a carpenter to be a TV star was almost as daunting a prospect as marrying Frances Dirrane.

Frances was, like himself, a strong Catholic. Seven years of 'keeping company' with her without committing the mortal sin of adultery had been so easy for Myles that he had begun to have doubts about his manliness. In fact he was so slow in making up his mind to lose his virginity that Walter had called him 'the knock-kneed not-yet.' But if his gait was ungainly in life — he tended to stumble over his own feet — he was the opposite of awkward on stage. Like all born actors, what was impressive about him was the physicality of his intelligence: if a character had to be, say, bowlegged, Myles was able to convince an audience that his heels were glued together and a barrel could be rolled through his legs.

Walter, however, was not in favour of barrels in the theatre, partly because the Belacqua Players' stage was too tiny to accommodate much furniture. If a prop could be done without, Walter would do without it. He had once told an interviewer he had been profoundly influenced by Alan Simpson's 1957 production of 'The Rose Tattoo' by Tennessee Williams, which had brought the police onto the stage of the Pike Theatre in Dublin. In court the guards gave evidence that they had seen the actress Anna Manahan dropping a condom on the floor. But, Alan Simpson said, because he knew the possession of contraceptives was a criminal offence, he had made sure that Anna had not possessed such a thing — she had only pretended to drop it. This, Walter told the interviewer, was a high point in the history of Irish metaphysics. But for once he was on the side of the police: in the kind of theatre he was committed to, seeing was not believing but the other way round. This had led the interviewer to describe Walter's directing style as 'magic minimalism'.

When it came, though, to the production of 'The Dumb Waiter', a dumb waiter was a prop that could not be done without. This was where Bunnahowan had played its part.

Frances Dirrane's father, whose name was Florrie, had built the house to his own design. Design was not Florrie's forte, but he was a master craftsman and determined that Bunnahowan would be the best house he ever built. In 1948 the concept of feng shui was unknown in Kinvara, but even so one didn't have to be a Chinese geomancer to be puzzled as to why Florrie had arranged the house so that the sun never shone in through its windows. Also, rather than cement blocks, he had gone for reinforced concrete, shuttered and cast. The house was as solid as a rock. Solider in fact: all the limestone of the nearby Burren, one of the wonders of the world, might one day dissolve and be washed into the sea along with its rare orchids, but Bunnahowan was here to stay. Concrete, though, was not cosy. The only insulation was wallpaper or paint, and as a result the house was, Walter Leary said, 'colder than the rectum of a corpse'. It was also oddly high. Florrie had worked in New York and he wanted something 'with a bit of height to it', so Bunnahowan was four storeys tall and, like a skyscraper, taller than it was broad, and the windows in the fourth storey were only half the size of the windows in the storeys below. The house gave the impression of looking down on what it looked down on, that is the road to Gort. The impression reflected Walter Leary's view of the world: he did not think much of it.

As a result of doing repairs on the decaying mansions of the local gentry, Florrie had also got the notion that it would be nice to have the kitchen on the ground floor, the dining room on the floor above and the dinner transported between them by dumb waiter. The notion proved impractical, especially in the winter when the Dirranes had to huddle around the Aga cooker for heat. By the time Walter saw the dining room it had been disused for years. Removing the dumb waiter had been simple — Myles Fury was a carpenter after all.

From the start Mrs Dirrane disliked Walter. The first day she met him, he had stalked around her kitchen, one arm across his belly, the elbow of the other arm propped on it, an arrangement that enabled him to keep the end of his cigarette close to his lips. The cigarette worked away like the beak of a hen pecking the dirt, up and down, up and down, little puffs. And Walter had dropped ash all over her freshly washed red and blue diamond tiles. And once, without so much as a by-your-leave, he had picked up an old soup tureen from the dresser, turned it over to see what was written on the bottom, and put it down with a bang, saying loudly, 'Mmmmm'. And he had called her 'my dear'. And he had long hair, curling up on his shoulders. And he wore a cravat, scarlet with a yellow paisley pattern. And — worst of all — he smelt like a baby's bottom dusted with Johnson's talcum powder. Perfume on a grown man. It wasn't right.

Six months later Mrs Dirrane died. At the end she was still asking what had become of her dumb waiter. It had not been returned, and never would be. Myles had not brought it back from Edinburgh, as promised. Instead, he had gone straight to London to act the psychopath. Mrs Dirrane had had a lot of time for Myles. He'd sit down with you and drink a cup of tea and tell you about his relatives — that was the sort of man of man you wanted your daughter to marry. Mrs Dirrane refused to believe Myles had taken up with another woman, and if he had itself, wasn't Frances to blame, keeping him on the long finger all those years. She should never have let him out of her sight. It was only at the last minute that she had gone to Edinburgh, as a surprise, but it was she who got the surprise when she arrived at his digs and caught Myles in a compromising position with his new girlfriend, in the same bed.

Mrs Dirrane said she wouldn't be at all surprised if Walter had put Myles up to it. Frances had burst into a terrible storm of tears and said her mother was an ignorant old woman and she would never speak to her again. Mrs Dirrane had pursed her lips. Frances was on the rebound; there was no talking to her. Three months later she had married Walter. Mrs Dirrane hadn't been well enough to attend the wedding, and even if she had been, she wouldn't have gone.

She was wrong, though, to allege that Walter had put Myles up to it. He was beyond doing anything that could be described as deliberately evil. At the most important times in his life he operated instinctually. He had not encouraged Myles to go to London to become a soap opera psychopath — why would he deprive himself of his best actor? All he had done was to begin telling Myles how excellent his acting was, which he had never done before, while at the same time harrying him day in and day out about his performance as Ben in 'The Dumb Waiter'. Then, halfway through rehearsals, he had made a radical decision. Instead of playing the psychotic Ben, Myles would now play the paranoid Gus. Actually, the distinctions between the characters were hair-thin when considered in the light of what united them: Pinter's language. Walter said this language was charged with a perverse homoeroticism — there was nothing wrong with directing the cast's attention to that, surely; it was a directorial insight, after all. But the effect of the switch on Myles was electric: the hair-thin distinctions were overloaded with current and got all sniggled up.

Then, a week before the play opened, Walter had brought in a new stage manager. This young man wanted to become a director, but now all that he had to recommend him was his energy, his willingness to please and his good looks — he was tall and had gloriously curly auburn hair. As against these qualities, he was extravagantly emotional, mentally unstable, hysterically gay, histrionically repressed. All Walter had done was ask Myles to look after the young man and be sympathetic to his uncertainties about his sexual identity. And, when they got to Edinburgh, he had booked them into the same boarding house. That was all.

Although the play had not won any awards, one of the London reviewers had described the acting as 'extraordinarily febrile' and another had said the production 'crackled with electricity'. It was enough: the Arts Council had coughed up a substantial capital grant for the new Belacqua Theatre and a modestly comfortable salary for its Artistic Director.

All Cory knew about all this was that once upon a time her mother had been engaged to a failed actor who had become a derelict in London and died of the drink. She did, though, know about the dumb waiter because, behind a pinned-up piece of muslin, its absence yawned a black hole in the wall of the dining room, which had become her father's office and, for the last twenty years, his bedroom.

As Will drove up the rutted track that led to the house, he saw Walter sitting at the window of this room. Walter gave no sign of seeing him. Nor did Cory give any sign of seeing her father.

Her mother, though, hurried out to greet the visitor and usher him into the kitchen. She had heard all about Will — Cory made a small grimace — and was delighted to meet him at last. He must be parched, he had to sit down and have a cup of tea immediately, and a little biscuit. The kitchen was filled with the smell of lamb fat melting in the low heavy heat of the Aga. Mother and daughter had not kissed. They had acknowledged each other perfunctorily, as if they had been separated by the length of the morning only. Will noticed, though, a change in Cory. She asked her mother easy questions with the faintest air of expecting to get complicated answers. Had she aired the bed? Had she changed the sheets? And so on. Mrs Leary answered the questions obediently and in be-tween times went on talking to Will. But he soon realised that she was not listening to him, to Cory or, even, to herself. She was like the queen in a beehive, turning this way and that, radiating out from her abdomen messages she does not understand but that her offspring are able to decode and obey. But that wasn't apt: she was not queen here, and her daughter was not obedient.

The kitchen was neat and tidy, but nothing in it was new. The pine chairs, the table, the dresser, were as old as the house, and homemade too. What was plastic, the white goods, had long since discoloured to ivory. Not long after Cory's birth something had stopped.

On the drive down Will had asked would they be sleeping together; she had uttered only a disbelieving 'huh!'. Now as they climbed the steep stairs — there had been a carpet on them long ago — he knew better than to ask.

Nor did he ask about what was on the walls: framed posters

for plays, theatre programmes, and newspaper cuttings, yellowed with age and foxed with spots of paper-rust.

His room was in the attic. The only furniture was a chest of drawers and an iron bed covered with a turquoise-coloured candlewick spread. On the chest stood a delph ewer in a delph basin, decorated with a pale pattern of reddish-brown Persian roses. In the ewer lay the casing of a dead fly, last year's by the look of it.

Mrs Leary had something in common with Will's mother: she couldn't cook. A glutinous brown soup with rubbery cubes of tinned carrot suspended in it was followed by tough mutton, wet turnips, lumpy mashed potatoes and a dessert of shop-bought lemon cake with chocolate chip ice cream. Will ate it all up greedily. The taste of grease that the mutton left in his mouth was familiar, even nostalgic, as was the bottle of Piat D'Or Mrs Leary had bought in his honour; it and she were just like his mother: thin and sharp, yet vague.

There was nothing vague about Walter. After the soup course, he came down, unsummoned, from his room, opened the door and stood on the threshold silently, with the air of having left momentous business behind him.

Cory said, 'Daddy, this is Will, Will Ferris.'

Walter threw his arms out wide and proclaimed, 'I always dress up to welcome a new writer into our theatre.'

He was wearing a pair of voluminous black trousers, low in the crotch and held up with a polka-dot tie, and a stained alpaca jacket over an open-necked checked shirt, which was actually the jacket of his pyjamas.

It was obvious where Cory had got her pointed nose and freckle-dotted skin: they were Walter's. But his pointedness was bony, and what was golden in her was liver-spotted in him, and his mane of hair, unlike her shining mouse cloud, was grey, thin and rigidly swept back, like the striations on a much-weathered sea shell.

'Nice to meet you, Mr Leary,' Will said.

Walter's eyes narrowed. 'William,' he said, 'William Ferris.

That's a good Protestant name.'

'Daddy,' Cory said, 'your dinner is getting cold and he's not a Protestant.'

'I hear you're a bard,' Walter said. 'Like the Swan of Avis. Or is it Hertz? Ah, wine,' Walter said, spying the Piat D'Or. 'You must be a very important young swan, mister. Unlike me.' He began to sing, 'There once was an ugly duckling, with feathers all stubby and brown.' Then he stopped, stepped back, said, 'Who knows what happens next?' and went out.

'I forgot the gravy,' Mrs Leary said.

'It's grand,' Will said.

'I can make some if you like.'

'No, really, thanks very much.'

'I have the granules.'

'The what?' Cory said.

'The granules. Erin gravy granules. I got them in Galway. They're quicker than Bisto.'

'For god's sake, Mother.'

'It won't take a minute.'

'No, no, Mrs Leary,' Will said. 'No gravy, thanks. It's lovely without it, honestly.'

As Mrs Leary made the gravy, Walter came in again, this time without stopping in the doorway, sat down and began to eat in a desultory fashion but quickly, peckingly. The business he had left behind him was a pint glass of gin and tonic. It might have been water the way he drank it. Will, too, had gulped down his wine as if it was water. Mrs Leary and Cory, being non-drinkers, had neither of them seen the need of offering him a refill. The need grew desperate the more Walter spoke.

'I mislead you back there,' he began.

'Sorry?'

Walter said sharply, 'Don't say sorry, say pudding.' Will made a noise that wasn't a word. Walter went on, 'When I said Hertz, I was thinking of Avon. The Swan of Avis, fortunately for him, had nothing to do with car rental companies.'

Will, who had never heard Shakespeare described as the Swan of Avon, made another noise, this time of agreement.

Cory said, 'Daddy.' Then she said, 'Who is the consultant you saw?'

'Mr Njinga,' Mrs Leary said. 'He's from South Africa, or is it Nigeria?'

'Did you ever hear,' Walter said, 'the story of Micheál MacLiammóir and the oranges?' He gave the Irish version of Michael all the fullness of its roundness: Meehawl.

'No,' Will said. Fortunately, he knew that MacLiammóir had been a barnstorming actor famous for 'The Importance of Being Oscar', a one-man show about Oscar Wilde.

'It was at the height of the apartheid business,' Walter said. 'And Micheál was one day at the market in Moore Street doing his shopping. In full fig, of course, and fancy dress. The green carnation, the toupée, the slap, the atropine in the eyes to make them glitter. Well, he said to this old hawsie, these are nice oranges, but, tell me, are they from South Africa? Yeah, says she. Oh, says Micheál, I couldn't buy them. I know what you mean, Mr MacLammermoor, says she, I don't like touchin' anything that's been touched by them niggers either, but sure I do have to make me livin'.'"

Will choked on a lump of mashed potato. What was funny was Walter's sudden piercing sideways glare at him, as if he were an eagle about to stoop from on high straight down on a rabbit.

Mrs Leary said, 'Would you like a glass of water?' Will shook his coughing head and poured himself some wine, apologetically.

Cory said, 'Did Mr Njinga show you the angiogram?'

Walter said, 'That's the word I was looking for. I couldn't remember it. What's the other one, with the balloon?'

'Angioplasty.'

'That's it. That's the one for me.'

After a pause Cory said, 'Not a bypass then?'

After another micro-silence, Walter said, 'They're going to blow me up. And not a moment too soon apparently. Or they'll put in a stent. Is that what you call it?'

Cory said. 'Yes.'

'What instrument do you play, William?'

'I play the guitar, Mr Leary.'

'Ah. The guitar. Where would the modern world be without it?'

Cory said, 'Putting in a stent is a very safe procedure.'

'Disappointingly so by the sound of it. Unless I get a stroke in the process.'

'Fat chance of that,' she said, and they smiled at each other.

Later, trying to reconstruct this conversation in his notebook, Will had a nagging feeling that he had forgotten something important. He had a recollection of Walter saying, 'I'm an eyeless, boneless, chickenless egg', which was a line from an anti-war song, but the memory had got tangled up with what followed. Walter had asked did he know 'Surabaya, Johnny', which was also a kind of wartime song. The asking was merely a pretext for what grew into an increasingly bitter rant about the events that had led to him being suddenly ousted as Artistic Director of the Belacqua.

'There wasn't anything sudden about it,' Cory said as they drove away the next morning. 'He'd taken to the bottle big-time.'

That wasn't how Walter told the story of his production, much stripped-down of course, of 'The Threepenny Opera' by Bertolt Brecht. In his version the fault could be traced back to America. The heartland of capitalism and — he gave Will another eagle look — of 'twangling guitars' had done for him. Thanks to Ronald Reagan, not to mention that murdering bitch Maggie Thatcher, neo-liberal notions of competition had been introduced into Irish society, specifically into the Arts Council.

'Competition, how are you,' Walter said, 'our lickspittle Paddies couldn't win a competition to find their own balls.'

'Have some cake,' Mrs Leary said. 'It's lemon-curd.'

Walter went on, 'Brecht, they said to me. Who's this Brecht fella? But he's a communist. Nobody in Galway would want to go to an opera by a communist, a German one too. That's too highbrow. What we need is art for the people, culture for the community.

'OK, I said, let's do "Darby O'Gill and the Little People". Little did I realise then that I had been nurturing a viper in my bosom. The whole thing was a set-up.'

The viper was the former curly-haired stage manager who, though Walter didn't say so, had seduced and destroyed Myles Fury.

But then, as if bored, Walter suddenly got to his feet, saying, 'Up my lemon-curd cake I wish to bring, but I'll spare you the pleasure of that performance. I have to go to Gort.' He offered his hand to Will, said, 'It's been interesting to hear your views, but if you want my advice, take up the tuba. Fare thee well.'

What happened then was embarrassing. While Mrs Leary asked Will did he want coffee and proceeded to make it and also to switch on the television set and turn it up loud, Cory followed her father out into the night, trying first to persuade him he was too drunk to drive, then to wrestle the keys off him. But the door of his car slammed shut with a blast of exploded air and he rattled off down the rutted track to Gort. Cory came back and sat down to watch the nine o'clock news as if nothing had happened, but the dots of her freckles stood out on her skin, which had grown paler, faintly blueish.

The night had passed without further mention of Walter. Mrs Leary talked in a garbled rush about many things, mainly her brothers, one of whom lived in Philadelphia, the other in Missoula, Montana. They had only been home once since their mother's funeral, but they had brought herself and Cory out to America three times and paid for everything.

At the mention of money Cory said she was going to bed because she had to be up early to be at work in the hospital at nine o'clock. Will knew this was untrue — she had been given the weekend off to be with her sick father. To his incredulity, they had then gone down on their knees and recited the rosary. Will had only come across the practice once, in his mother's parents' house in Allihies in the far west of Cork. As he struggled to keep up with the prayers, he thought of the old religion and its traditions retreating to the furthest edges of the island. For centuries the Irish had gone to bed with little cries, but now they had nothing to cry about. The only thing beyond Ireland these days was the Atlantic, easily crossed for shopping-trips to New York. A wild wind was blowing around Bunnahowan, but the kitchen window cast its light across the rushy fields as if creating a pathway for the religious and once neighbourly past to come in by. It was hard for Will to do without laughing what the Dirranes and their neigh-bours had once done devoutly: to kneel on a blue and red tiled floor praying to an Aga cooker, an enamelled yellow cast-iron god set into a niche of heat-blackened concrete. It was odd, too, to see how upright Cory was, kneeling with her arms across the back of her chair, while her mother bent over the seat of hers, paying out the brown beads of her rosary like a fishing line. Perhaps to avoid catching his eye, Cory had covered her face with her hands. The weeping redness of her gnawed thumb gave him a pang of sorrow.

Then she was nodding to indicate that it was his turn to say a decade of the Sorrowful Mysteries. He got through the Our Father, stumbled through the first Hail Mary, then remembered the next nine, but miscounted and was beginning on an eleventh when Cory intervened and started the Glory Be to the Father, which he took up and finished properly.

Two things had happened after they went to bed.

Just before daybreak he dreamt he was on a small raft in a storm having sex with Maeve MacNamee. The sail on the raft was a key, shining brightly against the dark clouds roiling in the sky. Maeve was furiously demanding, but he couldn't satisfy her. Then he woke up and instantly realised it was not Maeve who was with him but Cory. She had stolen into the room — a creaking floorboard had woken him — crept into the bed and, without saying a word, wept warm tears onto his bare chest.

Earlier, he had heard the crunching of gravel as Walter's car returned. Walter was safe, if no one else was. Cory had gone down to let him in. He had clumped up the stairs and gone into the room that had a hole in the wall for a dumb waiter. After some minutes he had re-emerged, stood on the landing and shouted up at Will, 'Tá na Gaeil fucáilte ag na capitalists.' The sound — Thaw na Gwale fucawlta egg na capitalists — was as coarse as the meaning: The Irish have been fucked by the capitalists. Then he had gone back into his room, slamming the door, once, twice, three times. Was it any wonder that at the end of the rosary Cory and her mother had prayed so fervently?

> *Hail Holy Queen, Mother of Mercy,*
> *Hail, our life, our sweetness and our hope.*
> *To thee do we cry, poor banished children of Eve.*
> *To thee do we send up our sighs, mourning and weeping*
> *in this valley of tears.*
> *Turn then, o most gracious advocate, thine eyes of mercy*
> *toward us; and after this, our exile, show unto us the*
> *blessed fruit of thy womb, Jesus.*
> *O clement, O loving, O sweet Virgin Mary.*
> *Pray for us, O holy Mother of God, that we may be made*
> *worthy of the promises of Christ.*

But much later, when Will was thinking what 'this, our exile' could mean, he remembered the smile that had passed between Cory and her father over the fatty lamb at the dinner table. It was complicit. Could that be why Cory was so pure?

28

CORY WOKE HIM in the dark with a cup of tea. When he got down to the kitchen, her mother was bumbling about as if she hadn't been to bed at all. As they were leaving, she dipped her fingers in a small heart-shaped pot nailed to the jamb of the door and sprinkled him with holy water.

'Don't be a stranger,' she said. A stranger, he supposed, was someone who would not return.

The night had widened to a ghostly grey and then stopped short before it could turn blue. But as soon as they emerged from the shadow of Bunnahowan, the greyness gave way to the rising sun. For Will, dazzled by the dew-wet silver road going east, the journey was blinding. For Cory, cut off from what she had long since left behind her, the small fields and stone walls passed by unnoticed. She was talking more than usual, but not feverishly. She avoided fever. She was the opposite of her fevered father. As an explanation, that was too simple. It was true, though, that her character had been constructed as an answer to his, or in correspondence with it. The one word she didn't use was disappointment, but it pervaded everything she said about him. She was disappointed not so much because he was a hopeless alcoholic as because he was a proud one. The pride that underlies the alcoholism of a certain kind of intelligent drinker was in him geological, and molten. There had been a brief period when he had joined Alcoholics Anonymous, but he had never spoken at meetings — he was too proud to be ridiculous — and, really, he had only gone for the drama. His resolving to be sober had been poignant for Cory, and not keeping his resolution had made her angry, but wasn't there in the anger of a thirteen-year-old girl an added poignancy? There was. And she had traded in it. Disabusing her of the notion of being a victim had occupied Walter for most of her teenage years and had ended only after she had escaped to medical school. By then she had realised, he thought, that poignancy was merely sentimentality for the butter-hearted. Walter was too flinty for that. So, too, was Cory, at last. He was proud of her flintiness. She had taken on his pride. Her not drinking, which he called teetotalitarianism, certainly wasn't humble. And as for medicine, it must be nice to be a saint and a well-paid member of the middle-class at the same time.

But if she wasn't humble, what was she? Cory herself didn't know, and so she gave it no name. It was just one of many commodities she refused to trade in with her father. But, still and all, Walter knew the score, and she knew it too. Knowing was the language they had in common. Like the Gaelic he had been brought up speaking, there was no commercial use for it, but it was a badge of difference, and Walter was, after all, a native speaker. Being different might be a free market, but if so it was exclusive. And it had become free for her, too. Or so he thought, mistakenly, because she despised knowingness, or intelligence, if knowingness came to that, even more than she despised being condescended to. Her pride and disdain were, if anything, greater than his, though she knew — she couldn't not know — that being proud and disdainful meant it was almost impossible to be what she wanted to be, which was simple. Simple. What a word that was. One might as well aspire to be a drop of water. But while it was true that the human body was almost wholly composed of water, the few per cent of whatever else it was made of, the residue, the sediment, the sludge of sentiment, muddied the spring.

And, of course, when it came to her mother, the whole intelligence thing fell flat on its face in the pigsty. Try as she might,

Cory could not prevent herself thinking little of and disbelieving in her mother in the same way as she thought little of and disbelieved in her mother's religion, while still practising it every Sunday. In this faithless faith, if God the father was invisible, up in his room with the hole in the wall, then God the mother was down in the kitchen and obvious all over the house. But it was next to impossible to make her out — like her talk, she was as undifferentiated as her Erin gravy granules.

There was another word, related to disappointment, that Cory used a lot that morning. The word was money. As they were driving down the steep rutted track, Will had said, 'If you don't mind me saying so, the house could do with a lick of paint. Pink would do a lot for it.'

She said, 'Paint costs money.'

Bunnahowan needed more than paint. The pebbledash was ballooning on the walls. Slabs of it had already fallen off, leaving behind an atlas of unknown cement islands. In a top-floor window a stone had starred a pane of glass. The crack was backed with cardboard, much buckled after a dozen years. And to one side of the house, some fifty yards away, a giant bite had been taken out of the hillside. Growing around the edges of the scar were droopy stands of purple loosestrife.

Everything — including the window, which Walter had broken with a stone one night when Frances had locked him out — had its price, but Walter would not pay it. He was fanatically parsimonious. Although he had just had to have Bunnahowan, getting it didn't mean having to spend money on it, not even if raw sewage stood in the potholes at the bottom of the track — when it rained heavily the septic tank overflowed. Meanness explained the kitchen too: he had not bought as much as a tin opener since Cory was born. Anyway, he didn't buy; he borrowed. Had Will ever seen the notices in country shops: 'Please do not ask for credit as a refusal may offend'? It might have been devised for dealing with Walter. But it was Frances who had had to put up with the offence. At first, of course, she hadn't been refused: the Dirrane name was good in Gort and Kinvara. But debt led to dependence and soon shopkeepers from Ballyvaughan to Portumna were offending her. There were still places in the counties of Galway and Clare that would refuse her custom, even if she held out the money in front of her in a cleft stick.

When Walter was not at home, he was generous. But the generosity was of a peculiar kind: he bought drinks the way a medieval monarch scattered coins before him or laid hands on those with the scrofula: if you got a gold testoon or a touch, that was because you were either a serf, or scabby, or both, and either way you were expected to be grateful for ever. Also, Walter gambled. Occasionally he won; usually he lost; always he exaggerated. What was bad had to be the worst. As it was with the horses, so it was with his health: not only did he not need a bypass, it was quite possible that Mr Njinga had diagnosed him in a lounge bar.

Walter's principal financial losses, though, were on a much larger scale. He had mortgaged Bunnahowan to the hilt, and then, to keep up the repayments, he had begun to sell off the twenty acres. This was before the boom. Even so, he had sold the land cheap, mostly to farming neighbours as rough grazing. One neighbour had opened a gravel-pit — that was the scar on the hillside — and then abandoned it: in those days no one needed gravel. Much more recently another neighbour had sold on the five acres that bordered the road to a developer, who had secured permission to build a hundred townhouses on the site.

By now they were on the other side of Ballinasloe; the silver road had dried to grey; the fields were bigger, and fewer of them were enclosed by stone walls. The next, and last, thing she told him was said in a tone of voice as flat as the country they were driving through.

One day when she was eight Walter had come home early and passed out in the bath. Waking up, still drunk, he had gone to bed. After an hour, unable to sleep and shivering with the cold, he had crossed the landing and carried Cory back to his room.

Will said immediately, 'Did he abuse you?'

Just as quickly Cory said, 'I knew you were going to say that.'

The answer was no. All that he had done was tell her a story. Making up stories was something Walter was good at, and this one, which was about a little girl who lived alone in a castle, was familiar to her, and, of course, it connected with how she lived in Bunnahowan.

For the first three years of their marriage Walter and Frances had slept downstairs in the parlour — her father had converted it to a bedroom after emphysema stopped first him and then his wife from climbing the stairs. Because he had installed high up on a wall an electric fire that looked like the mouth of a shark with a cord hanging out of it, the conversion had not improved the room's appearance, but the fire gave off some heat. For that reason, and for the reason, too, of laziness, Walter had decided to sleep there rather than in the main bedroom upstairs. As soon as she was old enough, that room had become Cory's. The change of scale was great: she had quit a cot for an enormous mahogany bed with a canopy — the canopy had battlements notched in it, which was the origin of the castle story. Her grandfather had carpentered the bed on the spot; it was too massive to shift. By rights Walter should have taken over the room for himself after he had left Frances in the parlour, but again he was too lazy, and anyway the dumb waiter suited his disused spirit.

On the first occasion Cory had been scared by her father hugging her and mumbling and getting lost in the story, but she had fallen asleep and woken up back in her own bed. The second time she panicked. What made her cry was his smell: he hadn't had a bath, he stank of decaying meat. Hearing the crying, Frances had run up the stairs, burst into the room, dragged Cory out of the bed, and demanded to know what he was doing to 'my child'. Walter had said she wasn't her child; she was nobody's child. Then he had started slapping Frances about the head and trying to wrestle Cory out of her arms, but his feet had got mixed up and he had fallen over and hit his cheekbone on the ledge of the dumb waiter. Enraged by the sight of his own blood, he had picked up Frances and tried to bundle her through the dusty piece of muslin that covered the hole.

'That's terrible,' Will said. 'He could have killed her.'

'No, he couldn't. The lift was stuck. The pulley, the wire rope, was rusted solid. Anyway, I grabbed on to the sides with my hands and feet and legs and wouldn't let him. I still have the scars. Haven't you noticed them?'

'Jesus, look out!'

29

Who made the world and what did he make it out of?
If he made it out of you, are the two little scars on your face,
the small scar on the back of your hand a trace effect of the
material, or are they as I think, the sink and indents of the
Shade finding a place to lie down in, the way a blind man
expects when he put his hand out into the air it will be shaken?

USUALLY, WHEN WILL started a new song, he had an idea that
was in some way or other musical. This was different. Trying to
work out how the stuff Cory was made from had affected or been
affected by what had happened to her had confused him into
prose. This was as far as he could go. Anyway, what was the Shade
and why had he capitalised it? And though it rhymed with face,
what was a trace effect? He had asked Harry, who said it was a
technical term in linguistics. That was no help. Will turned back
the pages of his notebook and read what he had written.

> 'I still have the scars,' she said. I said 'Jesus, look out!' but
> it wasn't the scars that made me say the Holy Name, it was
> the steering wheel. It just turned in my hands, and next
> thing the rear-end swung out across the road and then we
> were nose-deep in the nearside ditch. God made Sundays
> and thank God he did because if there'd been oncoming

traffic, we'd have been creased. Lucky too I was listening so hard I was only doing about 30mph.

It was easy to see why we'd skidded: the front wheel had caved in and twisted to the left. That's what comes of being hit by a Lada. Cory was trembling like an aspen leaf, but after a few seconds a car came up. The woman in it, Mrs Dargan, was going to church but she missed it like a Christian and rang her brother and out he came from Athlone in jig time. His name was Edgar. A long droopy guy in overalls with just one black tooth sticking out of his mouth and a groove in his lip made by the cigarette he had clamped into it. Edgar said he'd have to get a tow-truck and it'd be tomorrow before he could do it. Cory said that was grand, she'd get the train from Athlone, but Mrs Dargan said Edgar wouldn't dream of it. Edgar looked like he'd be happy to dream of it for a month of Sundays, but Mrs D said Cory was a doctor and she had to get back to work, the country's Casualty Departments were a disgrace, thousands of old people were dying on trolleys 'night, noon and morning'. So there was no dreaming for Edgar.

I went off with him and we towed the car to his garage. The job was going to take him at least two hours, so he dropped me back to his sister's Bed & Breakfast, The Ponderosa. Ugly name for an ugly place, brand new, surrounded with an acre of cobble-block. Garden full of gnomes and leprechauns. House painted daffodil yellow with PVC windows. Inside it was coming down with knick-knacks, souvenirs of thatched cottages, ballerinas made out of glass, mirrors with stuff written on them, glossy pine floors, flowery carpets, stripey sofas, cushions with lacey edges. A conservatory on the side like a plastic church. I forgot: pictures of Padre Pio all over the place.

Anyway Mrs D insisted we have 'a proper breakfast'. Rashers, eggs, sausages — a heart attack on a plate. Afterwards she and C sat out in the conservatory drinking tea and talking like a pair of old hens. Never saw Cory like this before. I don't know what came over her. She told me afterwards that Mrs Dargan's first name is Edith, surname Templeton, a Protestant. It was her Catholic husband who had 'a special devotion' to Padre Pio — much good it did him because he died young of cancer. It was testicular, so they had no children. Maybe that's why they were talking like mother and daughter. Which I didn't hear because Mrs D said that if I wanted I could go upstairs and have a shower. I was still covered with filth from getting the car up on the low-loader. It was one of those useless dribbly electric showers that deliver one thickness above a mist. But afterwards I swear I never felt cleaner or better. Out the window off to the side of the Ponderosa I could just see the Shannon.

Silver mother river, flow on forever,
Flow further on than father.

I don't know anything about the Shannon. Why is that? The whole country is divided in two by it, right up the middle. So that we're nearly two islands really. No, it's like a sexual opening. The Shannon is the national vagina. If so, the County Clare is the Mount of Venus. Which means the clitoris must be Loop Head. Oh, give us a break.

Anyway when I went down, I asked Mrs Dargan was it possible to walk by the river and the next thing I know she has all these maps out on the table specially for hikers and she's planning a route for us. The Callows is what the area is called. Up the Callows to Rindoon, that's the way we went. She even drove us to the start. I've never met anyone so like a Fairy Godmother. With her coat like a cloak and her grey hair sticking out from under her Sunday-best pointy hat, she looked the part, too.

And the walk was like a vanishing trick. A hundred yards up the river all industrial noises had gone and we were back in a world that could be a 1,000 years old, except that Ireland was all trees then. You could hear a dog barking a mile off, and the sky was a bright blue with big white clouds standing up tall and still as if they were painted but when you looked again they'd moved across the sky. I said May was my favourite month because you had the feeling that everything you hardly knew you hoped for was going to happen, but Cory told me an old saying: 'Ne'er cast a clout till May is out.' What's a clout? A loincloth? A swimsuit?

> *Don't put your Speedos on*
> *Until the spring has gone.*

Cory said when she was a kid, she taught herself to swim in the quarry beside Bunnahowan. Rainwater gathered in it. It got the sun all day so the water was warm except in the middle where it suddenly got deep. I said, you taught yourself, does that mean you went there on your own, and she said yes. I was going to say, wasn't that dangerous? But then I didn't, I don't know why.

> *In those remote and distant years*
> *The theatre-father of your fears,*
> *A dumb show colder than a stone.*
> *A pool you swam in on your own,*
> *But, unafraid of depths you knew about,*
> *You dived down deep, and airiness won out.*

Is this too heroic? Maybe. But when it comes to thinking about Cory nobody sees her as clearly as I do. Why is that? In a storm of butterflies you wouldn't see one moth, but when you know it's there, you see it. That's her.

He stopped reading and closed the notebook with a feeling that was not entirely unlike guilt. Sometimes he felt guilty when he thought of Cory. And often her purity filled him with trepidation.

30

Truth as you exist I found you.

SPEAKING TO HIM about sex — it had only happened once — his father had said, 'Women are all the same. They only pretend they like it.' And he had looked heavenwards, as if Polly might be up there, looking down on him disdainfully. Of course, what Paul thought was primeval, but when you applied what he said to the mad women of Cork, he wasn't far off the mark. Even at their clingiest, like Sheevawn Rogers, they had a way of making you feel that only for the fact they needed a man on an ongoing basis for some obscure reason, they'd flatten you like a Lada crushing a hedgehog on a country road. Will had had to escape them. They stuck to him. Evil was adhesive. But were Dublin women any better? Someone like Maeve MacNamee was worse, probably, because she was so upfront about her desires and cared even less than a Corkwoman about whatever ball-bearing being she happened to be flattening. Will preferred to praise the girl with the turn in her eye — what was Vanessa's real name? He'd forgotten. Oh yes, Betty.

Cory was different of course. But how? He didn't need to know. That was the secret. As she began, so she went on. The New Year would be old before she told you about it. Hadn't it been that sunny day swimming at Hawk's Cliff in March before she revealed she had gone to Emmet's studio to have her portrait painted?

This confession, though it didn't sound like one, hadn't worried Will. He wasn't jealous. That particular evil didn't adhere to his rubber soul. But within a week of being told, he had gone for a walk down the river and dropped in on Emmet, quite casually, in passing.

There was no portrait to be seen in the studio, but then the place was in rag order. That only bore out what didn't need bearing out: as an artist, Emmet was a messer. But if he believed sex in art was hostility and aggression, as he had said in Keogh's pub, then it followed that he went the same way about sex in action. That is, with Cory. Had he? If so, the fool, he had nothing to show for it.

Inspecting Emmet's studio had been an electrically prickly business, but Will was only half-aware that the banter between them, if two bantam cocks stalking around each other could be called bantering, had not been taken in the spirit in which it was intended. It hadn't occurred to him that Emmet, like Cory, would notice he was being condescended to. Well, maybe it did occur to him, because when he said that the studio reminded him of Ossie's mother's new bathroom, which she had described as 'minimalisht', Emmet had bridled. Only a total thick, he said, would describe him as a minimalist. Actually, he was a maximalist. And either way, what he did was 'more relevant than plucking a fucking banjo'. Although this was, as repartee, less rapier-thrust than sabre-slash, Emmet was pleased with himself. He had won another duel.

Will shrugged — why should he care? If Emmet wanted to win a Lonsdale Belt for relevance, he was welcome to it. He acted like he was already Champion of the World, or of the Anti-World. But he wasn't grateful for his gift. He treated it the way he treated women. You didn't have to fuck the heart out of a female to prove you were a winner — that way sorrow lay.

There were many reasons why Cory filled Will with trepidation. For a start she was orderly, yet she had a poor sense of direction, and she was always losing her phone, her car-keys, her house-keys. Stuff that connected her to the outside world. Stuff she didn't want to be tied down to. Him maybe. She was very fastidious.

And yet, for all her fastidiousness, she often chewed bits of paper and left the pellets in unexpected places — he found one on a glazing-bar of the window in the bedroom and realised that she must have stood there for a long time looking down on Leeson Street, like the hawk moth and the swallow, unobserved.

She was also shy, modest, prudish. She wouldn't let him see her naked, yet she allowed him to come in and talk to her when she was in the bath — but only on condition he didn't look at her. Since she liked to soak for long periods, this caused him an excitement that was almost unbearable. Her no-need-to-know was one thing, but what about his low-need-to-look? Maybe not seeing was believing. Anyway, even if she hadn't told him about going to Emmet's studio, she had come to Leeson Street on New Year's Day. And what's more, she had stayed the night.

To stay the night — or, as they used to say in Cork, to stop the night — was what she had done, and after talking for hours they had brought the morning in by falling asleep together, still wearing their clothes, underneath the fruit-and-flower curtains, wrapped in each other's arms, because even though the gas was on full, all the rings and the oven too, and the flat was filled with the snore of its heat, Cory was still freezing. Will, for his part, felt he was suffocating, but when he raised his head from her childishly sweet-smelling neck, he could breathe the air of the second day of the New Year whistling thinly in through the unclosable window. And her hand, when he put it under his shirt, was like a goldfish resting on his ribs, cold but alive.

It could have been otherwise. This Titanic could have sunk in Cobh, the cove of Cork, even before it set out into the Atlantic.

Will had, like Emmet, prepared food for the goddess. In a *Daily Telegraph* colour-supplement that had been used to line a drawer in the kitchen dresser, he had spied recipes for what the magazine called 'classic Roman dishes of ancient times' and hurried down to Tesco to buy the ingredients. The soup was supposed to be based on 'a carefully de-fatted chicken stock' flavoured with pounded fresh thyme and garlic, but he had used a Knorr stock cube, and, lacking a mortar and pestle, had chopped the garlic and thyme, which was dried, with a knife. The soup tasted of salt, sulphur and must. The magazine said wild boar could be substituted 'at a pinch' with pork chops but there could be no substitute for its flavouring: juniper berries. Tesco had juniper berries. But juniper berries tasted of nothing.

'You're a very adventurous cook,' Cory said. But she did little more with the soup than stir it with her spoon, and she seemed unwilling even to poke at the black-speckled meat, soaked in oil yet cardboard-dry. The only thing she did eat was the dessert: a bunch of grapes. Will told her, reading from the fat-stained supplement, that the Romans used to train their vines to grow up into the branches of elm-trees.

'That's interesting,' she said.

And it was interesting. For as long as it lasted. But then he ran out of information to impart. He had been embarrassed from the beginning; now he was in agony. And of course Cory didn't drink, which he had forgotten, so the bottle of German hock he had bought for her (only €3.49 but dear at the price), instead of disinhibiting them both, inhibited him the more, because it would be bad manners to keep swilling it down like a drunk in front of a nun. But the silence didn't seem to bother her. She sat straightbacked on the wooden chair wearing her crombie coat, biting her thumb and smoking a cigarette. That surely was a subject for discussion. Had she noticed that nowadays it was mostly women who smoked in the street? No. No? Well he had, and he had come to the conclusion that they were making a point. They were doing it in order to show they were browned off with being lady-like. Maybe lady doctors, who knew about lung cancer, smoked for a similar reason: just as their sisters rejected femaleness by smoking in public, women doctors courted death in defiance of medical common sense. These were complex ideas to explain. They were difficult ones, too, in the circumstances. Since meeting Cory on the boardwalk at O'Connell Bridge, he had begun to have an inkling that saying anything non-factual risked, like the smoke now trickling out of her mouth, getting up her nose. Why this should be so, he had no idea: he was only trying to be objective; there was nothing personal in anything he said. Still, it would be better to stick to the facts. Besides, the silence was excruciating.

'Did I ever tell you,' he said at last, 'about the time I was in jail?'

'No.'

But she didn't ask why or what for, which would have allowed him to make his confession. After a long level look at him, she said, 'And I'd prefer if you didn't.'

This was like being with her on condition that she not be looked at. As a theme it was to appear and disappear and reappear during the months they lived together in Leeson Street. The other main unmusical subject, also unspoken, was whether they were a couple. She had never formally moved into the flat; she just stayed when she was not in one hospital or another. Will had been under the impression that she was doing an internship, but the two months each she was doing in surgery, psychiatry, general medicine, obstetrics, and paediatrics (which he thought had something to do with feet), were actually called 'clinical rotations' or 'attachments'. She was attached to a rotation; Leeson Street was merely a stop on the roundabout. Anyway, when she stopped the night, she was often so tired she slept in the front bedroom on her own — the back room, although it had a double bed, was too cold. But not for him, of course.

If only that was the only reason. But it wasn't. There was a multitude of other, truer reasons. None of them was fixed. Like the universe, they, as individuals, were continuously evolving. Even when things stood still, as for moments they sometimes seemed to, they were moving. Or one or other of them moved, and the other flew. Then they were flying together. They flew in a humming-bird confusion. But it was mostly he who hovered in front of her, balanced on a beak longer than himself. This probe was maladapted for its function: although it vibrated intensely, not only did it remain stock-still in comparison to the wings of his desire, which were whirring so fast they were invisible, it was about as sensitive as the vivified wood of a real bird's beak — and its equivalent of a humming-bird's tongue, when it flickered out, was not retractable. The seed of the male cannot go home again. An orgasm cannot be taken back. The shudder he felt then was a once off, or whatever the number of once-offs in a shudder is, and it was followed by a sudden turning-aside, a dropping of one shoulder and a vertiginous falling out of sight, satiated but unsatisfied. And the flower that he hovered in front of, though it was more welcoming than any tropical datura, say the jimson weed, because of the absence of any rankness in its smell, and though Cory's scent, her own mixed with Chantecaille, was more exotic than that of the West Indian Red Jasmine, the perfume of which is called frangipane — that was old Italian for broken bread — and though the flower it came from is as delicate as the honeysuckle — what a word suckle is — this flower was, after all, invisible to him, and was to remain so until the afternoon at Rindoon, because she wouldn't let him look at her naked, except for the occasional glimpse, which was cruel, like the time when she had stepped out of the bath into the rough towel he was holding, with his head turned aside. It wasn't that she teased him deliberately. No way. Quite the opposite in fact. She meant it when she threatened not to allow him into the bathroom ever again, because as he wrapped her in the towel, he had looked down at her dark down, even if ever so swiftly, as he had been forbidden to do and had sincerely promised not to.

Or maybe she had only half meant it.

Half meant it because, while sex in her mind — like the scars on her face — could not help but be associated with injury, with the forbidden, or the foreboding, she could also not help but be caught up in the atmosphere between them, whatever 'them' referred to — her scars and his (broken nose, thick eyebrows), his sex and hers (invisible), her self and his self, or all three at once. Because none of these distinctions was fixed.

Within narrow bounds, nothing else was fixed either. Some nights they went out to the cinema; or they walked on the bank of the canal, either up towards Portobello or down towards Ringsend; or they watched television, especially if an old movie was showing;

or they listened to records on the Philips Dansette — Cory liked Jack Buchanan's strangulated singing. But she didn't care to go to the Baggot Inn gig on Monday nights, or to any of the other gigs in pubs that he was now getting. Sometimes they read; sometimes they talked, in or out of the bathroom, often late into the night; sometimes they were silent. Sometimes, but always without prior arrangement or even an understanding, they went to bed together.

For Cory, the past was like the theatre: she only went there when she had to. She acted in fact, as if she had no past. It was as if, Will felt, the vine had not climbed up into the branches of the elm-tree, but had grown there without a root, like mistletoe.

Eventually, though, he had come to understand that there had been other males in her life. No-hopers most of them. But there had been one real man. He was almost as old as her father — Will stayed mute — a teaching professor, a consultant paediatrician. 'A bunion specialist?' No. The relationship had lasted a matter of weeks only, then Daddy Doc had returned to Mammy Doc. But he had written letters. Cory had not replied. She had burnt them. Unlike Emmet Roche, she didn't preserve her relics.

None of these men, all of them boys really, had got far with her. Really, all she wanted was to be — Will found the word in the dictionary — companionate with him. But sleeping with her companionately was like having a sword between them, a sword that slashed an uncrossable abyss through the middle of the bed. When he thought of other explorers being lost there, like himself, Will did not feel compassionate towards them: he wanted to punch their heads hard. Not to be the only traveller lost in the Grand Canyon was infuriating. But he didn't think of these men as menacing; they were dots of masculinity so pale they were almost invisible, like the white berries of the mistletoe in the virgin gloom of Cory's unpollarded elm-tree. Daddy Doc did matter, though. When Cory told Will — they were in bed, fully dressed, on a sunny afternoon in March, when the snow was all melted — that she had touched the Doc in the same way as she was touching him now, he had shuddered desperately. She knew what she was doing of course.

She knew all the steps up the stairs, as it were from the cellar to the skylight. Without having studied the manual, she knew how to launch the rocket. But she didn't take pride in her handiwork, which is what this was. Vulgarity didn't please her. Nothing vulgar pleased her. But she would, sometimes, lock her free arm around his neck and kiss him hard while he came.

And occasionally she would allow him reach the same end by the French doors of frottage, a word that Will learned around this time from Harry O'Gara, who said it reminded him of froth and the age of consent, both of which he avoided like the plague, thank you very much.

Somehow that act, especially when her back was turned, inclined to annoy her more than the masturbation, and they got as near to fighting over it as they did to anything. She because it was impersonal; he because it was too personal — you couldn't win in the frottage business. The whole thing was childish — worse actually, since at the height of its delight, the infant doesn't feel inferior to the cause of its laughter. The sensible adult, though, can't help feeling low about joy, or humbled by it anyway. They could have looked pragmatically at this procedure, which anyway was rare, and decided to agree that the impersonal could be personal, that is usefully laughable, and therefore jointly, if unequally, pleasurable, but only if the excitement of the experience for him was created by her willingness to accept it as such. But there were too many variables in the formula — their wants were unequal for one thing — and inevitably the squalidity triumphed, which, after all, was probably the pleasure the tawdry comedy of it pointed towards in the first place. Unfortunately.

Even their kissing had in it some of these elements of uneven exchange. After an initial period of reluctance, Cory had realised that she liked to be kissed. French kissing she had never liked. The delicacy of tongues had been too intimate for her: unlike frottage, you couldn't pretend it was going on behind your back. But now having his tongue leaping around in her mouth like a new-born lamb, as he described it, was, well, it was OK. And it was OK, too, when without being asked — the thrill was the unexpectedness — she darted the tip of her tongue against his. Sometimes when she did that, she could feel he wanted to submit, to pull her over on top of him — that was submission? — and to make of his mouth an empty hall that she could fly into like a bird from the night outside, if she wanted to. But she didn't want to. It made her gasp for air; she couldn't breathe. But not being able to draw breath meant that she was speechless, which, in turn, meant that she didn't have to find words to say when, for example, she did climb on top of him and his long hard-muscled boxer's thigh was clamped tight between her thighs and for a moment she was moving against it. But only for a moment, or maybe a few moments of wordless panting, in which nothing, well, almost nothing happened. Nothing much would happen either when, for another, more usual, example, she would have his hand locked between her legs. About this there were all sorts of unspoken rules. The main rule could be reduced to two words: Outside Only. He could touch her outside her skirt, jeans, slacks, nightdress, or silky pyjama bottoms. Sometimes, very rarely, she would allow him go further: to touch her inside whatever she was wearing but on the outside of her tights-and-pants. Sometimes, even more rarely, on the outside of her pants only, the material of which, usually cotton, was so thin it was almost like — but 'almost' was miles too close and he would have to stop, stop, stop. Momentarily she'd be in a rage. She hated him.

She hated him too — these were separate occasions — when he would tell her what he would like to do with her. These were complex negotiations in which bravado and his usual imparting of objective information, mixed with a dirty-raincoat shame and a mackintosh flasher's daring, very Barberous, plus a small amount of innocence, atom-sized and citified, a certain wheedling, and a general breathlessness, were all muddled up together.

'You're the only person I've ever met who can bully and cringe at the same time,' she had said to him once, and now she said it again. That had been said about his servility, but that couldn't be connected to what he was asking her to put up with, surely, could it? Well, no. But as with all nice distinctions, it was too tempting not to spread it around, even when the sequence was wrong, like butter on jam; or it was out of kilter with the possible, like a tsunami in Oklahoma where the corn was as high as an elephant's eye; or it was unheard of, unimaginable, unnatural, unthinkable, like...

'Like, is this for real?' Will said.

The thing was it was unreal. Never mind that apparently she had never had an orgasm, not only with anyone else but even with herself — she had never tumbled the frangipane — it was crazy that someone like her, whose business was bodies, and who, anyway, had seen a great many films, should think that something as pure and beautiful as teasing her clitoris with the tip of his tongue was unthinkable. But the unthinkable was what she never thought. It had never occurred to her, not in her wildest dreams — anyway she didn't have dreams that were wild.

That was why, when, in a sun-warmed hollow on a grassy bank outside the abandoned medieval city of Rindoon, overlooking Lough Ree, the King's Lake, having come close to being killed on the road to Athlone, she was glad just to be alive, and glad, too, to have fled the mad death-in-life voice of her kingly father crying up the stairs in the concrete house of the Learys on the road to Gort. That was why when she had waded into the river with her skirt bunched up and then got out and took off her wet cotton pants, and the tip of his tongue did to her what she had never dreamed of being done in her wildest dreams, and her hands, thrown out wide, could no longer hold onto the grassy bank, and her eyes could no longer be kept tight shut, because the blue sky with its towering and seemingly motionless white clouds opened them, and the gravity of the unseen moon on the other side of the world dragging her down to earth was overcome by the upper half of her body, the clothed half, rising up towards the point of liberty, that was why she clasped his head in her hands and cried out, 'Don't do that, don't do that.'

As for the complement — that she might do to him what he had done to her — Will knew better than to ask her to return the compliment. Just because she went to church every Sunday, it didn't necessarily follow that she was a Christian. But neither of them was disappointed. There was no bitterness between them. They were joined together by the faintly musky scent that comes off the condensed fluid of desire, the pure drop of more-than-water that carries both the egg of creation and the one seed fated by chance to rise up to unite with it in time.

That was why he wrote in his notebook: Truth as you exist I found you.

31

'You're leaving me then, are you?'
'Jesus, you are such a bitch.'
'What!?'
'You heard me. Fuck off, you brassboun cunt.'
'What did you say?'
'I said: You're a traitor, a fucking turncoat. We
didn't get rid of enough of your kind in 1921.'

THERE WERE THREE different conversations here, but they were sequential and related in the sense of the old saying that 'One word borrowed another.'

'You're leaving me then, are you?' Sheevawn Rogers had said. Her tone was more steely than pathetic. Will had got the point, and he was hurt, furiously. The fury was the cause of what followed on the SeaCat to Holyhead and after that in the port of Holyhead. But Sheevawn could hardly be blamed for those events, though Will did blame her.

To go back to the beginning, he was furious about his birth. Being born in October and Polly not sending him to school until he was almost six years-old meant that by the time he left school he was getting on for nineteen. Then, although he had just enough points to get into the Cork School of Music, he had hated being taught what he already knew — 'boring, boring, boring' — almost as much he loathed having constantly to avoid bumping into his mother. Polly was like the tune in Ravel's Bolero: fucking everywhere. So he had dropped out. Then he had joined a band — 'a stupid punk band' — and quit within weeks because they insisted on finishing every gig with a version of the Sid Vicious version of '(I Did It) My Way.'

Then he had moved in with Sheevawn in a house near the university. Sheevawn, who loved being in college and studying economics, had minded Will calling her 'a breadhead' a good deal less than she did his having it off with one of her housemates. After she had thrown him out, he had gone off busking down the length of France — 'a more stupid country than it thinks' — until he arrived in Barcelona in time for the Sonar festival. This was 'boring, stupid and coming down with trendy breadheads,' but he had heard a good piano player called Agustí Fernández playing at a club in the city — of course Fernández was too good to be in the festival proper.

The outcome of this year, utterly wasted in the opinion of Paul and Polly, was that he had to forget about education, look for a job on a building site or in a chip shop, stand on his own two feet, get out of the house, and in short 'Stop the nonsense!' He had broken his mother's heart and seriously disrupted his father's routine. But the outcome of the outcome was that he was to get a last chance. His parents would support him while he worked spare time and studied full-time for a Bachelor of Arts degree in University College Dublin, where Ossie was about to begin his second year. The Gleesons had installed him in a nice flat in Sandymount, and Will could stay there, sharing the rent. In theory.

The theory had not been put into practice. The day before he left for Dublin, he had met Sheevawn walking by the Lough. More than a year had passed since he had screwed her housemate, but he had written a poem of apology from France, which began: 'I pass in the street and nobody knows me,' and Sheevawn now accepted that that bitch had (cat-scratching quotes with her fingers) 'seduced' him. So, after they had drunk a few cans of beer by the Lough — it was like being young again — they had gone back to her house. The girl she was now sharing with had set a trap for mice without telling Sheevawn. Finding a mouse dead in it, Sheevawn had screamed. That, and what followed, was the origin of the song he had sung at the beginning in the Baggot Inn. Then, as a result of being comforted with kisses, she had wanted to make love in the old way, to be seventeen again. But Will had declined. Why he didn't know. Maybe not taking advantage of the offer was moral — good of him, good for her. That was when Sheevawn said, 'You'd better scuttle off to Dublin then,' adding that he was an egomaniac — hadn't he noticed that in his French so-called poem there was no mention of her? Yet again, and for the last time, she had sent him away with his tail between his legs. Plus a furiously regretful erection. The fury was partly at himself for being such a pompous prat, partly at her for insulting him and his good intentions. 'Jesus, you are such a bitch.' But above all he was furious that he hadn't torn her pants off and given her — as she ironically pronounced it — 'the wan thing' she and every woman he had ever met said men were only interested in. So he had gone downtown in search of someone he could vent his sexually righteous fury on, failed to find anyone, and instead staggered home, threw up in the washbasin in the bathroom, and fell asleep in his clothes.

The only thing that filled him with greater rage than the moral squalor in which his parents lived was saying goodbye to them. 'We spend our lives forever taking leave' was a line by Rilke that he often quoted at this time, but 'taking leave' was a ritual utterly different to Polly stuffing a hundred quid into his breast-pocket and acting like a hypocritical hen when what she really wanted to do was kick up a stink about the stink he'd left behind him in the bathroom. So he had left Cork still in a fury.

The fury was not much abated by three weeks at University College Dublin. The place was full of students. Students were stupid. So was Ossie Gleeson. For instance, this band that he was managing: they were called Our Buzz.

That was a dead giveaway: they were an out-and-out boy-band, or would have been, except that all four of them played instruments, quite passably too, and wrote their own songs — which they called anthems.

'If you ask me,' Will said, 'they're more like orgasms in a plastics factory.'

But Ossie didn't ask him. He had been too busy spending his father's money on getting the band's look right: hair teased, t-shirts torn, denims slashed at the knee, teeth whitened, plus a course of Ritalin for the drummer, who had a bad dose of acne; then a portfolio of professional photos, low on smiling, high on brooding; a four-track demo CD; an elaborate sound-desk; and finally, most expensive of all, a series of backing tracks, commissioned from professional musicians, including violinists, which guaranteed decent live performances. Ossie's strategy was to start small, then go big as word-of-mouth spread. Who knows what heights they might climb to? Actually, though he didn't say so, certainly not to Will, Ossie had his eyes fixed on the Eurovision Song Contest.

What he did tell Will, acting blasé but hardly able to contain his excitement, was that a well known A&R man in London had heard the demo record and expressed an interest. Ossie had acted decisively: Our Buzz would fly to London and he would follow on the SeaCat with their equipment in a hired van. Would Will come? All expenses paid. Maybe he'd even play for the A&R man, who had, you know, a really good ear.

'You want me to be your roadie,' Will said.

But he went.

The trouble began early. In the airport Ossie had confiscated a small quantity of cocaine from the spotty drummer. 'Are you mad?' he'd said. 'Do you want your career to end before it starts?' But back in the Hermitage, Will had snorted the coke and drunk the most of a bottle of champagne Mrs Gleeson had had delivered by courier, along with a big bunch of flowers, to wish Osmondo good luck in the Big Smoke.

Then he had rung Sheevawn. All he would say to Ossie afterwards was, 'The bitch blew me out again.' So he had drunk some cans in the van on the way to Dun Laoghaire.

Will thought the SeaCat was 'cat' in the Cork sense of the word, meaning crap. It wasn't a boat; it was a shivering shopping centre. It had slot machines, a cinema, a café, a lobby with high ceilings, a bright red and blue carpet — and a bar. Which was full of Manchester United fans travelling to a match in the English midlands.

Ossie knew the situation was hopeless and went off to the cinema.

Will stood at the bar drinking pints of Heineken and shots of vodka mixed with Red Bull — 'I need the caffeine to stay awake' — discussing with the supporters the character of their hero and his fellow Corkonian, Roy Keane.

'He's autistic,' Will told them. 'That's the only explanation. Either he's fucking autistic or he's an out-and-out plain fucking criminal. Keane is a criminal. He's a fucking thug. The cunt is a fucking psychopath.'

Actually, he did not think any of these accusations was true. It was merely that Manchester United fans invited contrariness and when it came to being contrary, Will didn't need an invitation. Actually, when it came to Keane, Will was a hero-worshipper. Roy was everything an artist should be: single-minded, determined, all of a piece, ruthlessly human. When you saw him storming up the middle of the park, radiating to other great, but lesser, players, like Paul Scholes or Ryan Giggs, a ferocious electricity that commanded them to obey his call, follow his fanatical will, break down the resistance of the opposition — which, by the very fact of opposing him must be morally weak — their weakness was the secret! — and then, having occupied their territory, burst into their castle and shatter the shite out of it. When you saw that happen, it brought tears to your eyes.

Actually, Will had never seen Roy play except on television. He wasn't interested in soccer, he couldn't be bothered. Still it had to be said, and he did say it: 'The cunt is a fucking psychopath.'

He felt a tap on his shoulder. A man wearing a white cap with gold braid on it was saying, 'Kindly moderate your language, young man.'

'Who the fuck are you?'

'I said, watch your language. There are women and children here.'

'Would you ever fuck off, you silly cunt, you and your sailor's hat.'

'What did you say?'

'You heard me. Fuck off, you brassbound cunt.'

The man disappeared. Will turned back to his United fans. They were looking at him with newfound respect. He had important things to say to them about the function of aggression. Mad and all as he was, that fucker Keane wasn't mad at all, he was the sanest man in Ireland. In the middle of his madness he was 'cold like ice like fire'. That was a song. Did they know that, Manfuckingchester Ufuckingnited fansyfuckers? It was a song, it was like leading with your head in boxing, when what you should really be doing — 'Here, hold my drink till I show you' — was keep your lead hand straight out, jab-jab-jab, even when you were going backwards.

It was very peculiar to be going backwards and demonstrating your jab going forwards, and yet at the same time to be going upwards. So lightly, so effortlessly.

Ossie, returning from the cinema, entered a magical silence in which only Will's voice could be heard. The whole place had grown still. And the Manchester United fans, having created a boxing ring for Will to demonstrate his art in, were frozen in time, as if under a spell. But as Will danced his Muhammad Ali shuffle and jab-jab-jabbed his straight right, four sailors advanced in a phalanx, seized him by the arms and legs and, led by the gold-braided officer in the white cap, bore him Up Up and Away.

Will was too surprised to struggle. All he could do was look open-mouthed at each sailor in turn. One for the right leg, one for the left leg. One for the left arm, one for the right. The symmetry was astonishing.

It was a long journey. But it seemed short. Down dimly lit steel corridors and narrow steel stairs, unvisited by the travelling public.

Just as he finally managed to say, 'Hey, what the fuck is going on?' he was heaved onto his feet, propelled forward, and a steel door was slammed shut on him. And as it closed, the light, what light there was in the belly of the beast, was extinguished.

The SeaCat takes ninety-nine minutes to catamaran across the Irish Sea, so Will spent roughly an hour in the blackness of the steel box, and during that time, instead of cooling his heels, he barked his shin on something sharp. After roaring many fucks of fury, he discovered, by feeling it with his hands, that Stena Sealink had provided its prisoners with a chair that had only three legs. Good enough for them too. But all this humiliation, plus claustrophobia, scalded Will's heart and set it boiling.

'What's this then, Paddy?' the policeman in Holyhead asked.

This was the last straw that broke the back of the drowning camel. It had been bad enough to be grabbed by the same four sailors and frog-marched onto dry land. But the land wasn't dry. Through a window in the terminal Will could see lamp-standards, standing stalky in lashing rain, shining wanly on the hell-dock of Holyhead.

Travellers straggling in a queue to board the SeaCat stared at him. Will had something to say to them: 'Fuck off back to Ireland.' But he said it only because neither the ship's officer nor the sailors would answer his questions, not the general ones about what was going on, nor the particular ones, which related to Ossie Gleeson, his van, his going to London et cetera.

'What the fuck are you looking at?' he inquired of the queue, but answer came there none.

'What's all this then, Paddy?' the arriving policeman said.

In Will's opinion, the lowest of all low things in all the world, lower even than an informer, was an Irishman who had become an English cop. In fact this policeman was half-Welsh: his mother was a Griffith from Pwllheli. But he had been brought up in Cork and his name was Pat Murphy. Pat was fat. Not in the loose way policemen over-fond of their bacon and cabbage and chicken tikka masala are fat. He was bursting-out-of-his-skin fat, fat with hypertension, fat with barely suppressed rage, fat with what used to be called choler. He was choleric was Pat. He had anger management issues. In other words, he was a most unpleasant man. That was why he was still an ordinary constable at the age of forty-two. He had once been a sergeant, but his issues had become an issue and he had been demoted. More immediately relevant was the fact that despite having left his native city at the age of thirteen, Pat had acquired only as much of a Welsh lilt as was sufficient to accentuate the Cork brogue of his upbringing.

As soon as Pat asked him, 'What's all this then, Paddy?' Will identified the accent as coming from the region around Watergrasshill.

'I know you,' he said.

'You what?' Pat said, alarmed. He was alarmed because a motorist he had once amused himself by abusing had uttered the same sentence. The motorist had turned out to be a magistrate. Pat's excuse to his superiors was not a good one: 'The road was dark.'

Now, to 'You what?' Will responded by reciting a series of questions that have been known to irritate people from his native county.

'Are you from Cork? I am, are you? I am, I am. Do you eat potatoes? I do, I do. Skins and all.' (You is pronounced 'oo'. Skins is pronounced 'shkins'.)

Pat dimly remembered these questions but did not relate them to his origins. However, they freed him from alarm at being known. Turning to the ship's officer, he said, 'What's going on here then?'

'He's drunk and disorderly,' the ship's officer said. 'And he used foul and abusive language.'

'For fuck's sake,' Will said.

'In front of women and children.'

'What year is this?' Will asked. 'Nineteen-forty-eight?'

'Shut it, Paddy.'

'Don't call me Paddy,' Will said.

'Shut the fuck up.'

'If I shut the fuck up, how can I tell you what's going on?'

'Paddy, I'm going to have you.'

'Did you ever hear of habeas corpus?'

'What did he say?' Pat asked the officer, bewildered.

Will said, 'Habeas corpus, you gobshite. They locked me up

without it. And you're a quisling.'

'What did you say?' Pat said.

'I said: You're a traitor, a fucking turncoat. We didn't get rid of enough of your kind in 1921.' At this stage Will had begun to sense that he had, maybe, gone too far. 'I'm entitled to habeas corpus,' he added weakly. 'I'm entitled to a fair trial.'

This weakness may have been the cause of what happened next. It certainly allowed Pat the time to hitch up the side of his tunic and unclip from its clip his truncheon. With which he now struck Will a smart little blow on the side of his left knee. This was a mistake from Pat's point of view. It was a mistake because Will's reaction — following a short hop into the air — was automatic. As soon as he returned to earth, he took a step backward and at the same moment whipped out a straight right hand, a classical counter-punch, which caught Pat, unclassically, beneath the chin, full on his Adam's apple. Pat uttered a sound like that made by a hen which has swallowed a large pebble, 'Uhwockh!' Then, like the animal he much more closely resembled — a bullock — he went down as if poleaxed by an electrically fired bolt in a slaughterhouse.

The Stipendiary Magistrate said he would have quite understood if this case had not come before him. Such an unprovoked assault on a member of the constabulary might more properly have been dealt with on indictment by a superior court. That Mr Ferris had no previous convictions, 'at least in this jurisdiction', cut no ice with the bench. Nor had he displayed any hint of remorse, maintaining instead a sullen and brazen silence. Also, the plea of mitigation entered by Mr Gleeson, while heartfelt, was incoherent, irrelevant and indeed counter productive: the claim that the defendant was an artist, so-called, rendered his behaviour all the more reprehensible. Well, he intended to teach Mr Ferris a lesson he would not soon forget. In the circumstances of what amounted to aggravated assault, which could have caused grievous bodily harm, even death, he had no hesitation in imposing the maximum sentence on 'this dishevelled and dastardly Hibernian bully'.

32

'I'M ONE OF the worried well,' Harry said. Will fished his notebook from his satchel and recorded the sentence. The notebook added to Harry's worries: he had not realised that what he said was being taken down and might be used in evidence against him. It was silly to be paranoid about such an absurd possibility, but from then on he was to become wary of what he said within Will's earshot. Not cautious though. That would be to go against his nature.

The odd thing was that what started him worrying was something that amused him.

Working late one night in Brown Thomas's, he had overheard two assistants talking about their holidays while they were stocking up the shelves in the perfume counters.

'I didn't go anywhere really,' the first one said. 'I was only, like, with me aunt in Staines.'

'Staines? That's a funny name for a place. Where's that?'

'It's in England.'

'It's not.'

'It is so it is. It's near London. In Middlesex.'

'Middlesex? That's gross.'

The girls — identical blondes with fake tans the colour of simnel cake — had ur-Dublin accents, the kind that turns on pronunciations of 't': sibilantly dental in 'aunt'; unvoiced in 'what'; and metamorphosed in the already mysterious 'It is so it is' into 'Ir is so ir is.' But far from 'That's gross' being intentional, it had just bubbled up out of the girl's subconscious, and it probably had more to do with the distinctions she was making between the parfum and the eau de toilette than with gender identity, proving yet again, if proof be needed, that as far as segmental and suprasegmental phonology are concerned, intonation is one phenomenon whose domain extends beyond morphology. (Harry was now self-educating himself in linguistics — which was why he had been able to explain to Will the meaning of 'trace-effect'.)

But hearing the girl's tone of voice, Harry had begun to worry about his own geography. He was Middlesexed all right, but gross? A bit plump maybe. But then so was the Sibyl who said it. And she was veiled in a cloak of Chantecaille Frangipane. She was supposed to be stacking the stuff, not squirting it all over herself. Chantecaille cost a fortune. That worried him too. His moroseness was shrouded in smells. He was sensitive to stinks.

And to stains.

Harry was used to saying that he had run away from home at the age of sixteen. But this was only partly true. He had been running away since the onset, the onslaught of puberty. And he had run with bad company. Long before he had reached the age of consent, he had been known, biblically, by many priest-like men who wanted to deprave him, though none as tormentedly as Father Philomena, the Druid of Dungarvan, who had been caught red-handed, whereupon he grew fat, or fatter, and killed himself. If that episode had not frightened Harry — for some reason he was afraid of nothing sexual — it had taught him that there has to be a limit to hazardous behaviour. He had met quite a few queer folk, and some straights too, who acted otherwise. These crazy birds flitted romantically around death. To them, the danger of dying added zest to life. Although a few of the few had got more lemon juice than they bargained for, most of those had stumbled into extinction. The vast majority of masochists, in Harry's experience, were far too sensible to chase their orgasm into the morgue. And yet he had always had a soft spot for those who took a bet on death and lost their shirts on the gamble. Did Vanessa Banim, née Betty O'Hara, fit into that category? Maybe. But if she did, it was not a shirt she had lost but her modesty vest, the finest linsey-wool, made in Belfast, a souvenir of childhood, well hidden away in the bottom of a black plastic sack.

To say that Harry had run away from home was only partially true. Once, when he was six years old, he had been sent to an actual Home. It had happened because his mother, Moira, a shop assistant in Clerys, had a problem with what she called 'me nerves', and his father, Paddy, a merchant seaman, had a problem with what he called 'the drink'. Torn between a distraction and an abstraction, Harry had been lodged briefly in an orphanage, and then fostered out to a nice family in Bray. After three months he had been sent back to his parents. Being at home was nicer, just about. But by the time he had reached his teens, he had decided he preferred chaos to comfort: the aesthetics were more interesting.

Home was certainly chaotic. Moira had twice gone to live with other men. The first of these lovers, a gentle soul who had problems with both his nerves and the drink, had crumpled under the pressure and emigrated to Australia. The second lover had been sober and sane, but he had soon developed a homophobic abhorrence of Harry — an irrationality more than normally irrational since Harry was only twelve at the time.

Paddy, when he wasn't at sea, had stayed on in their tiny house, an Artisan's Dwelling in Stoneybatter, in the centre of the city. After a year living with the homophobe, Harry had gone home to Dad. The least you could say about Paddy was that he had had too much experience of the way life swung on the ocean wave to have anything against homosexuals, though he did call them arse-bandits.

Moira had then shot off to Australia to join her first lover. Harry had visited, stayed for a year, and then returned to Dublin. The fact that his father had gone to sea was OK with him, but his social worker was concerned, alarmed, outraged that a fourteen-year-old boy should be living in a house on his own. Before she could do anything about it, Paddy came back again. But then he went off again. The social worker couldn't keep up and had let Harry's file lapse.

By the time Paddy had been promoted to captain, the drink had given him a grog-blossom nose, smoking had similarly thickened his lungs and he had been forced to come ashore for good. In retirement the anger had ebbed out of him and the delicacies of his brain had begun to reveal themselves, like the claw-prints of seabirds in petrified mudflats. He had taken up painting as a hobby. His subjects were two: landscapes of an inland, sunny, waterless, unpeopled Ireland; and — somewhat less unreal — tropical seascapes, moonlit, stormy, in which a castaway, always the same one, held out imploring arms to the ship from whose canting deck the waves had just now swept him, and which always passed on, oblivious, scudding still before the wind. Most of Paddy's time, though, was devoted to creating a replica of Isambard Kingdom Brunel's steamship *The Great Eastern*. Built exactly to scale — a hundredth of 692 feet — it had six masts, a hand-sewn suit of sails, and three functioning miniature engines, one each for the paddle wheels, the propellers, and the steering, as in the original. The model was pond-worthy, but it had never been launched because one night an embolism had sailed out of Paddy's lung into his heart and he had collapsed onto *The Great Eastern*, breaking its keel.

The newspapers had briefly reported the unusuality of a man lying dead and unnoticed in Stoneybatter for four months. They had got it wrong. Since Harry had visited his father, as he always did, on the second of February, his birthday, and the body had been discovered at the end of April, the maximum possible number of days was eighty-four. Still, for reasons of hygiene, the Captain had been hurriedly cremated, the workshop cleared of the wreckage of *The Great Eastern*, and the lower forms of life exterminated. Apart from a smell of Jeyes Fluid, all that remained — and Harry had only seen it briefly, in the company of a public health official called Quirke — was ineradicably imprinted on the floorboards. Were it not for the broken boat, the outline of the body could have been drawn in chalk, as in a murder mystery, but while the shape of the head and the crooked X of the arms and legs were discernible, the torso had dissolved into a sprinkle of Aleutian Islands, an archipelago of fat.

Fat, like stains, was a word Harry did not like to think about.

To avoid distressing his mother, he had only told her — the irony was not lost on him — the bare bones of the story. Anyway, Moira did not want to know: Stoneybatter was too literally descriptive of her experience there. She was interested, though, in what was to become of the house. Neither of them wanted to keep it. Harry, advised on the legalities by Maeve MacNamee, did not say he was entitled to two-thirds of the estate. Instead, he had offered to share the proceeds of the sale fifty-fifty. Moira had agreed. But he worried about his behaviour: a few years earlier he would have given her the house lock stock and barrel.

Something worryingly selfish was also happening in Brown Thomas's. Throughout his working life, Harry had behaved irresponsibly. In all the cities he had lived in — New York, London, Paris, Madrid, Milan — he had shuttled between department stores and fashion houses without a care in the world. Like an anarchist without any theory of anarchism, he had been devoted to the excitement of it only, which he had fuelled with sex, or sexual comedy, and, for a while, with cocaine. He had been a messenger boy, then a window-dresser's assistant, then a window-dresser. But now his experience had caught up with him. Management had noticed his impatience with bad buying and slow selling and how well he understood the quicksilver glooms of the retail business; plus he seemed to know anyone who was anyone anywhere, especially in the rag trade. So he had been taken out of window-dressing and put into a tiny windowless office.

All his life Harry had got his way by using his charm. It was a shock now to be able to use power without persuasion. More often than not he could say 'Do this' and it was done, or 'Buy that' and it was bought. But power was charmless, and no charm meant no magic, and no magic meant no affection. Looking after lesbian men with HIV was a fundamental part of his Middlesex vocation, wasn't it? But ever since he had got this new job he had begun to suspect that his caring was really a form of vanity, or worse, that he disdained the diseased, it was their own fault. Too long a practice of the work of tenderness had brutalised him. It was another reason for worry. But almost immediately he had begun to make money for the company. Profits for Brown Thomas meant bonuses for him. He had never been poor, but that was because he had always lived on the run, like a gypsy, consuming and discarding, keeping nothing except his address book and his CD collection. Now far more money was coming in than going out, and when Stoneybatter was sold he would have, if the house-market kept soaring — people were mortgaging their souls to buy rabbit hutches — at least a quarter of a million quid to provide for his future. Provide for his future? Was he, who never thought of tomorrow, to have one? What about the moment he lived for? Well, for the moment, he would stay on in Aungier Street. The only new thing he did was to go out — with Gay Chevara — and buy himself a couple of Etro suits. A suit for the suit he had become. It was the Middlesex thing to do.

'I'm worried about you,' Ernesto said. 'You'll be getting married next.'

Marriage was for people who lived in Staines, not for Harry. But he was growing old and ugly: he had the beginnings of a potbelly and he was on the brink of being thirty and all he had to celebrate was the knowledge that what is beautiful is not oneself. Oh woe. Oh worry, worry, worry.

'I'd rather die,' he said. 'Let's have a party.'

33

Hence when Hera and Zeus disputed whether the pleasures of love are felt more by women or by men, they referred to Tiresias for a decision. He said that if the pleasures of love be reckoned at ten, men enjoy one and women nine. Wherefore Hera blinded him, but Zeus bestowed on him the art of soothsaying.

AN ICEPACK AFFORDED Cormac Healy some relief from bone-pain. Or it did when he could find the ice. In his dump in Nelson Street there was no fridge. In Waterloo Road, though, he could occasionally — when there wasn't the other wan thing on his mind — wrap a teacloth around the ice-cube tray from Maeve's freezer compartment and clap it on the wound. But it was easier being patient with his oozing leg than with Maeve. Impatience with her boiled beneath his skin, like a bubble of super-heated gas in molten lava, and when it came to the surface, as it did one Monday night in the Baggot Inn, the blast hurt only himself. The cause of this explosion, the prick that burst the bubble, was, as usual, Will Ferris.

Instead of being his usual sullen monosyllabic self, Will had actually spoken to his audience — that is to the ones who had been able to get in. Crowds of fools were now flocking to see him. Announcing what he had sung or was going to sing was usually as far as he went, but tonight he said he was going to read a piece he had found in a book by Apollodorus.

'Who's he?' Cormac said.

'A Greek writer,' Maeve said.

'Never heard of him.'

'That's because you're thick,' Maeve said.

When Will had finished reading, he said, 'Makes you think. Made me think anyway. I've been thinking about it all day. Nine to one is some odds.' Some of the fools clapped their hands and laughed knowingly. Will went on, 'Blinded him no less. The punishment hardly fits the crime, does it?'

Again the fools chortled and clapped, and one of them, a man entirely unloved, whooped.

'What the fuck are they laughing at?' Cormac said.

Maeve looked at him sideways and said, 'They're laughing at you, sweetie.'

'What do you mean?'

'Everyone knows what a hammer-man you are.'

'Well, fuck you too,' Cormac said, jumped to his feet and bullocked his way through the crowd.

Outside it was still bright. The blue of the sky, as sometimes happens after a day of uninterrupted sunshine, had turned pearly. It would have made a sober man restless. Where was he to go? Smokers were clouding like midges outside Doheny and Nesbitt's and Toner's and the bar further down on the other side of street, past the Tesco supermarket. What was the name of that kip? Because he never went there, Cormac didn't know. He was sick of pubs. In his mind's eye he saw himself walking up Baggot Street as far as the canal, then instead of crossing the bridge, taking the path beneath the trees. There, if he had a mind to, he could lie on the grass, lean on his elbow and look at the waterhens, dopey fuckers, scooting about, making vee-shaped ripples on the still untroubled water.

These imagined lookings didn't last long. There was no question of lying on the bank of the canal. Walking that far couldn't be done, not with his leg throbbing like this. So he went across the road to the pub near Tesco's that he didn't know the name of.

He had stood so long in the doorway of the Baggot in the hope that Maeve would come out looking for him. Hopelessly. He knew her too well for that. Other no-hope thoughts insisted he think them too. Would she say I'm sorry? No hope. Let's go home to bed? No hope. No-hopers were rushing around inside his brain like little black Velcro-clad rodents, snapping at each other, sticking together and tearing themselves loose, traces of each contact adhering like fine hairs to their skin-hooks.

Cuntooks.

This Velcro beast of a word clung to him. It was not a new one. But recently it had started worrying at him with its needle-sharp teeth.

While he had been in the Mater having his titanium joists adjusted, Maeve had sent him a postcard. It had been delayed for days, and when it finally arrived, a hospital administrator, an old geezer wearing a cardigan under his suit, had delivered it personally. The postcard was enveloped in a white envelope. As he handed it over, the geezer said, 'I'll have you know, Mr Healy, this is still a Catholic hospital.' There was bitterness in his 'still' — a younger but (of course) more senior administrator had warned him against saying anything to this degenerate that might be actionable. Nowadays the dirt-birds would have you up in the High Court for breaching their human rights if you refused to deliver their filth for them. What was the country coming to?

The legend on the postcard was unobjectionable. It read:

Herm of Hermes
Attributed to Boethos
Hellenistic, ca. 100-50 B.C.
Bronze, H: 103.5cm (40¼in.)
© 1993 The J. Paul Getty Museum, CA

The photograph showed a bronze stature of a shovel-bearded Dionysos wearing a turban-like headdress of loosely wound ribbons. The pupil of one of his eyes was yellow, made of ivory — the other one had fallen out somewhere along the road to the Getty Museum in California. This man-god had no arms and no legs. Beneath his shoulders all he had for a body was a squared column of sharp-edged bronze. But out of the middle of its smoothness erupted a small bag of balls and a worm-like penis.

That was bad enough, but what the geezer had most objected to was the message on the card.

> *Hi Cuntooks!*
> *Remind you of anything?*
> *Even if that bastard hospital*
> *did this to your little Willy*
> *I still have a hot slot*
> *for a decent prick.*
> *Keep on truckin!*

The geezer, though he had misread the last word as 'fuckin', had seen 'Cuntooks' clearly. It was one of Maeve's favourite words. Of course, prickteaser that she was, she knew well that the message would give Cormac the horn, guaranteed cast-iron, or Type One Titanium. That was OK by him but, because his own balls felt like they were encased in bronze, it was also cruel.

Maeve was cruel. The cruelty of the things she said made flitters of his heart. With one word she could shrink it small as a goblin and send it flying up into his throat. The way the leprechaun pulsed was addictive, like the mad rush you got from cracking poppers, a gay sex trick she had heard about from Harry. That sort of jazz wasn't up Harry's alley any more, or so he said. Yeah, right. For Cormac the hit he got off her cruelty was irresistible, but, after a while, exhausting, draining, will weakening. Will! That bastard again.

Cormac sat at the counter of the nameless bar and drank a pint of stout with a double Jameson Crested Ten as a chaser. The ecstasy he had taken on Saturday was all but gone out of his system. Tomorrow was odds-on to be a Blue Tuesday. He took a pill out of his breast pocket and popped it. 'The Drugs Don't Work': Will Ferris had sung that song just now in the Baggot, and as he was singing he had given Cormac a mocking look. And he'd looked at him too when he read out that nine-to-one crap. Of course the snake knew what Maeve had been doing to him. And half the laughing fools probably knew it too. Did Emmet Roche know? Emmet wouldn't be seen dead in a wormhole like the Maggot Inn if Will Ferris was in it. But Harry O'Gara, where was he? He wasn't there either and he hung around Ferris like flies around shite. Poor Harry, poor little ferrety fucker with his curly hair and his little short footsteps — no wonder they were short with those cuban-heeled boots he wore all the time. To make him tall. Some chance. He was too small for his own good. But you could talk to Harry; he was a decent skin, even if he was a nancyboy. Where was he now that he needed him? Probably up in Leeson Street babysitting little Cora Leary.

Why Maeve had called Cory Cora was a story in itself.

From the age of fourteen Will Ferris had despised the piano, because Polly had tried to ram it down his throat. But now that Harry had given him a recording of Leif Ove Andsnes playing Janacek's 'On an Overgrown Path', Will had decided he had to play the piece too. So he had bought an electric piano, sight unseen, sound unheard, from a guy in Stillorgan — which Harry said was a very pianistic place to live — but the Saturday afternoon the instrument was to be collected, Cory's car had broken down, yet again, so Will had rung Maeve to ask could she go and collect it.

Cormac said, 'You cannot be serious.'

But Maeve was serious. 'Something came up,' she said. 'There's a Yank in town Harry wants Will to meet.'

'Yank my granny,' Cormac said. 'Let him do his own yanking.'

'It's no skin off your nose,' she said. 'You can give me a hand carrying it.'

'Me carry Will Ferris's piano? You must be joking. I wouldn't piss on him if he was on fire.'

'Come on, be generous for once in your life.'

When Harry heard this story, he said, 'Maeve MacNamee would give you the shirt off your own back.'

Her generosity was one of the things that most interested him. Instant, impulsive and careless as it might seem, it was calculated. In this instance the payback for delivering the piano was getting the chance to run a jealous eye over Cory Leary's domestic arrangements.

Did Will know that that was the price? Probably. But if so he knew unknowingly. Typical.

Was that how his own altruism worked, Harry wondered. When he was stony broke he had been a giver. Now that he owned Stoneybatter he had become a taker. He was taking bread out of his mother's mouth. That was selfish. Selfishness was the basis of everything. It was naturally selected, according to *The Origin of Species*, a copy of which he had recently been given by a rather sweet old professor in Trinity College. Harry had glanced through it, but only long enough to wonder why a person would sometimes sacrifice his personal life for the sake of another person if the real reason for doing it was impersonal. These days, personal death, like the dissolving of human fat, was a subject he couldn't prevent himself thinking of. Survival was the same delusion he supposed Vanessa had been directed by when she had overdosed on her sugaring diabetes pills. Why had he continued to visit her when she didn't know he was standing there at her undulating bedside? That was like asking him how he was serving the survival of the species when he had no intention of reproducing himself. He was a member of a strange charity: Gays Against Evolution, a not-for-profit organisation. Anyway, he had recently arrived at the hospital to discover Vanessa had been removed to Belfast, after which he had heard no more of her. Nor had he rung Doris Dalkeith to find out. More selfishness.

Cormac knew he lacked for brains. That pretentious ponce Will Ferris had once said that Harry was the cleverest man he'd ever met. But in Cormac's opinion, when it came to dealing with women, by which he meant Maeve, he had more intelligence, that is experience on the ground, than Harry would ever have. Tonight, though, was not the best of times for being intelligent. No matter what he drank, thoughts of Maeve squeezed his heart small and spat her pulsing into his throat. She gave and gave all right, but what she gave was less interesting to her than watching the person she was giving to. She was a desperate watcher. And just because she said she had done something didn't necessarily mean it had happened. Or so Cormac hoped. Hoped and didn't hope. Because the question he often asked himself about Maeve was, or should have been, simple and straightforward: was she or was she not bent?

If there was one thing among the many things Maeve understood about men, it was the hold the lesbian fantasy has over their dirty little imaginations, though in her opinion imagination was too big a word to be applied to stuff that was so narrow and depthless. If Cormac was to believe half of what she said, half the women in the world spent half their time with their tongues halfway down the throats of the other half. But he didn't believe a word of it. To his certain knowledge when it came to same-sex sex, most women began with a 'no thanks' and ended with a 'yuk'. In real life it'd be like a girl going to bed with her own mother. Those were depths normal people didn't sink to.

But closer to the surface it wasn't uncommon for Maeve to announce, 'I dig with both feet', and to act as if she meant it, snogging gay girls in clubs, the butcher the better, to show them who was boss. It certainly gave Cormac the horn when he saw it, as it was meant to. But he wasn't born to be a looker-on. He was who he was — 'a Limerick woolly-back', according to Maeve — and what he felt was what he felt, full stop. What puzzled him was that stuff that properly belonged in porno magazines, real women would do for real in strobe-lit clubs like The Pod, not to speak of in the grey light of ordinary day.

Gay men puzzled Cormac too, but differently. As long as they didn't frighten the horses — whatever the hell that meant — it was grand by him. For one thing, men in love with other men, like Harry O'Gara was in love with Will Ferris, were only putting on an act, and in five minutes, if they had a notion to, they'd be panting after somebody else. That wasn't a prejudice. Cormac didn't prejudge homos, for the simple reason that since the beginning of time commonsense had always passed the same verdict on them: if you were queer you were always going to be found guilty. You had to pity the poor pansies, but, sweet arse of Jesus, they were always looking for notice, like that prick Will Ferris. It was the same with Maeve french-kissing dykes in The Pod and even the lesbo stuff she said to provoke him in bed: it was only for show, aimed at the audience. But there was other stuff she did that she didn't talk about, stuff that was private, which was aimed — where? Was it aimed inwards or outwards, or was there some other direction between out and in? Some other ditch, some other bog?

These tangled thoughts were as close to abstraction as Cormac could get. That is to say, not even close — except for the ditch and the bog. By now, two pints and two Jamesons later, the LSD he had swallowed, mistaking it for a Valium, had begun to take over from the alcohol and decaying ecstasy in his brain, and where he found himself, without knowing it, was a kind of ditched and scrubby bogland, brown as the mahogany bar-counter which, without knowing he was doing it, he was staring at. This low-skyed and high-horizoned landscape was twilit, stormy, yet windless. He was staggering, one stiff leg dragging, through dense thickets of dwarf bushes. Dwarf-willow, dwarf-birch. The bushes had tiny shiny olive-silver leaves the size of a fingernail on a very little little finger. Millions of them, millions of little-finger fingernails.

'Wow,' he said, and his little wow was a little laugh.

Then he was remembering the who-who wail of the ambulance carrying Vanessa up Waterloo Road and the look on Harry's face. He had turned away, left Harry on his own without a word and gone back into the flat.

There, sitting on the couch goggling at *Neighbours* on the goggle-box, was Thomas the Tinkerboy.

No, it couldn't have been that day because the kid had scarpered with the Marietta biscuits before the ambulance had gone. Which irritated Cormac, as this kid always did. You could hardly turn around with seeing him sitting there like a Rumanian leprechaun. So on this occasion, whenever it was, Cormac had said to him impatiently, 'For Christ's sake, where's your father?'

Thomas answered, 'My fadder is died.'

'What?'

'My fadder is died. But my modder got a new stereo.'

A stereo?'

'And a radio.'

For the number of words spoken consecutively by Thomas this might not have been a record, but it was the most Cormac had ever heard from him. Usually his speech was toneless, maybe because of his harelip. Now the tone indicated that he understood that while a new stereo might not make up for having a dead father, the addition of a radio was compensation galore.

Yes, that had been another day. On the day he was thinking of there was no broken-ribbed Vanessa Banim hurtling through the streets in an ambulance, deaf to its wooing. Then, while Thomas was watching the TV, Cormac had crossed the bog-brown expanse of the shabby Turkish carpet to the kitchen, and there he saw, quick as a slurred click of the white-faced electric clock on the wall above their heads, three women.

The central figure in the tableau, which instantly dissolved, was Missy, Thomas's sister. She was standing straight, except for her head, which was tilted slightly to one side, as if interrogatively. Her almond eyes, beneath heavily mascaraed eyelids, were looking back in the direction from which her head was tilted. In the direction it was tilted towards, on Missy's left side, was Mazee, Thomas's mother. She was gazing in the same direction as her giant daughter — at Maeve. If there could be said to be any expression on Maeve's face, it was one of sternness. But these eye-exchanges were seen by Cormac only momentarily. What his fast-shuttering stare was instantly drawn to was Maeve's right hand. The hand was fixed on the dome of Missy's left breast. Whether the breast was being lightly moulded, or gripped tightly, or clawed and turned fiercely he couldn't say, in part because the freeze-frame was instantly unfrozen, and in part because the hand's lightness, or heaviness, or activity, or inactivity, was made vague by being sunk in the fluffiness of Missy's jumper, the pile of which had been compiled out of some kind of industrial wool, a frizzlingly lemon-coloured fake angora.

Cormac's mouth was dry.

On the mahogany counter stood his stout glass, empty but for a bog-pool scurf of yellow foam on the bottom. Inches away, miles away, was a glass of water. Reaching for it he knocked over the stout glass.

The barman was browned off having to put up yet another drug-freaked young fella hardly three or four years older than his own son talking to himself. He would give his boy a good clip on the ear if he went the way this desperado was going. And on a Monday night too.

'That's enough for you, avic,' the barman said. In Irish 'avic' is the sound 'a mhic' makes, a vocative that means 'O son'.

In the fingers of one hand he gathered up the unbroken stout glass, the whiskey glass and the water glass with two nerve-scraping *gsrecqs*. Then he dumped them, with one nerveless *ggddsh*, into the dishwasher, safely.

Cormac, startled, stared. The barman had a yellow eye. Just like the statue of the herm in the postcard. Torn in four, that god was now mouldering in the dump at Ballyogan, or whatever dump the black-sacked rubbish of Waterloo Road mouldered in.

Maeve had, of course, not denied that she had, yet again, allowed herself to be fucked by Ultan McGrath.

It had happened when Cormac was back in hospital. How could she deny it when the bastard badger had left his trail behind him? Under the bed. A hat. A green felt hat with a feather sticking up out of the hatband, which Cormac, a week out of the Mater, hunting for his boxer shorts, had found in the dust. And lying beside it, like a message from some dusty hell of dried seed, a condom. Knotted. Who else but Ultan McGrath would take the time to knot a condom?

Cormac rang Maeve at work. She said, 'It's none of your business what I do in my private life.'

How could she say that now that they were engaged to be married? The engagement, she said, was a joke; both of them were jarred at the time. She hissed this, not venomously like a snake, but because someone was coming into her office. Then she had hung up. And thereafter her mobile went straight to voicemail.

'Hello, hello, hello.'

Maeve was a whore. Goodbye to her and goodbye to Waterloo Road and goodbye to the whole shebang of love. She was a ride. And he would tell her so. He'd write her a note and put it in an envelope with the used condom and leave it on her bedside table. No, no, he'd deliver it personally to the Attorney General's Office. Addressed to: Maeve MacNamee Slut Slag and Solicitor. He rampaged around the bedroom looking for paper to write on and hit his shin on a chair. It was while he was lying on the bed trying not to writhe in agony — because writhing was worse agony — that he emptied out his inside pocket and saw, amid the raggedy slab of unpaid bills, the postcard of the Herm. As he extracted it, a suspicion of the truth touched him, as faint on his fingertips as a nipple of bronze under a mile of lemon-coloured angora. He stared at the picture. The truth stood proud the way the balls bulged out of the dead flat bronze. Of course! The sham in the card was the spitting image of Ultan. Except that the Herm's beard was thicker, they were dead ringers. The whole thing had been a cruel joke.

'You want to make a show of me in front of the whole world,' he said. All of two days had passed and most of Saturday. Then she had rung and he had come around to Waterloo Road in a taxi.

'What the hell are you on about?' Maeve said. 'They look nothing like each other.' But she had to admit to herself that the Herm and Ultan did indeed look alike.

'Everybody is laughing up their sleeves at me,' he said.

'Cormie, baby, you're crazy.' It was the diminutive, which had been last used by Vanessa, that led to the postcard being torn up.

'You've done it now,' Maeve said.

'You did it out of spite, just to spite me, just like you....'

'Just like I what?'

He had been going to say 'just like you felt up that knacker', but he had stopped short because his fury was not, then, without limits. Hope was the limit. And it always would be, because, as Maeve well knew, the horn is always hopeful. And eventually — later that night — she did get him to finish the sentence. Because he could not make out her face in the sexual dark and because she never denied anything, he believed her denial. He was, she said, out of his cotton pickin' mind to think such a thing. Anyway, it wasn't Missy she fancied; it was Mazee, the mother. But that was a joke Maeve didn't pursue further — she'd already gone too far in going too far. Any further provocation might have led him to wonder how come she knew without asking who 'that knacker' was.

Lucky for me, she thought, Cormac is slow on the uptake.

But it did occur to him now in this bar he didn't know the name of. The flash of the revelation was momentary, though. There were too many other flashes firing through the synapses of his brain for any follow-on questions.

He might also have asked why she hadn't asked who the everybodies were who were laughing up their sleeves at him. She didn't have to ask. The news had spread rapidly through Government Buildings. Luckily, when it happened it was lunchtime and the office that Ultan shared with two Clerical Assistants was occupied by him alone. For that reason what everybody was talking about was only the end of the story. Maeve knew the start and the middle too, because Ultan had rung immediately to tell her.

'He just opened the door, stuck his head in and, do you know what he did?'

'No.'

'He threw my hat at me.'

'Your what?'

'My hat. He threw my own hat at me. You know, the Alpine one. With the feather? I bought it in Vienna.'

'Really?'

'Yes. In a hat shop off the Ringstrasse. There was a sale on.'

'You got it cheap,' she said.

But Ultan, not getting the joke, said, 'I can't remember. It was three years ago. But I was attached to that hat, you know, and I was relieved to get it back, so I just said thanks. It never occurred to me there was going to be trouble about it.'

'A lot of things don't occur to you.'

'I know, I know.' Ultan lowered his voice, unnecessarily in the empty office, 'That hash blew my mind. I'm going to have to give it up.'

'Ultan, get back to the hat.'

'Well. I'm not used to this kind of thing, you know. I'm not used to having people waving their walking sticks at me and warning me to keep my snout out of their business. Those were his precise words. Well, I can tell you, the penny dropped then.'

'Did it?'

'It did. I realised the hat was at the back of it. He must have found the blessed thing in Waterloo Road and put two and two together. Do you get my drift?'

'Mmmm. So what did you say?'

'Well, I said, this really isn't the time or the place to discuss this particular subject. And do you know what he called me?'

'No.'

'A four-letter word beginning with C.'

'I know the word you mean.'

'Well, I said, I don't think that language is appropriate in the circumstances. On top of which it's inaccurate.'

'That's a persuasive argument.'

'I agree, but it didn't work with Cormac I'm sorry to say. He used more of the same kind of abusive language. Words beginning with F and B. But he was really quite incoherent. And just then, what should happen but the door opens and who walks in only Sheila.'

'Who?'

'Sheila Loughnane, my Principal Officer. Haven't I told you about her?'

'I don't think so.'

'She's a very interesting person. Her PhD is in statistics from Harvard and she's done some amazing work on the distribution of —'

'Ultan, Ultan.'

'Yes?'

'It's immaterial where she got her doctorate. What I'm interested in is did Cormac say anything.'

'To her? To Sheila? No. Why would he?'

'Did he mention me? Did he use my name? That's what I want to know.'

'Your name? Oh, I see what you mean. No, no, I don't think so. I understand your concerns. But no, I don't think he mentioned you. In fact, on reflection, I'm certain of it.'

'So what *did* he say?'

'Well —'

'Well what?'

'Well, he called me a blankety-blank badger.'

'A what?'

'A fucking badger. Oh yes, and he said I should stick my hat where the monkey stuck his blankety-blank nuts. It was very embarrassing. Sheila was mortified.'

'Pity about her. So, was that it?'

'Yes, but when he went out, he slammed the door so hard behind him the whole building shook.'

'Christ.'

Given a choice between bone-pain and paranoia, Cormac would probably have chosen the pain. At this stage of this night, though, his paranoia was, like the effects of the acid, in its infancy. The notion that the entire civil service was chuckling over his cuckolding was, for loudness, less loud than the slurred click of the electric clock in Maeve's kitchen.

One way or another all his delusions related to his jealousy. But realities that were not at all delusory were also snapping at his sore heel. Hard to explain to himself, they were impossible to explain to others.

In Nelson Street, for instance, a tap had leaked all winter, but when the plumber came to fix it, the fool — a Dublin Jackeen of course, not a proper Pole — had insisted that a replacement washer could not be bought anywhere for love or money.

'They haven't made these things,' he said, 'since Noah's Ark was a rowing boat. You'll have to get a whole new tap. And would you look at the state of these pipes, they're as old as Methusalem.' To prove the point, he had given the pipe a tap with his spanner and it had fractured, and, because the fool had forgotten to turn off the mains, water had spouted all over the flat.

This work was going to cost money upfront. The landlord wanted a written estimate. In the meantime the water would have to be cut off. Cormac had spent a week ferrying buckets of water from a standpipe in the indescribable Gehenna out the back of the house. By the time the plumber returned, the yard had flooded, and while the standpipe was being fixed, some kind of vacuum had been created which sucked mud and gravel up into the tank in the attic, and as a result gravelly mud had exploded out of the taps, and then ceased to flow at all. The plumber had promised he would fix it as soon as he got back from his holidays — a fortnight in a place he called 'Lanzarohe' — but on the plane home he had suffered a deep-vein thrombosis and retired to recuperate at an apartment he owned in Kusadasi, Turkey. Another plumber had then been employed and he had fixed the tank, but no one had told him about Cormac's washer problem. The tap remained unfixed still.

At work, too, there were un-understandable problems. Cormac had been summoned to the office of the ancient in charge of Human Resources, a Higher Executive Officer called Tadhg. (The 'a' is pronounced like the 'i' in 'thigh'; the 'hg' makes the same sound as the 'g' in 'gig'; and the 'd' in the middle, like the 't' in Lanzarote, if you are a Dubliner, is silent.) Cormac could not grasp why, although he was there on foot of a complaint relating to Dr Sheila Loughnane — not made by her personally, but by the Association of Higher Civil Servants — Tadhg had made no further reference to the door-slamming incident. He had gone on and on about the absence of a sick-leave certificate for the afternoon Cormac had skived off with the Latvian or Lithuanian or whatever the fuck nationality that minger was. Plus he had not yet supplied certs for his recent stay in the Mater. Nettled by Tadhg emphasising 'stay' as if it were a holiday in the Canary Islands, Cormac had said, 'For fuck's sake, I was having my fucking leg shortened.' That kind of language had caused Tadhg to purse his lips. He had then raised the matter of a sensitive file (the Finance Act 2005, Miscellaneous Provisions, Stamp Duty, Proposed Amendments) that had been marked out to Cormac by the Registry, which was now missing. This was potentially a serious threat to the financial security of the State. Finally, Tadhg said, he had received a report that a member of the public, a distinguished property developer, who happened also to be a personal friend of the Minister, had come upon an officer stripped to the waist, shaving himself in the departmental lavatory.

At the end of the meeting Tadhg had referred to 'your probationary period'. Some days later Cormac suddenly understood this to mean he was on probation. Why? For what? What had he done? He didn't know. But he had begun to develop an awareness, at once dully woolly and razor keen, of one of the most horrible truths of existence: shit not only happens but it is chain-linked. There were shitty links between the perished rubber ring of a washer, the noise of gravel in a lead pipe, the bronze balls of a Grecian herm, the sick-leave regulations of the civil service, the feathered hat of a fucking fool, and a quick shave in a Department of Finance lavatory. With a glob of soap globbed out from the departmental dispenser. Reddish-purplish soap. Like something exuded from a necrotic leg. Not to mention the frizzly lemon of industrial angora. They were all connected one to the other in sequence.

But why?

The why of it all was that fucker Ferris. Without Will there would be no Ultan. No second-hand Stillorgan piano carted up five flights of mud-coloured stairs in Leeson Street. No sitting listening to Cory Leary referring to Ferris as 'the boy'. And Maeve, nice as pie, pretending she was talking about Thomas. Oh, sorry. Asking was her name really Cory or was it Cora. And then, when the flustered girl was saying she was sick listening to Will singing the same songs over and over again, Maeve had said, 'Poor little Cora, my heart bleeds for you.' Giving a little frightened laugh, Cory had said, 'Oh, I'm not complaining really.' And Maeve said, 'Sure we know that, pet, don't we?', and Cormac said, 'Yeah,' though he hadn't a notion in a bog what it was he knew. Then, as they were leaving, Maeve had kissed Cory, really nicely, saying, 'All this and an electric piano too. Aren't you the lucky woman?'

Driving off in the Volkswagen, Cormac had said, 'She never even asked did we have a mouth on us.'

To this Maeve had replied, 'She doesn't drink. But I bet she wishes she did now.'

Cormac didn't mind Cory. She was all right, nothing to write home about. He couldn't see what Maeve was in such a snit for. Maybe she was annoyed by the flat. It was just so show-offy, just like the ferret Ferris himself, with neat stacks of CDs and books everywhere, the table set out with pens and pencils in jars, and a pile of lined sheets for music, as if Will was a real composer instead of what Emmet Roche said he was, 'a sham with a banjo'. Plus the place was sparklingly clean, the bottles were gone, there was some kind of a big white coarse linen thing, a throw, thrown over the tattered couch, and new red and white check curtains on the window, and a vase of fresh flowers, white freesias, on the windowsill. None of this was Will of course. It was all Cory. Which was another reason for Maeve ripping the shit out of her, because Waterloo Road was like a cave you burrowed into, grand and warm with the glowing red of the gas fire and the yellow light of the standard lamp. But draw the curtains in the morning and it looked like the inside of a whore's handbag and smelled like an unswept pub after a tinker wedding.

All the same, the old-fashioned advertisement for soft drinks that Maeve had found in a bric-a-brac shop and sent to Cory anonymously through the post was definitely going too far. It wasn't funny ha-ha; it was funny peculiar. The advertisement showed a sweetie with big tits in a 1920s swimsuit simpering over the legend:

Little Nora
Cordials and Squashes

Nora was Cora was Cory. Would she get it? Maeve said she'd love to see her face when she opened the envelope. Cordial little Cory. Squashed! *Tssss*.... Like the air escaping out of a balloon.

Tssss wasn't the sound Cormac's fist made when it went through the window in Waterloo Road. That was a *Kerrack*! But as he withdrew the fist there was a *tssss*, no, less a *tssss* than a twang, inaudible but imaginable in the ear, as the glass severed a tendon at the base of his thumb. And the road wasn't even Waterloo. It was Raglan. But why he was there Cormac couldn't explain, not to the irate residents, not to the police from Harcourt Terrace, not to the ambulance men, not to the Accident and Emergency staff at St Vincent's Hospital. Nor the next morning to the Dublin District Court either. But the judge gave him the benefit of the Probation Act.

34

EMMET ROCHE COULD not conceive of joy except as the offspring of anguish. This baby might be fathered in the usual way — there was no doubt about that part of it — but it had to be motherless, or the mother had to be not present at the birth, away from the manger. That was a lot to ask. The contradiction stood in the middle of his road to joy like a block of concrete, man-sized, and he was bound to crash into it, and invariably did, usually as soon as he had set out. But the blockage also had a practical function. It worked as a yardstick, a standard of comparison, like the holding up of the curved spatula of his huge thumb to measure an object he was engaged in painting. If the object was, say, the brute, the lamp in his studio, the blockage stopped him being blinded by the light. Of course, if he held the thumb too close to the bulb, it burned. But that kind of pain could be useful, and indeed he had made use of it while he was painting his 'Naked Light' series. Four of the series had been shown in a gallery in Pimlico, a part of Dublin largely unknown to anyone not living there. The gallery was small, a kind of hallway, and because the pictures were big, it was impossible to stand back to look at them.

'Suits me,' Emmet said. 'Just what I want.'

The only review of the show had appeared in a listings magazine. The critic, a History of Art student, had written that she had never thought paintings so yellow could look so black. That was an interesting observation, and in return Emmet had been interested enough to invite her to his studio. And up the ladder into his sex-nest. She had gone, too. But on being woken in the morning by a flash of light, she had almost leaped through the trapdoor in her hurry to escape.

When Harry was told this story, he said, 'Did you ever hear that old Rolf Harris record, My Boomerang Won't Come Back?'

The quivering critic had been just one of many girls who had climbed the ladder between January and June. But none of them had left behind a relic their host thought worth preserving. Host was the right word. After his failed attempt to return her tissue to Cory, Emmet's relationship with it had changed. It became Religious. It possessed Real Presence. Holiness adhered to it. Even in texture it was not unlike the disk of papery-tasting material that changes from bread to bleeding body at the Mass. But Emmet had never given any thought to the meaning of sacrifice, though in snatching back the tissue from Cory he had perhaps come close to the meaning of it.

As well as with transubstantiation, Emmet had a blind spot with painting. He couldn't budge beyond the technical. Technique was something Will Ferris was also grappling with. While both of them had Luddite tendencies — Will hated phones and Emmet (at the end of the day) hated electric light — their attitude to less actual machinery was directly contrary. The main machine of difference was influence. Will's instinct, which he knew was absurd, was to not let influence work on him at all. He resisted it. For Emmet, though, the influencing machine was galvanic: his frog would not twitch without it. Like many painters older than himself, he was wired to Pablo Picasso, or to that Picasso for whom violence and tenderness run side-by-side, Siamese twins joined at the hip by anxiety. But Emmet, anxious to avoid letting the influence show, said that Picasso wasn't really a painter at all; he was a sculptor who moved colour around in blocks. To be seen properly, these blocks had to be at least an arm's length from the eye, and the more the viewer was disconnected from them, the better they worked.

It was a bit like looking at buildings — up close, say a nose away, they vanished. But never mind the nose. What about the length of a big prick? That was the way to engage with paint. Stick it in and stir it around. Get in close. Get in tight. That was what Jackson Pollock had exploited. Forget the fact, Emmet said, that some of the stuff 'the Yankee dauber' painted was twenty feet long. Standing back you saw the smallness of him — at a distance all he did was diagrams for dance steps. You saw him best up close — in, say, a hallway in Pimlico. Then the paint swamped your peripheral vision; there were no edges left or right. The way out was the way in.

'You lay it on a bit thick, don't you,' Will had said, peering at a sun-spot in the yellow hell of a Naked Light painting propped against a wall in Emmet's studio. This was towards the end of his unjealous visit in search of the portrait of Cory.

Emmet had replied, 'I hate thinness.'

'Is that a fact?'

Emmet, who had an unerring instinct for causing offence, said, 'Thinness is for niggers. Anorexia is for Ethiopians. I have no intention of starving to death. In fact, when I die, I want to be buried in paint, buried up to my bollix in it.'

'You'll come to a sticky end, my boy,' Will said.

But by the time the subject of being buried next came up, a great deal had changed in Emmet's style.

Almost every form of contemporary art, especially if was in any way conceptual, annoyed him. However, the kind of stuff Leonard Rivers did — huge teacups and heroic insects — did not annoy him in the slightest. The concept was so slight and the images so superficial, as slick as the shiny paper they were printed on, they amused him. You had to hand it to Leonard, though, because, despite his pansy locks and his pansy theories, he didn't mind being told his hair and ideas were pansy bollocks.

'Do you know what your trouble is?' Emmet asked him one day in the NCAD cafeteria.

'What?'

'You lay it on a bit thin,' Emmet said, and laughed.

'Ho ho,' Leonard said.

'The sort of stuff you do, it's got no depth. No blood. No life. It's art for zombies. There's no cunt in it. You've got to have cunt in your work.'

'Thank you for sharing that insight with me,' Leonard said.

'That's OK. I'm just trying to be helpful. You see, what you're doing is shite. Flat shite too. Just like this art-magazine arse-paper here. Look at it. A shiny fake Vermeer photograph. Vermeer with varnish on it. I could do this in my sleep, Leonardo, even if I took a ton of Valium before I went to bed.'

Emmet was mistaken, but not wrong. In the copy of *Flash Art* he was flapping at Leonard, what looked like a photograph of a young woman with a hoop earring was actually a painting by Gerhard Richter. No matter, Emmet said; it was still only a cheap photo-realist trick. Leonard then bet one of his own photographs that he couldn't do it. What! Not only could Emmet do it, he would get the result shown in that Cathedral of Conservatism, the annual exhibition of the Royal Hibernian Academy. Which he did.

There were other changes, though, that had to happen first.

Emmet hated the police. This was not surprising. His mother's family had fought on the anti-Treaty side in 1922 and in 1969 they had walked out of the Mansion House with the faction that was to become the Provisional IRA. Peace Process or no Peace Process, the cops were lackeys of the Free State.

On his father's side the hatred of the police was less political but it had eventually proved more costly. In the early 1990s Mr Roche had augmented his income from his butcher's shop by selling Angel Dust to local farmers. Although the feeding of this hormone to beef cattle was legal in the United States, it was illegal in Ireland, largely because no one in the European Union would eat Irish hamburgers if they were reared on the same principle as Arnold Schwarzenegger. For that reason the gardaí, armed with a search warrant, had rampaged through the Roche family home one dark winter's night and found the Angel Dust stashed under Emmet's bed. Emmet had kicked a Detective Sergeant on the shin and called him a 'Blueshirt bastard', though he had no idea who the Blueshirts were (a neo-fascist gang of bully-boys in the 1930s, or anti-communist defenders of democracy, depending on your upbringing). The Detective Sergeant had given Emmet a clip on the ear and called him 'an impudent little brat', which wasn't accurate as far as 'little' was concerned: this thirteen-year-old was big and he had monstrously big feet and he was wearing big hobnailed boots. But his mother had screamed blue murder. She had rung the *Limerick Leader*, which newspaper had quoted her to the effect that the gardaí were more brutal than the Gestapo. When Lily repeated this opinion in court it had not helped her husband's defence: the judge had fined him £30,000. That was a lot of Angel Dust, and paying it had impoverished Emmet's teenage years.

But politics didn't interest him. Nor did money — the Apollo Gallery had sold only one of the prints, and he could not make up his mind whether he was pleased or annoyed when he learned Maeve had bought it as a present for Cormac after he had severed the tendon in his thumb. By then Emmet's own injury, the hand he had cut butchering the sheep, had been so long healed, it didn't occur to him or to Cormac to remark on the coincidence. Nor had it occurred to them, until Harry pointed it out, that their injuries were not dissimilar to Vanessa's.

'Big deal,' Emmet said. A connection between three cut hands had about as much substance as the notion that there are three persons in one god. It was a ball of smoke. Of course smoke, unlike god, actually existed. In comparison to god, it was definitely there, it was as real as the cloud of spores a rotten toadstool puffs out, each spore of which could form itself into another little mushroom, the whole ball of them clumping together and growing ecstatically into a luminescent ghostly shadow.

Just like the one on the X-ray of his mother's lung.

In September Lily had gone to her GP complaining of tiredness and breathlessness. Because these symptoms were not associated with weight loss, the sawbones had decided that what she was suffering from was fatness and paleness and prescribed exercise and iron tablets. In mid-February Lily had managed to mishear what she was told by her consultant and to convince herself that, probably due to an influx of foreign nationals into Limerick, she had contracted tuberculosis, a mild strain amenable to being cured by antibiotics.

> *It's a hot slow consumption.*
> *Killing you by degrees.*

Without being aware of the coincidence, Will Ferris had sung that blues by Sleepy John Estes in the Baggot Inn. It was yet another reason for Emmet to hate him.

Even during chemotherapy, Lily had contrived to keep up her conviction that she had TB, or maybe an associated pneumonia. Her family had no stomach for telling her the truth. The chemo tired her out and she often went to bed in the daytime, watching television, reading Robert Ludlum, smoking long black cigarillos, and falling asleep. Emmet had taken to going home every weekend. While he was there, his brothers made themselves scarce, and his father removed himself to the shed in the yard, where he marshalled his cures for scour, hoose, warble fly and other diseases of animals. These medicines were legal, fully patented, or had patents pending.

Emmet being left on his own in the house with Lily was not unlike pelting down the highway in the middle of which stood the block of concrete he called joy. Fortunately, his own room, downstairs, was far away from hers. There he worked on the painting that was going to teach Leonard Rivers a lesson. It was small, 'a bloody mantelpiece picture'. Carrying it up and down on the train had influenced not just the size but also the medium: instead of oils, he was using quick-drying acrylics. Another kind of dryness benefited him: no inspiration was required. This was non-gestural work. No thick splodge straight from the tube was needed or called for, no quick drip, no sudden flick of the wrist so that the tip of the impasto leaned over slowly, not as stiff as a meringue or as soft as Miracle Whip, but more toothsome than either. This rigid Richter way of painting in glazes, with brushes as fine as the fluff on the belly of a mongoose, with not a bit of loose scumbling to amuse yourself with — you could do it in your sleep. In fact you couldn't do it any other way. 'Paint without paint.' That was one of Leonard's Zen Buddhist bullshit rules. Bloody pansy Brit. But one thing was true: you could paint this way without thinking about it, yet while you did it, you could blank out everything else in your head. Almost.

Almost because, when he did have to go upstairs — she banged on the floor with her shoe or rang him on his mobile — Lily was bound to annoy him. She would start telling him in fine detail the plot of her latest brick of a book, wander off into a memory of meeting her husband in Kennington Park in London, and then by some hidden chain of associations — was it because the Oval cricket ground was nearby? — start telling him things he didn't want to know about ovarian diseases, then arrive at a whine on the menopause, on hot flushes, on being an old biddy at the age of fifty-three when your life was hardly half over. And then she was off on a rant about what the English had done to Ireland, because the episode of *Fawlty Towers* that featured an Irish builder was a slur on the people who built their bloody country for them. Who was it played the part? He was very good. But thin as a rake. Apparently skinny women didn't get as many hot flushes as fat ones. At least she wasn't plump now.

'David Kelly, that's who it was,' Lily said. 'I love David Kelly. He's a gentleman, but he's too skinny.'

The room, as well as stinking of smoke, was littered with litter. It was as bad as his studio. Worse in fact, because Lily had a longer career in accumulation.

'For Christ's sake,' Emmet said, 'look at this.'

He had opened the door of the wardrobe in search of the family album that contained the photograph of him in his First Communion blue suit with the long-tailed white rosette on the lapel, and an avalanche of shoes tumbled out of it.

'Look at what?' Lily asked. On the television at the end of the bed an ancient repeat of *Neighbours* had started. She had long nurtured an animosity against one of the characters, a constantly hard-done-by fat man with glasses.

'It's ridiculous,' Emmet said.

'I know,' Lily said. 'Nothing ever happens to him. Why can't he be knocked down by a bus or something?'

'What are you watching that crap for?'

'I like the tune.'

'It's crap.'

'But I miss Kylie.'

'What?'

'Kylie Minogue. She got it too and she never smoked a cigarette in her life.'

This was the first time Lily indicated that she knew. Sitting on the floor surrounded by unfashionable footwear, Emmet said, 'What the fuck do you want forty pairs of shoes for?'

'Don't swear, Emmet.'

But Emmet said, 'It's fucking criminal.' Then he took the shoes downstairs and spent the rest of the evening polishing them till they shone.

His brothers thought he was mad, but then he'd always been odd that way, and the oddest of all the signs of his madness was his art. Mickeleen was the least scornful, not because he was tolerant but because, being older than Emmet by ten years, he regarded all his doings as childish. The painting nonsense was real mammy's boy stuff, like a kid sitting on the floor and splothering his own crap on the wall. Emmet was a queer kind of a yahoo all right, but at least on the National Question he was sound as a pound.

Actually, Emmet thought the National Question — whatever else it was, a united Ireland wasn't a question — and all other forms of politics were beneath contempt. Like his mock-Gerhard Richter painting.

'It isn't worth a roasted snowball,' he said to Leonard Rivers on Varnishing Day at the RHA Annual Exhibition in the Gallagher Gallery.

'Well, I think it's terribly good,' Leonard said. He had just returned from putting a blue Not For Sale dot beside the photograph Emmet had chosen as his prize for winning their bet.

'Of course it's good,' Emmet said. 'It's the best thing in the entire show, but that doesn't mean it's good.'

'Who's the girl?' Leonard asked.

'I can't remember,' Emmet said. There was a sense in which this could have been true: he might have forgotten whose rounded hipbone this was, whose delicately cross-hatched patch of pubic hair, whose softly under-muscled flesh, whose skin, the palest of pearly blues and dawn-ruddied pinks, whose dusty pink nipples, slightly puckered from the cold — he might have forgotten because in painting them it had been as if each of the features of the body had personality and the owner of it none. This body belonged to no one in particular; it was nameless, pure, uninfluenced corporeal being. But of course he did remember whose flesh it was, and why all that could be seen of her face was through her splayed fingers. The hand had been raised in a defensive gesture against the flash he had photographed her by while she was asleep in the dawn's early light. But the way she reacted you'd have thought she'd been shot not with his Nikon but with a Kalashnikov.

Emmet went home early. Not because he minded being praised by a number of Academicians, including Patrick Pye, a kind of shaggy-bearded biblical anchorite, who said the painting was 'spiritually terrible'. Since Pye painted religious subjects in a Byzantine style but after the manner of El Greco (which was weird, like prophesying the past), Emmet had taken the remark as a compliment. Nor did he go home because the wine had to be paid for — with hundreds of exhibitors flocking to the Varnishing Day, buckshee drink was out of the question. No, he went because he had to catch the first train to Limerick in the morning and someone called Kevin was staying the following night in the studio and the key had to be left at a pub in the North Strand for him to pick up.

After Cory had sat for her portrait, Emmet had made no attempt to contact her. He dreaded something. The dread was worse because the cure for it was Cory, but that meant the cure was the disease. Eventually, after a week he had rung her. If it had been five, even six days later, it might not have mattered. But letting the week go by was the killer. So was making the call in the morning. Durrr-dur, durrr-dur, durrr-dur. Before she could answer he had had to rush out to the primitive jacks in the yard and shit an explosion. Oh joy! Oh pain!

Another week passed and then he rang again. When she said 'Hello', he hung up. His tongue was wooden and would not utter. Had he given her his number? He couldn't remember. Number remember remember number. His numbed brain would not allow him to. But she must have known it was him because his name would have come up on her screen. So he had changed his phone settings to private. And waited for her to call. An hour, two hours. A day, two days. On the third day he rang again and again heard her voice.

'Hello. Hello. Hello. Can you hear me?'

For an instant he felt otherworldly. It was like praying in reverse: he wasn't launching a plea into outer space; outer space was pleading with him. He was God the Receiver. Might he be the Answer to her Prayers? His answer to that hopeful question was to thumb-jab the End Call button.

But though it was a joy-pain, ringing Cory could only be indulged in sparingly. He had once called at three o'clock in the morning just to hear her speak from her sleep. But she had said, 'Please leave me alone, whoever you are.' Whoever you are? Whoever he was, he felt ashamed. So he had stopped calling. As god had done with the world, he left her alone.

None of this meant that he didn't see her every now and then. In the ordinary way they met and spoke, but always in company. Cory didn't socialise much. She came, collected Will, and went.

One evening in April — the first evening it was warm enough to sit at the tables outside the Bailey in Duke Street — as she watched the pair disappear into the crowd, Maeve said, 'They don't run with our gang, do they? They're not one of us.'

'He acts like he was doing you a favour,' Cormac said. 'Meeting that prick is like meeting with an accident.'

'You'd know about accidents,' Maeve snapped. She had mistakenly taken his 'you' to mean herself, who was unfavoured.

When Emmet arrived back from Limerick on the Monday, he got a call from Leonard Rivers. Why had he sloped off so early? Didn't he know the RHA had awarded him a thousand euro prize? It was a new award, funded by the collectors Victor and Rachel Treacy, for the best painting by a first-time exhibitor.

Emmet spent a good part of the day ringing people to tell them what the idiots in the Academy had done now. Why not come to the opening? Apparently it was a huge scrum of middle-class wankers, a bit like the Oscars in Hollywood, and in his speech he'd tell them that, by Jesus he would.

There were, in fact, no speeches. Nor was there any prize giving. And the only man in a tuxedo was Emmet. But he didn't mind sticking out like a burned thumb. Actually, he was pleased — the tuxedo was a kind of satirical thing to do: a real artist in a monkey suit thumbing his nose at the unreal apes of the RHA. Ossie had given him the idea: because of the ripped armpits he had been obliged to buy the tux Will had worn at Farmleigh House. It fitted Emmet better too — he wasn't deformed, a pigeon-chested banjo-plucker. And to point up the mockery, Ossie had finished off the ensemble with a long white chiffon scarf.

'You look very nice,' Cory said on the opening night. It was Monday and Will was singing in the Baggot, so Harry, her babysitter, had persuaded her to come with him.

'Absolutely fabulous,' Ernesto de Mahon said.

'Write it down,' Harry said vaguely. He was looking at Emmet's painting. The gesture of the hand hiding the naked woman's face reminded him of something, but he couldn't think what.

'You look fabulous too,' Emmet said to Cory.

'Thanks,' she said. 'Congratulations on the prize.'

'It's you that deserves it. I mean the congratulations. You got qualified I hear. You're a real doctor now.'

'No, it's only the first part.'

'You'll get the second part, no problem. And the third and the fourth.'

Emmet was exalted. It was easy to speak to admirers. Prizes brought you prizes. That was how success worked. Something else, perfectly ordinary but magically appropriate, would come out of his mouth next. He just knew it. So, he sensed, did Cory. She was wearing a very feminine suit, not very doctorly, and her newly cut hair, short, thick, the colour of a golden mouse, shone with health, as did her water-dotted skin, and the whites of her eyes were shining too. So he wasn't happy to be distracted by Harry tugging his sleeve and saying, 'Do you see what I see?'

'Good Christ!' Emmet said. 'This is unreal.'

But the red dot beside the painting was real. To keep off the bourgeoisie, he had priced it at an outrageous five thousand euro. But they had not been kept off. And the painting had been bought not just by any passing architect with a blank space over his sofa. No, the buyer was a billionaire builder of apartment blocks with a seat on the Board of the Irish Museum of Modern Art. It was Ernesto who found this out, but he had to go to Doheny and Nesbitt's with the news because by then Emmet was in the back snug drinking champagne with Cory and the damage had already been done.

Doing the damage had taken only the few minutes Harry had spent on the other side of the road in the Baggot Inn telling Maeve and Cormac to come, quick. But Will was singing his version of Stephen Foster's 'Oh Susanna' and the stillness of the room could not be broken. Harry thought how startling it was that such a racist ditty could be made to sound so blue.

> I jumped aboard the telegraph,
> And travelled down the river,
> The electric fluid magnified,
> And killed five hundred Nigger,
> The engine bust, the horse run off,
> I really thought I'd die;
> I shut my eyes to hold my breath,
> Susanna, don't you cry.

Just as this was being sung, Emmet was saying 'I think you're just amazing.' He said it not only because he thought it was the very first time in Cory's life that she had ever drunk champagne, but, infinitely more important, that she was doing it just for him. 'A little glass, a mouthful, just for my sake, just for me,' he had said. She didn't say she had more than once drunk champagne with an eminent clinician much older than herself. Those bubbles had given her a rush, as if time was made for rushing through heedlessly, but the pain in her head afterwards, a thin and persistent drone like the tone that whined through the consultant's self-obsessed letters, had dismayed her and for that reason, and for family reasons too of course, she had stopped drinking.

'*Sláinte agus saol,*' Cory said, raising her glass.

Emmet responded, '*Saol fada agus bás in Eireann.*'

For people from families in which the Irish language was respected it was not unnatural to follow a toast of 'Health and life' with a wish for 'A long life and death in Ireland'. The wish was a reminder of the Great Hunger when a million people had starved to death or died of the fever and another million had emigrated — in those days expiring of old age at home in your own house was worth wishing for, if unlikely. Things had changed since then. These days people were less interested in dying than they were in dieting. But in the opinion of some thinkers, the appropriately named John Waters for one, the memory of the Famine has been repressed, and the repression, a huge psychic bruise, has defined the character of the Irish people ever since. The hurt, in the opinion of Tim Pat Coogan, a thinker bulkier than water, was inflicted by the British people, or, more generously, by their ruling class, bureaucracy and government, a sizeable gang. They had used the failure of the potato crop to commit a deliberate act of genocide. The disaster had produced in the Irish soul such a bewildering variety of textures and densities that the character of any individual Irish person is bound to be inconsistent and unpredictable, not to say prone to outbursts of irritation. Even so, what Emmet did after expressing the wish that Cory would die in Ireland was surprising, even to himself. And it so surprised Cory that at first she did not react, except visually: she felt something but she had to look to be sure she was feeling it. Yes, there was no doubt about it: on her thigh, in her lap, was Emmet's enormous right hand. Her widening eyes lifted and locked onto his gleaming granny glasses. In his gaze was a combination of questioning, adoration and triumph and on his lips a smile of lascivious realism, as if to say, 'I hardly need to ask, since we both know we're beasts, but I'll ask anyway: How about me riding the arse off you?'

'Emmet,' Cory said at last.

'Yeah?'

'What do you think you're doing?'

'You're gorgeous,' he said.

'Emmet,' she said, 'take this away.' She lifted the weight of his hand off her leg. It rose quite easily. Emmet did not resist. Rather than resisting, he assisted. He was helpful, he was submissive, as in the very last instant before crashing into the block of concrete, he always submitted. But no sacrifice is perfect without the words to go with it, and Emmet had them.

'I'd like to fuck you,' he said.

'What?' Cory said in a whisper.

'I'd like to fuck you,' Emmet repeated, adding in the one breath, 'until your teeth fall out.'

Emmet was not at all unused to young women, bright ones especially, telling him to get his paws off them. That was part of the game, a stop on the trip, a step in the dance, and often enough not the last one either — he would gleam at them before, and he was pretty sure he would gleam at them after. But Cory laughed. And being laughed at by his ideal woman robbed him of his strength, unmanned him on the spot. This wasn't the usual misfortune, the usual collision with the pre-cast concrete. He could take that, just as, in another sense, he could take a photograph of a naked art historian and, far from being bothered by her reaction, be pleased with it, as if he were an eagle and her hand was a perch he could perch on while he pecked at her eyes, her puckering nipples, her dim pubic patch, her general private downiness. But what he would have done usually — say something even more outrageous — he couldn't do. All he was capable of doing now was staring at Cory, whose head was turned away, for a long number of seconds.

During these seconds, Will, on the other side of the road, was singing about Susanna that 'the buckwheat cake was in her mouth, a tear was in her eye.'

Thinking about the disaster afterwards, Emmet pinned the blame on the language. Instead of saying 'I'd like to fuck you until your teeth fall out,' he had meant to say 'until the fillings in your teeth fall out'. It was just about possible to fuck someone so hard her fillings would loosen. But her actual teeth? That would indicate homicidal force, and death. Or extreme old age. Which was a horrible thought. No, no, it wasn't Cory as a corpse or a crone he was referring to, it was her buck-rabbit front teeth upon which she could only deliberately close her lips. He loved that she couldn't help it. It was what he most loved about her: her helplessness. That tender thought could have saved him a lot of anguish. But Emmet didn't think it for long. Thinking about being saved was not something he did. He was vulcanised against vulnerability.

Anyway, the time it took for Harry to go to the Baggot Inn and to come back with company did not take as long as the explanation of what happened in the interval.

The first of the new arrivals to speak was Maeve. She said, 'It's like a funeral in here.'

Emmet said, 'What?'

She said, 'I thought you'd be dancing on the table.'

Just then Will arrived. At the sight of him, Emmet jumped up, punched both fists at the ceiling and cried, 'I'll give you dancing!'

The emotions that went into this utterance were even more complex than the standing up, the placing of one foot on the stool he'd been sitting on, of the other one on the table, followed by the first, and all without knocking over as much as a glass. That was simple. For emotional complexity Emmet might have been mimicking the raising of Lazarus. Actually, once upon a time, while looking at a painting by some Renaissance pansy, Signorelli maybe, he had imagined what that miraculous event would have been like, in the homeopathically unlikely event of it ever having happened at all. From a dim and frowsty tomb he had imagined a dreepy looking Lazarus emerging slowly into the blue day, blinking at the brutal sun. Emmet had not thought that the logic of this awakening pointed not towards fright but joy. Nor did he think that an old man's nightly terror of soon being dead must not have been the experience of Lazarus revived. To have been a real miracle Lazarus would have sprung into his second death like a baby being born, new and renewed, not whinging but singing, 'Here I go again, I hear those trumpets blow again,' like the Angel Gabriel, courtesy not of Will Ferris but of Latouche, Fetter and Duke, non-fictional songwriters.

Fortunately or unfortunately, none of the staff in Doheny's saw Emmet dancing on the table in the back snug — had they seen him, he would have been barred. Then Ernesto arrived with news of the identity of the billionaire buyer of the painting. More champagne was ordered. Will said to Emmet he was glad for him, genuinely, but he had to go back to the Baggot to sing for his supper. Although his fee had gone up to a hundred euro, that was probably less than the cost of these bottles of bubbly. With a movement of her eyes, Cory indicated that she wanted to go too.

At closing time Emmet went home alone. The night was warm, the sky a velvety black. Everything in his head was fuzzy. He was exalted by his success, infuriated by Will Ferris mocking him, contemptuous of the buyer of the painting. Most of all, though, he was destroyed. He had cocked up with Cory and now he was crestfallen. Those fillings! He could have bitten off his own teeth. Mistakes have themselves as excuses, but he had no excuse. He was worthless. The intensity and novelty of this feeling stopped him on the Matt Talbot Bridge. The soundless Liffey flowed slowly beneath him. Could he unsay what he had said? Could he undo what he had done? Could he go back and start again? No. Like the river, he went on further into the dark. The desolation of where he lived flattened what remained of his spirit. This was a place of oblivion, of abandoned factories and weedy yards. This was development land, a brown field site. It might have a future, but now, like his soul, it had died back on itself.

The street lighting on the quays was poor. The long blank concrete wall behind which he lived was always in shadow. Pierced through it was a short passageway that led to the steel door into his studio. In the pitch dark of the passageway, fumbling for the key that hung from his belt, he felt a presence behind him. There was no sound. But he knew instantly that only the shape of a man could add weight to the shadows in this way.

And as soon as he knew it, he heard a voice. 'OK, Kevin,' it said. 'Don't move.'

35

CORY WAS SILENT in the same way as she went to Mass but didn't pray. If she engaged with people she often did so wordlessly. If she was asked for advice, she was slow to give it. If attacked, she didn't defend herself. As far as sympathetic engagement went, it wasn't a case of always the bridesmaid never the bride. No, she didn't go to the wedding at all. Was she ungenerous then? Maeve MacNamee said she was mean. This puzzled Harry. But he asked himself was there any evidence of Cory ever doing anyone a kindness? Well, the way she had behaved towards Emmet, and not just while his huge hand was laid on her lap, but afterwards, was kindly — she hadn't told anyone. And when she did tell Harry, the following January, nine months later, she did so for a reason: Emmet had come to Leeson Street and said it was OK with him if she spilled the beans to the police. It was something she should do, in fact he begged her do it.

'Beg my barney,' Harry said. 'A blind man on a galloping horse could see that spilling the beans is the last thing he wants. What Emmet wants is the Heinz off the toast and back in the can. Can't be done, can't be done.'

But Cory had not helped the police with their inquiries. Had she been thanked for it? No. Was that mean or what?

Cory's meanness had first come up on one of the few occasions — fewer after the hand in her lap — that she was in Emmet's company. On a night in May when it was again warm enough to sit outside the Bailey, Maeve was saying she was sick of buying drink for Cormac. Why was he always broke? If his bogger friends hadn't blabbered so many lies about who was driving the other car, he would have got the money for his leg long ago. Now, though, he should make certain sure to do better with the severed tendon. It was disgraceful that that ape in Human Resources had threatened him with suspension. Cormac should have slapped an injunction on him for even mentioning it. She'd have done it herself if she wasn't in the Attorney's office; she couldn't shit on her own doorstep.

Harry noticed Cory's slight wincing at the image. So did Maeve, which was yet another reason to stick it to her.

'What's brown and sticky?' she said to Cormac, but not to him.

'What?' he said, but not as an inquiry.

'A stick.'

'What the hell are you talking about?' Cormac said.

'You might not know this, gobshite, but pain and suffering are worth money even when they're your own fault.'

'That's crazy,' Emmet said admiringly, as if struck by an idea that was new to him.

'Yes,' Will said. 'I like it. And while you're at it, you should sue the owner of the house because Albert Einstein here put his fist through his window.' Harry saw Cory narrowing her eyes at Will in warning.

'You'd be surprised what pain and suffering covers,' Maeve said. 'But what we're talking here is Constructive Dismissal.'

'Con is the operative word,' Harry said after he'd listened to the scheme. It was completely off the wall, not at all like Maeve. OK there was a way to bring a case to the Equality Authority if Cormac had been dismissed. But he hadn't even been suspended. He was out on sick leave, wasn't he? Harry could see that Cormac was furious about his leg and his monumental hand, encased in plaster of Paris, being bandied about by Maeve. He resented it almost as much as he hated people pitying him, and her for not pitying him. But it didn't make sense — or did it? — that he would present his medical records and a solicitor's letter to the HR department claiming he had been constructively dismissed.

'I haven't got my medical records,' Cormac said. 'I haven't even got a sick-leave cert.'

'You what?' Maeve said.

'I told you before,' Cormac said. 'My consultant has gone off on his holidays to Ethiopia or some other Third World fucking country.'

'That's no problem,' Maeve said, hooking her hair behind her ears with her thumbs. 'Cory here can write you a cert, can't you, Cory?'

'Hey,' Cormac said, 'that's a brilliant idea. Why didn't I think of that before? It'll get the HR monkey off my back.'

'What's up, doc?' Maeve asked Cory, who had lifted her coffee-cup and sipped from it.

'You're not my patient,' Cory said to Cormac. 'I can't write a cert for you.'

'Oh come on,' Maeve said, not beggingly.

Cory was silent.

Ossie Gleeson said, 'That'd be a breach of medical ethics.'

'Give us a break,' Maeve said to Cory, not beggingly. Cory sipped at her coffee again. Maeve said, laughingly without a laugh, 'Oh Cory, only a saint could be as mean as you are. Anyway, what's the big deal? Any old sawbones will write a bloody sick-cert for us. That's the easy part. The hard part is the crooked solicitor. Where the hell are we going to find one of those?'

At the time Harry was surprised that Will had not reacted to Maeve's cattiness. Perhaps he hadn't heard — Duke Street was crowded with noisy passersby; or maybe he simply hadn't got it — he wasn't feline, he lacked felinity. At any rate the subject had been dropped. That wasn't like Maeve either. Usually she returned to things: she was a bitch with a bone, a cat with the memory of an elephant. But why had she said Cory was as mean as a saint? Saints weren't mean, were they? Saint Sebastian, for instance, always looked like he'd welcome a few more arrows into his marble-white body; to stiffen his resolve or something. Harry, who had gone off sex, put the image of the first gay martyr out of his mind. But Maeve was a schemer; he wouldn't put it past her to have contrived the whole conversation just to get a shot off at Cory. Why? Why did she do it? Because of her obsession with the hero she hated. She'd kill for Will. It was a weird way to be obsessed since she didn't want him back, nor did she desire him, not really, though her non-desire was very physical: she was hung up on his body, or rather on his presence. Well, Harry thought, so am I, but even I don't shadow him the way she does, I don't go as often to hear him sing — which drives Cormac around the bend — and she doesn't do it, like me, for the love of beauty. Art for art's sake is not Maeve's bag. She wouldn't know a song from a hole in the ground. What was it then? Harry remembered the way Will sang:

> *I had a dream the other night,*
> *When every thing was still;*
> *I thought I saw Susanna,*
> *A-coming down the hill.*
> *The buckwheat cake was in her mouth,*
> *The tear was in her eye,*
> *Says I, I'm coming from the South,*
> *Susanna, don't you cry.*

Will had a way with him. He had the power to make you feel the grief and the grit of the buckwheat at the same time. That was what Maeve saw in him. She had had a taste of the cake, and she wanted the tear too. All at once.

Someone else had taste. In New York Harry had known Sykes Milstein when he was just an office boy working for his father in the rag trade. But now he ran a top-notch jazz club in the Lower East Side and he had his own record label. Harry had introduced him to Will in the Westbury Hotel — it was the Saturday afternoon of Maeve collecting the electric piano in Stillorgan. Sykes had only been overnighting in Dublin so it was just a meet-and-greet, the making of a connection that might be useful some day. The dynamic had been curious: it was as if Sykes had been presented to

Will for his approval and not the other way round. Fortunately, he had passed the test and Will, though he had no guitar, had sung for him, right there in the hotel room, a bunch of songs, all new.

Would he come to New York? He would. Would he record for him? He would.

And Sykes had been as good as his word. He had gone so far as to arrange the necessary P Visa. But no further: on the Immigration Service computer up had popped Will's criminal record. Mr Ferris was barred from entering the United States. Forever.

Had Will told Cory? He said he had. But if so, why had he asked Harry not to tell her about it? Maybe instead of 'tell' he had said 'talk to'. There was a difference. Either way it was a sensitive subject.

But when it came to kindness what was the difference between Cory and Maeve? Come to think of it, there wasn't just the two of them in it. Vanessa Banim had to be included as well, even though in the brain stakes she was a non-runner. But, as Harry knew, intelligence has nothing to do with charity. At this time he was listening constantly to a recording of Schubert songs by Dietrich Fischer-Dieskau. Not his favourite singer by any means — too much finish — but Harry loved the way he spoke the prologue to *Die schöne Müllerin*, particularly the up-and-down way he said the line, *wer mehr gibt, als er hat, der heißt ein Dieb*. It meant, 'He who gives more than he has is a thief.' That suited Miss Banim. Certainly she was a thief — she had even stolen her own name — but she had, equally certainly, given more than she had. Her all and her hat, too. But how could she have had such a brass neck and at the same time been so girly-girly? She was a doll, not Meissen, but cheap and Chinese, garishly painted, made to be broken and thrown away in the same way as Cormac had thrown her stupid book through the window of Maeve's flat. Harry continued to feel the shame of that day. He didn't hold it against Cormac — wasn't he working himself up to smashing his fist through the glass of someone else's window? Although the shame was shared, it was not diluted by sharing but concentrated, like being part of a lynch mob. They had all despised Vanessa as much as they loathed her miserable soup, the miso with the frayed scallions and the tabasco. And the Yorkshire Relish. Thick and brown. But the most shameful of them all was Ossie. He had just sat there fright-smiling, looking for the nearest ditch to ditch Vanessa in. And from that moment on, her days were numbered.

Harry had never really liked Ossie, with his doey eyes and his bulky mother beating everyone out of her way with the trunch of her husband's money — the one time he'd met her, she had treated him like he was the original Gay from Outer Space. And though Ossie followed Will around like a spaniel, at the end of the day, when night fell on the Irish Sea, he hadn't been loyal. All right, you couldn't blame him for being a nitwit during the Holyhead court case — in the brain stakes he carried the same handicap as Vanessa — but afterwards he had bolted off to London like a shot from a shovel. Ossie had the soul of the manager of a boy-band. This verdict was as harsh as the Welsh judge's on Will, and Harry knew it, but he made no effort to be lenient for a reason other than the underlying one: the disloyal spaniel he disliked in Ossie was not far from the sarcastic lapdog he feared in himself. The surface reason was something Emmet had told him: the chiffon scarf that had finished off his RHA tuxedo had come from the underskirt under Vanessa's rubber butcher's apron. Ossie had cut it up. He was his father's son: there was a streak of the ruthless draper in him.

What Harry didn't know was why, following prolonged ringing of his doorbell, he had opened the door, in his kimono, to be faced by Emmet in tuxedo and chiffon scarf, and why Emmet had gone wordlessly away. He had asked, but Emmet would not tell, not him, not anyone, not now, not ever.

36

EVEN IF EMMET had confessed his crime, Harry wouldn't have been able to understand it. The reasons for this inability related to Current Affairs. If Harry had to watch the news on television, a device in his brain was activated that turned the faces of politicians into a jelly-wobbling chessboard and their utterances into an audible custard. This was especially true of anything to do with Northern Ireland. His mind was untroubled by the Troubles. Although repression is said to lead to overflow, it does not always produce a high arching spurting forth. No, it leads more often to a mean, messy, dribbling ejaculation. For history, as now, currently, for sex itself, Harry felt distaste, if not disgust. Of course, for most of the 1990s he had been out of the country. Even so, if he had ever heard of the murder in Adare, Co. Limerick, of Detective Sergeant Jerry McCabe by the Provisional IRA in 1998, Harry had forgotten it.

But Emmet hadn't. In the passageway when he heard the wrong name whispered in the dark, he instantly remembered that if Kevin hadn't actually shot Jerry McCabe, he knew the shooters.

'For fuck's sake,' was what Emmet said to the Special Branch detectives when they stood him up against the wall to search him for weapons. And found drugs.

'For fuck's sake,' he said again when they took him to headquarters in Harcourt Street and he saw the face of the cop who came into the Interview Room. It was the detective whose shins he'd kicked in Limerick for confiscating Daddy's Angel Dust.

The detective was now a Superintendent. The intelligence report he was looking at had Emmet Roche down as an artist. Did artists wear evening dress and hobnailed boots at the same time? Were all artists riddled with self-pity? He asked the question because within half an hour this one was saying his mother had lung cancer, with an expression on his face that it was the fault of the police. This young galoot was like all the other young galoots. Special pleading was what they did when they were helping the Special Branch with their inquiries. They talked. They were afraid not to, unless that is someone had put the frighteners on them. Another truth that experience had taught the Super was guilt by association: Robert Emmet Roche might not be as bad as Mickeleen Roche, but he was his brother's keeper. This worked both ways: as Cain slew Abel, Mickeleen would personally slay Emmet, or allow him to be slain, if he squealed.

It was three o'clock in the morning. So far Emmet had said nothing useful. To speed things up, the Superintendent employed an old tactic. He left the room. After an hour Emmet was told he was free to go. He cheered up. But when he was being taken down to be released the Super suddenly reappeared in a long dark corridor. The slightest lifting of his head sent the escort away. Another lift directed Emmet into a cramped cubicle blue-lit by a halogen lamp.

'Sit down there like a good man,' the Super said, indicating a chair by a steel desk. 'Now,' he said. 'There's no audio or video recording in here. This is just between you and me. You, me and nobody else. Do you understand that?'

Emmet nodded.

The Super undid his watch and laid it on the desk between them, carefully. He then took from his jacket pocket a pair of black leather gloves. Emmet's eyes began to blink. The Super put on the gloves, drawing each finger down over each finger, carefully. Then he laced the gloved hands together and raised them over his head, as if stretching from weariness. In stretching, his jacket opened and Emmet saw, as he was meant to see, a holstered pistol. The Super remained in this position until, on the count of ten, he crashed his fists down on the table. Emmet jumped. So did the Super's watch. It turned over and lay face down on the metal of the desk.

'Now,' the Super said. Then he opened a drawer in the desk, took from it a large manila envelope and pushed it towards Emmet. 'Now,' he said. 'Take a look at that.' And waited.

Emmet took a look.

The Super meant to say next, 'That's what your friends did for Ireland. What do you say to that now?' But, with the photographs splayed out in his hands like a deck of cards and without a word said, Emmet looked like he was about to cry. When the Super saw his expression, something unexpected happened: sorrow overcame him too. But while he was remembering that Jerry McCabe had been a friend of his, Emmet was saying to himself, 'I'm going to get hit with these black fists in these black gloves, and I'm afraid, and what I'm afraid of, far more than dying like the body in these bloody pictures, is that I'm going to wet myself.'

It wasn't fair. And that he didn't know Vanessa Banim had feared the same thing — that wasn't fair either.

Emmet had not much to tell. But all the same he told it. Was Kevin's number on his mobile? No, of course not. Still, the scent was fresh. In return, the Super said he'd forget the cannabis and the cocaine. No charges would be laid against him. Emmet really was free to go.

It was this freedom that brought him to Harry's door at the dawning of the day. There was a touch of the priest about Harry, and a priest, no matter if he was spoiled, could listen to your confession and, maybe, give you absolution for becoming a tout and an informer. So when Emmet looked at him, it was forgiveness he was looking for. But then he turned on his heel and went away. He was too guilty to confess to anyone.

37

IT WAS IN HARRY'S character not to find shame shameful. But how could he look so understandingly on sexual cruelty — for instance the torture of Cormac Healy by Maeve MacNamee — and yet cast such a cold eye on Ossie Gleeson cutting up Vanessa Banim's petticoat? The answer was pettiness. Sexual passion wasn't petty. Was it?

As for money, Harry thought it petty too. OK it was fundamental, like sex, but secondary. Money came after sex like a wolf went after a lamb. It was a man-thing. Sugar Daddy owned the pot and if you wanted the taste of honey you had to lick his spoon. In Maeve's case, of course, it was a woman-thing.

Long before Thomas had said his father was 'died' but his mother had got a new stereo, Maeve had been giving charity to him and his family. Harry said, 'You've taken them to your heart,' but it was truer to say that she had taken them into her flat. There she fed them, gave them cash, clothes, cosmetics and copies of *Hello!* magazine — just the sort of charity a dysfunctional family needs.

The cosmetics were literal and, like the origins of the word, they were to be cosmic for her, and for others who were drawn into their field of gravity.

One evening in April when Harry dropped into Waterloo Road — this wasn't unusual; he was often on walkabout — he found Thomas, Missy and Mazee sitting on the couch watching *Neighbours*.

The theme tune was concluding that neighbours should be there for one another because that was when good neighbours become good friends. Harry had seen these ones on Maeve's sofa before, perhaps not often enough to qualify as friends but certainly for them to ignore him. This time, though, Missy's face cried out not to be ignored. Her complexion, which was unusually fine, now glowed more porelessly white than usual, and her lips were painted a bright scarlet. Maeve had made her up to look like a Pierrot, or a clown in a mask, like Vanessa in fact. And with Vanessa's cosmetics.

Harry said to himself, Hello!

Nothing the family did was usual, but they usually came to Waterloo Road once a week, together, singly, or in some combination of two. Not infrequently Thomas arrived on a Saturday morning, early and alone. Whoever opened the door would be greeted by the stare of his unskinned almond eyes and be obliged to take from his hand the held out note. Realistically, it could hardly have been the same note and yet it was always as tattered as ever it had been. He was looking for money and, failing money, anything he was given — or could take. Maeve hadn't noticed the disappearance of a pair of emerald earrings, a Swatch Watch, a digital camera, a fifty euro note, and an antique handbag belonging to Vanessa, but after she caught him carrying off a jumbo-sized coffee jar filled to the brim with coins she did identify what else had disappeared.

'Just because you give the kid your heart, you can't expect him not to take your money,' Harry said. 'But I agree with you, it's very upsetting.'

'You always agree with everyone,' Maeve said sharply. 'You're so innocent it's sick. And I'm not upset, I'm in a red rage.'

This conversation took place as the coda to an evening in Ossie Gleeson's new apartment in Ballsbridge. In return for her being supportive during his grief over Vanessa, Ossie had allowed Maeve the use of it while he was off in Ibiza with a gang of guys from his old school.

'What's the huh! for?' she said.

'Nothing,' Harry said. He had nearly said, 'He can go to Ibiza, but he was too weighed down by sorrow to make it out to the hospital to visit his comatose former girlfriend.'

In her day-to-day behaviour Maeve was placid. She moved slowly, even languorously, like a large deep-sea creature, but when something excited her attention, when a silver fish tailed off from a shoal of other silver fishes, she would snap up the straggler in a convulsion of energy so sudden the prey had vanished before the darkness knew it. Then she would continue on as before, violet-eyes goggling, sardonic lip turned up at the corner as ever.

On this twilit evening in Ossie's apartment looking out on the blue Dublin Mountains, she was unusually restless. In the family of her emotions guilt was not a member, but in the last few days she had been nagged by a feeling that had an incestuous relationship with shame: she wanted to confess. Like Harry, she regarded nothing sexual as sinful. On the other hand she had a more developed understanding of transgression than he did. She used it liberally, like chili in her violent stews. Used was the operative word. With her, transgression was at one with being used. Like salt in seawater, there was no separating them. But the transgressive was for others, not for herself. The sin was theirs, not hers. That was why the temptation offered by Missy had taken away her breath, as if she was a creature from the depths of the ocean sucked up suddenly into the weightless air. The effect was a ballooning out of her mental structures, followed by their collapse onto themselves. The inflation part of the process, which took all of two days, had begun to happen while she was, quite innocently, making up Missy's face — the innocence was relative, just as the using of Vanessa's cosmetics had been relatively thoughtless. Had she deliberated on any of this in advance? No. And when she said, 'Close your eyes,' there was nothing deliberate about it.

Missy, who was sitting on the edge of the bed in Maeve's bedroom, did what she was told. To apply the greasy blue eye shadow to the girl's lids, Maeve put her hand around the back of her head, just to steady it. The hair was thick but coarse to the touch, because the slick gel that kept Missy's fleece of ringlets in place had dried out. Fleece was the right word: the ringlets gave her the look of an unshorn sheep. But Missy was no lamb: she had been drinking vodka with Mazee in the morning and in the afternoon she had smoked some gear in an abandoned flat in Foley Street with people she knew, sort of. Missy had a slight lisp: on the rare occasions she used the word 'heroin' she pronounced it 'hahwin'. Her usual word was 'geah'. If she had been told opium was extracted from the heads of poppies in Afghanistan, she would not have understood that the country existed. Plus she had never seen a poppy. All that was unreal. But gear was real. It was brown powder. That was simple.

Missy was not simple. With her head held back and white neck exposed, she may have looked like a lamb about to be slaughtered — but she was not about to be anything other than what she was. And though she may have smelled a little bit stale-smoky, she was wearing a lot of a perfume called 'Joy' and her breath had a faintly caramely scent — along with the vodka, she had drunk a couple of cans of Coca-Cola, and had gone on drinking it all day. But what she did now only an unsimple being could have done — she opened her mouth and flicked out her pinky brown tongue.

Whether the invitation came before or after the temptation, or vice versa, is unclear. The most that can be said is that Missy's tongue darted out and an electrical current rushed up Maeve's spine. What can be made clear, though, is that Missy had not opened her eyes. She didn't have to.

When Missy's tongue was withdrawn, Maeve followed it with a thrust of her own; a thrust that was like the spear a primitive hunter darts at an animal that has retreated into a cave. After a few seconds, 'as long as a shortness of breath' as the poet has it, Missy drew back, opened her eyes and said, 'Get off me, you.'

For Maeve to be transported sexually was always the last thing on her mind, or in her sensations. Energy, like good things, which come in small parcels, travels light. It carries a very small suitcase. It isn't staying the night. It isn't really going anywhere; it's there already. That was how Maeve regarded transports, erotically. But, like energy, she had no time to spare on theory, quantum or otherwise — it could only lead to religion, and she did not believe in God. Unless, that is, there was a No-God, a Non-Creator whose purpose in the world was wickedness. Because only an unimaginably wicked intelligence could have created a world as wicked as this one is.

In the days after this exchange of spit, a change occurred in Maeve's inward metaphors. She had never thought of sex as anything but a one-way street, with the traffic coming in her direction. Now for the first time the flow was reversed. For the first time her gnostic beliefs were tested to destruction, or near to it. That was why, when she spoke about what had happened, she did so sincerely.

'I am so evil,' she said to Harry. 'Do you think I'm evil too?'

The sequence of events that led to this question began the day after the french kiss when Missy got a call on her mobile inviting her to Ossie's apartment. Maeve had a plan. But as soon as she opened the door, the plan fell apart. For a start Missy's outfit — high-heeled red sandals, skin-tight powder-blue jeans, white gypsy blouse with a low scalloped neckline, a cut-away bright orange cardigan — clashed with the colour scheme of the flat. Mrs Gleeson had had the place done up to look like a suite in a boutique hotel. Everything was in shades of beige, sage, chocolate brown and maroon. The one bright thing in the whole place was the bed: a slab of whiteness that glowed whiter than Missy's make-up. And when she was lying on it, as she soon was, she had a look about her that was primitive, prehistoric, aboriginal, or, in the Australian sense, from a time that coincided with the first series of *Neighbours*. In any event Missy lay there, eyes shut, hands folded over her lap, ankles crossed. Maeve, who was wearing only a loose silk wrap, lay down beside her. Leaning on her left elbow, she put her right hand loosely on Missy's left breast, lightly kissed her on the lips, parting them with the tip of her tongue, slightly. Then she stopped.

She stopped not because it was not exciting. Excitement did come into it; or rather it had come prepared to come into it, like a thief in the night breaking and entering a premises. That prospect had excited Maeve. She was charged up, but the charges had flipped.

Instead of feeling Missy, she felt like her. And Missy was as old as the hills, and about as excitable.

Actually, Missy was beyond excitement. The truth is she wasn't all there. An interruption to the umbilical oxygen supply at birth had scrambled her brain slightly. Her social environment, too, had not been friendly to the sense of otherness that fosters the strangeness of sexual excitement. That did not mean she had no romantic feelings for others. She did have them, but they were felt by a roughly nine-year-old child. It was as if she was a Barbie doll playing with 'My Little Pony': the pony was pink and she was a princess, the star of a provincial gymkhana in comic-cut Britain, but really the rider of one of the four horses of the Apocalypse. Was she Conquest, War, Famine, or Death? The closest to Missy was the red horse of Famine. She was over-fed but starving. The nearest she had ever come, if not to bliss, to the source of pleasure was gear. But even heroin depends on circumstances, and hers were famished. Certainly she had never experienced orgasm. And even more certainly she was not going to experience it for the first time with a solicitor from the Office of the Attorney General.

Maeve herself was aware of little enough of all this. But the Famine she understood. She had known about it from way back. Was that why she stopped? She stopped because she could not go on. She had thought, in her usual way, of giving sexual pleasure, of provoking it until the power of it came back, briefly, to herself. But now she wanted it the other way round: to be given what could not be asked for. That want could only be offered, not supplied, and Missy wasn't offering.

'It was the best sex I ever had in my life,' Maeve said to Harry. He didn't realise that this was a lie. Beyond the initial tongue-tipping there had been no sex at all. Unless that is, Maeve's surrender, her consoling embrace of the stone god, was sexual. In its uselessness as consolation maybe it was.

After the great non-sex, Missy had said, 'Mazee says give us like five hundred quid, OK?'

The details of how this sum was withdrawn from the ATM

in the Tesco supermarket on Baggot Street with the use of two cards, Laser and Visa, and the unwisdom of paying out what could be the first instalment in a scheme of blackmail hardly registered with Harry. He was too busy thinking about what was going to happen next.

The reason they were lying on Ossie's kingsized white bed was to look at the home-cinema-sized TV fixed to the bedroom wall. Presumably it was a coincidence that what was on, with the sound turned down, was an episode of *Sex in the City*. Maeve couldn't have contrived that in the same way as she was contriving now, absentmindedly and casually, to pluck at the crease on Harry's Etro trouser-leg in an up-and-down but progressively ascending pattern.

He was more than surprised to realise he was supposed to do with Maeve, or rather vice versa, what she had supposedly done with Missy.

'I am so evil,' she said. 'Do you think I'm evil too?'

'Well, sweetie, let's say I don't think you'll ever get to heaven.'

'No?'

'No, not this way anyway.' He looked at her eyes, then at her plucking hand, then at her eyes again. 'It's not natural, you know.'

'What?'

'This.'

'Oh this,' she said, shaping her hand gently around his genitals.

'Are you enjoying yourself down there?'

'Are you?'

'It's brilliant fun, thanks. But, do you know, I don't think Mr Mouse is going to come out to play.'

She was leaning on one elbow, staring at him. Her gaze was neither hard nor mocking. It might have been beseeching, but it was too voracious for that.

Slightly tightening the looseness of her hand, she said, 'I could just eat you up.'

He said, 'Without salt?'

'I don't need salt.'

As Harry felt, despite himself, the stirring of an erection, he said, with a harshness that was new to him, 'Baby, you're a fish out of water.'

Maeve didn't attach any significance to this — what did Harry know about fish? Practically speaking, not a bloody thing. Anyway, what people said or did she never held against them. She was too practical for that. People do what they have to do. So did she. Taking, for a good example, a couple of days' annual leave the weekend before St Patrick's Day in order to go to London was something that, practically speaking, had to be done. And nobody had noticed. Certainly not Will Ferris. Eighteen weeks, or whatever it was, had been too long, too close to the legal limit.

So, almost instantly, when Harry brushed her hand away, she said, without anger, 'And you only want what you already have. You're a cowardy custard.'

Afterwards, as he walked home to Aungier Street through the gentle summer air, Harry thought he should buy himself a place to live in, not piss-elegant, like The Gallops, but with a view of the mountains or, even better, of the sea. Then he thought of Ibiza and Ossie Gleeson swimming in the blue of the Mediterranean while Vanessa dripped cloudy yellow urine into a bottle. But why should he suddenly feel angry? He wasn't an angry young man, was he? Not any longer. He was getting too old for anger. That was what boys like Cormac Healy and Emmet Roche had in common. Will Ferris too. They were angry and young and men. Not like Middlesex him. They wanted what they didn't have. They had more in common with Maeve. She was a shameless male bitch. And she wanted him to be Missy. That was what women did: they dragged you into their hole and ate you up. They did to you what had been done to them. And at that moment he realised that the heat he felt was shame. This was new to him. They were newborn bastards together. Who was primitive now? No wonder he had come to hate sex.

38

The falling snow is closing golden eyes,
And the soul in its old clothes is
A god alive, as rich as Jesus was,
A king alone, a temple cat.
The weak night fades, the icy roofs arise,
And everything renewed enblazes us.
What we live by we don't look at.

BEFORE HE WROTE this in his notebook Will had written 'Darkness falls on the temple of what happened,' and scored it out. It wasn't that the line was too romantic — snow falling was even more so. Nor did he object to 'temple'. One of the reasons he carried the word over to the new song was that, recently, while browsing in a bookshop, he had found a history of ancient religions which contained a photograph of an altar in a Roman temple recreated in painted plaster. It showed two vestal virgins making mystic signs with their hands while a young priest was pulling back a bull's head by hooking his fingers in its nostrils. In his other hand was a knife for slashing the rearing animal's throat — its two front hooves were off the ground. What had struck Will was the crudity of the colours, which the book said were true to the original. This was religion as a Walt Disney cartoon, simplified, rough and ready, yet refined. Crude refinement — that was, visually, the style he wanted vocally, as an addition to the dry, bitter and reduced tone he used now. So, when the assistant wasn't looking, he tore the page out of the book.

Cory said he was mean — how would he like to buy something and discover it had been vandalised? The next day she had gone out, found the desecrated book and bought it. Her gift was a rebuke to him and a kindness to a stranger.

Will had told this to Harry and Harry had told Maeve. Maeve had said, 'Oh god, she is a saint,' and made a circular motion with her hand away from her mouth in imitation of waves of vomit pouring out of it.

Anyway, the reason Will had rejected the line was because darkness falling wasn't right for what had been a daytime event: what he and Cory were living by and couldn't look at was the sun.

The cat wasn't theirs. It lived on the roof-valley that ran the length of Lower Leeson Street around the corner into Pembroke Street and around another corner into Fitzwilliam Square. At dawn it would squeeze through the skylight, which Cory left open for that purpose, descend the white ladder, cross the landing, creep in the door and curl up on their bed.

It could hardly have been called a stray. Around its neck it wore a leather collar from which hung a dull metal disk with 'Bituit' engraved on it. Cory had Googled the word and learned that Bituit had been a barbarian king in Roman times. Monarchy suited this cat: it was old and kingly, and there was a crown-shaped patch of white on its black head, but the crown was set askew, as if it had slipped to the side, which made Bituit look befuddled. There was a mobile phone number on the disk, but when Cory rang it, a robotic voice said the number was not in service. Even so, it was likely that this cat had two sets of servants at its beck and call.

Although Cory looked after it, gave it food and shelter, it treated her with disdain. As if to make the point, it attached itself to Will, who gave it nothing, and followed him faithfully around the flat.

'It's not an it,' Cory said. 'It's a he. Like you. And there's no law against giving him a bit of a stroking now and then.' But when he did stroke it, she said, 'Don't ruffle his ears. He's not a dog. Cats don't like that.'

But Bituit did like it. Ruffling his ears caused him to purr like the engine of a car revving in neutral. And when Will was practising on the piano, he would sometimes leap up onto his shoulder and lie there, tail twitching. Once he had even climbed on top of Will's head. Cory had tried to take a picture with her phone, but her hand had shaken and the image was blurred. Anyway, Bituit did not look as if he had performed the trick for their amusement, or for his own either. His impassivity was sourced in another universe. It made Will uneasy. The cat didn't do anything for anything like a human reason. Why did he purr when he took no pleasure in it? Will stared at him for as long as a shortness of breath. When Bituit blinked at last, he seemed to contract his head, to be for an instant not there at all. He vanished when he stopped looking. Maybe that's the reason, Will thought, he reminds me of Cory. The closing of her eyes as she fell asleep while looking at him happened at the same speed as Bituit's. 'Darkness fell on the temple of what happened.' But first her eyelids slowly trembled like snow falling, and the hazel of her eyes was gold-flecked.

'You're so romantic,' Cory said. 'You're a hopeless romantic.'

Since crossing the Shannon, they had taken to sleeping on the mattress in the room where the swallow and the moth had died. The back room had a big double bed, but it was cold and dark by comparison. As the spring moved on into summer, the heat and brightness in the front room went on increasing. Some after-noons, when the sun shone straight through the window, it was so bright nothing could be seen for the silver glare. But just before that happened, everything sideways was lit up clearly.

Not that there was much to illuminate.

The only furniture was the mattress and a lamp on the floor. The walls were painted a green paler than spring grass. A furrow, probably dug by the edge of a chest of drawers, showed that once upon a time these walls had been painted blue. And beneath the blue was the chalky cream of gypsum. In the two hundred years that had passed since the house was built, maybe longer, the room had only been painted twice. In the light of the afternoon sun the furrow had an old shadow. Everything with an edge had a shadow, or a shine. Even a speck of glass that had somehow found its way into the room lay winking on the floor. Will crawled out of bed and picked it up. He rolled it between thumb and forefinger. It was perfectly round. Was it some kind of bead? Or was the roundness the result of erosion by the sea? And if so, what beach had it come from, and how? Before Cory, it could have been part of the room's history, most likely that of the tenant, now dead, who had written on the kitchen wall the record of a conversation he had once had with someone nameless. The couple had probably broken many a bottle in their time, which might have explained where the speck had come from. Except that now it had to be new because one of Cory's things was that she was as clean as daylight. No, daylight was clear. That too, then. She had cleared and cleaned the flat of everything left over, worn out, blotched, forgotten and dirty. With the old torpedo-shaped vacuum cleaner she regularly sucked up the dust almost before it had time to settle. If a thing remained, even if it had no use, it was given a place and remembered.

Partly as a result of being constantly in transit, and partly because she had so little money, Cory owned almost nothing. Other than the clothes that she stood up in, she had accumulated little by way of a shell. Which is not to say she was soft. No, because she had left home so young, she was hard. Now, though, since she was at last earning a living wage, she had begun to acquire some of the things that make life less unyielding. Her first indulgence — really, it was a necessity — were bedclothes. There was no romance in sleeping wrapped up in an old curtain. So she had bought a duck-down duvet and good Egyptian cotton sheets. Their newness and snow-cold cleanness made Will horny. What he loved most about Cory, maybe, was that she was simple, with the result that when she did something that wasn't simple, it was more exciting. It wasn't that she didn't care about her clothes, or her looks, or her figure, or her weight. It was just that they didn't define her as a woman, or as a human being. It was simply as a human being, he thought, that he thought of her. Her body was merely — of course not merely — the shell of her self. Shell and self fitted each other perfectly.

She wasn't perfect. She had her limitations, of course. Her habitual silences, for example, and the embarrassment they created were sometimes used not to create space for herself, which was fair enough, but to wield power over the people who got into that space, himself included. But these limitations were better thought of not as limits but as edges, margins, frontiers, the boundary line on which the wind hits heavy. Even if she was from the west, Cory was a North Country Girl. She expected that the air coming down from the North Pole, or in from the Atlantic, or out of the great empty plains of North America would be freezing cold. Naturally, she wrapped herself up against it. But there was something in her, too, that disregarded the winter. At the outer edge of her limitations, which in physical terms was her skin, she was as cold as the woman with the raised torch, the Statue of Liberty. But she gave back what she was given. And she wasn't that cold either. Far to the south the Gulf Stream was revolving the wheel of its heat around the Bay of Mexico and wafting up to the North Country boundary line warm currents of air that smelled of the mesquite bush. Of creosote. A faintly tarry smell. 'Tarry' was also an old-fashioned way to say stop, stay, delay a little longer. That was not Cory's cry. Her cry was, 'Come now, now, now, quick, quick.'

Later, when she read this in his notebook, she cut it out with a scissors. Still, she left in the passage where he said it came as a surprise to him that she took to buying clothes 'to flutter the feathers of Eros'. The ruse wasn't patently obvious. She would never have dreamt of buying, never mind wearing, like Maeve, a satin-ized catsuit, scarlet and glossy and slashed to the waist in a deep vee. Cory was a bit of a prude. This was, it seemed to him, another of her failings. But then one day she did buy something for its sex-iness. It was a linen suit made in Japan by a designer whose name he heard as Mickey Yaki, cut on the bias and, according to Harry, 'beautifully structured, à la Madelaine Vionnet'. The colour was almost mauve, a moderate purple, but the cuffs and the hems were trimmed with a narrow ribbon of raw silk, the pinkish colour of which was almost as pale as lavender. Will had a set against lavender — it was effeminate. Come to think of it, why did effeminate men, like Harry, like lavender? Why did they mimic women as if women were their trimmings only? And why was it he had never met a woman who was like a man like that? True, femininity was the origin of effeminacy, but they were entirely opposed in practice. In this case the effect of the raw silk against the dyed linen was nothing if not feminine. Male as he was, he had to admit he would never have been capable of imagining it.

The shock of the suit was, first, that Cory would wear something so womanly. Secondly, it was the deliberation with which she did it. Thirdly, it was the offhand manner in which she revealed its secret, the way as it were she played the trump card in her hand. With her hand, too, as it happened.

It happened on a grey-sunny afternoon in May in McDaid's on Harry Street. Through the pub's high doors he saw her coming towards him from the far pavement, and for a few seconds, until she came out of the glare into the gloom, he failed to recognise her. With her mousey hair newly cut short, she might have been a slightly dumpy Swede or a German. Dumpy? A little potato dumpling. No, no, he had never thought she looked like that. She was a human being. That was what made her interesting. He had respect for her. She was respectable, not suitable.

Later, in his notebook he wrote, 'Respect. Re-spect. Worth looking at twice. That's what respectable means. That's what Cory is. And that's what I want to be. In fact it's what I am. I am a respectable person.' He meant to put the twice-looked-at line in a song he would write soon. But the idea somehow made him feel gloomy. 'Renown,' he wrote, 'is a lesser form of respect, and it's shameful, like a peacock spreading out the eye-filled fan of his tail as if to say, "Here for inspection is my erection". That's why a peacock looks so anxious. Because if he won't get up on the pea-hen, some other cock will. So if he doesn't show off his erection, she will judge him unsuitable to be the father of her children. Then he won't be able to reproduce himself and he'll die alone and be no more. Well, I'm not going to wave my cock tail in the air.'

Will was superstitious too. About his desire to be famous, which was magical, he felt ashamed. Fame was like wanting to be looked at in the moment of death. So, because that would be unlucky, he never went back to the line about Cory being 'worth looking at twice', and he never wrote the song.

In McDaid's, though, he must have thought she did use to look a little like a carelessly wrapped parcel. Because now she didn't. The suit had been so well cut by Mr Mickey Yaki that she could have passed for a native of Japan. It was a miracle of packaging, which is, after all, what the Japanese are good at. Will was so proud of this new Cory — the few customers in the bar looked enviously at her loveliness and knew it was for him, not them — that he acted as if he was used to being attended on by beautiful creatures, women of the world, plainly not virgins. Torn between the old and the new, between beauty and ugliness, hers and his, he stood up, gave her his stool and leaned his elbow on the bar.

'OK,' he said. 'What do you want? Coffee? Ballygowan?'

'Aren't you going to say hello?' Cory said.

'What?'

'I think I'm getting hay fever. I've been sneezing all day.'

She had been expecting him to say the suit and the haircut were nice and instead he had stood up gracelessly and plonked his ugly elbow on the counter. It was time to teach him a lesson. She pulled up her skirt.

Had she done this with a provocative pout it would have been next to no good. But doing it as if she was not aware she was doing it was excellent. Anyway, she had indeed been sneezing all day, and now she could feel a sneeze coming on. Luckily, under her skirt were shorts of the same material as the rest of the suit, trimmed with the same silk, and in a little pocket, high up on the thigh, was a tissue, which she took out and blew her nose with.

Much later that afternoon, Will said, 'Aren't these what they used to call in the old days hot pants?'

'How would I know?' Cory said.

But she did know. It was just that she kept silent about what she knew.

39

ANGRY WAS A word very like energy. The difference was two tabs of e. A mild pain can last a long time; an intense one passes. Emmet couldn't bear mildness. Although he had been often enough tempted by tenderness and the weaknesses that go with it, such as clemency and pity, he sensed they could last only as long as a mild pain, when all he was interested in had to last forever. So he had resisted the temptation. All the same, when he was hungover or coming down from ecstasy, or both, which was often, he had a sharp eye for things that had been caught in the tender trap.

'Thanks for the memory. Shut the door behind you.'

This note was propped against an empty wine-bottle on Maeve's coffee table. He had woken up on her couch with a piercing pain in his head.

Why was he there? And what day was it?

On the floor lay a copy of *The Sunday Times*, dated 19 June 2005. That was yesterday. He felt less than half the man he used to be. It couldn't last, this pain. But it did last. It wasn't the pain, though, that led him at last to fall to his knees on the mattress in his studio, and slowly, a dead-weight by then, to topple sideways.

This had happened before, hadn't it? Yes, when the murdered sheep had poisoned his hand. Then the wriggling world, scurrying on its dead-white legs, had got into him, spreading its toxins through his soul, which was anyway contaminated from birth by the original sin of conception, filthy dirty thing. His true soul, though, was part of the First Light, and for that reason uniquely self-conscious.

But that was still a long way off. Now, the pain merely annoyed him into firing bolts of cold water at his head in Maeve's bathroom. When he straightened up, the sensation that someone was looking at him was too fleeting to stop him staring at himself dripping in the mirror. What he failed to remember was that Maeve had told him she had had the same sensation one night in March, just before St Patrick's Day. Lying in the bath, she had felt all of a sudden the displacement of silence that follows the withdrawal of a spy. She had stood up, the hot water falling off her as if guilty at becoming so quickly cold. The weird little box-like window high up in the wall was open. Poking through it, a long thin finger of air was long-fingering her frizzling skin. Throwing on her pink robe, she went to investigate, and saw in the cold stone passageway that the old stepladder that had lain for a lifetime on its side against the wall had been lifted up and was leaning beneath the window.

Emmet dried his face and staggered out of Maeve's flat. On the way home he went into the National Gallery. The wooden floors were sprung and under the tread of his hobnailed boots they quivered like a trampoline. No one could see beautiful things as sharply as he saw them, but today only one picture stopped him in his tracks. The name of the painter, the well-known Something-or-Other Chardin, didn't matter. Chardin was too useless for his name to count. He was only a mantelpiece man. What didn't matter either was the subject of his painting: a plump boy laboriously learning to write, watched over by a chinless skivvy, the blue sleeve of her dress picking up a paler blue from the creamy white of her bodice. Emmet could do that. What annoyed him was the solid woollen paint on the boy's cap. How had that been laid on? Was it blobs of impasto levelled off with a spatula or a turn of the thumb? No, it was too old for that. Old? It looked old, but then so did all the pigment in the painting, despite the youth and bloom of the subject. He was tempted by this technical tenderness; it was as if the way the paint had been applied was the answer to what was going on between the anorexic skivvy and the fat kid. But he had not stayed looking for long. Art would not bring him to his knees. And he refused to consider the cause of his pain. What happened was bound to happen. It was a consequence of allowing himself to be tricked by Maeve MacNamee. She had burgled his premises. Broken and entered and left without leaving a clue. No ladder. Nothing stolen either. A perfect robbery. Unlike that bitch Vanessa. But he was aware — an awareness like that which just knew when he opened his mother's wardrobe an avalanche of shoes would fall out if it — that Maeve had stolen something from him. What could it be? What could it be?

It was not until his mother had gone into remission that Emmet understood how inexpressibly futile his ambitions were. Lily had got out of bed and begun, slowly at first and then with increasing speed, to run around her old haunts, chattering huskily, smoking her long black cigarillos, and complaining gaily, 'Oh, I wish I was as young as I feel.' Her consultant in the Regional Hospital had said, 'It's a miracle,' muttering as he bent his head to the next x-ray, 'if you believe in miracles.' All the same the futility of her optimism had been diminished by the pride she took in Emmet winning the Treacy prize at the RHA — for a picture she had not seen — and in the commission he had now got to paint the wife of the billionaire on the board of the Museum of Modern Art.

'Ten grand he's getting!' she said to friends and neighbours. 'What's the country coming to?'

She was much more excited by the news that a lectureship in the National College of Art and Design was soon to be advertised and that the Director had told Emmet that, all things being equal, the job was his. Emmet didn't know, though, if he wanted the position. Lily was incredulous. Like all her ancestors, she nurtured a deep respect for two words whose roots reached right back to the Famine: the words were 'permanent' and 'pensionable'. Emmet might object to being called a civil servant, but with the grace of god a civil servant was what he was going to be. He didn't know how lucky he was. But that, she said, was Ireland for you, and, really, she could hardly have been more proud of him if he had shot a policeman.

By the time Emmet woke up it was the afternoon. By eight o'clock that night, in Hartigan's on Leeson Street, the piercing pain in his head had been replaced by nausea. To kill it, he ordered rum and blackcurrant, with a Bulmer's cider on the side to cut the sweetness.

When Cormac came in, the first thing he saw was Emmet retching into a wad of tissues. 'What's wrong with you?' he said.

'I'm dying,' Emmet said.

Dying, though, was a measly word for the feeling he felt at this unexpected sight of Cormac. Did Cormac know what he was now remembering? If the thought of Cormac's existence had risen while the memory was being created, which was when Emmet was tearing the pants off Maeve, which it hadn't, in all likelihood he would have said, 'I can't stop now.' But seeing Cormac limping into Hartigan's, he realised the thought should have come to the surface, walking stick and all. If it had been as real then as the man was now, he wouldn't have done what he had done. That was a pity; he regretted it. Not regret like a nice Chardin painting hanging over the mantelpiece. No, regret like falling into the blazing fire in the fireplace. Because he liked Cormac. Cormac was OK. They were pals, buddies, brothers under the skin. For a wretched retching moment, he saw Cormac as he saw himself: the hero, once loved, now betrayed.

Although she was a crap dancer, Maeve was into clubbing. Being stoned out of her brain, though, wasn't really her thing. A bit of blow, an occasional tab of ecstasy, that was it, usually. But on this Monday night in RíRá's — *rírá agus ruaille buaille*, pronounced ReeRaw ogus Rooilla Booilla, is the Irish for 'uproar and ructions' — she was on a mad buzz. Buzzing on Bacardi Breezers and a big bag of coke she'd scored on the street outside the club. Scoring on the street was not her thing. Nor was cocaine. It didn't worry her, though.

'I've got no worries,' she said. 'That's the difference between you and me, Emmet baby.'

But Maeve did have worries, which she certainly wasn't going to tell him about. The curious thing was she didn't tell herself about them either. At one and the same time she was capable of non-thought and deep calculation. She was also capable of another impossible trick: she calculated with lightning speed but she did it cold and slow. Unlike Doctor Cory Leary, she was not like water, which finds its own level, and yet she moved with the logic of water. Where self-interest was concerned, which was everywhere, she changed as a water-clock changes: drip drop, fill to full, trip the trap, click, escape, and flow. All things being equal, a clepsydra is predictable. Maeve, being human, did not work like clockwork. Normally, it wasn't in her nature to be overwound and run fast, but Cormac, her fool, had interfered with the mechanism.

What could she do about it?

She would have to cut his balls off.

That was regrettable, not least because, despite his small size, Cormac had, as far as courage went, balls big enough to be fired from a cannon. But he had gone too far. Off they would have to come. No two ways about it. There were no half measures in the castration business.

It was true she had provoked him. But provocation was inescapable. It was built into her clock's escapement. How else was she to respond to being threatened? Was she not free to sleep with whomever she liked? She was. Even if hats with feathers were flying and departmental doors were slamming. Even if, especially if actually, thumb tendons were twanging. It didn't matter that her freedom of choice was reduced to her right to choose Ultan McGrath, a man with, when it came to boldness, balls the size of raisins.

So she had had sex with him yet again.

In response, Cormac had taken a taxi to Firhouse. When he arrived at the McGrath sliver of beige brick, he hesitated. A knock on the door suddenly seemed too aggressive. So he rang to challenge his rival to come out and fight like a man. But Ultan didn't answer his phone. Orla did. She said he was away for the weekend at a conference of statisticians in Athlone. Who was speaking? Cormac identified himself. Oh yes, she had heard about him. Did he want to leave a message? He did. The message was that he was Maeve MacNamee's fiancé and if Ultan ever laid hands on her again — a child began crying in the background — he was going to fucking kill him. Orla had looked out the window of the upstairs room that was too small to turn around in, where she was going through the history of the websites visited by her husband on his laptop, and seen an unevenly weighted man, a short leg on one side and a plaster-of-Paris cast arm on the other, hirpling away down the street on a walking-stick.

Orla was distraught. But when Ultan returned home, she said nothing. Over the weekend she considered what to do. By Monday she had made a decision. Luckily, there was a family friend in whom she could confide. Her father, who had once been a senior civil servant, had a high opinion of Tadhg Deeney's judgement. Tadhg, Daddy said, was no great brain — that was why he had gone into Personnel (which was now Human Resources) — but he was a safe pair of hands, a strong Catholic, a Knight of Columbanus. Solid as a rock.

In one respect Tadhg was indeed rock-like: as he listened to Orla's story, the distressed sound he made with his tongue against his teeth was like two bits of wet gravel knocking their irregular edges together while falling down a series of steps. Dth dth. Dth dth dth. Dth dth dth dth dth.

Something would have to be done. Tadhg would think about it. He would get back to her.

The first part of the something did not really need to be thought about for long. Within the hour he had rung Cormac Healy, requesting, no, requiring him, to return from sick leave and present himself for interview. Tadhg had been planning this interview anyway. The present schemozzle had merely brought it forward. The outcome had already been contemplated, reluctantly then, less so now: the invalid would be examined by departmentally appointed consultants, and then invalided out for good. Not to put a tooth in it, leg or no leg, they would give him his marching orders. Thank you and good night.

The second part was a matter of some delicacy. To be delicate without knowing other delicate people is impossible. This was a law of civilisation so well known to Tadhg he did not need to formulate it. There were many such laws. They ranged from a prohibition of murder to not shaving yourself in the Department's lavatories. If these rules and regulations had one thing in common, it was a distaste for cornerboys. In recent years, unfortunately, there had been slippages in this regard. In the old days, for instance, well-brought-up people would not have given the time of day to the likes of the Sinn Féin leaders Gerry Adams and Martin McGuinness. These so-called rebels were in fact cornerboys of the deepest dye. A right pair of raparees. Not only were they, like nature, 'red in tooth and claw', they were actual Reds. Bolsheviks. Nowadays, nonetheless, they were in and out of Government Buildings like yo-yos. But *c'est la vie*. Ours not to reason why. But mark my words; it will all end in tears. In the old days, too, any kind of monkey business, that is anything below the belt, was grist to the Department's mill. And, contrary to what some Holy Marys thought, there had always been plenty of filth in Ireland. Adultery, the Irish for which is *drúis*, pronounced drooish, had not begun with Bishop Eamon Casey, who had fathered an illegitimate, excuse me, a non-marital child, on an American woman called Annie Murphy, who was no better than she ought to be. No, indeed. But monkey business had not begun with that episcopal ape. Droooooish had caused trouble to Personnel Officers since the time of Moses. In those days a toe-rag could be struck down with a thunderbolt from Jehovah, but even today there were ways of stepping on the dirt bird with your spawg (a heavy boot): you could, for instance, allocate him an office without a phone, or shuffle him off to inspecting warble-fly in Toorawaddy, County Mayo. Whatever suited the situation, departmentally speaking.

So Tadhg had spoken a word in the shell-like ear of someone he knew in the Office of the Director of Public Prosecutions. This person, no names no pack drill, had then spoken to another someone in the Office of the Attorney General.

The report back was that Miss MacNamee was well-thought-of, very capable, going places, a bit harum-scarum in the clothes department, a bit too keen on the bottle — nowadays of course lassies were fond of a jorum — but she had her head screwed on. She knew her onions. She was, probably, biddable so.

Tadhg had then made a call on what he called the steam telephone to the someone in the AG's Office. Treading on another department's territory in this fashion was quite a liberty to take, but, sure, if the Yanks were doing it down in Shannon, wasn't an Irishman entitled to do something similar up in Dublin? Anyway, 'extraordinary rendition', no matter what the bleeding heart liberals said, was only common sense, another subsection of the universal law: what else would you do with Al Qaeda cornerboys but bundle them onto a plane, fly them off to some Toorawaddy and oblige their warble-flies to be inspected?

Tadhg and the AG's someone had then taken tea in the Merrion Hotel (pricey but worth every penny). The very next day the AG's someone had called Miss MacNamee into his office for a consultation on a tricky bit of Corporation Tax legislation — for all the relevance it had to the matter in hand, it might have been an amendment to the law on the licensing of bog canteens — and before her bottom had warmed the seat, he had steered the conversation around the corner to the cornerboy in question. How long was she in the AG's Office now? Nine months? Ah! (A smile and an unspoken pregnant pause.) How was she finding it? Grand. Good good. They were a nice tight little department, weren't they? One big happy family. Not like some other departments of state. In such bloated organisations cohesion and discipline could easily become a problem. Why, he had heard the other day of a case in point. Was it in Agriculture or Justice? He couldn't remember. Anyway, the story concerned a young officer who had offered physical violence to another officer. By way of a threat of lethal force. He had in fact offered to kill his colleague. The offer had been made indirectly. Through a third party. Outside the service. How would a bright young officer advise the Secretary General of a Department to deal with that kind of carry-on? The offender's feet, Miss MacNamee said, wouldn't touch the ground before he was out the door. Ah, the AG's someone had said. And paused. Threats against the person were a breach of the criminal law, of course, and the gardaí should be notified *instanter*. But, *festina lente*, make haste slowly; you had to consider that there might be what you might call collateral damage to the Department. Who knows what kind of thing could be behind this kind of thing? If there were counter-allegations of, say, bullying, you could be down in the High Court in the morning. That was true, Miss MacNamee said. Or it might be, the AG's someone said, something more personal. What if, for example, the officers in question were engaged in hanky-panky? With each other? No, no. With someone else. In the same Department, Miss MacNamee asked. Oh yes. Definitely. Or in another Department. I see what you mean, Maeve said.

'But do you know what I said then?' the AG's man said to Tadhg as they again took tea in the Merrion. 'I said — by the way these what do you call them, *petit fours*, they're very tasty — I said what would this third person say to the Secretary if he raised the matter with him, or her as the case might be, of course. And do you know what she said?'

'That you should mind your own business?'

'No. She might have said that, but she didn't. She looked me straight in the eye and she said, cool as you like, "I'd say to him, there's no law against barking up the wrong tree, but, you know, there is a law against slander".'

'Well well,' Tadhg laughed. 'That beats Banagher, and Banagher bate the world. Miss MacNamee is one smart cookie.' Just because he was old-fashioned didn't mean Tadhg wasn't up-to-date. He had all the modern lingo at the tips of his fingers. And when he rang Orla all he said was, 'The job is Oxo. Say no more, say no more.' Orla didn't need to know what had been done, and to give her credit she hadn't asked. As they say in the Irish, *Is leor nod don eolach*. A nod is enough for the knowledgeable.

To be palatable, Oxo cubes require dissolving in boiling water. The instant Tadhg's cube was plopped into her cup, Maeve had understood that she was in the soup. But she was also in the dark. The water was hot and certainly salty enough — about 98% by the taste of it — but where was the beef? For all she knew, the Oxo might be a vegetarian bouillon. Marmite. Or miso. Miso with Yorkshire Relish. Yum-yum. For a few moments Maeve remembered Vanessa. Both of them were in the dark, but as far as Vanessa was concerned, a nod wasn't as good as a wink to a blind horse. She was gone beyond nods and winks, or horse riding, or hanky-panky.

Maeve was livid. With the system? No, what would the point be of that? She was livid with Cormac. It had been the easiest thing in the world — sex was the easiest thing in the world, so much so that sometimes, like now, using it made her feel weary — to find out what he had done. The cheek of him. Not only did he think he had the right to lay down the law about whom she could lie down with, but also to threaten to kill Ultan McGrath, and, worst of all, to issue the threat through a third party, his sainted wife. That was another kish of brogues entirely. Dragging Miss Frigidaire into it went beyond the beyond.

Cormac said, 'Are you threatening me?'

'Yes.'

'You and what army?'

'I don't need an army,' Maeve said. 'You'd better listen to me now, because I'm only going to say this once. What I do with other people is none of your business. Right? If you don't like it, well, I don't want to see you around here any more. Have you got that?'

Some time after she said this, while they were standing by the bed, Cormac had turned away dismissively with a wave of his hand. Although the blow with the plaster cast was glancing, by morning the muscle below her shoulder was stiff and a dingy bruise was spreading beneath the skin.

But after the strike had been struck, around midnight, they were back in bed again, and Cormac was consumed more completely than he had ever been consumed before. Had he been historically minded, it might have occurred to him to think of this last time making love with Maeve under the old rules as being akin to the way that gladiators in the Colosseum cried out to their Emperor, 'We, who are about to die, salute you.' But Cormac was not interested in history and he did not know that the purple dye that stained the robes of the Emperor was made from the crushing of a mollusc, the murex.

Maeve wasn't history-minded either. But the flood of sub-surface emotions pouring through her riverine being dislodged pebbles in her memory. Dth dth dth.

One of these memories was a line from a film she had once seen, the rhythm of which, though she changed the words, she reproduced exactly.

'You're not afraid, Cormac Healy,' she cried. 'You glory in cruelty.'

The comedy suited the occasion. She didn't care for being sodomized — not for the shame of it: shame was the grease of others — but when a man has lost his footing and is rolling over and over down the flood, it is sensible to let him feel he is standing on solid ground. That, indeed, he is the ground. Solid rock. Volcanic, rhyolite, andesite, black basalt. Obsidian before it glassifies. Anyway, Cormac really was a furious lover, as furious as the Zeus who blinded Tiresias. And Maeve thought just as Hera did. And she shivered as well. She shivered like never before, like a fast still river. Still, still. So it really was a pity about him, and about his balls, the fountains of generation, having to be cut off.

Afterwards, mollified but defeated, Cormac said to himself but in her hearing, 'I don't know why we do these things.'

And Maeve thought, Well, it is a pity because, really, I do love him.

40

AFTER DRINKING in Hartigan's until closing time, Cormac found himself in Emmet's studio smoking a joint. They had not been speaking about women, so, as well as not being sure he was hearing rightly, because of the boom of Kraftwerk in the background, he did not know who Emmet was referring to when he shouted suddenly, 'I love her, I love her.'

'What's that?'

'I love her,' Emmet repeated, not so loud, but savagely.

'Who?'

'Nobody you know,' Emmet said, staring at Cormac, savagely. Then, after a long pause, staring at the red-hot tip of the joint that he was almost burning the tough skin of his thumb with, he said, 'I hate people.'

He said this because the night after RíRá's, he and Maeve had taken a taxi to his studio.

'Do you actually live here?' she had said. 'What a kip.'

After that, a little later, she had said, 'Let's see what you're made of.'

And after that again, much later, she said, 'I don't believe it.' What she didn't believe was that he had screwed Cory Leary. 'I don't believe it,' she said admiringly. 'You gave her one, did you?'

'What?' Emmet said, raising his nose from the coke.

'I don't believe it. You're a liar.'

'Who're you calling a liar?'

'Tell me about it. What was it like?'

Emmet did not answer. Instead, he got up and danced until he fell. Then he got up and danced again. He might as well have been, like his father once was, a labourer in London, one of MacAlpine's Fusiliers, living in Kennington and dancing in Cricklewood. Hadn't his old man, before he became a butcher, dug the tunnel for the Victoria Line by day and by night slept in a wardrobe lying on its back? That was a story Daddy Roche liked to tell. But the mirrored door of the wardrobe had been left open. Exile was for him a social condition, and not, as it was for Emmet, a condition of nature. The fate of the son was, in the son's opinion, the sadder fate by far. And now on this dirty nose-candied bank of the Styx, it was to become the saddest of all the fates the son of man is heir to.

He had been lying with Maeve on the mattress in the studio. She didn't believe he had done the deed with Cory. What was she like in bed then? He wouldn't say. To keep his King Kong hands off her, she got up and went to the trestle table where, amid a forest of paintbrushes growing in coffee-jars, she knew there was a Bacardi Breezer. Which she drank from.

'You're only a liar,' she said. She shouldn't then, especially not standing there naked from the waist down, have laughed at him and said, 'Who do you think you are, Will Ferris?'

Not only had he told her the truth, he had shown it to her. In a snow-white rage of cocaine he had displayed the second drawing he had made of Cory. She was on her knees, looking upwards with an evilly sluttish look in her drugged eyes, and in her mouth, or just coming out of it, in both senses of the word, was a crowing cock. His.

'I believe you, I believe you,' Maeve said. 'Thousands wouldn't, but I believe you.'

After that, she put her hand back through her legs and brutally thrust the same cock into her. Emmet was offended. He didn't like to be treated roughly. Rough was his way. So, in the midst of the horror of the betrayal of Cory, he went mad, leaned his forearm hard on

Maeve's neck and, as near as damn it, raped her. Did she fight him? No, she sighed. She didn't care. It wasn't Emmet she was thinking of. She was having done to her what only Will Ferris should have been able to do.

The truly dark impulse does not star in its own play. When Emmet woke up it was daybreak, grey-greased with the melancholy of disgust. Beside him on the mattress, Cormac was asleep, his head thrown back, his plaster-of-Paris arm cantilevered out over the filthy concrete floor. Although the air was woolly and too warm, the piercing pain in Emmet's head had gone. All things that could be clarified were clear to him now. When I'm dead, I'll be glad to be dead. This thought didn't come to him in words. It was more like a drawing, in charcoal, of a haunted house. Quick as a mild pain, quick as tenderness, quicker than clemency, he shut it out of his mind.

Cormac, who had not been breathing, now sighed a long impatient sigh, and then ceased to breathe again.

They had spent a long time talking in the night. Not talking. Arguing. But intimately. There had been one thing they agreed upon. That thing was Will Ferris. He and he alone, Cormac said, stood between him and Maeve. Not Ultan McGrath.

'Ultan who?' Emmet asked.

'Big guy with a foxy beard. Looks like a badger.'

'Oh him.' Emmet was a little amazed that Maeve had had it off with such a wanker, but he didn't say so.

For his part, Cormac was more than a little amazed that Emmet had the hots for Cory Leary, but he didn't say so. He did say, though, and Emmet agreed, that Will Ferris was a cunt.

Now, lying on the mattress in the dawn's early light, Emmet saw clearly that he had lost his beloved for good. He had lost her by showing her to Maeve. At the climax of his play, his star, which he had always thought of as a brightly shining thing, as being part of the original First Light, had not shone. It had been mingy, mean, a dribble, a ragged ruffle on the surface of a leaden puddle, with not a glimmer or a gleam off it. This thought was only a zeptosecond long, the billionth of a trillionth of a second it had taken the light to cross the distance between Cory turning into Maeve, between the poor and the pitiless. Cory was poverty-stricken. That was why he loved her. Emmet knew that now. But he had given Maeve a nail and a hammer to crucify his love with. And she would use it. He couldn't allow himself to think that thought for long. He could think, though, about the poisonous shadow that had invaded and occupied the two women, and joined them together. Will Ferris was that shadow.

The air felt like felt.

When Cormac woke he got a start. Beside him on the mattress and shaking his shoulder, Emmet was staring into his eyes. It was a mad stare.

'What day is it?' Emmet said.

'What?'

'What day is it?'

'How the fuck should I know?'

'It's not Tuesday,' Emmet said accusingly. 'This isn't Tuesday. It's Wednesday.'

'So what?'

'I'm missing a whole day.'

'What?'

'I missed an entire day in my entire fucking life.'

'What are talking about?'

'Somebody stole my life.'

'You've lost it,' Cormac said and closed his eyes.

They were both crazy. And neither of them was a fox.

41

'YOU'RE AN UNGRATEFUL young pup,' Harry said.

'I have this weird feeling,' Will said, 'that you're annoyed with me.'

'Annoyed? I am beside myself. You can't make a career out of scoring own goals. When are you going to cop yourself on?'

'I don't know. Maybe never.'

'He's only a ponce,' Cormac said and went off to search for Maeve.

'That's another own goal,' Harry said. 'Why do you have to annoy everyone all the time?'

Kiely's in Donnybrook was packed. It was not a pub that Cormac would have been in on any night of the week, and on this Friday night it was annoying him. The place was full of rugger buggers, beefy jocks with blond-streaked hair sticking up, self-confident as a stiff prick. The main reason for annoyance, though, was that the kip was full of Will Ferris's fan club. One of them, the chief fan, Toby Bowen, was now talking to Maeve, pressed up against her by the crowd. It was a good thing for Toby that he was a rat-faced little queer. Otherwise he'd have been a candidate for castration.

'Toby Bowen, gay?' Harry said later. '*Au contraire, mon chou.*'

'What the fuck are you talking French for?' Cormac said.

Toby Bowen was, in fact, the reason why they were all in

Kiely's pub this Friday night. Although he was still only nineteen, Toby had a business card, frequently produced, on which he described himself as 'DJ and Event Organiser.' He was known, too, as a musician. Up in his bedroom in his parents' house in Clontarf he sampled, Aphex Twin-like, other people's sounds. It was not those mixings, though, that would in the future bring him in a steady stream of income. It would be the music of Will Ferris, or to be exact, a song of his, which began:

> Who made the world and left no trace
> He made it out of you.
> The scars that mark your hands and face
> Are his creation too.

It was as an Event Organiser that Harry had hired Toby. For his thirtieth birthday, which was to be celebrated on Midsummer Eve at White Rock beach in Killiney, Toby would supply, in addition to the sound system, two kegs of Guinness, one of lager, one case of red wine, one of white, gallons of bottled water and a variety of nibbles, including a big bag of boiled sweets for the dancers. When the free drink was drunk, Toby could open a pay-bar. Could he DJ too? He could, but not until midnight, not until after Will had done the first hour.

'Will who?' Toby asked. 'Not Will Ferris? Oh my god.'

So, on the Monday night that Cormac's tendon had twanged, Harry had introduced Toby to Will. The back room of the Baggot Inn was empty, except for the barmen clearing up. Slouched on the raggedy undersprung banquette, Will didn't want to be told that he was 'just such an amazing singer'. What he wanted to know was where he could buy a decent second-hand amplifier. Toby said he could get him one, no problem. Then Will wanted to know where he could get a decent recording machine, not big but broadcast quality. Toby said the recorder, being digital, wouldn't need to be big; it was really the microphone that mattered. Actually, he had examples of what Will was looking for in his shoulder bag and produced them on the spot. Harry said the mike weighed a ton and was obviously a serious instrument, but he didn't believe a thing half the size of a packet of cigarettes — 'It's a Sony mini-disk,' Toby said — could record a sound that would be audible to a passing bat.

If the barmen had been asked, they would have said, what with all the banging of stools being stacked and the *gdashing* of glasses into the dishwasher, that they hadn't heard Will singing and accompanying himself on his electric piano. But when Toby played back the mini-disk through the crackly amp they did hear it, and one of them, whose shirt was tight-stretched over his fat belly, leaned on his sweeping-brush and listened.

Toby said that, in exchange for the recording, he'd give Will a present of the Sony and the microphone.

Harry said, 'Toby!'

Toby said, 'There's five hundred quid's worth of stuff there.'

Will said, 'It's a deal.'

Harry said, 'You're crazy.'

What happened then was simple. Toby uploaded the song onto his website and, though he faded out the ending, the fragment had been downloaded a thousand times in the first week. Then Toby had sent a copy of the song to a friendly DJ on a local radio station, and the DJ had aired it on the hour every hour, which was something since the pirate worked a six-hour slot. Another DJ had heard it and he had gotten in touch with Toby, who had asked Will's permission for the song to be played.

Harry said, 'Are you crazy? Of course you'll let him play it.'

The him, after all, was John Kelly. Not only did Kelly probably know more about all kinds of peculiar music than any other DJ in the universe, he was also legitimate, and he was listened to nationwide: every night between eight and ten o'clock his 'Night Train' was broadcast by RTE. And because state radio was obliged by law not just to get permission to play but also to pay for playing 'He Made It Out Of You', Toby had asked Will would that be OK.

Will said, 'Send the money in a plain brown envelope.'

'Your father is over the moon,' Polly said on the phone. 'He listens to John Kelly every night. And do you know what?'

'What?'

'I met that Mrs Gleeson the other day and you'll never guess where she heard it. On the Larry Gogan Show.'

'So I believe.'

'Well, I went straight home and told your father and do you know what he said?'

'No.'

'He said, "Who's Larry Gogan?"'

'Larry Gogan is the oldest disc jockey in Ireland, and the best.'

'Sure, boy, your father knows that. He was only making one of his jokes. Really, he's as proud as Punch. So am I. I couldn't be prouder if you got a job in the symphony orchestra. Weren't you the fooleen to give up your studies?'

'Thank you and good night.'

'What are you talking about? It's only the middle of the day. Which reminds me. Is Cory there?'

'No, Polly. She's at work. It's the middle of the day.'

'Do you know what else that Gleeson woman said to me?'

'No.'

'I never liked her. Jumped up draper's wife. And as for brains, the only thing she has between her ears is mascara.'

'What did she say?'

'She said she heard you were doing a strong line with a specialist.'

'A specialist?'

'A hospital consultant. And do you know what she said then?'

'No.'

'"I suppose they'll be naming the big day soon." The cheek of her. I felt like giving her a good slap for herself. But, do you know, if she's saying it, the whole of Cork will be saying it soon. Anyway, what would a lovely girl like Cory want to be marrying an omadawn like you for? Oh my god, will you look at the time? Birdie must fly. Bye bye bye bye bye....'

After Larry Gogan played the recording, requests had started to come in to RTE dedicating the song to people who were sick in hospital. By then, after Harry had worked on him, Fergus Menton was enthusiastic about it too. Fergus had not forgotten Will's rudeness to him in the Baggot Inn, but he was willing to pretend to forget because, like Harry, he adored being close to talent. Which was why he was so good at being a researcher for the *Late Late Show*, the most popular TV programme in the country.

At first the show's presenter, Pat Kenny, had not been interested. Ferris was just another singer-songwriter plugging a record. But Fergus had the idea parcelled up as a package. Not only is Will Ferris maybe the new Bono, but also he is discovered in a pub by Toby Bowen, a teenage genius with a website, who is maybe a new Paul McGuinness (manager of U2). And the song is an anthem, a kind of religious anthem, a hymn to a her. Are the cubs of the Celtic Tiger turning their backs on materialism and turning their eyes to God? There was an angle there.

So Will and Toby had been invited to appear on the Late Late. The song would be sung and Pat Kenny would follow it up by talking to Toby, who was planted in the front row of the audience. But a technical glitch — just before Will was announced, his piano wouldn't amplify — had caused panic in the control room. Hearing the news through his earpiece, Pat said, quick as a flash, 'And to top off our show I can promise you a real treat. If the name Will Ferris doesn't mean anything to you now, it soon will. It's his first time on TV and he's as nervous as a bag of cats. But I can tell you, well, all I can tell you now is that this is a guy with something to say for himself. Hang about. Now, I know what you people are really interested in: our give-away quiz....'

You had to hand it to Pat: he was a pro; you'd have thought he was reading it off an idiot board.

This was fine as far as it went. But in the event another glitch, this time in timing, meant that after the song was sung, they were up close against the clock. So Pat went over to talk to Will and Toby only got a close-up, unexplained.

'Will Ferris,' Kenny started, then stopped for a micro second longer than the length of comma, to indicate that he had been overcome and was just now waking up to find it hard to find the words to say, 'That was just heavenly.'

'Thanks,' Will said, scowling.

'Really intense.'

'Yeah?'

'Absolutely riveting. *He Made It Out Of You*. Divine title.'

'Thanks.'

'It's a love song, but it's very spiritual, isn't it? An anthem. Would you say it has religious overtones?'

'Depends what you mean by religious.'

'What do you think it means?'

'Well, you've got me there. I wouldn't say it's heavenly, though, or divine.'

'I get the impression that you're not too happy with the state of things, with Celtic Tiger Ireland.'

'No, I'm as happy as Larry. I'm as happy as Larry Gogan. Anyway, that Celtic Tiger stuff, that's just tabloid talk. Real people don't talk like that.'

'Real people? Who would they be?'

'Ordinary people. They know who they are. The plain people of Ireland. They haven't sold out to the tabloids. That's only a media thing. It's only media airheads that talk like that. Prattlesnakes. That's what I call them. Prattlesnakes.' Will stopped long enough to realise that he had woken up and didn't quite know what had come over him. 'Of course,' he added, 'I don't mean you, Pat.'

Somebody in the audience tittered. But the tittering hadn't spread. Pat was too much a pro to allow that to happen. True, he didn't care to be condescended to by a mumbling brat with what looked like a lavatory brush sticking up on the top of his head. But Pat didn't care that much. What he cared about was getting back to his desk, phoning a complete stranger, asking him or her a simple question that only a deaf-and-dumb bonobo would be incapable of answering, e.g. 'How much are penny apples?' — though as Larry Gogan had told Pat from an eternity of experience quizzing the plain people of Ireland, you'd be amazed how many of them thought the answer was 'Two pence' — then telling her or him that she or he had just won a Renault Mégane. Thus ending another great *Late Late* and freeing Pat to drive home to Dalkey. Alone again, naturally. Which was the title of a really good song, by a real genius, Gilbert O'Sullivan, not Will Ferris.

Harry telling him in Kiely's that he was an ungrateful pup didn't bother Will much. All that mattered was that he had sung well. And as he moved through the crowd of well wishers towards his parents and Cory's parents — Paul thought Walter was 'a gas man' — Maeve MacNamee stopped him. On the other side of her, Cormac was haranguing Toby.

'Well,' she said, 'everybody loves you.'

Will said, 'Pat Kenny doesn't.'

'Pat Kenny is a prattlesnake.'

'No, he's not. He's a brilliant broadcaster and a very mannerly person.'

'Well, you taught him a lesson he won't forget in a hurry.'

'The only lesson Pat could have learned from me is: Don't talk to shitty people.'

As Will peeled off and departed into the crowd, Cormac, coming into earshot, said, 'What did he say?'

'He said I shouldn't talk to shitty people, like you,' Maeve said.

The pause for the comma was not half as long as a microsecond. Then she linked her bare arm with Toby's and pressed herself against him. So what if she was a baby-snatcher? Cormac Healy had to be taught a lesson, yet again. Everybody loved Will Ferris, but nobody loved him the way she did.

42

IT WAS ST JOHN'S Eve. In the morning Cory had rung Harry to wish him a happy birthday and to apologise for not being able to go to his party. It was the first week of her first ever real job and she couldn't be late for work — she was the most junior junior doctor in St Michael's in Dun Laoghaire and straightaway she'd been rostered for night duty. Harry had said that that was OK, he would grant her an audience at another occasion. These days he was indulging another of his enthusiasms, this time for the new Pope. John Paul II had died at the end of April, and immediately he had become obsessed with his replacement. Pope Benedict, 'Il mio caro Ben', as Harry called him, was clearly as gay as a lark, he had a gorgeous secretary, a priest called Gregory, and he wore Prada shoes. Harry's birthday present for himself was to go out and buy a pair, the exact same shade of papal red, 400 euro, and cheap at the price, because he had got them for half that. Of course he had been in love with the old Pope — how could you not be in love with a real man? — but on homosexuality John Paul had been that worst of all authority figures, 'a backward upright straight', whereas Ben, even if he was supposed to be conservative, would be bound to look kindly on those who were bent in the same Grecian direction as himself. He certainly wouldn't say of gay goings-on as John Paul had that, 'These acts have no finality.'

When Cory told this to Will, he said, 'That's all very well, but what the Pope was talking about is getting pregnant, and when it comes to that, these acts, whatever they are, really don't have any finality.'

She said, 'Do you know what? You make me laugh.'

St Michael's was little more than a cottage hospital, but at four o'clock in the morning of her first day there it seemed huge. The whole institution was her responsibility, or at least she was the only doctor who was awake in it. As dawn was breaking, she had gone out of the back entrance to escape the hospital heat and breathe the coolness of the new day. There, in a side street, she had come upon a hidden terrace of single-storey houses with gardens in the front. Each house had one window on either side of a hall-door with a fanlight over it. The grass in their little front gardens was tightly shaven, and spindly rosebushes top-heavy with flowers were beginning to have their old-fashioned perfume drawn out of them by the freshening air. One of these houses would suit her. It's not for nothing, she thought, that I'm my father's daughter. She knew what Walter knew, and at the end of her shift when she drove back to Leeson Street through the rush-hour traffic she felt light-headed with his knowledge and her freedom, the promise of going home when everybody else was going to work. And she was her mother's daughter, too, because Will had to be taken care of. This was absurd: the idea that she should mind a man was fantastically stupid, but someone dumb enough to dismiss the chance of a record deal in America simply because he didn't like the producer needed minding. Besides, playing at being a housewife was comical too: getting Will out of unravelling jumpers and sweaty tee-shirts into a clean shirt every day, and to hear him raging about being made to getting the wrinkles out of it — he had no idea how to use an iron — amused her. But clean shirts were as far as she would go in nannying him; after that he was on his own.

Work wasn't the only reason for bringing Will to the party early. Performing in the open air was not something he had done 'since my busking days', as if that was a hundred years ago, so he wanted to check out the venue and the new amplifier which

Toby Bowen had rung Cory to say he had found for him. Toby had rung her because Will still refused to have a mobile. Some things would never change. The reason the amplifier was new and not second-hand was because Toby was now selling a download of the original recording *He Made It Out Of You* on his website — business, like the amp, was booming. To be honest, the amplifier was a down payment on royalties, but it was also insurance, a soft hand under the golden goose.

'Do you know where you are?' Cory said as she rounded the bend on to the Vico Road. Will said he did, of course. But, of course, he didn't. If he had known, she wouldn't have asked. And when he asked her why she asked she wouldn't tell him, of course.

'Talking to you,' he said, 'is like doing a crossword without the benefit of having the clues.'

It was only when she parked the car and they had walked up the road that he recognised the path down to Hawk Cliff where the wash from the SeaCat had lifted her up and landed her on her feet, miraculously. That was months ago. He couldn't be expected to remember the path, which was invisible in the half-dark. What he didn't know was that Hawk Cliff and White Rock were so close to each other. A hundred yards along the road another path led down to the beach. They had arrived; they could walk there from here.

I don't get it, he thought — what's the mystery?

Cory was thinking too. She didn't expect him to remember anything but the miracle of the wave, which anyway was not a miracle. He couldn't have known that a moment had occurred as she saw him looking at her breast, blue with the cold, when she had realised that things had gone too far to stop now, and that of all the peculiar men in the world, she was going to have to trust this particular one. That he was allowed to sleep with her didn't mean she trusted him, of course. And it wasn't the cold alone that made her shiver. It was March then. She had only known him since January. Plus a few days in December. And of course there was the first night she had ever seen him, the Baggot Inn in November. Then there was a day in May on the bank of the Shannon. But if this was happiness, the sequence was disjointed, gapped but linked, packed full and in some peculiar way empty, so that she felt that there had been no past, no actual time, when these things actually happened, and yet now in the middle of the summer she had the evidence that they really had happened, and in the correct order too, inevitably, as if prearranged.

'At least you look the part,' she said The loose white shirt with the neck open suited him. All he needed was the flowing locks and he'd look like Lord Byron, or Percy Bysshe Shelley. But Will's hair would never flow: if she didn't cut it regularly, it grew straight out from his head, like a dirty blond Rumplestiltskin. She looked at her watch; it was quarter past ten; she had to be at work in fifteen minutes. It was still daylight, but the air was thickening and across the other side of the bay the Sugar Loaf, Three Rock Mountain and Bray Head were turning from navy blue to black, sharp-edged against a pale sky, pearly at the join with the land, but darker above. The sea was flat calm, indigo-coloured, and the tide was on the rise, motionless but brimming.

When they reached the end of the path, they crossed the railway bridge and stopped to look at what lay beneath them. Toby Bowen had done a good job. The food and drink were set out on trestle tables under white awnings and all around the cove he had strung rope-lights, which blinked on and off like fireflies in the gathering gloom.

Toby had told Cory his plan for staging the performance but it was only now that she understood it: the stage was a shelf of rock jutting out into the water with a cement platform on top — at full tide swimmers used it for diving from — and at eleven o'clock all the lights would be switched off except for a single spotlight high up on the cliff. The spot would pick out Will and he would seem to be floating in mid air, singing above the sea on what by then would be almost an island.

'Look,' Will said. Harry was walking across the sand towards the sea. In the near-darkness the red shoes could not be seen, but his cream linen suit and broad-brimmed straw hat were visibly elegant.

Cory stepped back out of sight into the shadows. 'Come here,' she said.

'You could at least give him a wave.'

'If he sees me, I'll never get away. I have to run.'

'Give me a kiss then.'

'There,' she said and pecked him on the cheek.

The protective wall of the bridge was made of metal much dented and sprayed with graffiti. Cory being forced back against it caused it to bend enough to produce an almost inaudible creak.

'Now,' Will said. 'That's what I call a kiss.'

'Get off me, you,' she said.

Again he pushed her back against the metal wall. Again, after a few seconds, a few more than the first time, she broke away.

'Fuck off, Will Ferris,' she said furiously.

Then she ran across the bridge and up the path to the road. She was going to be late for work. If she had had any sense, she'd have parked the car closer. What difference did it make to bring him to Hawk Cliff first? None. But what difference would it make if she was a few minutes late? None. She slowed to a walk. None, that is, if the car started. Well, if Will Ferris could have a new amplifier, she could have a new car. And if your aunt had balls, she could be your uncle. But they really did need more reliable transport. Something with a boot big enough to take the amplifier and the guitar. Although she hadn't said anything yet, she had already made up her mind on a station wagon. But he deserved to be told. She would do it when she got home in the morning. What he would get then he would deserve. For slamming her up against a wall like that, she'd finish him off. She would get her own back.

The air was cooling, but a still warm moon was rising low in the sky. The track of light that it cast shone more brightly silver on the sea than the floating golden stone it came from. She stopped briefly. Yes, she had heard a sound: it was the waves far below, rustling together like silk excited to speech. The path was breathing in the dark a sharp nettle scent, as if the way to go was a warning. She went on. There was something else Will needed to know. Tomorrow she would tell him why what he said about the Pope had made her laugh. He was just like Benedict: he hadn't the faintest idea what he was talking about. Or maybe he did. And maybe he was right. How could you not fear what joy had shown itself to be the key to? But the Pope had never taken a chance on happiness in his life, and he'd never counted the days afterwards — what did he know of finality? My god, she really was late, and it was all Will Ferris's fault.

As she ran along the Vico Road, an approaching van passed her, slowing down.

View of the Vico Road pathway looking towards Dalkey

View of the Vico Road path with entry to railway bridge at left

TRANSCRIPT OF EVIDENCE

Friday 27 January 2006: Evidence of Benedict J. Quinn

Sworn. Examined by Mr T. Greeley S.C.

1. You live at Duras House, Seafield Road, Killiney, County Dublin, isn't that right?
   — *That's right.*

2. You're a retired merchant seaman, a ship's captain?
   — *Like my father before me. I'm a sailor's son.*

3. I see. You are a widower, Mr Quinn, and you live alone?
   — *That's right.*

4. Now, on the night of the 23rd of June 2005, can you tell the court where you were?
   — *I was in my workshop, in the shed, in the garden.*

5. What were you doing there?
   — *I was building a ship. Not a real one. A model. Ships in bottles. It's my hobby.*

JUDGE: That's an age-old tradition amongst seafarers.

Witness: Well, I'm not the first man to do it.

6. Mr Greeley (to Witness): So you were making a model. What happened then?
   — *I heard a racket.*

7. A racket? What kind of racket?
   — *A noise. Boom-boom-boom.*

8. And this booming noise continued for some little while, did it not?
   — *It went on for, well, it just went on and on, and it was late and it was annoying me.*

9. It was annoying you. What did you do then?
   — *I thought it might be coming from the beach, so I went down there to have a look.*

10. Is the beach near your house?
    — *A couple of minutes' walk, maybe less.*

11. According to your statement, the beach was deserted, isn't that right?

— There wasn't a sinner in it, bar myself.

12.   I see. But though you could hear this booming noise more clearly, you still couldn't identify the source of it, is that right?

> *— Well, I knew it was coming from the direction of the White House.*

13.   The White House?

> *— The White House. It's down the end of the beach. It used to be a tearooms. A man called Homan ran it, a decent sort he was too, hired out boats, did a bit of lobster fishing, only he died there not so long ago, and the place is closed now. It's a bit of a ruin to tell you the truth.*

JUDGE: Mr Greeley, I fail to see what bearing Mr Homan or his ruin has on this trial.

Mr Greeley: Thank you, judge. I believe that we are about to show its relevance.

14.   Mr Greeley (to Witness): As I understand your evidence, you had walked down the beach and discovered that the boom-boom noise was not coming from the White House, is that right?

> *— Yeah, it was coming from White Rock.*

15.   JUDGE: The White House and the White Rock?

> *— White Rock, your lordship, it's the next beach to Killiney, but you can't see it, if you get my meaning.*

16.   Mr Greeley (To Witness): There's a headland between them, a rocky headland, isn't that right?

> *— That's right. When the tide is out, you can walk from Killiney beach to White Rock, but when the tide is in, you can't. And you can't see what's going on there either.*

17.   The only way you can get to it then is from the Vico Road, isn't that right?

> *— That's right. So I thought I might go and have a look.*

18.   How did you do that?

> *— Well, I went up...*

JUDGE: I hope this is not going to be another long journey.

19.   Mr Greeley: How long did it take, Mr Quinn?

— About ten minutes. There's a short cut.

20.   A short cut?

— Yeah, a path. Under the railway bridge, up by Bono's house.

21.   JUDGE: Whose house?

— Bono's.

Mr Greeley: Bono, my lord, the lead singer with U2, the band.

JUDGE: I believe I've heard of them.

22.   Mr Greeley (to Witness): Can you describe this path?

— Well, it goes up between two walls. It's very steep. Dark and dirty.

23.   And can you tell the jury what you saw on this dark and dirty path?

— I saw two people, just there near the top.

24.   Can you tell the court what these two people were doing?

— They were in a clinch.

25.   A clinch?

— Yeah.

26.   They were courting?

— Well, I don't know about that. He had her up against the wall. They were having it off I'd say.

27.   I see. And what happened then?

— Well, when they saw me coming they ran away. The bird ran up towards the Vico and the bloke ran down the hill towards the train station.

28.   Can you describe this bloke, this man?

— Not really. All I can say is that he was wearing a mackintosh.

29.   He was wearing a mackintosh, that is a raincoat. But it was a fine night, was it not?

— Yes, that's why I noticed it.

30.   May it please the court; no trace of this person has ever been found, despite the best efforts of the authorities. Now, Mr Quinn, the woman who ran away towards the Vico Road, did you see her face?

— No, she had her back to me.

31.   But she was recognisable, was she not?

— You couldn't miss her. She was wearing this white get-up, white

jeans and a white top, all white. Well, it was dark, so they could
have been a different colour, maybe yellow or something, but they
looked white.

32. Do you see that person in court today?
    — *I do. Missy there. That's her.*

33. The witness is referring to the accused, Marilyn Rovinj, also
    known as Missy. Mr Quinn, can I ask you this? Were you not
    surprised to come upon two people, as you put it, having it
    off outside Bono's house at this unearthly hour?
    — *Not really. There's people there morning, noon and night. The*
    man never gets a minute's peace with them. They spend their
    time writing their names on his walls. So that's what I thought
    this pair might be up to. Waiting for Bono and writing graffiti.
    As well as the other thing of course.

34. I see, I see. So, Mr Quinn, you saw this woman running
    up towards the Vico Road. What did you do then?
    — *I went after her. I didn't follow her, do you get me? I just went*
    in the same direction.

35. I understand. And when you got to the Vico Road, what did
    you see?
    — *I saw cars. And people. Lots of cars and lots of people.*

36. How many cars would you say?
    — *I don't know. They were parked every which way along the road,*
    up on the footpath and everything. You'd only see the like of it on
    a sunny weekend. And there was taxis coming and going.

37. I see. And how many people were there, would you say?
    — *There must have been fifty, sixty, maybe a hundred, I don't know.*

38. And what were these people doing, Mr Quinn?
    — *They were going down to the beach, to White Rock.*

39. There is a path down to the beach?
    — *That's right.*

40. Mr Greeley: At this point, judge, I think it would be helpful
    if the jury could consult the photographs of the area in the
    booklet they have been supplied with. Now, Mr Quinn, can
    you tell the court how these fifty or sixty people, this crowd,

were making their way to the beach?

— *They were going down the path there.*

41. It's a tarred path, it's got tarmac on it, isn't that right?

— *Yes.*

42. There is a photograph taken from the bottom of the path, looking back towards the road, isn't that right?

— *That's right.*

43. And there is a photograph looking down the path, isn't that correct?

— *Correct.*

44. But there is also another path, isn't that right?

— *That's right.*

45. Can you describe it?

— *It's narrow, and steep, like the one at Bono's place, only it's got more steps.*

46. These paths meet at the point where they cross the railway bridge, isn't that correct?

— *Correct.*

47. May it please the court, the steps have been counted and there are sixty-one of them. That's a very steep climb, Mr Quinn, but easier to go down than up, isn't that right?

— *I've done both in my time. I'm pretty fit for a sixty-eight year-old.*

48. Very good, very good. Now, could you tell the jury what you did then?

— *I went down the steps. Or I tried to anyway.*

49. You say you tried to go down, Mr Quinn. What prevented you?

— *Well, when I got near the end of the steps, I saw they were blocked.*

50. The steps were blocked. How were they blocked?

— *With a van. There was a van, a Hiace, parked right up tight against the steps. I couldn't get past it. I was gobsmacked.*

51. You were gobsmacked. Why was that?

— *Well, I never saw a van there in my life, or a car. It's wide enough, but it's not a road. For one thing, the path is blocked off up at the road with a barrier. There's a kind of a pole, you know, a steel pole across the opening. It's got a lock on it.*

52. Judge, the jury will hear evidence in due course that the lock on this barrier had been broken. Now, Mr Quinn, your way was blocked. Can you tell the court what you did next?
— *I didn't do anything. I just stood there looking at what was going on.*

53. You stood there looking on. It was dark of course. Could you see clearly?
— *Well, there was a good moon, and the van's lights, the headlights, were on full. They were blinding the people.*

54. The people coming down the path were blinded by the lights. I take it then that the van must have reversed down the path, is that right?
— *That's right.*

55. Tell me this, Mr Quinn, were the lights on inside the van, that is in the cab?
— *No.*

56 So you couldn't see whether there was anyone in it?
— *There was someone in it all right, only I couldn't see them, but I could hear them, or I heard them when the racket stopped.*

57. What racket?
— *The boom-boom.*

58. The booming noise that had brought you there in the first place?
— *Yeah, the closer I got, the more I could hear it. Boom boom boom, it was that loud it made your insides, what do you call it, vibrate.*

59. This noise was so loud it made your insides vibrate?
— *Yeah. It was like an earthquake. I don't know why they call it music.*

60. Indeed. And then it stopped. The music stopped, is that right?
— *That's right.*

61. And then you heard, what did you hear?
— *Shouting. In the van. There was women shouting in the van, two women.*

62. And what were these women shouting about?
— *Money. Something about money and not getting paid. I don't*

know, I couldn't make it out properly. But they were effing and blinding good-oh.

63. They were cursing? They were swearing?

  — *Like troopers.*

64. Now, Mr Quinn, let us turn our attention again to the path. As I understand it, people were streaming down the path, is that right?

  — *Yeah. Well, when I got there they weren't streaming. They were stopped. They were in a kind of a queue.*

65. Why was that, Mr Quinn?

  — *The only way they could get down to the beach was they had to go past the van and they were stopped, or going slow anyway. It was that narrow, like a bottleneck.*

66. The van created a bottleneck. That was a convenient way of ensuring that only people with invitations could get into the party, wasn't it?

JUDGE: That's a matter of opinion, Mr Greeley. Let's stick to the facts as the witness knows them.

Mr Greeley: Judge, I was about to ask the witness if he saw signs of a security presence there, whether or not this queue was being organised and marshalled.

JUDGE: Well, ask him then.

67. Mr Greeley (to Witness.): Was this queue organised, Mr Quinn? Was there security? Did you see what is popularly known as bouncers?

  — *Well, there was a guy there all right, but I couldn't see him clearly. The van was blocking my view. All I could see was people queuing up and then going across the bridge.*

68. Very good. What was the atmosphere like?

  — *It was grand. It was like a lot of young fellows and young ones, girls like. They were well tanked up I'd say. They were carrying on, you know, shouting and laughing and generally acting the maggot.*

69. Acting the maggot? They were having a good time; they were having a party?

— *Yeah.*

70. And what happened then, Mr Quinn?
    — *Well, the queue had cleared; do you know what I mean? They'd got past the van and the path was empty, so I thought, that's it. I'd copped on it was one of those rave things, do you get me? So I thought, that's it, I've seen enough, let the guards sort it out, and I headed off home.*

71. But you didn't go, did you? Can you tell the jury why?
    — *Well, I saw this couple. A man and a woman.*

72. I see. You thought they were a couple, did you?
    — *Well, there was a pair of them in it.*

73. There was a pair of them in it. Were they going down to the beach?
    — *No, that's why I noticed them. They were coming the opposite way, up from the beach.*

74. They had come up from the beach, crossed the bridge and were going up the path, is that right?
    — *Yeah. Except they didn't go up the path. They stopped in front of the van.*

75. So you could see them clearly by the headlights, is that correct?
    — *I could see her all right.*

76. How do you mean?
    — *Well, you could hardly not see her. She was wearing this mini-skirt thing. Skirt is too big a word for it. I've seen bigger belts on a judo wrestler. She must have been petrified with the cold, not that it was cold.*

JUDGE: Mr Quinn, would you please confine your evidence to what you saw. Kindly refrain from expressing your opinions, however colourful.

Witness: Fair enough, your honour.

JUDGE: And please do not refer to me as your honour. I am simply a judge.

Mr Greeley: Yes, yes. Members of the jury, there is no dispute about the identity of the young woman in question. Her name is Maeve MacNamee. Miss MacNamee will give evidence later in this trial. As for the young man, his name is William Ferris. There are questions about his identification that I will return to later.

JUDGE: That is a separate matter.

Mr Greeley: Yes, separate is the word for it.

77.   Mr Greeley (to Witness.): Now then, can you describe Mr Ferris for the jury?

— *Well, tall. About six foot. Well built. Big chest on him. Blondie hair, sticking up, you know. He was a bit of scruffbag.*

78.   A bit scruffy?

— *Yeah, his shirt was sticking out. And he had a guitar. He was carrying a guitar in a case.*

79.   This is the guitar that was found the following day floating in the river. Can I ask you—?

Mr O'BOYLE S.C. (for the Defence): Judge, judge, I wish to make an application. This is quite improper.

Mr Greeley: There is no argument that the guitar was found —

JUDGE: Mr Greeley, there is an argument. There is a legal argument. Ladies and gentlemen of the jury, I will have to ask you to retire for a little while.

[THE JURY RETIRED AT 11.17 A.M.]

JUDGE: I hardly need to remind the media, but I will, that nothing may be reported of what is said here in the course of legal argument. Not one iota of it, not even a hint. Is that understood? Very well. Now, Mr O'Boyle.

Mr O'Boyle: It is grossly improper for Mr Greeley as an experienced Senior Counsel to refer to the evidence of other witnesses while leading a witness.

Mr Greeley: I did no such thing.

Judge: What were you doing then?

Mr Greeley: I was about to establish how the guitar case was being carried by Mr Ferris.

Mr O'Boyle: Reference was made to the guitar being found.

Mr Greeley: The jury knows that from my opening address.

Mr O'Boyle: Well, they know it, but Mr Quinn doesn't. And now, before he can open his mouth, the prosecution has told him not just that the guitar was found but that it was in the river Liffey, eight miles away.

Mr Greeley: What possible influence could that have on him?

Mr O'Boyle: I suppose we have to be thankful Mr Greeley did not imply that the guitar was thrown into river by Miss Rovinj.

Mr Greeley: I never implied any such thing.

JUDGE: We have already heard legal argument about that matter.

Mr O'Boyle: And you ruled it was improper.

JUDGE: I know what I ruled, Mister O'Boyle, I don't require to be told.

Mr Greeley: The guitar was found. There is no argument about that.

Mr O'Boyle: It's been reported in the newspapers. That doesn't make it a fact.

JUDGE: That's enough.

Mr Greeley: Can I say that I regret any discourtesy to the court or indeed to my learned friend? I was merely trying to establish whether Mr Quinn was aware of —

JUDGE: Mr Quinn's awareness is irrelevant when it comes to any evidence but his own. You should have stuck to the point, Mr Greeley. I would be obliged if you stick to it from now on. However, unless Mr O'Boyle wishes to make a formal application, I will merely note it now.

Mr O'Boyle: With leave to re-enter?

JUDGE: Yes, yes. Very well. The jury can be recalled.

[JURY RETURNS 11.24 AM]

JUDGE: Thank you for your patience, ladies and gentlemen. We are going to begin where we left off. Mr Greeley?

80. Mr Greeley (to witness): Mr Quinn, you have given evidence that Mr Ferris was carrying a guitar case. Can you tell the jury how Mr Ferris was carrying this case? Was it under his arm, for instance?

    — *No, he had it slung over his shoulder, like on a strap.*

81. His hands were free?

    — *Yes.*

82.	Now Mr Ferris and Miss MacNamee had come up from the beach and they were standing in front of the van. What were they doing there?

— *They were talking.*

83.	Talking?

— *Yeah. Well, she was, I don't know, maybe not arguing with him, but she was saying a lot anyway.*

84.	You couldn't hear what she was saying, though, could you?

— *No. The boom-boom had started up again. It was the same old same old, so I couldn't hear them.*

85.	Yes, yes. You couldn't hear the words, but you did observe the conversation. Would you say from Miss MacNamee's behaviour that she was being vehement? That is to say extremely intense, or strident?

— *I wouldn't go that far. It was, like, normal enough. She was gasbagging at him. That's about all it was.*

86.	Gasbagging, I see. So she was just gasbagging. And can you tell the court what happened then?

— *I heard this shouting. No.*

87.	No?

— *No, first of all I should have said they were kissing.*

88.	They were kissing each other?

— *Well, she kissed him. Now I wouldn't say she was bet into him exactly but —*

89.	Bet into him?

— *No, but she was giving him a good smacker.*

90.	I see. Now, you said earlier that the first thing you heard was shouting, and you then corrected yourself and said you saw the couple kissing. Can you say which came first?

— *I can't really. They were close together. It might have been the same time even. I couldn't say.*

91.	Very good. Now, can you tell the jury who was doing this shouting?

— *Well, it was like lads, kind of like jeering. You know, lads having a jeer.*

92. Lads having a jeer. There was more than one lad. How many?

    — *There was two of them.*

93. Can you describe them for the court?

    — *Well, they were twisted.*

94. Twisted? You mean drunk.

    — *Drunk as lords. One of them, the little one, he was like a cripple.*

95. A cripple?

    — *He had a walking stick and a plaster cast on his arm. Rolling all over the place he was, he was that far-gone.*

96. There is no argument about the identity of this person. It was Mr Cormac Healy. And the other person, can you describe him please?

    — *Well, tall, big burly chap, greasy hair, little glasses.*

97. This is Mr Emmet Roche. That is accepted. Both these gentlemen will give evidence in due course. Now, Mr Quinn, can you tell the jury what Mr Roche was doing?

    — *He was setting fire to the place.*

98. Setting fire to the place. What place?

    — *The bushes, the bushes there beside the path.*

99. And how was he doing that?

    — *With matches. He was lighting matches and flicking them into the bushes. Then he, like, I don't know, I'd say he set fire to the whole box of matches and he threw it away from him, like, you know, like he had to, like he was dancing to get rid of it.*

100. I see. Can you tell the jury what Mr Healy was doing at this moment in time?

    — *He was coming down the path, waving his stick.*

101. Waving his stick? In a threatening fashion?

    — *Well, I don't know. You could say he wasn't too happy at the carry on, the kissing and all that.*

102. And Mr Ferris, what did Mr Ferris do?

    — *Well, he sort of went to meet him, in that direction anyway.*

103. And would you say Mr Ferris was angry, behaving in a threatening fashion?

    — *No, not a bit of it. He was laughing.*

104. Mr Ferris was laughing?

    — *Yes.*

105. Let me get this straight. Mr Healy had his stick raised and Mr Ferris was laughing. What happened then? Was a blow struck?

    — *Yeah, but not by Healy.*

106. Not by Healy? By whom then? Who struck the blow?

    — *Ferris. It was Ferris struck the blow, but it wasn't Healy he hit. It was the other fellow.*

107. What other fellow?

    — *Roche. Ferris hit Roche, but he didn't start it, you see, because Roche came at him like a mad bull, and he gave Ferris this great push that knocked him back. He knocked Ferris flying, and he went bang into the van, so Ferris came back and Roche made to push him again and Ferris just stuck out his right hand and down Roche went, like a sack of spuds. Or at least I think he went down.*

108. JUDGE: Mr Quinn, don't tell us what you thought, just tell us what you saw. Did Mr Roche fall or did he not?

    — *Well, I don't know, your honour. I saw him getting a smack in the gob, like he'd run into a brick wall, and then, it was like I was looking at him one minute and then the next thing was the whole place went up.*

109. JUDGE: The whole place went up. What do you mean?

    — *It was like the bushes went up in a flash. I don't know whether there was like a gust of wind or what, but the bushes just burst out into flames.*

110. Mr Greeley (to Witness.): The bushes burst out into flames. Now, Mr Quinn, let us try to be quite precise about what happened next. What did you see?

    — *Well, I saw these two women, the ones that were in the van —*

    Mr O'Boyle: I object.

111. Mr Greeley (to Witness.): Let me deal with Mr O'Boyle's objection. You say, Mr Quinn, that these two women were in the van, but you are only surmising that, isn't that so?

— No.

Mr O'Boyle: No, no.

Mr Greeley: Mr Quinn, you misunderstand the point.

JUDGE: Mr O'Boyle, when I come to give my charge to the jury, I will address this matter. As of now, I am minded to allow the witness to say that the two women he saw were the same women he believes had earlier been arguing in the van.

112. Mr Greeley: Mr Quinn, do you understand his lordship's point?

   — Yeah, but it was them all right.

JUDGE: Be quiet there. This is a serious matter. I will not have people sniggering in court. Just answer Counsel's questions, Mr Quinn. Try not to express your opinion about them.

Witness: OK. I get you.

113. Mr Greeley (to Witness.): Now, can I ask you to describe these two women?

   — Well, one of them was the one I saw at Bono's house, the one in the ringlets.

114. Missy Rovinj. And the other woman, can you describe her please?

   — Well, she was half-naked.

115. Half-naked?

   — Yeah. She had no top on.

116. Now this was remarkable, was it not?

   — It's not the kind of thing you see every night of the week.

Mr O'Boyle: This is more of it.

JUDGE: I am losing my patience. Go on, Mr Greeley.

117. Mr Greeley (to Witness.): Can you say anything else about the appearance of this half-naked woman? What did she look like, her age and so on?

   — About forty, I'd say, maybe forty-five. Blonde. Long blonde hair. Smallish woman. Smaller anyway than the daughter.

118. Can you identify her in the court?

   — That's her there.

119. The witness is indicating the defendant, Mrs Margaret

Rovinj, known as Mazee. Now, Mr Quinn, can you tell the court what Mrs Rovinj was doing when you saw her first?

— *Well, I don't know what she was doing, I don't know what she was up to, but she was raging.*

120. She was raging?

— *She was in a fury. Like she was going to burst. I don't think she was screaming, only she was like she couldn't get the screams out of her. But I only saw her for a couple f seconds. Like I said, it was all going on at the same time, and I'd hardly seen her and then the next thing the fire started. It just blew up and I was looking at that. That's what got my attention I suppose.*

121. You say you were looking at the fire; what did you see there?

— *I saw the fellow running into the bushes. Young Ferris.*

122. Young Ferris ran into the bushes?

— *He ran right into the fire, straight into the flames. That's what I saw.*

123. And what did you see then?

— *I heard this scream, a loud high scream it was, and I looked and there I saw the young one with the ringlets. She was running up the path and your woman without the top, she was going after her.*

124. Going after her? Do you mean she was chasing her? Was Mazee, that is Mrs Rovinj, chasing after her daughter?

— *I don't know about that. I wouldn't say she was. It was more like she was following after. But then I was looking at the fire too, so I didn't see, if you know what I mean.*

125. There was a great deal of speed and confusion and the sequence of events may not be clear in your memory, Mr Quinn, but you are clear that you saw Mr Ferris plunging into the flames and after that you heard a scream and saw Missy running up the path, followed by her mother, is that right?

— *That's right.*

126. Very good. And what happened next?

— *The next thing is the young fellow, young Ferris, out he comes out of the fire, and there was like smoke coming off him. You could see it in the headlights. And he was carrying, well; I didn't know what it was at the start. And then I saw, you could have knocked me down a feather, it was this young kid.*

127. A young kid? A boy?

— *Yeah. He must have been in the bushes. God knows what he was doing there. In the fire he was. He was sitting in the middle of the fire.*

JUDGE: Mr Quinn's surprise seems reasonable to me. What was the child doing there at that time of night?

Mr Greeley: He was playing with an electronic toy, a Gameboy.

JUDGE: Mr Greeley, the question was rhetorical. Continue please.

Mr Greeley: Beg pardon. The jury will hear evidence in due course that this boy is Thomas, the son of Mazee Rovinj.

128. Mr Greeley (to Witness): Now, when Mr Ferris came out of the bushes with the boy in his arms, can you tell the court what happened next?

— *Well, there was all this smoke, but from what I could see the women attacked him.*

129. The women attacked Mr Ferris?

— *Yeah. Only I don't know if they were attacking him really; they were kind of tearing at him. Tearing the boy off him.*

130. Now let us get this straight. By 'the women' whom do you mean?

— *Missy and Mazee.*

131. But not Miss MacNamee? Let me re-phrase that. Where was Miss MacNamee at this time?

— *Well, she was there all right, but she was trying to get them to lay off.*

132. To get them to lay off? That is to stop them attacking Mr Ferris?

— *Yeah. They were shouting and screaming. The young one and her ma were screaming.*

133. Could you hear what they were saying?

— *They were cursing him. Calling him a pervert. That was the one word I heard. Pervert.*

134. JUDGE: Mr Quinn, can I ask you to clarify something for the jury? How far away were you from this incident?

— *Twenty or thirty yards.*

Mr O'Boyle: Thirty yards is fifty per cent further than twenty.

JUDGE: That's why I asked, Mr O'Boyle. The jury should be aware that Mr Quinn's evidence may have to be tested on the ground as it were. That remains to be seen. Let's hear the evidence first.

135. Mr Greeley (to Witness): You say Mr Ferris was being attacked, torn at, or let me put it like this, beset by these two women. By Mrs Rovinj anyway and her daughter, and that Miss MacNamee was also present. Would that be a fair summary of your evidence?

— *Yes.*

136. And while this was happening what were Mr Roche and Mr Healy doing?

— *I don't know really. I'd say they were like looking on, like they were having a laugh at the whole schemozzle.*

Mr O'Boyle: The witness says he really doesn't know, then he imagines something, then he asserts they were having a laugh.

137. JUDGE: Do you hear that objection, Mr Quinn? You can only give evidence on what you saw and heard, not on what you imagined or supposed.

— *Sorry about that.*

138. Mr Greeley (to Witness): Can you say for certain that Mr Roche and Mr Healy were looking on and laughing?

— *I can, I can. That's right.*

139. And Missy and Mazee Rovinj were trying to tear the child away from Mr Ferris, out of his arms, is that right?

— *That's right.*

140. What happened then? Tell the court what you saw.

— *Can I say what I heard first?*

141. What you heard? What did you hear?

— *I heard the engine revving, I heard the engine of the van revving like mad.*

142.	I see. The engine of the van had been idling all this time, hadn't it?

— *Yeah. But now it revved up like crazy, like he'd put his foot right down on the floor.*

143.	I won't ask you who this 'he' was. At this moment in time you hadn't seen anyone in the van, had you?

— *No.*

144.	Tell us what you did see.

— *OK. Well, the van just leapt forward full pelt.*

145.	Full pelt? You mean at top speed?

— *It went off like a rocket. And the brakes were screeching. That van, burning rubber she was, she flew up that path like nobody's business. Straight at them, straight at the crowd of them. But the funny thing was, you know, they all scattered, they got out of the way in jig time, I can tell you, but the funny thing is, that young fellow, young Ferris, he just stood there. Didn't move, didn't budge. Not an inch. He looked like, I don't know, like he was thinking of something else, like he wasn't bothered he was going to be run down.*

146.	Did you see him being hit by the van, Mr Quinn?

— *No, I didn't see that. I couldn't. My view was blocked. I couldn't see it for the van. But the last thing I saw he was standing right in front of it.*

147.	Very good, very good. Now this is an important point: did the van brake, did the driver of the van apply the brakes?

— *No.*

148.	No?

— *No. He went straight through the guy.*

Mr O'Boyle: I object. The witness has already said he didn't see what happened and now he says —

JUDGE: Yes, yes. Mr Greeley, you asked did the driver apply the brakes. The answer was no. Go on from there.

149.	Mr Greeley (to Witness): As far as you could see, the van went straight through where Mr Ferris was standing, is that right?

— Yeah. Then he stopped. Further on he stopped. The van stopped.

150. What happened then?

    — Well, I was like, I thought, Jesus Christ, and I came down the steps where I was, I came down off the steps and I went up towards the van.

151. How far away was that, would you say?

    — Maybe forty yards, maybe fifty.

152. The van had gone past the fire, past the burning bushes? Had it gone into the dark?

    — Well, now that you say it, I suppose it had. But I could still see it, there was a lot of smoke, but I could still see the brake lights, you know, the rear lights.

153. So you went towards the van. And what happened then?

    — I saw this guy coming at me.

154. You saw this guy coming at you?

    — Yeah, and the others were running away from him.

155. The others were running away from him. What others?

    — The young fellows and the young one.

156. That is Mr Healy, Mr Roche and Miss MacNamee?

    — That's right.

157. But not Missy or Mazee or the child, Thomas? Where were they?

    — They were around the front of the van I suppose.

158. No, no, don't suppose. Did you see them?

    — No. But I saw someone else.

159. Someone else. Can you describe this person, please?

    — Blocky fellow, squat like. Built like a brick, you know. He was coming at me.

160. Do you see this man in court today?

    — That's him.

161. The witness is indicating Tomas Rovinj, the third defendant. Now, Mr Quinn, you say Mr Rovinj was coming at you?

    — Yeah, like a bull.

162. Was he carrying anything?

    — Yeah. He had this huge cleaver and he was kind of making swipes

at the air with it.

163. He was making swipes at the air. What kind of cleaver was this?
    — *A butcher's cleaver.*

164. A butcher's cleaver. So what did you do then?
    — *Well, I ran. I don't mind telling you, I turned around and ran back the way I came. Up the steps.*

165. And did Mr Rovinj follow you?
    — *No. He wasn't interested in me. He was after the others.*

166. He was chasing after Mr Roche, Mr Healy and Miss MacNamee?
    — *Yes.*

167. Where did they go? In relation to you, where were they?
    — *They ran across the bridge, down to the beach.*

168. But Mr Rovinj didn't follow them, did he?
    — *No.*

169. Can you tell the court what Mr Rovinj did?
    — *Well, he ran across the bridge, but he didn't go all the way, if you know what I mean. He went about half the way and he was banging the cleaver on the walls.*

170. The bridge is enclosed between metal walls, a wire-mesh actually, a grille, isn't that right?
    — *That's right.*

171 And you saw him hitting the grille with the cleaver, is that right?
    — *That's right.*

172. And was he doing anything else at this time?
    — *He was roaring, like an ape.*

173. Could you see Mr Roche, Mr Healy and Miss MacNamee at this point?
    — *No. They'd scarpered. They'd made themselves scarce.*

174. No, no, that's an opinion. You didn't see them, you couldn't see them, isn't that it?
    — *That's it.*

175. And what did Mr Rovinj do then?
    — *He ran back up the path.*

176. And what did you do?

   — *Well, I went up the steps and I kept going. To tell you the truth, I was scared shitless; I was scared out of my wits. I wanted to get out of there, so I kept on going up the steps. But then I thought, well, I thought, you know, that young fellow, he must be, I thought he might be still.... Well, I thought I'd go back and see could I give him a bit of a dig-out.*

177. A dig-out. You went back to see could you give Mr Ferris a helping hand, isn't that right?

   — *Well, I suppose I did. I wasn't acting the hero or anything, you know. Anyway, your man, I thought your man with the cleaver, he's not coming after me, so that's why I went back. I wasn't in any danger. There was no fear of me getting hurt.*

JUDGE: Mr Quinn, if I may say so no one in this court doubts your courage, but try to confine yourself to what you saw.

Witness: I wasn't that brave, your honour. I can tell you that for a fact. I only went a bit of the way. And I wasn't in any hurry either. I didn't run, I was walking because, you know, I was looking for something, because I thought if I meet this boyo I'm going to need something to defend myself with, and so I was walking along there nice and easy and my foot hit something on the path and when I picked it up what was it but the walking-stick, young Healy's walking-stick. He must have dropped it, or maybe he threw it away I don't know.

JUDGE: That may be a reasonable speculation, Mr Quinn, but it is a speculation nonetheless. Please don't speculate.

Witness: OK.

178. Mr Greeley (to Witness.): You picked up this walking stick. Was there anything you noticed about it?

   — *There was blood on it. There was blood on my hands.*

Mr O'Boyle: I object. The witness could not have known it was blood.

JUDGE: Mr Greeley, ask the question.

179. Mr Greeley (to Witness): You didn't know it was blood at the time, did you?

   — *No, but I soon found out.*

180. What do you mean by that?

— *I mean when I got home and washed my hands there was blood on them. I saw it in the water, the water ran red, or brown, and I remembered the stick when I picked it up, it was wet like.*

181. JUDGE: Mr Quinn, you will be examined on this matter in due course by Mr O'Boyle, but can I ask you to help the jury with an obvious question, which is this. In your evidence earlier you say you saw Mr Healy waving his stick and approaching Mr Ferris, isn't that right?

— *That's right.*

182. JUDGE: But you did not see Mr Healy strike Mr Ferris, did you?

— *No.*

JUDGE: Thank you. That's very helpful.

183. Mr Greeley (to Witness): You can't be sure that you didn't touch something else that had blood on it, can you?

— *Well, I'm pretty sure.*

184. You're pretty sure. In any event you picked up the walking stick, and what did you do then?

— *Well, do you see, I went towards the van and, like, the doors were open, the back doors were open.*

185. The doors of the van were open. Could you see anyone inside it?

— *I saw Missy and the kid.*

186. Can you recall what Missy was doing?

— *Well, she had her back to me. She was standing up and leaning over the seats there, you know, the front seats, like she was looking out the window, the windscreen.*

187. And the boy, Thomas, what was he doing?

— *He was sitting there on the ground, on the floor of the van, and he was like playing the what do you call it?*

188. The Gameboy. He was playing with his game. Is that right?

— *Yeah. Do you know what I'm going to tell you? When I saw that it stopped me in my tracks. It was queer, like he didn't notice anything was going on. And the next thing around the side of the van came your man.*

189. Mr Rovinj?

    — *That's right. The very man.*

190. How far away was Mr Rovinj from you at this point?

    — *I'd say maybe fifteen, maybe twenty yards.*

191. So, Mr Quinn, from a distance of fifteen or twenty yards you saw Mr Rovinj. Can you tell the court what he was doing?

    — *He was carrying the young fellow. He was carrying young Ferris.*

192. I see. Can you describe what he did?

    — *Well, it all happened so quick you know. It was like he came around the side of the van, and he banged into the door or something. Anyway he looked like he couldn't get a right hold on him, on the young fellow, like he was falling, or maybe he was fighting.*

193. Mr Quinn, your evidence on this point is extremely important. Please do not say 'like' or 'maybe' in your answers. Can you tell the court was Mr Ferris fighting or not? Was he moving?

    — *Well, I've thought a lot about that, but it all happened, it could only have been a couple of seconds, and to tell you the truth, I don't know was he alive or maybe he was just being, like, flung about.*

194. He was maybe just being flung about. Can you say what happened next?

    — *Well, your man just fired him into the back of the van.*

195. Mr Rovinj just fired Mr Ferris into the back of the van. And what did he do then?

    — *He jumped in after him and they took off.*

196. They took off. Who is they?

    — *The van. The van took off. The doors were swinging like billyo, so the mother must have put her foot down.*

197. No, no, you cannot say who was driving the van.

    — *Well, it had to be Mazee. It couldn't have been anyone else. That only stands to reason.*

198. It's the woman not the name, Mr Quinn. It's the very fact of

her being a woman at all that is the difficulty; don't you understand that?

— *I don't get you.*

199. You didn't see who was driving the van, so you can't say it was or it was not a woman when you don't actually know, can you?

— *I don't see why not. They never found the young fellow's head and still you know he was murdered.*

JUDGE: That's quite enough.

Witness: Sure, we wouldn't be here otherwise, would we?

43

THERE WAS, CORY said, something special about her father's performance after the funeral. That night in Leeson Street Walter had given a virtuoso recital of his troubles with Bertolt Brecht and the Arts Council, a performance he had swelled out with a version of 'The Threepenny Opera', sung in mock German. Even Will's mother, who thought he was a dreadful person, had laughed. Walter had been sober, well dressed, closely shaven, and smelling of talcum powder, but one of his shoes was black and the other was brown. The next day he had got up at dawn and gone off without a word to the early opening pubs; then he had taken the train to Galway, but only reappeared in Bunnahowan a week later.

Will's body had been found in the sea off Howth in early July. Now it was the middle of January. In the intervening months Harry had seen Cory almost every day, usually at night — she had gone back to work as soon as she could. He had often wondered did she know that he knew that Maeve MacNamee had come to see her in October. Almost four months had passed before Cory mentioned it.

If not then, why now?

Most of what she said wasn't news to Harry. But hearing what Emmet said when he put his huge hand in her lap in Doheny and Nesbitt's snug was something he hadn't heard before.

'He didn't say that,' Harry said.

But he did.

Nor had Harry heard that when Maeve came to Leeson Street she had brought flowers and a box of chocolates.

'That's gross,' he said.

Maeve had said the reason she had come to talk to Cory was to say that Emmet was cracking up. He was racked with remorse. His jealousy had started it all, none of it could have happened without him, he wanted to apologise, but he didn't know how. His head was wrecked. And of course his mother was terminally ill. On top of which the police were asking questions about Missy Rovinj and how well she knew Maeve. Had Cory heard anything about that?

Harry said, 'You didn't tell her I told you about their lesbian thing, did you?'

'Of course not.'

Cory had told Maeve nothing. Nor had she said anything to the guards. The explanation was simple: they hadn't asked. Miss MacNamee was not a suspect; she was immaterial; she didn't matter.

But that was October. Now it was January. The night was cold. Cory's head was hot and her body, clogged with baby, was about to burst. She had asked Harry to call because that morning a cardboard tube had arrived in the post.

Harry fingered out the photocopied image that was inside the tube.

The objects in the background were vague, indicated with washes of shadow and a few lines of ink: a steel table, an aluminium ladder, an industrial blow-heater. But the figures in the foreground were pin-sharp. Emmet, though, looked more imposing than he did in real life, like a Greek god in fact, and Cory, naked and down on her knees, was looking up at him with a look of abandoned adoration.

'Well,' Harry said, 'I always knew Emmet was an animal, but I fail to see why he's doing this.'

'It's not him, it's Maeve.'

Harry had to agree, eventually. And eventually he said, 'Really, at the end of the day, Maeve is a naughty girl, but she's hardly Satan, is she? I mean she doesn't have to have her hooves pared to fit into her Manolo Blahniks. You shouldn't get worked up about it. What's the point of paying twopence for a penny apple?'

That had worked in bringing down Cory's temperature — it appealed to her to have her own deflationary principle applied to herself. But by the time they arrived at this point, the drawing had been reduced to ashes in the fire and all she wanted to do was go to bed. She had to be up early in the morning: it was her last day of work before going on maternity leave.

That had been the last time she had spoken to him about Maeve at any length. She would occasionally ask had he seen the others, but the only one she was interested in was Cormac. That was because he had sent her a letter saying he was sorry, which was all the more pathetic for being semi-literate. The compensation for his leg had come through and he had fled to London where he was working in the public library in Hendon and drinking himself sober, or so he told Harry, and so Harry hoped. Another thing in his favour was that he had rung Orla McGrath to apologise for threatening to kill her husband. Before she could put down the phone — Cormac was incoherent and she was scared — he had heard a baby crying in the background. A new one.

Harry said, 'Master McGrath knows which side his bread is buttered on. Everything will turn out boring in the end. That is, if the booze doesn't get him first. But even when he's stoned he's cautious, not like Master Roche.'

Emmet was permanently high on coke, smoking gear, motoring around town like a car bomb looking for an excuse to explode. To be cruel to women and yet to want pity from them was a hard road to drive on, but driving in a storm of expensive snow was bound to prove fatal — though only to Emmet himself. Personally, hopefully.

44

HARRY RANG MAEVE the following morning. At lunchtime they met in Iveagh Gardens.

'This is weird,' she said.

'You look awesome,' Harry said.

She was talking about the weirdness of there being such a large park in the centre of the city that she had never been in, that she hardly knew existed. He was talking about her appearance. She was thinner, better defined. In the old days she had gone in for swirling patterns and bright colours; now she was wearing a navy blue cashmere coat and a grey silk scarf.

In a grove of dusty trees a broken statue of a Grecian woman stood on a plinth. Until they arrived there they had been walking and talking in the distracted yet attentive way of people who are soon to cross a frontier. In no particular order, he said that all the best young lawyers had got Alexander McQueen coats for Christmas; that he was still looking to buy a place with the Stoneybatter inheritance. She said if she'd known they were going for a walk she wouldn't have worn these heels; that she had taken out a huge mortgage on a flat in Whitefriar Street; that Ossie Gleeson had gone to Goa.

Harry said, 'So I hear. Maybe he'll send us a postcard. Or a parcel. A cardboard tube, with a surprise in it, or was that Emmet's idea?'

'Hold on,' she said and stopped beneath the statue.

'Are you coming,' he said, 'or are you just breathing heavy?'

'Harry,' she said, 'you're not as funny as I used to think you were. Or maybe as you think you are either.'

'Thank you for that insight.'

'Have you got something to tell me?'

'I just want to know why you're doing this.'

'You don't know?'

'No, I don't.'

'You're too innocent of course. Well, go back to your girlfriend and tell her to lay off me. And while you're at it, have a good cry on her shoulder.'

'She isn't my girlfriend.'

'Maybe she would be if she knew what you're really like.'

'Surely not.'

'What does that mean?' She had tilted her head slightly and was looking at him sideways out of her speculative violet eyes.

'I'm fairly sure you mean if she knew what I was really like she'd think I am a very mean person.'

Maeve smiled. 'Oh Harry, if you're so clever, why are you so weak?' Tucking the end of her scarf into the cashmere coat, which released a faint waft of a perfume he didn't recognise — it was called 'Joy' — she said, 'It couldn't be a gay thing, could it?'

Then she turned, piano-trilled goodbye with her fingers, and walked off, swaying comfortably on her too high heels.

He looked up at the statue standing on the plinth. The broken woman was faintly smiling. As ever.

45

A JUNIOR SOLICITOR for the prosecution had rung to say that
Dr Leary was, after all, required to give evidence in person; her
affidavit was not acceptable to the defence. They wanted to discover why a person not related to Mr Ferris by blood or marriage had
been allowed to formally identify his body.

Before she had time to think, Cory said, 'Am I supposed to be
happy about this?'

'Happy?' the solicitor said. 'In what sense?'

'In the sense that I'm going to have to make an excuse for myself.'

'No, no, not at all. Nothing like that will be necessary.'

'Nothing like what?'

'Well, like your relationship with the defendant. I'm sorry, I
mean the deceased.'

'I know what you mean. And do you know something else? If
your legal friends want to ask me about my private life, they won't
like what they hear.'

'I beg your pardon.' In the solicitor's begging there was genuine
begging but also a hint of asking this hysterical woman to give him
a break.

What Cory took was the hint. She said, 'Tell them to ask me
who abused Missy. Tell them to ask me that, and I'll give them
their answer.'

And she put down the phone as if it was coated with slime.

Within a week of the call the cardboard tube had arrived. Part of the reason for showing Harry its contents was to find out did he know Maeve had sent it. It was obvious he didn't. Cory was ashamed of herself. It was almost as shameful as suspecting he would think Emmet had done the obscene drawing from the life. Still, even though Harry was innocent, she hadn't told him what she had said to the prosecution solicitor. In part to conceal her lack of trust. In part because he didn't need to know.

In the event she had gone into court and sworn an oath to tell the truth and uttered only one word. Mr Greeley, for the prosecution, had asked had she identified the body as that of William Ferris. She had said yes. Mr Greeley had sat down. Mr O'Boyle, for the defence, had stood up and asked what her relationship to Mr Ferris was. Before she could answer, the judge wondered was it being proposed to establish that the identification had been mistaken. When Mr O'Boyle said no, the judge said that if the witness's relationship to the deceased had not impinged upon her identifying his remains, the nature of that relationship could have no bearing upon the correctness of the identification, obviously. Mr O'Boyle replied, with respect, that it had a bearing in law. The judge said he was familiar with the law, but it was logic he was concerned with here; counsel could not say no and mean yes, or vice versa, because in that case the law of unintended consequences would come into play.

At this point Mr Greeley had pointed out that the witness had gone pale.

One of the grounds of the subsequent appeal was that the judge, while quite properly allowing Dr Leary to receive medical attention, had excused her from giving further evidence, and in doing so had, quite improperly, remarked that a lady in her condition should never have been called in the first place. However, the Court of Criminal Appeal held that it was not necessary to make findings in regard to the matter, despite the fact that the learned judge had made errors both in law and in logic.

In relation to the testimony of a psychiatrist for the defence that the defendant was suffering from a personality disorder, the Appeal Court found that the judge had adequately explained to the jury the meaning of the term *mens rea*, the legal definition of the guilty mind, and he had properly charged the jury with deciding whether the defendant, having been found fit to plead, had the *mensrea* necessary for a verdict of killing with malice aforethought. The judge had also correctly instructed the jury on the question of whether events following the killing were or were not premeditated and connected essentially to the intention to kill, if that intention existed.

Well, Harry had thought at the time, you might run a man down with a van in a momentary fit of pique, but cutting his head off and throwing it into the river Liffey was not the sort of thing you did on the spur of the moment.

The jury had found Tomas Rovinj not guilty of murder but guilty of manslaughter. When the verdict was announced, he had made a peculiar noise. Manslaughter? Man's laughter. But it was less a laugh than a brief whinny of disbelief. He didn't believe he wasn't guilty, or he disbelieved he wasn't innocent, or both at once, or neither. The judge had given him twelve years to think about it.

Missy and Mazee had not appealed. There had been a trial within the trial and the judge had ruled they had not been properly cautioned and as a result their statements were inadmissible as evidence. They had subsequently pleaded guilty to lesser charges of assisting an offender and withholding information, for which they had got two years each. On their release they had gone to England, leaving behind young Thomas, who had been taken into care.

The story had died down then. But in 2011 the *Financial Times* had published a profile of an Irish billionaire who owned a large lump of central London and was now in court for bankruptcy. As an example of his unconventional style of management the FT had pointed to his Head of Corporate Legal Affairs being a woman still in her twenties who had been a witness in a sordid murder trial.

Her title, Harry said, was a euphemism for 'body-slave', but the way the case was going the billionaire might need Maeve to keep him out of jail for fraud — and then the slave would be him. She was marvellously manipulative, as Emmet Roche had discovered. She had schooled him what to say to the guards (nothing about her) and in court (nothing about her) and then, as soon as the trial was over, she had ditched him.

Harry had, he told Cory, 'made it up, sort of,' with Maeve, though he didn't say this had happened a couple of years earlier. Anyway, on the rare occasions they bumped into each other nowadays, he had the impression she was looking at him as if he belonged to a world she couldn't quite remember.

Harry saw Cory rarely enough too, because she had moved to Cork so that the child, Ruth, could be close to her grandparents. That was generous of her. Nonetheless, Will's mother was constantly complaining about Cory's standoffishness. Will's father said nothing. If he had said something, it would have been that Polly and Cory were not unlike each other, and Ruth was the image of them both, though less dogmatic. She was a very lovable child, just like poor old Walter Leary, God rest his noble soul.

On a bright summer's day almost exactly three years after Will's death, Walter had collapsed onto the floor of a bookie's shop in Gort and died in a litter of beaten dockets.

At the funeral a man had emerged from the large crowd of mourners to say, as usual, 'I'm sorry for your trouble. Your father was a great man.' When she asked him who he was, he said in an English accent, 'Tell your mother Myles Fury was asking after her.' And then he had stumbled away, too drunk to walk straight. When Frances heard this some days later, she had wept. Cory was upset too — she had never seen her mother cry before.

It was during this time that Cory began to suspect Harry disapproved of her, that he saw her as moralistic, intolerant, judgmental, a professional widow, older than her years. But he had changed too. Once upon a time he had expected people to act queerly, as if god had made them to amuse him, but now he had a look in his eye as if he'd found out that the world was not queer, it was straight, in the sense that it went straight through you, like a van driven by a Rumanian maniac.

But, Cory thought, I'm not as prim as he thinks. She was as wanton as the next woman, including Maeve MacNamee. If she wanted she could be like her — but not vice versa. In her mind this pair of female opposites rubbed up against each other like small, excited animals. Images of no one she knew occupied her then. Sandpaper skin scraped her neck. A harsh voice instructed her. A hand she pretended was not her own knotted in her hair. Then the sun was shining into the front bedroom in Leeson Street. That was why she had chosen to rent a tall house in Montenotte and why she slept on the top floor: from the window the river Lee could be seen opening its way to the sea. But why a hill in Cork should be called Night Mountain she didn't know, not least because it looked towards the sun and the houses stacked on the slope had a southern feel to them, which reminded her of Italy, though she had never been there. She had a longing for the land where lemon trees blossomed and golden oranges glowed in dark green leaves.

But daydreaming had nothing to do with remembering. Anyway, it was demeaning to act, or be treated, as if the only conceivable way to solve a problem like hers, or any woman's, was to find a new man. She remembered an old song Will used to sing:

> *If all the young ladies were hares on the mountain,*
> *The men with their hounds would be out without countin'.*

Well, that was the impression men liked to give, but more often than not it was the ladies who were out hunting with their hounds, savage dogs they were too. For years she had brooded over Maeve's hatred of her. And now, seven years on, she had found out from Harry about the abortion. Well, if the truth were told, what Will called 'the wan thing' was what all men were interested in, and women hated them for it. So she and Maeve were sisters under the skin. And Vanessa Banim too. They lived in the same world, the ancient world of the first earthquake and the first eclipse, long before grapevines were trained to climb up into the elms, but not before women died giving birth to a foreign body that had taken them over. Maeve had done her dying on a table in a London clinic, paid for in advance, by Visa card. Cory wondered if the foetus was the half-brother or half-sister of Ruth — but how the disorganised cells in the steel bowl had been organised, those who had seen for themselves, if they had looked at all, had long since forgotten.

It was February. Harry had come down to Cork for Ruth's seventh birthday. That night they stayed up late drinking wine, looking down at the river, and he told her he had slept with Will. No, not slept. Had had sex with. At the time both of them were, he said, 'infantilised by alcohol'. It was Will who suggested the experiment: he wanted the experience. But those few minutes had not been magical. Anyway it had happened in early December, long before Cory moved in to Leeson Street. The reason he was telling her now was that at the time he had told Maeve. He hadn't been able to keep it to himself. The knowledge was a secret, but the secret had become the knowledge. When they went up to bed it was way past midnight. As they separated to go into their own rooms, they embraced. Ten minutes later she tapped on his door, opened it slightly and said, 'Can I come in for a minute?' But it was many minutes later when, looking up at him, she said, 'Is this all that different?' Then she went back to her own room, took two aspirin and a sleeping pill, drank as much water as she could swallow and slept.

In her dream she thought she was awake and listening in the house, but this house stood by itself in the shade of a giant oak tree on the sunlit bank of a narrow river. At the end of a long autumn silence she heard a diminishing series of clattering sounds, like a heavy stone falling haltingly through the branches of the tree. Then the river bounded like an emptying artery, rushing onwards and widening until there was no land left in sight. The sky was low and lit by a livid, bruised moon, and in the troughs of the waves a man's head was rolling. His voice was familiarly reedy and she recognised his hair, grown long from the grave, but still standing up straight. The song he was singing she had never heard before, and yet she knew it. It said they would never meet again in the way they had once done. And then, swiftly but over a long fixed time, the voice faded and the head was borne away by the flood, growing smaller and smaller, until at last it disappeared from view.

This time when she woke she was awake. The house was the house. She went to the window. A single star hung low in a clear dark blue sky. She had been wrong all her life. The conviction of being better than other people that she had learned from her father she had paid him back in kind, with disrespect. And she had made little of her mother too, mourning and weeping in this vale of tears. She had been asking to be cut down to size, and she had got what she wanted: humility had been forced on her. And now look at what she had done. It was cold and she was naked and wrong. Wrong, like a bell. Wrong, wrong. But self-pity was no pity. She shivered. The opposite of guilt could just as easily be true, even if it couldn't be innocent or pure. Will had said to her once that everyone had two names but she had none — she was a woman not a name. Everything of value she had experienced was connected to everything that had the same kind of value in life generally. So she decided then to be devoted, in the old sense, not to Will Ferris in particular, who she knew now was dead at last, but to some third person singular in him, in others, and in herself, who would remain always in sight, like the Morning Star, so-called, if that was what this star was.

She drank more water from the tap. It was as cold as wine straight out of the fridge. Colder. Harry had said her kisses were sweeter than wine. That was a cliché. She should have told him they were the opposite. But she hadn't had to. He was far too clever not to know. Or to take what had happened tragically, or seriously. She got back into bed. In the afternoon she would drive him to the station. He should find himself a nice man and settle down. She had a good mind to tell him that, too. And then she would never see him again. Probably. But of course she wouldn't say anything. And in any event they were bound to meet. Sooner or later. Next year anyway. And then they would put more water into the wine. He didn't believe in miracles. Nor did she. She would fall asleep now, dreamlessly with any luck, and when she woke again she would have the same name and be the same woman, more or less.

ACKNOWLEDGEMENTS

I thank my niece Dr Aoibhinn Lynch for advice on medical matters in this book; Dr Serena Condon for bringing me into the Rotunda Hospital more than forty years ago; Rachel and Victor Treacy for generously lending me accommodation in which parts of the book were written — in the past they endowed a prize for painting through the Butler Gallery in Kilkenny but the Royal Hibernian Academy prize here is fictional. I am grateful to the Office of Public Works for appointing me in 2007 as the first writer-in-residence at Farmleigh, the government guest-house in the Phoenix Park — the Farmleigh event described here is fictional. I thank my daughter Clare for typesetting and designing the book; my daughter Camille for promoting it; and, above all, my partner Mary Shine Thompson.